QUEEN'S MOMENT IN THE SUN

QUEEN'S MOMENT IN THE SUN

JR ZINK

CHAPTER 1

Hinds County, Mississippi – Summer 1865

The driver halted the black carriage in front of the plantation house. Dark-haired, blue-eyed Aaron Johnson, dressed in a suit and top hat, stepped down onto the dusty driveway and assessed the columned house, in need of a coat of paint and roof repairs. John Johnson, similarly dressed, emerged, stood beside his half-brother, and looked around the property.

"This one is more neglected than some of the others," said John.

"Doesn't appear to have been ravaged by the Union soldiers," said Aaron.

They walked up the stone front steps and knocked on the door. A Black woman answered. "Yes, sir?"

"I'm Aaron Johnson, here to see Mr. Grayson."

"Come in," said the woman, leading them into a parlor with bare floors and a brown water stain on the wall. Their footsteps echoed in the sparsely furnished room. "Please make yourself comfortable. I'll let him know you're here."

A large man with a bushy beard appeared after several minutes. "I'm Elliot Grayson."

"Aaron Johnson." They shook hands. "Thank you for seeing me. I was encouraged by your letter and hoped we might find a mutual arrangement to benefit us both."

"Well, you're not the first carpetbagger who has tried to swindle me, but I'm willing to hear what you have to say," said Grayson.

"I appreciate your openness and your directness," said Aaron.

"Who's this?" said Grayson.

"This is John. He's accompanying me on my travels with his own objective. He's looking for someone, a former slave."

Grayson looked at John. "Who's that?"

"Her name is Jenny. She would be about fifty years old," said John.

"No one here with that name."

"Might be called something else now. I haven't seen her in twenty years or more."

"She light-skinned like you?" said Grayson.

"No, she's dark. She worked on William Reed's plantation, Western Magnolias, in Greenville in the 1840s. She was sold at the slave market in Jackson sometime after that."

"Doesn't ring any bells. Can't help you," said Grayson.

"While you two conduct your business, do you mind if I talk to the Black folk here? Maybe they know something?" said John.

"That would be all right. Their quarters are out back. You can find your way."

"Thank you, sir." John bowed his head and made his way to the front door.

"How did you end up with him?" said Grayson.

"He was born on my father's plantation in Scott County, Kentucky. I'm doing him a favor, kind of a repayment for his years of loyalty," said Aaron.

"Christ, since they were freed, they all feel they're owed the world. We fed 'em and clothed 'em and looked after 'em for years. They want the world handed to them on a silver platter. They think freedom means they can sit around and do nothing, but they're learning that freedom means working for a living like the rest of us. What a fiasco. It's been hell since the Union armies set them free. And ones like him; go traipsing off to look for long-lost ones. What's that going to accomplish? If they ever find them, how will that help either one?"

"Well, John's determined to find his mother," said Aaron. "He has means and has spent considerable effort looking for her."

"But that's not why you're here. Let's talk about what you have to offer," said Grayson, directing them to chairs in the corner of the room. "You said in your letter you were looking to invest in farming?"

"Yes, I'm looking to invest in a cotton farm here in Mississippi. I know that capital from the banks dried up during the war, and many landowners had to sell their possessions and farms to make debt and tax payments. Now that the war is over, the price of cotton is up, and prospects look good. I want to be a part of that."

"Are you looking to buy a farm outright or invest?" said Grayson.

"I'm interested in exploring either. But I'd prefer to buy."

"You want to run a farm? Cincinnati lawyer type like you?"

"I grew up on a plantation in Kentucky. I'm familiar with running a farm and managing the labor," said Aaron.

"Growing cotton is a far cry from the farming you got up North. Cotton farming is hard work. Takes a lot of labor all year long. Darkies hate it. Since they were freed, I can hardly get any to come work for me. They'd rather go into town and pal around with their friends. They're all looking for something easier to make a living at."

"How are you incenting them?" asked Aaron. "I know things aren't like they used to be."

"You got that right. Last year, I offered labor contracts. Damn Freedmen's Bureau agents telling them what they need to ask for in contracts. Any time it doesn't sound right to them, they run to the Bureau's office, and I have to go in there and meet with an agent. Agents comb through the contracts and make issues out of little things. I've accepted that they're free now, and I need to pay wages, but the

Freedmen's Bureau gets in the way."

"Other than the hassle of the Bureau, how has it been working otherwise?"

"Well, some of them have decided they don't want to just work for wages. They want their own land. Started with 'forty acres and a mule.'"

"How do you mean?" asked Aaron.

"Last year, a Union general took confiscated farms and parsed them out, promising every freed Negro forty acres and a mule to start their own farm."

"Right. General Sherman. I read about it, but I thought President Johnson rescinded that and took back the land from those families."

"He did. Thank God for Andy Johnson, but the problem is, the freedmen didn't hear about that part and 'forty acres and a mule' stuck. They believe they're owed some of the property that they worked. So some of the planters are trying sharecropping as a compromise."

"How's that work?" said Aaron.

"You make a contract with the family. Everyone in the family works for the year, and you provide a place for them to live, food, land, seed, animals, and tools. In return, they get a share of the crop's proceeds."

"How much?"

"One-sixth to one-half."

"One-half?" Aaron said.

"Look, I haven't gone this route yet, but that's what I'm hearing from others contemplating it."

"The economics don't work at one-half."

"I wouldn't think so," said Grayson. "But I see the potential. The workers share in the risk of the crop. If they don't work hard, their share is less. It's a way to, as you say, incent them. They like feeling like they own part of it."

"It makes some sense," said Aaron, "but it could also create problems if there's a bad harvest. They lose out too."

"I don't think they're smart enough to figure that out. Besides, what choice do they have? There are four hundred thousand newly freed Negroes in Mississippi. Most are roaming around, looking for a way to make a living. Poor whites are having just as hard a time. The war ruined our whole economy. Most stores and businesses went out of business."

"I understand. I'm sure it's been difficult," said Aaron. "What are you looking for in an investor?"

"I'm in a hole. I had cotton stored in my barn that I hoped to sell when the markets opened up to the North, but the damn Confederate government came and confiscated it; said it was their property, and I had to forfeit it to support the war. I planned to use that to pay for my seed and labor this year. I got the seed planted, but my funds are depleted. I have delinquent loans and no hope of another one from a bank. I need cash to pay the farm hands."

"How much do you need?"

"The wage is ten dollars a month for adult labor. I have about eighty field hands," said Grayson.

"That could be upwards of $10,000 a year," said Aaron. "Depending on the price of cotton and the yield of your harvest, there's no guarantee you'll recoup that."

"Well, that's why you're here, son. Cotton growing ain't for the faint of heart. Another thing I need is livestock. Yankees took everything I had: oxen, cattle, pigs. I need beasts of burden to work the fields and meat to feed my family and the hands. All the farms for miles were stripped clean of everything. We're practically starving."

"I'll make some inquiries back home. I have some connections that I might put to use. What are your other debts?"

"I don't want to go into all the details. If we do a deal, we can get into that. Suffice it to say, I need four good years, and I can dig myself out of the hole I'm in. After that, I'm profitable."

"There's a significant amount of uncertainty in that forecast," said Aaron.

"Son, I know that. I've been doing this my whole life. You

educated Northerners think you can come down here and save the world that you destroyed. Created quite an opportunity for yourselves, didn't you?"

"Mr. Grayson, the Confederates started the war, if you recall."

"To save ourselves from becoming the prey of the North."

"Forget that. Doesn't matter," said Aaron, trying to bring calm back to the negotiation. "I can help you. Allow me to help you by investing in your crop. For every dollar I invest, you give me ownership shares in the plantation. We'll be partners and in this together, win or lose. I like to win."

"I gotta be honest. I'm trying to figure you out. Raised in Kentucky, educated, lawyer. Hard for me to trust a Yankee."

"Don't think of me as a Yankee. My mother was from these parts. Mississippi is in my blood. She married my father from Ohio, and I ended up in the North. I understand why the men of the South did what they did to protect their way of life. I saw my family's Kentucky estate destroyed by the Union army. I know what you've lost, and I'm happy to help rebuild the South and make a profit in the course of it. Besides, you're about out of options. Take my offer."

Grayson sat back in his chair, face reddened and looking defeated. "I'll think about it. This a handshake deal?"

"It will be a handshake and our words as men of honor, but I'll draw up a contract. Too much money for this to be just a handshake. I'll need records of your last couple of years and an accounting of your finances," said Aaron.

"Let me sleep on it."

"You do that, but I need an answer this week. I'm talking to some other men about their farms."

Grayson nodded his head. Aaron stood, and they shook hands.

"I'm staying at the Spengler House in Jackson. Send word once you make your decision."

#

While Grayson and Aaron met, John went to the servants' buildings behind the main house. He found two rows of cabins along a dirt walkway. Two elderly women, dressed in threadbare loose dresses, sat on a porch, one cracking nuts in a wooden bowl.

"Good morning," said John. "Might I have a word with you ladies?"

"Who are you?" said the non-nut cracker, patting her hair and smiling at the handsome John.

"My name is John Johnson. I'm looking for someone." He stepped up onto the porch and removed his hat. "I don't want to trouble you any. Are you the only two here today?"

"Most of the rest working in the fields. A couple of the old ones are inside. They feel too poorly to work. Who you looking for?"

"A woman. My mammy. She was sold in Jackson about twenty-five years ago. I'm trying to find her."

"What's her name?"

"Jenny," said John.

"Don't know any Jenny. Any other names?"

"Jenny Johnson, maybe? I'm not sure. When I was a boy, about twelve, we were living on the Given House plantation in Kentucky. Mammy was sold downriver to a family on Western Magnolias, a farm here in Mississippi, up in Greenville. Master there was William Reed. I went there, but only the house servants remained. They told me Jenny was sold at the auction house in Jackson about ten years later. I don't know where she went after that. I've been to a dozen plantations around Jackson. No one has seen her after that."

"What does Jenny look like?"

"It was so long ago. She was pretty when she was young. Darker than me. Not too tall. She worked in the house, not the fields."

The women shook their heads. "So many torn away from their babies. I lost six children myself. I'm sorry I don't know nothing to help you. I wish I could."

John said, "I'm sorry, too, for your babies. When they sent my mammy away, I was determined to find her. Over the years, I thought about her, where she might be. When Mr. Lincoln freed the slaves, I felt a renewed sense of hope. I've been searching for weeks now. I was foolish to think I could do this. The country is too big, and the masters spread us around on purpose. Just one more way to keep us under their control."

The woman nearest him smiled at John. "I'll bet Jenny'd be proud of you. Growing up in the middle of all this. Trying to find her. Becoming a fine young man. You travel all the way from Kentucky?"

"Cincinnati. Before the war, I was freed and went North."

"Where's that?"

"It's in Ohio. You take a riverboat up the Mississippi and then up the Ohio River. About four days' journey."

"Things better there? In the North? Some of ours went that way after the war."

"It's supposed to be. Better for white people. Still hard for us. Good-paying jobs are scarce," said John.

The nutcracker said, "Things are better now that the war is over and we're free. The field hands are all being paid. We have money to buy food and clothes, but those things are hard to find. Even Mr. Grayson's family doesn't have enough food. That how it is up North?"

"Plenty of food if you have the money, but most Black folks don't have enough. We're trying to educate everyone. Teach them to read and write. That will help them get better jobs. We're starting up schools for the children and teaching the adults."

"The Freedmen's Bureau opened a school over in Jackson."

"That's good. That's important," said John.

"There's a new Negro church too. Just for us. We can ask there about your Jenny."

"I'd appreciate that. And will you ask the others who live here? If anyone remembers anything?"

"Oh yeah, we'll ask."

"I'm staying at the Negro boarding house in Jackson. You can find me there."

#

The carriage pulled away, leaving John and Aaron on the dusty street in front of Aaron's hotel. Many nearby buildings were still piles of bricks or burnt remnants from General Sherman's attack the previous year. Brick chimneys were the only building remains above the rubble across the Jackson city center.

"I've done all the looking I can do," said John. "The Freedmen's Bureau doesn't have any record of her. No one has seen her. I didn't realize how difficult this was going to be."

"It's a big country," said Aaron.

"I think I need to go home. Get back to work," said John.

"Are you sure? You won't find her there. We know she was here. There's a trail, and you just need to find it again."

"She could be anywhere," said John. "I don't know where to go from here. She may not even be alive at this point."

"I'm sorry," said Aaron. "I know how long you've thought about finding her."

The two half-brothers looked at each other; they rarely saw each other this way. Each thought back to the day as boys when John's mother was ripped away from him. Neither could make sense of it at the time. John vowed to find her. Aaron continued with his life and pushed the day's ugliness to a place that didn't hurt. Their journey together to the South had resurfaced the memory for both of them.

"Thank you for bringing me on this trip," said John. "It would have been much more difficult to do this alone. The people here have been pretty hostile. I'm grateful."

Aaron broke his gaze and looked at the ground. He felt the shame of what his family had done to John and his family. "It was nothing."

John said, "It wasn't nothing. I know that."

Aaron looked up again at John. He was never one to vocalize his emotions. He wasn't sure what he felt. After all that had transpired between them, he was amazed that John could still treat him kindly.

Unable to formulate words, Aaron nodded.

John nodded in return.

"I'll be staying a while longer," said Aaron. "I think Mr. Grayson and I will be making a deal. If that happens, I'll send for my family. When are you going to leave?"

"No reason to delay. I'll catch a steamboat tomorrow," said John.

"All right then."

The two men shook hands, then John started down the street, walking around the crowds of unemployed white men. He nearly collided with a man, stepping out of the way at the last minute.

"What are you looking at?" said the man.

"Nothing, just minding my own business," said John.

"Keep your eyes to yourself. Don't you disrespect me, boy."

"I'm not looking for any trouble," said John.

"Best not be. Git."

John hurried on his way, putting his hands in his pockets, and clutching his remaining greenbacks. He saw a long line as he approached the shanties in the unofficial Black neighborhood. Three men handed out bread and bags of cornmeal from a cart with a Freedmen's Bureau sign hung from its side. The line was pushing forward in spots, people anxious that the rations would be gone before they reached the cart.

He crossed the street to the boarding house, where he had been sharing a room for the last few weeks. A small group stood in front, listening to a man who held a newspaper in his hand. "They're calling them the Black Codes. The new state government passed them. The vagrancy law says that by the second Monday of January, everyone must have a contract with an employer for a job or be fined $50. If you can't pay the fine, you'll be imprisoned unless you find a planter to pay the fine for you."

One of the men said, "How are we supposed to pay fifty dollars? Who got fifty dollars? None of us. That puts us under the thumb of those old masters again, owing them that debt."

Another man said, "There's plenty of work growing cotton. You gotta go back to the farm."

"What if we don't want to be a farmer no more?" shouted a man.

"There ain't nothing else to do. What you gonna do?"

"These are their tricks to get us back to working cotton."

"What choice we got?"

"Freedman Bureau will help you make a good contract. You gotta do it."

"Ain't right."

"What else in the new laws?" said a man in the front of the group.

The man read from the newspaper, then summarized, "One dollar tax on all Negroes every year for in-dig-nent Negroes."

"What's that?"

"*Indigent*," said John. "It means poor. It's to raise money to help feed and care for poor people."

"Who's going to make sure that money goes to poor people?" shouted one man.

"That be the government," chimed in another.

"Shit. Other than the Union army and the Freedmen's Bureau, I don't see any government helping us."

John stood on the stoop of the boarding house and surveyed the block. It seemed hopeless. He wondered how much of the South and how many Negroes were in similar situations. He was glad to be going home.

He walked up dark stairs and down a narrow hallway to his room. He sat on the thin mattress of the bed and put his hands in front of his face. He started to cry silently. When the Union won the war, and the slaves were freed, John had hope. He was building a life as a free man in Cincinnati. He had believed the next ray of light would be finding his mother.

He broke down for the first time in years, muffling his sobs in his hands.

CHAPTER 2

Aaron sat in his hotel room, writing notes in his journal, and making calculations regarding Grayson's farm and the investment that would be required.

He answered a knock at the door. A middle-aged Black woman with shiny skin and large eyes stood in the hall.

"Excuse me, sir. Mr. Johnson?"

"Yes, that's me."

"I have this letter for you. Was delivered this morning," said the hotel worker.

"Thank you," said Aaron, taking the note.

The woman looked at him longer than was respectful.

"What is it?" demanded Aaron.

"Excuse me, sir, your name—Aaron Johnson. I knew a boy by that name."

A sense of familiarity dawned as Aaron looked at the woman's face.

"In Kentucky. Master William's farm. William Johnson." She studied his face.

Aaron stood, stunned.

"Are you William's son, Aaron?" she said.

"I am."

"It's me, Jenny. You remember?"

"Uh, yes. John's mammy."

"That's right. John. You and John. I remember you two

played together. You have a look like him, both with the same daddy."

"Step in here," said Aaron, looking both ways in the hallway. He closed the door. "Don't talk about such things. That was a long time ago."

"Is John still with Master William?" said Jenny.

"No. He's here. Looking for you," said Aaron.

"My baby, John, is here? Where?" she said, voice quivering.

"Over at the Negro boarding house."

Her eyes brightened. "John's here in Jackson?"

"Yes," said Aaron. "But he's leaving today."

"Oh, my word. Mr. Johnson, I'll take leave of you now. I need to go see my John."

"You should hurry. Catch him before he's gone."

"Thank you, sir." Jenny bowed slightly and hurried to the door.

As Aaron watched her leave, a wave of sentimentality came over him. He thought back to his youth and summer days playing with John, his valet and only companion on the big plantation in Kentucky. They played like brothers, but as he grew up, his mother taught him to distance himself from the servants and put them in their place, below the entitled class he was born into. He remembered the day when John's mother was sold down the river. He recalled John's distress and his own confusion as to why the Black and white world of the plantation had to be as his mother explained. He felt the loss of his own mother, taken by fever. He felt betrayed by his father, who had two bastard sons—half-brothers he didn't know about as a boy. John, who he felt shame toward; and Max Mueller, the German boy who grew up to be a better man than he was.

#

Jenny pushed past the ever-present men lingering in front of the boarding house and went inside. "I'm looking for a man;

his name is John."

"Who's this John?" said the desk clerk.

"From up North. John Johnson," said Jenny.

"He left this morning."

"Where did he go?"

"He took his bag with him. Headed for the train station. Said he was off to Vicksburg to catch a steamboat."

"No. How long ago did he leave?" she said.

"He left at first light."

Jenny raced through the streets to the edge of town. The train depot was a new building, one of the first public buildings to be rebuilt. She ran into the crowded lobby and looked around. She pushed past the patrons waiting at the ticket window and addressed the man behind the counter. "Has the morning train to Jackson left yet?"

"Hey, what do you think you're doing?" shouted a man, eyeing Jenny with disdain. "What the hell, damn Negro."

"I'm sorry, sir. I got to find somebody getting on that train."

"You can wait in line like everyone else. Negroes think they're now above us?"

Jenny ignored him and addressed the ticket agent. "Sir, the train to Jackson? Has it left yet?"

"No, there's a problem on the tracks. None of the Jackson trains have come or gone this morning. Everything's backed up," said the agent.

"Where is the Jackson train?"

"It will be on track two."

"Where's that?"

"Down there," he pointed.

"Thank you, sir," Jenny rushed toward the track. The station was packed with frustrated passengers. She saw the signs indicating track two and started scanning the faces; they were all white. She pushed her way to one side of the station, looked around, then drove back to the other side. She received jabs and sneers as she maneuvered through the mass of people. She climbed atop an empty spot on a bench and searched the entire room. The only Black faces she found were the porters and attendants.

Jenny started wailing, quiet at first, then raising to a full scream at the top of her lungs. The room hushed as people looked at the crazed woman on the bench. A policeman started moving toward her, pushing through the crowd.

She looked at the room full of unsympathetic, hateful eyes and stated loudly, "I've got to find my son. Please, somebody, help me. Please. I can't lose my baby again. Do none of y'all have any warmth in your heart?"

She screamed, "Sweet Jesus, please help me find my John!" The onlookers remained silent. The policeman was almost to her.

"I'm here," boomed a voice across the room. John stood in an exterior doorway. The crowd and officer turned toward him.

"John," cried Jenny.

"Mammy," said John, his voice breaking.

She jumped down and drove through the crowd. John shoved people aside, drawing return pushes and curses. As they met and fell into each other's arms, the onlookers stepped back, staring. Tears ran down both their cheeks, and they shook with sobs of relief.

A murmur turned into a din in the room as the police officer reached them. "All right, let's go. No one wants to see this. Outside." He roughly pushed them through the door into the sunshine. "What the hell do you think you're doing, disturbing the peace of the good folk of this town? What are you two doing in the train station anyway? You've no business in there."

"Sir, I am waiting for my train," said John, pulling his ticket from his breast pocket.

"Well, I can't arrest you for that, much as I'd like to. Your type is getting away with anything these days, but you," he sneered, poking his finger toward Jenny. "Vagrant hanging out and causing a ruckus. Let's go."

"Where you taking me?" said Jenny

"Over to the station. Lock you up with the rest of the troublemakers. Up to me, I'd sweep you all out of town. A lot of hassle keeping your kind out of the streets, getting in the way of restoring this town to the way things ought to be."

"Sir, she meant no harm," said John. "We've been apart for many years. Today we found each other. Can you find it in your heart to let our reunion be peaceful?"

"I don't give a damn about any of that. You're not from here. Where you from?"

"Cincinnati."

"A damn Yankee Negro. Just what we need, more of you. What are you doing here?"

"I'm here on business," said John.

"What kind of business?" said the officer.

"Personal business."

"Watch it, Yankee or no, I'll arrest you too if you get uppity with me."

"Sir, I'd like to propose that I save you the fuss of arresting anyone," said John. "If you let me pay you the fees for releasing her and let us be on our way, we can set this matter aside."

The officer looked at John in his suit. "You've got money to pay for her bail?"

"How much is it?" asked John.

"Twenty-five dollars should do it. Greenbacks; no graybacks. You have it?"

"Yes, sir. If I pay you, you'll let us go?"

"The jail is full, and the courts are jammed up. Sounds like an expedient resolution to this situation."

"Very well." John turned away and counted out the money. He handed it to the officer.

"Keep her from making any more trouble," said the cop, pocketing the bills.

When the officer was out of sight, Jenny pulled John's hands to her. "My boy has grown into an impressive man. You handled that cracker. How did you learn how to be such a man?"

"I've seen a lot in my lifetime. Watching white men taught me how to get along in his world."

"You're my boy. John. Oh, thank the Lord we found each other." They embraced. "Where are you going on the train?"

"I was going home. I live in Cincinnati. I'm a barber there," he said.

"My. I'm proud of you." She hugged him again. "I can't believe it."

They stood before each other, taking each other in. "What about Martha and Harry?" Jenny asked. "What happened to 'em?"

John guided them to a spot under the shade of a tree. "They're fine. They're living in Canada."

"Oh, the Lord watched over all my babies," said Jenny.

"They ran after Master William died," said John. "Master Lyle was getting ready to sell them down river. The Underground Railroad helped them escape to Canada. That was before the war. Martha writes letters. They're in good health."

"Mmm," Jenny closed her eyes. "They all right. I dreamed of you all. I dreamed someday we'd all be together again. But I didn't dream this. You're a man now. Not my baby anymore."

"I want you to come with me to Cincinnati. Live with me," said John. "We can have a better life there. The South is no place for the Negro right now. Winning the war and freedom isn't looking like the world we thought it would be."

"We're free, John. That's where it starts, and now we can decide where we want to go from here. I got the choice of where I want to go. Before, I didn't have that choice. I choose to go with you, and I'm free to do that."

"We'll build a new life together there. You'll see. I've been dreaming of finding you for almost twenty years. You ready to leave Mississippi?" he asked.

"Nothing is keeping me here."

"Do you have any new family? Or anyone you don't want to leave?" asked John hesitantly.

"No, after Ray, I never took another husband."

"Ray, he was Martha and Harry's daddy?" said John.

"Uh huh," Jenny nodded. "Master Lyle say Ray getting too uppity and sent him to Western Magnolias. I was crying and sad for a spell, but I had my babies to think of. No good come of moping around about something I couldn't do nothing about. Master William, he started up with me again after that. I lived in the big house and had it easier than the field workers. Then Mrs. Johnson found out about Master William taking to me, and that's when she sent me away too."

"I remember that day," said John. "One morning, you were just gone. No good-bye, nothing. I was so afraid and alone, but I didn't let anyone see it. I wouldn't give the Missus that. Master William, he was sad about it, too, I could tell. He told me it would be all right. Then Martha moved into the big house and took on your duties. Master William, he did take care of me, sort of. He never let Lyle mistreat me. He let me continue my reading and arithmetic. He even taught me how to figure in the books. He never told anyone he's my daddy until after he died. He freed me in his will and left me a thousand dollars."

"He did?" said Jenny in amazement. "What you do with all that money?"

"That's when I moved to Cincinnati. I've been working in Mr. Watson's barbershop. I used some of it to come here to find you. I gave some of it to the Colored church. I still have some in the bank."

"Master William," she shook her head. "He took a liking to me, but he went along with how things were just the same. I'm glad he freed you."

"He went along with it, but I don't think he ever liked it—being one of the masters," said John. "After Mrs. Johnson died, he took Aaron, and they moved to his house in Cincinnati."

"Did you ever hear from Ray again?" asked John.

"No. When I got to Western Magnolias, they told me Ray had died soon after arriving there. Fever killed him."

"I'm sorry," said John.

"A couple of years later, I was sold to a plantation in southern Mississippi. When we were freed, I came to Jackson and started working at the hotel. So nothing is tying me here.

"People been dragging me from place to place my whole life. Now I decide. So I say let's go to Cincinnati."

CHAPTER 3

Ohio River, North of Louisville, Kentucky – Fall 1865

Max Mueller sat at the table amongst the other Cincinnati movers and shakers. The blond-haired, blue-eyed thirty-year-old had risen from his meager beginnings in the German Over-the-Rhine neighborhood to his place as a city councilman and business owner.

The Cincinnati and Louisville Mail Line Company had invited the influential men to be their guests on a trip to Louisville, Kentucky, aboard their brand-new steamship, the *United States*. The group included the boat company's treasurer; chamber of commerce members; the mayor, Len Harris; the city treasurer; and several other councilmen. They sat, talking, laughing, and finishing breakfast in the ornate two-story dining room in the center of the steamship. Brass fixtures, oil paintings, and fine carpets adorned the room, and an ornately carved balcony ran around the perimeter.

A man emerged from one of the balcony staterooms, his hair uncombed, pulling on his jacket. "Gentlemen," he called down to the group. "I'll join you momentarily." He briskly walked along the upper hallway, heading for the toilets at the end of the boat.

"It appears Nate enjoyed himself a bit too much last night," said the tenth ward councilman Joe Siefert. "Max, you should have cut him off."

"I'm not in charge of him," said Max. "The man sells

spirits for his living. You'd think he'd better manage his appetite for them."

"The packet company wanted to ensure we all had a good time. It was an extravagant evening," said Mr. Harris, the mayor.

"Mission accomplished," said Joe. "The service and the food were as fine as any restaurant in the city. Do you think their service will be this extravagant for all their passengers?"

"I'd venture they put their best foot forward to impress us and the members of the press, who they hope will print rave reviews," said another man.

"It felt good to celebrate again," said Joe. "Things were so dark during the war. It's nice to enjoy fine dining and see liquor flowing again."

The mayor leaned in toward Max. "I appreciate your helping influence Joseph Longworth to lease the city the land for the new reservoir. The city has gone back and forth on committing to the project for years now. Given our growth, we desperately need the new reservoir to ensure the fresh water supply keeps up with the population."

"I'm glad I could be of assistance," said Max.

"How are you connected to the Longworth family?"

"Joseph's father, Nicholas, was a mentor to me. Since he passed, Joseph and I have remained friends."

"Well, your connection paid off," said the mayor. "Given the size of the parcel and its location, we will be able to create a city park adjacent to the reservoir. It will be an oasis right outside the city. There are other projects I want to push through as well: a new hospital and an expansion of the sewers. We must push the city's conservatives to invest more aggressively in our future."

Nate Bartlett, the other fifth ward councilman besides Max, took the empty seat at the table. "Morning gents." His hair was still wet from his quick grooming.

They greeted and ribbed him as he arranged a napkin on his lap. A waiter offered him coffee.

"God, yes, please," said Nate. "A piece of toast and some

bacon, please?"

The boat's deep whistle blared, drowning out the conversation momentarily. "Better wolf it down, Nate; sounds like we're approaching Louisville," said the mayor.

"That band last night. They were terrific," said Nate. "Who are they?"

"Menter's Band. I understand they'll be regulars on the ship," said Joe.

"My wife thoroughly enjoyed herself. The best time she's had in a long time," said Nate.

"You seemed to be enjoying yourself as well."

"I won't deny it."

"Gentlemen, before we disembark, let's talk about what we might accomplish on this little goodwill trip," said the Chamber of Commerce president George Davis. "I had my office send word to the Louisville mayor's office yesterday before we departed, so they know we're on our way. Although this trip is a packet company excursion, I'm counting on you to represent the city well. Nate?"

"Me? What? Of course. I'm on my best behavior today."

The group laughed.

Max said, "Although we're not here on official business, the best outcome we could hope for is to persuade some of Louisville's leaders to agree that building better commercial connections between our two cities benefits all of us."

"Agreed," said the mayor. "The federal government has opened up trade with the South again, but the flow of goods is still a fraction of what it was before the war. I don't have to remind this group how important expanding our city's commerce to the west and south is to our future. We need to regain the growth trajectory we had before the war."

"The Southern economy is still in shambles. It will take years for them to rebuild what the armies destroyed. At the same time, they're trying to figure out how to restore farming with paid labor," said Joe.

"Granted, but we need to be ready for the resurgence in commerce," said the mayor.

"That's right," said Max. "We must anticipate, and frankly, we are competing with other cities in the West for market dominance. Louisville itself has growing industries. St. Louis, Chicago—they're all making public and private investments to grow their industries. Now with the railroads, our transportation advantage is fading quickly. The riverboats will continue to be a conduit along the Ohio and Mississippi, but the landlocked portions of the country are looking to the railroads. We have not kept up."

Max continued, "There's a group looking at investing in a railroad to connect Covington to the South, but there's no funding. In the meantime, we must cement trade routes between Cincinnati and Louisville because Louisville has the L&N Railroad. They control what and how fast goods move through their depots."

The chamber president added, "I think some in Louisville still harbor animosity toward the North for the blockade that was put in place during the war, preventing them from shipping items to the Southern states. It's in our best interest to build more collaborative relations between our cities."

The ship rocked, the chandeliers tinkling with movement as the loud whistle sounded again.

"We must be at the wharf," said the mayor. The men stood and straightened themselves in preparation to meet the Louisville leaders. They walked outside and stood along the boat's rail, scanning the waterfront and city behind it. The rains had cleared, and a bright, sunlit morning buoyed their hopes for the Queen City now that the war was behind them.

Once the crew tied up the boat and lowered the gangway, several men in suits greeted the boat's captain and the mail line's treasurer. The group talked for several minutes, and then everyone returned to the saloon for an address. The families of the city leaders stood around the upper railing. Max scanned and found his nine-year-old daughter, Lizzie, in her party dress, standing beside his sister Marie, the girl's caregiver. He smiled and waved, and Lizzie enthusiastically waved back.

The shipping company treasurer began, "Ladies and gentlemen. Thank you for joining us on the first official run of the *United States*, the newest and most luxurious cargo and passenger ship to sail the Ohio." The audience applauded. The treasurer continued his commercial message of the merits of the ship, which was now part of the packet fleet that regularly traveled between Cincinnati and Louisville. He thanked the city officials and their families for joining and welcomed the mayor of Louisville to say a few words.

The mayor stood in a conservative black suit and sported several pieces of gold jewelry, including a sizeable sparkling sapphire ring. "Thank you, Mr. Sherlock. On behalf of the people of Louisville, I welcome you all to the Falls City on this occasion to celebrate another link between our cities— one that signifies our shared place in our nation's transportation and commerce gateway to the West and South. We welcome you to walk our streets this morning, as the creator has seen fit to part the clouds and bring sunshine onto this event. I encourage you to sample our fine arts, dining, and entertainment. I am also happy to announce that we will resume the horse races at the Woodlawn track this spring. Please return and see the finest thoroughbreds in the world, many raised right here in the bluegrass country.

"I won't have the opportunity to officially host your delegation, as we only learned of your visit late yesterday and didn't get a chance to adequately prepare a suitable reception for guests as esteemed as yourselves. Please, let's make more deliberate plans to have our respective municipal representatives meet soon."

The mayor looked around the room as he concluded his remarks, "Once again, thank you for coming." Several started clapping, followed by the rest of the audience.

"What the hell?" said George Davis, the chamber president. "He's not formally receiving us? No reception? No chance to meet their councilmen?"

"That's it? That's southern hospitality? Pfft," said another.

"I'm shocked," said Max. "Is this an indication of their

lack of interest in working with us?"

"Did you see his ring? Southern men seem as interested in adorning themselves as their women," said Nate.

"Something doesn't seem right," said Max.

Tom Weasner, the council president, said, "Let's go see." He, Nate, and Max joined the two mayors, who were chatting with several of the Louisville men.

During the pleasantries, Nate recognized his brother-in-law, William Stokes. After a few minutes of talk, Stokes invited the Cincinnati men back to his house.

The Louisville mayor apologized, saying, "I'm afraid I have some urgent business to attend to and won't be able to join you."

Stokes said, "It's just a few short blocks from here. I can provide some light refreshments and drinks. I'd love for you to join me."

"Thank you, Mr. Stokes," said Max. "That's very kind of you. Will any of the alderman or councilmen be joining us?"

"No, I'm afraid not," said Stokes.

Max said, "Let me see who's up for a walk this morning. Excuse me."

He returned to the Cincinnati men. "It's bizarre. The mayor claimed some urgent business. However, Mr. William Stokes, banker and the brother-in-law of our councilman, Nate Bartlett, has invited us for refreshment at his home."

"Urgent business, my ass," said one of the men.

"This is an insult," said George Davis. "I'm staying here on the boat."

Most agreed, and in the end, only Max, Nate, and a few others took Stokes up on his offer.

Max and Nate conversed with Stokes as they walked south on Chestnut Street from the river. "Are things bouncing back for you?" asked Max.

"Shipping traffic to and from the South is nowhere near pre-war levels, but it's slowly returning," said Stokes. "There's just no cotton or tobacco yet, and there's no money for them to buy the goods we used to ship. The bright spot in town is that our population is exploding, and there's a building boom going on. Not enough places to house everyone coming to the city. Good for my business."

"Soldiers? Negroes? Who's moving here?" asked Max.

"Well, some of those," said Stokes. "The Negroes tend to live amongst themselves on the outskirts; they don't have money to buy houses in town. It's mainly Southerners moving here for job opportunities. It's a chicken and egg thing, though. Unfortunately, the men are coming ahead of the jobs, but I think we'll find a balance over time."

Nate asked his brother-in-law, "Can you shed any light on what that was about on the riverfront? Why do we feel like we just received a snubbing from your mayor and elected leaders?"

"Don't blame the mayor," said Stokes. "He was embarrassed and tried to make the best of the situation. When his office received the telegram yesterday that y'all were coming, council voted to put together a welcoming committee and hold a reception, but several of the aldermen objected. They objected to entertaining other city officials on the citizens' dime when more urgent needs go unaddressed due to a lack of city funds. They have to answer to the voters. You can see their point, can't you?"

"I see the point, but it was pretty cold," said Max. "A simple opportunity to meet the councilmen, even briefly on the ship… I don't think we were expecting a grand buffet. The packet company has wined and dined us sumptuously. Right, Nate?"

"I over-indulged on their hospitality last night," laughed Nate.

"You? Over-indulge? What a surprise," laughed Stokes.

"These aldermen?" said Max. "Do you think that's really what their concern was?"

"What else might it have been?" said Stokes.

"Any of them, maybe reluctant to cede any inch to their Northern neighbor?"

"Do you mean are any of them among the Confederates

who accepted the surrender but haven't moved from their positions on slavery or the national government's authority over the commonwealth?" said Stokes with a touch of sarcasm.

"You answered my question, then," said Max.

"I'm not naming any names," said Stokes, "but some are not happy with how the war played out and will not forget it any time soon. Kentucky declared neutrality, then aligned with the Union. What do we get for our loyalty? Occupation by federal forces and the Freedmen's Bureau telling us how to manage our affairs. We were doing just fine on our own."

"I don't want to get into it, but I believe Kentucky still has not officially recognized the Thirteenth Amendment freeing the slaves," said Max.

"Yes, let's not get into it. That's been a state's right to legislate since this country was formed. We're not going to resolve that this morning," said Stokes.

"Fair enough. I hear you say, though, that there are men who will stand in the way of Northern proposals on principle."

"There are many principled men in Kentucky who do not accept the outcome of the war, are angry, and are adamant it is their duty to restore Kentucky's prosperity," said Stokes.

"I appreciate your honesty," said Max.

"Let's lighten it up, boys," said Nate. "William, I'm feeling a headache coming on. Do you have something that will soothe me, or should we stop in at one of these coffee houses?"

Stokes pointed, "I'm in the next block. I've plenty to nurse that hangover, not to worry."

#

As the paddle-wheeler moved upriver toward Cincinnati, the men reassembled in the saloon, where the bartender served more complimentary drinks.

"That was insulting," said the mayor. "To be disregarded

in such a way."

"I must concur," said the chamber president. "Very disappointing."

Max said, "Nate's brother-in-law, Mr. Stokes, shared with us that the mayor and council had intended to receive us, but some aldermen voted it down. Given the dire state of their finances, they didn't feel that the city budget should be spent on entertaining other city officials. On further inquiry, it came out that some on the council may harbor continued ill will toward the North and our city as a competitor."

"Confederates on their council?" asked one of the men.

"Many in Kentucky refuse to accept the loss of their cause and have great animosity towards Yankees. The war's not over in Kentucky," said the chamber president.

"It's not just in Kentucky. The whole South resents what's been thrust upon them," said another.

"I can't say I blame them," said the chamber president. "We wouldn't like an occupation by a victor's armies, especially an army that includes freedmen. Nothing burns some of these boys more than to see Black men in uniform in positions of authority."

"It is quite a turn of fate. I understand why they're upset. Slavery is immoral, but that doesn't mean the Black man is worthy of political and social equality," said Joe.

Silence fell over the room as the band ended a musical number. Nate shouted across the room. "Hey, do you know 'Oh, Let's Get Out of the Wilderness?'" The men roared with laughter.

"The ongoing animosity adds additional challenges to our predicament," said Max. "We must find ways to reestablish our dominance as an industrial and transportation hub."

"President Johnson's Reconstruction plan will mend the government, but the hard feelings will take longer," said the mayor.

"Will it?" said Max. "Johnson's plan doesn't begin to address the risk that the Confederate leaders may regain the power they had and use it to re-establish the aristocracy's position. He's putting too much trust in the provisional governments he put in place to decide what's best for their states. He's pardoning almost everyone, including most of the Confederate leaders. All he's asking of them is that their new governments pledge loyalty and support the Thirteenth Amendment freeing the slaves."

"We just need to give Johnson's plan time. They'll come around."

"I think that's naïve. Trusting the former Confederate leaders to rebuild their states is like having the fox guard the henhouse. It will take more," said Max. "In the meantime, we need to be building our own routes to the South, so we're positioned to serve the Southern markets when they're flush again,"

"Should we do another trip back here, as the Louisville mayor suggested?" said the chamber president.

"Or maybe we should invite them to visit us?" said the mayor.

"That's a start. Louisville controls the movement of goods in and out of the South. I've encountered issues with goods transferring from steamers to the railroads in the past. It's a choke point. We need alternate routes," said Max.

"There's only one river to Louisville," said Nate.

"We have to move beyond the river. We need a direct railroad route to the South," said Max.

"How do we fund that?" said the mayor. "Since the wave of railroad failures in the fifties, Ohio law prohibits cities from raising capital for railroads through bonds. It will take millions."

"Unless we can find a group of investors to fund it privately, we'll need to get the legal restrictions on bonds removed. Can we start working on that in Columbus?" said Max. "We have a great opportunity in front of us. It's ours to seize."

#

Later that day, Max stood on the promenade deck of the steamer with his daughter, watching the shores of Kentucky. Lizzie's auburn hair blew in the breeze.

"What did you do in Louisville while I was at my meeting?" asked Max.

"We went to the canal and watched the boats. I drew this," said Lizzie, flipping back the pages of her drawing pad to reveal a sketch of a steamboat. It lacked detail but captured the key elements: decks, smokestacks, paddlewheel, and flags.

"You drew this?" said Max.

"Yes. I had to hurry. The boat was moving away."

"It's very good, Lizzie. I like how it seems to move with the water splashing under the paddlewheel."

The girl beamed with pride. "Thank you, Papa."

"Did you draw anything else?"

She flipped the page. "This is Celia. I drew her when it was her turn to play checkers. She didn't know I was drawing her."

"Another nice one. You're showing some talent for drawing. Keep practicing."

"I wish the boat would stop so I could draw the trees. They look like big balls until you study them and notice all the leaves," said Lizzie.

"It's beautiful, isn't it?" said Max, admiring the green shores and hillsides along the river. "What do you think of the steamboat?"

"It's magnificent. I like the feel of the wind blowing when we stand outside. I also love the sparkling chandeliers in the dining room and the candies on my pillow at night. The waiter let me have two desserts. I had pie and pudding. Can we ride the steamboat again soon?"

"It's a nice treat, isn't it? We won't make a habit of riding them, but if we have occasion to travel, we can take another one someday. We were very fortunate to be invited by the steamboat company. Many people never get to do nice things like this."

"Why didn't Mother come with us?"

"She had to meet with her committee," said Max.

"I wish she could see this," said Lizzie pointing to the scenery. "You and Mother met on a steamboat. Tell me again."

"Mother was moving from New York City to Cincinnati and was traveling with her mother, sister, and brothers. I was traveling home after some business in Pittsburgh. I saw her on the lower deck, looking at the paddle wheel and steam engine. We started talking and drew a liking to each other at first glance."

"Was the boat like this one?"

"It was similar. Less grand than this one," said Max.

"Why don't we ever see Mother's family?"

"It's regrettable, but your grandmother has chosen to remain distant," he said.

"Why?"

"She disapproved of your mother's choices—her advocacy for women's rights and her decision to marry for love."

"I won't make choices that will disappoint Mother," said Lizzie.

"I like that you show respect for Mother and me. You're a good girl. When you're older, you will get to make your own choices. We may not always agree with them, but we'll love you no matter what. Both of us will always love you."

"I love you too, Papa." Lizzie hugged her father's waist. Max kissed the top of her head.

CHAPTER 4

Paris, Kentucky – Fall 1865

The strapping blond-haired, blue-eyed young man walked from the stables to the general store on Main Street, whistling a tune, unfazed by the multiple bags he carried. He admired the clean streets, neat buildings, and serene movement of citizens in the small town, his new home. He greeted a woman with a smile and a "Good afternoon, ma'am" as he set his belongings in front of the grocer's store.

He went inside and addressed the clerk. "Good afternoon, sir. I'm Oskar Mueller with the Freedmen's Bureau."

"Yes, Mr. Mueller. Nice to meet you. Welcome to Paris. I'm Gene Rutherford. You're a younger man than I thought you'd be."

Oskar ignored the comment. "Mr. Rutherford. You own the building, correct?"

"That's right. Twelve years."

"You maintain a neat storefront and a tidy store. The whole town gives off a glimmer. It's a pleasure to be here. I'm looking forward to becoming part of it," said Oskar.

"We're glad to have you. Nice to see the government stepping in to corral the freedmen and get them better settled. It should help us all."

"It will take us a while to put things in place, but I know we'll make a difference once we do," said Oskar.

"I hope so. The freedmen seem pretty lost. They need to

get back to work. Sometimes I get a crowd loitering outside the store. You won't be allowing that will you?"

"Part of my role is to help them find work. I'll also have rations for those that are in need."

"They going to line up here to your office?" said Mr. Rutherford. "I can't have food lines winding in front of my store."

"No, the rations will be distributed from the warehouse. I'll be setting that up at the old Camp Bourbon army depot at the fairgrounds."

"That's good. Wouldn't be good for business."

"I understand your concern. I'll do what I can to minimize any loitering or lines. I hope you'll let me know if you see any issues." said Oskar.

"You can count on it."

"I have a meeting with Reverend Thompson at St. Michael's Church. I'd like to drop my things off in my office. Can you direct me to it?"

"Let me get the key." Walking to the office in the back of the store, Mr. Rutherford called out, "Louise, mind the front. I'll be right back."

A young woman came around the corner and took in Oskar. "Well, hey there."

"Hi."

"You're new to town."

"I'm Oskar Mueller. A pleasure to meet you," he said with a warm smile.

"What brings you to Paris?"

"I'm the new Freedmen's Bureau Sub-assistant."

"Sounds official. What's that?" she asked.

"The Freedmen's Bureau, we're responsible for helping the freedmen get established. I'm the head of the local office."

"So you're going to be around for a while?"

"Yes, ma'am. I'll be staying at the Duncan Tavern until I find a more permanent place to live. My office will be on the second floor."

"Well, welcome."

"Here we are," said Mr. Rutherford. "Louise, I'm going to show Mr. Mueller to the office upstairs."

"So nice to have you with us, Mr. Mueller."

Rutherford led Oskar to a door next to the storefront and up a flight of stairs. "The other tenants on the floor are an attorney and an insurance agent." He unlocked the door and led Oskar into a front lobby area with three offices off of it. The suite had polished maple floors and dark stained woodwork. A massive wooden counter sectioned off a waiting room from the rest of the space. Two of the offices had large windows with views overlooking Main Street. "There's a toilet at the back of the building. Assuming it meets your approval, I'll drop the lease off for you to sign tomorrow. I'll need payment for the first month's rent."

"I'll have to submit a request to Louisville headquarters with the lease," said Oskar.

"How long will that take?" asked Rutherford.

"I'm not sure. To be honest, this is new for me. It's the federal government. You can trust their credit."

"I need the rent, and I don't have a choice, do I?" said Rutherford.

"I guess not. I'll submit it as soon as possible."

"Need anything else?"

"No, thank you. I think it will be most suitable."

"You know where to find me," Rutherford said, closing the door behind him.

Oskar surveyed the room. He placed his hands on the counter and swung his legs over it as if he were performing a vault in the Turner gymnasium. He raised his arms, fists clenched and exclaimed, "Yes!" in a confident hushed voice. He was ready to get to work, helping the freedmen of central Kentucky step into their new place as free Americans.

#

Oskar knocked on the door of St. Michael's parsonage and

stood back. As he waited, he admired the four stained glass windows, depicting familiar Christian scenes in shades of red and blue.

A white-haired, balding man opened the door. "Good day. How can I help you, young man?"

"I'm Oskar Mueller from the Freedmen's Bureau. I'm here to see Reverend Thompson."

"Yes, ah, Mr. Mueller. I received your letter. Is there anyone else with you?"

"No, sir, just me."

"Are you the field office manager for the Bureau?"

"Yes, I am," said Oskar.

"You hardly look qualified to run an organization of such importance," said the reverend.

"I beg your pardon, but I'm a veteran of the Union army and have a bachelor of arts degree. More relevant, however, I am committed to the education and elevation of the Negro," said Oskar.

"Hebrews 13: God equips those he calls. Come in, Mr. Mueller."

The church secretary served tea as they settled into a conversation in the parlor of the parsonage.

"I've read of the mission of the Freedmen's Bureau, and I am encouraged that Congress has taken steps to do more for the freedman than President Johnson appears willing to do," said the reverend. "The Confederate sympathizers in our midst are giddy at the prospects of a former slave owner now in the White House, especially one who puts previous political adversaries in power. I pray that the Bureau will be successful and that it is just the beginning of Congress's measures to ensure that the wolves hiding amongst us don't re-emerge."

"Do you believe that could happen?" asked Oskar.

"Unfortunately, my boy, I do. In some ways, Kentucky waited until the war was over before seceding from the Union. The Whigs and Democrats are organizing to ensure their candidates maintain control of the local and state governments. The nation is focused on the secessionist states; Kentucky is not top of mind. I share this with you because we will need your help to shine the light on the problems."

"I appreciate your counsel," said Oskar.

"So, how can I be of assistance?"

"My initial priorities are relief efforts for the destitute, education, and helping the freedmen get fair wages as they go back to work. That will help both them and the farmers. I understand you have provided some education to some of the county's Blacks?"

"We have a Sunday School. It's religious instruction. About a third of the students are Colored. They may have absorbed some basic reading skills through it, but it's not education in the sense you suggest."

"We plan to open a school for children and night classes for adults," said Oskar. "For the Negro to advance, they need basic education. It is crucial for integration into society."

"Agreed. Beyond that, education is foundational to develop the whole soul; it advances an individual's self-respect," the reverend said.

"I have a teacher arriving next week from Cincinnati. Can you provide classroom space in the school building?"

"Hmm. Some parents would object to their children attending school in the same building as Colored children, so it will be better if you set up your classroom in the church basement."

"Are they not Christians?" said Oskar.

"You aren't so naïve as to believe that people universally accept the equality of the races, are you?" said the reverend.

"No, but I'm hopeful they will accept them once they sit side by side together."

"How have you come by your openness to the mixing of the races?" asked the clergyman.

"I was schooled by the Jesuits. I believe that each person is a deserving individual created by God. I fought amongst brave, Black men in the army during the war. The Negro deserves no less than any other."

"Your hope and youthful optimism inspire me. Acceptance will not happen without some anguish. It will require patience and persuasion on your part. Please let me know wherever you need help."

"I'm grateful. I can see where your experience and knowledge of the community will be helpful to me," said Oskar.

"Do you know how many students?" asked Reverend Thompson.

"No, do you?"

"We have thirty-one in Sunday school, but that's no indication of the total number of Colored children."

"I'm going to post some notices announcing the services of the Bureau that will include the school. How do I get word to all the farms and communities?" said Oskar.

"You can reach many by visiting the areas on the edge of town, where freedmen have set up camps. Deliver your notices to the churches. We can reach the faithful through the pulpit. News tends to spread quickly by word of mouth from there. You could put a notice in the newspaper, but few freedmen will see it there."

"But the planters will," said Oskar. "I want them to see the Bureau as relief for them too. I know I need to ease their concerns as well."

"I must apologize, Mr. Mueller."

"For what?"

"I judged you too quickly. Your youthful appearance. You bring energy, dedication, and a thoughtful approach to your vocation."

"Thank you, Reverend. Please, call me Oskar. I'm young enough to be your son." Oskar smirked.

The reverend smiled in return. "I'm grateful the Lord has sent you, Oskar."

#

The following week, Oskar acquired office furniture from the abandoned Union army camp at the fairgrounds outside of town. He met Captain John Hope, who had served in the local Hamilton Guard militia unit for the Union during the war and would be his liaison to the federal troops assigned to maintain order in the county.

He was also joined by two agents, both former military men, who would report to him—Joseph Hilduth from Boston and Thomas Elliott from Cleveland. The three canvassed the county and met as many freedmen as possible. They received and distributed the first set of food and clothing rations. They rented rooms in a house at the edge of town from a war widow, Mrs. Stewart, who would provide meals and do laundry for them.

On Friday morning, the three sat in the office at their desks, completing the paperwork required by the Bureau Officer's Manual so that the government had an accounting of the expenses and services provided. Oskar whistled as he totaled the number of food rations distributed on the form.

"Good afternoon. Is anyone here?" came a soft female voice from the lobby.

Oskar stopped in his doorway as he encountered a woman removing her hat, revealing golden blond hair. She shook her head, parting the strands and smiled at him. She wore a fitted dress that properly covered yet revealed her curves.

Oskar stood speechless for a moment, then said, "Good afternoon. Can I be of assistance?"

The other two agents now stood behind Oskar, gawking as well. Thomas pushed Oskar forward.

"Excuse me, boys; I'm looking for the Bureau Assistant," said the woman.

"I'm the field office Sub-assistant," said Oskar, walking forward to the counter between them. "I'm Oskar Mueller."

"I'm to report to the man in charge," said the woman.

"Yes, that's me."

"But you're the sub-assistant."

Thomas stifled a laugh.

"Agents Elliot and Hilduth, don't you have paperwork to complete before the weekend in your offices? I can assist the lady," said Oskar.

"Yes, sir," said Joseph.

"Yes, Mr. Sub-assistant," said Thomas. They broke into laughter as they shut the door behind them.

Oskar, now red-faced, said, "I'm sorry about them. I am in charge. That's my title, sub-assistant."

"I see. I apologize, Mr. ..."

"Mueller, Oskar Mueller."

"I'm Mrs. Albert... Your teacher."

"Oh, yes, Mrs. Albert. I'm sorry. I wasn't sure when you'd be arriving. Welcome." He reached out his hand.

She stepped to the counter. Oskar shook longer than typical, again losing himself in her presence. She withdrew it, causing him to redden again.

"I left my bags on the sidewalk. Could someone carry them up for me?" she asked.

"Yes, one moment." Oskar yelled, "Thomas?"

Thomas immediately opened the door. "Yes, sir?"

"Would you be so kind as to retrieve Mrs. Albert's bags from down on the sidewalk?"

"Happy to. Hi!" Thomas gave a wave as he walked past and through the door.

"Won't you come in? Please have a seat," said Oskar.

Oskar sat behind his desk, and she took one of the two wooden chairs facing him.

"How was your journey?" he asked.

"The trains were running a little behind this afternoon, but otherwise, it was a pleasant trip. It's beautiful countryside."

"It is. I'm amazed at how quickly I've grown used to the rural landscape. I'm from the city, Cincinnati, like you."

"Oh, how did you know?" she asked.

"From your profile. The Freedmen's Aid Society provided it to me. What part of town are you from?"

"My late husband and I lived on Seventh Street, near Plum."

"Oh, I'm sorry for your loss. You're not in mourning still?" he said.

"No. It's been two years. William died in the army. He contracted typhoid."

"That's horrible," said Oskar. "To devote your life to the cause and have it taken by disease. Again, I'm sorry. I was in the Ninth. I enlisted during the final year. I feel blessed to continue the fight for the Union in the Bureau now."

"Oh, I'm sorry. You look so young. Your service to your country is admirable," she said.

"As is yours. I'm delighted to have you here. We have over one hundred students ready to start classes."

"One hundred. That's wonderful. How many teachers are we?" asked Mrs. Albert.

"Just you."

"No, that can't be the case. I can't possibly instruct one hundred students by myself."

"One hundred and thirty-two," he said.

"What?"

"There are one hundred and thirty-two enrolled as of this morning. I just finished the form," said Oskar.

"How am I going to do that? It's too many. These are new students. Most have never been to school before. Oh, what have I done?" She put her hand before her mouth to shield her quivering lip.

"Mrs. Albert… Mrs. Albert," said Oskar.

"Yes?"

"It's going to be fine. We're going to do this. I'm going to help you."

CHAPTER 5

Cincinnati – Fall 1865

"I'm finished," said Lizzie, placing the last sealed envelope in the large pile on the dining room table. "It tastes terrible."

"Have a drink," said her mother, Annie Bennett Mueller, handing her a glass of water. "It will wash away the taste of the glue."

"It's awful," said Lizzie.

"Thank you for your service to the cause," said Mary Berry, Annie's long-time feminist friend.

"Who are all these letters going to?" asked Lizzie.

"We're mailing them to men and women across Cincinnati. It's part of a national campaign to win the ballot for women," said Mary. "Did you read the letter?"

Lizzie shook her head.

"Read it to me," said Mary, handing her one of the printed letters.

Lizzie read with Mary helping her with the words she didn't know.

Dear Friend:

As the question of Suffrage is now agitating the public mind, it is the hour for Woman to make her demand.

Propositions have already been made on the floor of Congress to so amend the Constitution as to exclude Women from a voice in the Government. As this would be to turn the wheels of legislation backward, let the Women of the Nation now unitedly protest against such a desecration of the Constitution, and petition for that right which is at the foundation of all Government, the right of representation.*

Send your petition, when signed to your representative in Congress, at your earliest convenience.

Address all communications to
Standard Office, 48 Beekman St., New York.
On behalf of the National Women's Rights Committee

E. Cady Stanton,
S. B. Anthony,
Lucy Stone

** See Bill of Mr. Jenckes, of Rhode Island*

"Very good. You're an excellent reader," said Mary.

"Lizzie, it's time you're off to bed. Say goodnight to Auntie Mary," said Annie.

"Papa didn't review my lessons," said Lizzie.

"He's at a meeting. He'll look at them when he returns. You can talk to him in the morning."

"Yes, ma'am."

"Give me a kiss," said Annie. "Goodnight."

After Lizzie retreated upstairs, Mary said, "She's such a beautiful child and so intelligent."

"*Precocious*, you mean?" said Annie.

"No, she demonstrates advanced poise and humility for

someone her age. She'll be a model new woman, like her mother."

"She's not much like me, I'm afraid. She tends to favor Max's reserved nature. I should be thankful, I suppose. She's rarely cross or argumentative as some girls her age are. I worry that she won't advocate enough for herself."

"She's a smart one. She'll do just fine," assured Mary.

"I think getting her into the right school will be crucial. Max and I disagree on what's best at her age. I've suggested she go east to a boarding school. He insists she stay close to home and remains in school at St. Mary's. I worry that the nuns won't challenge her and give her every advantage as the boys in the class. The Catholic Church is so patriarchal and stuck in its ways. No friend of the women's movement."

"It's something to keep your eye on. As former teachers, we know how the schools can relegate girls below their abilities," said Mary.

"Mm hm," agreed Annie.

Mary said, "I have come to appreciate that not all nuns are created equal. You've heard me speak of Sister Anthony O'Connell at the hospital; she taught me nursing. She is as strong a woman and an independent thinker as anyone I've met. She's been a driver in expanding St. John's army hospital into the new Good Samaritan Hospital. She's a force. She's helped me secure a head nurse position."

"Congratulations, Mary. That's wonderful news."

"I'll do less hands-on nursing and instead focus on guiding the other nurses."

Annie said, "You know. As horrible as the war was, I am grateful for the opportunities it gave women to demonstrate what we can do. And men now accept us doing things we couldn't just five years ago. You're a classic example."

Mary said, "You've been on the leading edge for years in your work helping Max run his business. I've always said you do more for the cause by working rather than campaigning."

"You've been a strong supporter and a dear friend. It's been satisfying, but I'm getting restless," said Annie.

"Uh-oh, what does that mean?" said Mary.

"Now that the war is won and slavery is dead, I have more faith than ever in man's ability to respect all people's rights. We can change things, but it won't happen without focused attention. I want to do more. I need to do more. Now is the time."

Annie placed the envelopes in a cloth bag as she continued, "I've been exchanging letters with my cousin, Elizabeth. This campaign she, Susan B. Anthony, and Lucy Stone are leading is brilliant. It makes so much sense to act now. Rather than fight in each state, we will focus on the national government and a constitutional amendment to secure women's rights through the vote."

"I don't want to dampen your enthusiasm, but it seems like a long shot to me," said Mary.

"I understand it's not a given, but we must seize the moment. Men will not do this for us. We must use the momentum for Negro suffrage to win universal suffrage for all."

"You're preaching to the choir, sister. I'm all in. I'll address these envelopes and do whatever I can, but I have tempered expectations."

"Look at what's been done for Negroes. Five years ago, we had hope, but we didn't expect all the enslaved would be freed, and we'd be talking about political equality with the vote."

"But look at the cost. And suffrage is not a given," said Mary.

"Yes, the cost was dear, but we won. The Southern aristocracy was crushed. The patriarchy must be next."

"What else do we do besides these letters? What does your cousin need?"

Annie said, "Congress is starting to debate additional constitutional amendments to help further secure Negro rights. As they craft these amendments, we must have our voices be heard, that women are no less due equal rights than Black men. Suffrage is so critical to gaining and keeping our rights. These letters will support a petition that Elizabeth, Lucy, and Susan will present to Congress. They're going to do a speaking tour. I'm thinking of joining them."

"You are?" said Mary, surprised.

"Yes. It's something I've wanted to do for years. I almost didn't marry Max because I knew it meant abandoning the chance to go on tour. He's been so supportive of all my work so far. I think he'll understand why I have to do this now."

"That's exciting. I'm happy for you. What about Lizzie?"

"Oh, Mary. It's tearing me apart. I want to support and encourage her, but I feel a part of me is suffocating by not doing work that challenges and excites me. It's so unfair that I have to choose one over the other. Men don't have to choose. It's never even contemplated."

"I'm sorry, dear. I can see you're conflicted." Mary placed her hand on Annie's.

"I am. I agonize over it every day. I feel guilty for even considering my choices. I look at my sweet baby and wonder if she feels I'm not giving her enough. What does she think of me as a mother? But for my sanity, I've decided I must do this. During the war, I had a long bout of melancholy, something I'm prone to. I felt so weighed down by the mundane tasks of home. Even the work at the shop, the accounting, the scheduling, and the correspondence became rote for me. I was so unhappy, and that affected Lizzie and Max too."

Annie took a deep breath. "Lizzie's old enough now and doesn't need me as she did. She'll see what I'm doing for all women and know I'm doing it for her too. She may not understand today, but she will."

"So you've decided then?" said Mary.

"I have. The thought of it invigorates me. I must do this now, but I need to figure out how to tell Max."

CHAPTER 6

Cincinnati – Christmas Eve 1865

Max held the door, then followed Annie into the Eichen Garten saloon in the German district called Over-the-Rhine. The bar was packed with partiers of all ages, mostly Germans, most drinking mugs of lager beer. The voices and laughter were joyous signs of restored peace in the country. Annie nearly stumbled as she was pressed into the crowd. She stood, hands at her sides, waiting for an opening. She said something to Max.

"What?" he shouted.

She spoke directly into his ear. "I can't move. I've never seen it like this."

"It's glorious, isn't it?" he smiled. Max slid past her, pressing against her backside, then pushed sideways through the crowd. Annie took his hand and followed in the gap he created. The night air felt refreshing as they stepped outside into the rear beer garden. The crowd was quieter in the open space but nearly as packed. As they worked their way to the family table in the center of the courtyard, Max acknowledged familiar faces with raised eyebrows, smiles, hugs, and kisses. They approached the table and greeted their family. Around the table sat Max's mother, Katharina, Max's sister Marie, her boyfriend, Wolf, and Max's brother Peter, the newsman home from Washington. As his youngest brother Oskar approached the table, Max hugged him. "Little brother. How goes the quest to reform the Rebels?"

"I'm getting things established. I want to tell you so much. I need a beer. You?" said Oskar.

Max said "I'll come with you." He made the motion of tipping a mug to the others at the table. They all nodded.

Oskar and Max pushed their way back inside to the bar, encountering old friends along the way. They went behind the bar, and Oskar greeted their sister, who now ran the saloon for their mother.

Helene hugged her brothers.

"This is tremendous," said Max. "So many people."

"It's going to be a long night," said Helene.

"You're taking tomorrow evening off and coming to my house for dinner, aren't you?" said Max.

"Max, I don't know."

"You have to. It's Christmas."

"We'll see," she said.

"I understand."

Oskar filled seven beer mugs and lined them up on the bar. He took four, and Max grabbed the others. Oskar took sips off the top of each foaming beer to minimize the spillage on their return to the table.

"Where's Mother?" Max asked Annie when they returned.

"She had enough of the crowd and went upstairs to bed," said Annie.

The Eichen Garten was a central gathering place for German families since Katharina and her deceased husband opened it in the 1830s. Max's family had lived in the apartment above the saloon.

Helene brought another round of beers and sat with the family as they caught up.

Annie said to Peter, "Tell us the latest from Washington. Will Congress do anything to better President Johnson's failing Reconstruction plan?"

"It's been a wild month since Congress returned from their six-month recess," said Peter. "Thaddeus Stevens and the other radical Republicans are livid that Johnson implemented his plan during the recess without any input from Congress. It was a chaotic first session in the House as the speaker refused to read the names of the newly elected Southern congressmen—they were blocked from joining the session. Congress fears that the quickly elected Southerners are the same bunch of traitors who seceded from the Union and sought to destroy the country. The Republicans are planning a series of acts to strengthen what they see as the president's inadequate Reconstruction measures."

"Do you see any movement toward suffrage for the emancipated?" asked Annie.

"Bills are being drafted, but nothing firm yet," said Peter.

"I'd like to see universal suffrage that includes women. Do you hear any talk of it?"

"There are a few senators from New England who might support it, but I don't see it gaining enough support. Congress is focused on the rights of the freedmen."

Annie said, "The Thirteenth Amendment abolishing slavery finally received enough states' approval to be ratified, so that issue is resolved."

Peter said, "Hardly resolved. There are still some state legislatures that haven't approved it—Mississippi, Kentucky, and others. Plenty of resistance remains. Oskar, how are you finding Kentuckians' sentiment? You're in the thick of trying to implement the reforms."

"It's very mixed," said Oskar. "Some are trying to co-exist with the freedmen under a paid labor system, and others still refuse to accept the war's outcome."

"The issue remains polarizing everywhere," said Peter. "President Johnson has, in effect, declared that Reconstruction is complete, and he's ready to move on. Congress has a different idea. Max, how would you characterize sentiment here in Cincinnati?"

Max said, "The newspapers are filled with daily updates and editorials. People read them and have opinions. Some think the Southerners need to be punished and prevented from regaining their power, while others have faith that the aristocracy of the South has learned their lesson and want a reconciled nation. For the most part, however, I think Cincinnatians want to move past Reconstruction."

Oskar said, "That is a luxury that the people of the North have. The war didn't destroy their cities; their children have schools, and their factories and shops provide jobs so people can feed their families. And they don't have millions of freedmen searching for their place in the post-war order. The whole nation must stay informed and engaged enough to help the people of the South rebuild their society with the freedmen in their new place."

"You're doing good work, Oskar," said Max. "The Bureau is fortunate to have men like you."

"I wish we had more. There's so much to do, and we don't have enough staff," said Oskar. "I have two agents and one teacher. A surgeon from the Lexington office visits once a week to provide for the health of the freedmen. The Western Freedman's Aid Society, led by Levi Coffin, here in Cincinnati, has been a godsend. They've sent clothing and other aid to supplement what the government provides. Any support you can lend to their efforts, Max, is appreciated. They have provided an amazing teacher who is inspiring to see in action. She's teaching more than a hundred Colored children to read. She works tirelessly, with an infectious smile that makes the days pass most pleasantly."

Annie said, "Oskar, you speak fondly of this teacher. Do I detect more than a professional interest in this woman?"

Oskar smiled, "She is an oasis of joy that nourishes me in the desert of the Bureau's work."

Max laughed, "How poetic. Oskar, are you courting this woman?"

He blushed. "Mrs. Albert and I are becoming acquainted with each other."

Annie said, "*Mrs.*?"

"She's a widow. She lost her husband in the war."

"How old is Mrs. Albert," said Max.

"Twenty-one," said Oskar.

"Where is she from?"

"Here, Cincinnati. After the war, she felt her calling was to return to teaching to help the freedmen. She, like me, has moved to Paris."

"Does Mrs. Albert have a first name?" said Marie.

"Catherine," answered Oskar.

"I'm happy you found someone," said Marie. "I worry about you there, all by yourself."

"Don't worry about me. My life is full of blessings."

Max raised his mug, "To Oskar. Freedmen's advocate, suitor, poet."

They clinked glasses and exclaimed, "*Prost!*" and "*Zum Wohl!*"

Marie said, "Wolf would also like to make a toast."

Wolf hesitated as all eyes turned to him. "To families. To all of you who have welcomed me like one of your own and to the new family that Marie and I will make together."

Helene said, "Are you saying? You and Marie?"

Marie nodded as she beamed, "Yes, we're going to be married."

They congratulated and cheered the couple.

"There's more," said Marie. "Wolf has applied for homestead land in South Dakota."

"Oh, Marie, Wolf," said Helene.

"Congratulations," said Oskar. "What made you decide to go west?"

Wolf said, "Since my discharge from the army, I've had little success finding good work. If I'm to have a family, I want more for them. The government is offering one hundred sixty acres to farm. After five years, you can apply for the deed to the property. I will receive three years credit for my army service so that the land will be ours after two years."

Helene said, "This is such a surprise—so much news. South Dakota is so far away. Have you told Mother?"

"No, we'll tell her tomorrow. We couldn't keep it to

ourselves any longer. I'm so happy," said Marie.

Max said, "We're all happy for you, both of you." They toasted again.

Annie smiled as her mind raced through the implications of Marie's announcement. Marie had lived with Max and her for the last eight years, keeping house and caring for Lizzie. They paid Marie a generous salary for a domestic, and it allowed Annie the freedom to work at Miller Industries and pursue her women's movement activities. She was indebted to Marie beyond words. She felt an unjustified pang of betrayal and then panic as her future plans imploded in her mind.

As the family sat and conversed, Max became quiet and glassy-eyed. Annie noticed and leaned into him. "What's the matter?"

"Nothing, Nothing at all. I'm counting my blessings." Max looked at his red-haired wife, the only love of his life. "Are you ready to go home?" He gave her a look that she recognized as his amorous yearning.

She wanted the comfort of him tonight. She nodded. "Let's go home."

#

After attending Christmas morning mass at St. Xavier Church, Annie, Max, and Lizzie took the horse-drawn omnibus to the St. Aloysius Orphanage for German children in Bond Hill, eight miles north of downtown. Max donated annually to the orphanage and a dozen other charitable institutions in town. Annie had purchased small toys and games, including tops, dominoes, jacks, and playing cards. They left Lizzie and the bag of games in the playroom with some of the younger children and joined the administrators and visiting parents in the parlor. A woman offered them punch and biscuits.

They approached the director, Fr. Ferneding, who spoke quietly with several children gathered around a Christmas tree. He stepped away from the children. "Mr. and Mrs. Mueller, Merry Christmas."

"Merry Christmas to you too, Father. I noticed work on the addition is progressing nicely out back," said Max.

"Yes, we're ahead of schedule. Since the war, our dormitories have been overflowing. More families, many now without fathers, can't manage. We're grateful for your generous donation. Thank you."

"We are blessed to be in a position to do it," said Max. "You're a busy man. How do you manage to be pastor at St. Paul's and your work here?"

"I am blessed with help at both institutions."

"Your tireless service is an inspiration," said Max.

"I confess, at my age, some days are difficult. I worry I fail to meet the Lord's and my congregation's expectations of me. I have asked the archbishop to allow me to focus my energies here at the orphan's home."

"You're leaving St. Paul's?"

"It's not imminent, but I hope in the next year or so," said the priest.

"You'll be missed Over-the-Rhine. You've had a meaningful impact on the community."

"You're too kind."

The orphanage secretary stood behind the priest. "Excuse me, Father. I'm sorry to interrupt. This is Mrs. Alice Schultoff."

The woman, wearing a bulging, too-small overcoat, bowed slightly. "Father, I just wanted to say Merry Christmas and thank you."

"Merry Christmas," he said, taking the woman's hand. "Are you visiting your child?"

"Yes, two. Lina and George."

"How did you find them?"

"Oh, they're well. Very well. I can see they're being taken good care of. They have plenty to eat here. They're smiling. They're warm. It was wonderful to see them so happy on Christmas."

"I'm glad you could be with them today," said the priest.

"It was the best gift I could ask for. I feel I'm such a terrible mother. I can't be there for them. I want to, I do," said Alice.

"It's all right, dear. Don't blame yourself."

"I miss them terribly. I know they have each other. There's some solace in that. I don't know when I'll be able to take them back. I'm trying. I'm trying to earn enough. It's so hard."

"We'll take good care of them until you do. I promise."

"Thank you, Father." She teared up. "Bless you."

"Bless you, my dear."

She turned and made a beeline for the door. Max followed her out onto the sidewalk.

"Alice," called Max.

She stopped and turned, tears on her cheeks. "Yes?"

"I'm Max."

"Hi." She wiped her tears with her sleeve.

"I heard you talking to Father Ferneding inside. I wanted to wish you a Merry Christmas."

"Thank you. Merry Christmas to you too." She nodded and forced a smile.

He took her hand and pressed twenty dollars in folded bills into her hand. "I'll pray that your children can come home soon." He smiled. "God Bless."

She looked at the bills in her hand. "Oh, thank you. God bless you, sir."

Back inside, Max and Annie mixed with the visiting parents.

Max said to Annie, "We can't build enough orphanages, churches, and asylums. We have to find a better way. We have to create opportunities for people to lift themselves up. People need to earn a living to earn self-respect. People need both."

"I know," said Annie.

"We need to take care of each other. Rich, poor, Black, white. I know there are problems across the country, but there's much misery right here in Cincinnati. Most choose not to see it."

"I know," Annie agreed again.

"I struggle with it. I admit I love my comforts—the new house we're building, the food we eat, the clothes I wear. Why was I blessed?" said Max.

"We do our part with what we have. We each do the best we know how."

"It's not enough. There isn't enough. All I know to do is to help where I can and make our city as vibrant as possible so more people can thrive."

"You've always been true to that." She patted his arm. "You're a good man, Max Mueller."

CHAPTER 7

Cincinnati – Spring 1866

Max sat at a barstool talking with John Niemes, the proprietor of the new Niemes Café on Vine Street.

"The place looks terrific," said Max.

"Have you seen the dining room?" asked John.

"Not yet. My friend and I will be having lunch when he arrives."

"It's on me. I appreciate your help with getting the approvals from the city."

"John, your investment is good for every citizen in Cincinnati," said Max. "A vibrant city with places like yours helps us compete with Chicago and St. Louis. This is a huge step up from your old saloon."

"Three times the number of seats."

"Congratulations," said Max tipping his beer toward John. "Whose is it?"

"Hauck Brewery's direct from wood to you," John said, pointing to the large keg atop the bar.

"It's good," said Max.

"How's the house construction coming?" John asked.

"It's finally underway. We had the original plans drawn up before the war but had to put the project on hold due to a lack of labor to work on it. Advancements in fixtures and materials over the last four years warranted a reworking of the plans. We hope to be in the house by the holidays."

A sleeve with a hook protruding from the end snagged Max's beer mug and slid it quickly down the bar and into the hand of a dark-haired man. He lifted the mug, downed the remainder of the beer, and slammed it back onto the bar.

John was taken aback and stared at the Irishman with the missing right arm.

Max said, "John Niemes, meet Patrick Sweeney."

"Nice to meet you," said Patrick. "Can I get a whiskey and another beer for my friend here?"

As John moved to get the drinks, Patrick rubbed his hook in a mock caress against Max's cheek. "How are you, governor?"

Max pushed his arm away. Patrick and Max had been friends since they attended school together as boys. "Quit. I'm well, thank you. You seem to be in better spirits this week," said Max.

"I am, thanks to you. John Steptoe has hired me to be his shop foreman and salesman for Steptoe and McFarlan," said Patrick.

"That's wonderful news. I knew you would land on your feet," said Max.

"I owe you for making the introduction. I think he sees me as a charity case. The only reason he's hiring a crippled former soldier is to do you a favor."

"That's not so. Your experience managing the furniture factory before the war will be invaluable to him. The work you and I did developing new machines to make furniture assembly more efficient is what he needs in his business. He's trying to build the next generation of tools for woodworking like I'm trying to develop metalworking and machining tools. Don't undersell yourself. He's hiring you for your brain, not your missing right hand."

"Always my biggest supporter," said Patrick. "Thank you. I owe you once again. I promise I'll repay you for all you did for Molly while I was in the army."

"I'm glad I could do it," said Max.

"Tell me, what's new with you?"

"Business is robust, city council seems to be in a cooperative mood around some of our proposals to enhance the city's standing, and our house is now under construction. I am blessed."

"Annie and Lizzie?" inquired Patrick.

"Lizzie is my sunshine. Annie is now energized around campaigning for women's suffrage."

"She insists on making noise about that?"

"Yes."

"She's a handful. You're a better man than me, putting up with that."

"Over the last decade, I've come to understand her frustrations," said Max. "I wouldn't want to switch places with women. They have the same need for accomplishment but aren't given a fair chance to pursue their own course. She has reconnected with her cousin, Elizabeth Cady Stanton, and latched onto the idea that the vote is the path to women gaining an equal footing with men."

"Hmm. I'm not sure most women have the need for accomplishment the way Annie does. Molly seems pretty content with being a wife and mother. She hated having to take in sewing and laundry while I was away."

"Maybe so," said Max. "But for those women who do want to do something else, they should have the opportunity. I'm thinking of Lizzie, your daughter too."

"My Katie's a good girl. She's not the type to ruffle feathers."

"Anyway," said Max. "I have tried to support her efforts, but she's taking it a step further now. She wants to go on tour."

"Tour where?"

"Around the country. She wants to join the women campaigning for women's voting rights."

"You're not going to let her do that are you?" said Patrick.

"I don't want her to go, but she has her mind made up."

"Max, this is where you need to put your foot down. You're the man. If she does this, she's not fulfilling her duty as your wife. Don't allow it. You're not considering it, are you?"

"I am," said Max.

"Christ. Your wife parading across the country with those other hens, riling people up and leaving you home to fend for yourself. How's that going to look to people? To your customers, to voters? It makes you look weak."

"I have to let her follow her heart. She's working to make things better in her own way, just like I do in mine. How can I deny her that? She's stood by me. When we married, we vowed to support each other."

"You're like a brother to me, but I'll never understand how you let your principles drive you against the face of common sense," said Patrick.

"I can't do anything else."

"I know. I surrender. This new development does give me pause to bring up the proposition I was going to offer you."

"What is it?" said Max.

"Doesn't sound like the time is right. Forget it."

"No, I want to hear it."

"Steptoe has asked me to visit some of the east coast factories making new machine tools to learn the latest trends. I thought you might want to join me. You could bring some of the ideas back to your business. It would be fun to travel together."

"I know some of the Philadelphia firms are adopting some of what they're doing in Europe. I would love to see them. I'll think about it. If I can't go, maybe I could send my engineer. When are you going?" asked Max.

"I haven't made plans yet. Let me know what you think."

CHAPTER 8

Hinds County, Mississippi – Summer 1866

Aaron moved his family into a rented house in Jackson. Elliot Grayson's family was still living in the plantation house. Aaron calculated that within two years, he could force Grayson out of the partnership and move into the house. Mary was hesitant about living in the country, but Aaron was confident she would soften in time.

Aaron rode along his daily route from downtown Jackson to the Grayson farm. Due to a lack of traffic and maintenance during the war, weeds had overtaken most of the road. He used the time alone in the cool of the morning to think and plan his day. He thought about the path that had brought him here. He had been born on a plantation near Georgetown, Kentucky, the son of a Southern mother, whose family had plantations in both Mississippi and Kentucky, and William Johnson, a Northerner who had an insurance business in Cincinnati. As an only child, his companion was the enslaved boy John, the son of his father and one of the house servants, Jenny. After his mother died, his father enrolled him in St. Xavier College and moved him to Cincinnati. He graduated, married, and practiced insurance law there.

When his father William passed, just before the war, his will revealed Aaron's two half-brothers, John and Max Mueller, a child his father sired with his German housemaid at the time. William bequeathed his estate to Max and Aaron and freed John. All three brothers ended up in Cincinnati and concealed their relationship from all but their closest family and friends.

During the war, Aaron's law practice floundered, and he engaged in business deals to sell contraband and arms to the Confederates. Max turned him in, and Aaron spent the last two years of the war in a Union Army prison. He signed President Lincoln's amnesty pledge and was released at the war's end, but found he was a pariah in Ohio's legal community. To provide for his family, he returned to Mississippi to invest his remaining inheritance in cotton.

He had come full circle, back to the South. He felt no affinity with either Northerners or Southerners. His parents' differing heritage and viewpoints resulted in a coldness in Aaron that prevented him from forming allegiances. He was plagued by feelings of aloneness and harbored insecurities that he learned to cover with hubris. He was confident this deal with Grayson would return him to his appropriate stature amongst the Southern planter class.

He thought of his half-brother John. As boys, they were playmates until his mother taught him his place was above the enslaved. He distanced himself from John and came to accept the commonly-held belief that Negroes were an inferior race, a step below immigrants, poor whites, and anyone not of the Southern aristocracy.

When he learned that he and John shared a father, it caused significant dissonance within him as he tried to understand their relationship. He dealt with the confusion by remaining distant and not deviating from society's expected relationship between a Black and white man. He agreed to have John accompany him on his journey south to look for his mother for several reasons. Deep down, he felt he had betrayed his childhood playmate, and the trip together was a sort of atonement. He also wanted to learn how emancipated men thought—valuable knowledge in his new role. He and John conversed during their travel together but maintained their aloofness.

John returned to Cincinnati with his long-lost mother, and Aaron hoped he might be happy now.

Aaron believed that revamping Grayson's slave plantation into a paid-labor farm would require incentives and rewards for the hands. A key motivation for the freedmen was ownership and a sense of control of their destiny. He felt he could accomplish this through a version of the sharecropping system. It would require a delicate balance of freedom, constraints, and economics. He was formulating his plan for the upcoming year. The 1866 season had already been put in motion, and he planned to fund the wages, milk Grayson of his equity, and pray that the harvest was good enough not to bankrupt him.

As he rode along, calculating cotton prices and monthly labor costs, a group of white men charged him from the bushes, forcing him to swerve his horse to avoid a collision. One of the men grabbed his reigns and pulled Aaron to the ground. Another shoved a gun in his face.

"Don't kill me," stammered Aaron. "What do you want?"

"Whatever you have," sneered the gunman in a Southern drawl. "Your money."

"All right," said Aaron.

The man pulled open Aaron's coat, checking his breast pockets. He pulled out Aaron's leather wallet, took the bills and threw the wallet on the ground. "What else do you have?"

"Nothing. That's all."

"You're a Yankee. A damn carpetbagger. Here to cheat us out of what the army didn't already take."

"No, I'm not. I'm helping Elliot Grayson on his farm," said Aaron.

"You talk like a Yankee. Dress like a Yankee. I hate Yankees."

"I lived in the North for a while, but my family's from near Greenville. Western Magnolias plantation,"

"Never heard of it. You a Negro-loving Yankee?"

"No," said Aaron. "I told you, I'm not a Yankee."

"Give me your ring," said the gunman.

Aaron looked at his wedding ring, then at the gun barrel still pointed at him. He wriggled the ring off and handed it over.

"You got a watch?"

Aaron unhooked the chain and handed over his pocket watch.

"Anything else?"

"No."

"Take his boots," instructed the man holding Aaron's horse. "We can sell 'em."

The gunman pointed at his boots with his gun.

Aaron angrily removed his boots.

#

Aaron regained consciousness and lay on the road, rubbing the knot on his forehead. He sat up and covered his eyes, shading them from the blazing sun. "Shit," he muttered. "Shit," he fumed again. He stood and waited for the dizziness to pass, then brushed the dust off his clothes and started walking back into town.

After retrieving a pair of shoes from home and reassuring Mary he was fine, he went to the sheriff's office. "I was robbed and assaulted on the road just outside of town. My horse and valuables were taken."

The deputy said, "Were you riding by yourself?"

Aaron nodded.

"Unarmed? What did you expect, then?"

"I didn't expect to be robbed by thugs. I've been riding that road morning and evening for months now."

"And this is the first time you've encountered marauders?" said the deputy.

"Yes," said Aaron.

"They're all over the countryside. Most of them are returning soldiers who can't find work. If you're going to ride in the countryside alone, you need to carry a weapon to protect yourself."

"I will going forward," said Aaron, "but what are you going to do about them? My things?"

"Do you know who these men were?" said the deputy.

"No. I've never seen them before."

"Not really much we can do, then."

"What are you doing about the raiders in the countryside? Patrols, maybe?" said Aaron.

"There's a lot of countryside," said the deputy.

"Well, shouldn't they be sought out and arrested? It wasn't that far from town."

"You can talk to the federal troops stationed here. Sounds like that's their job. The governor and president have tasked them with restoring order."

"Thanks, for nothing," said Aaron. As he stepped outside the station and closed the door, he heard the sheriffs laughing.

#

Aaron sat behind the desk in Elliot Grayson's study, relegating the owner to the chair in front of him. "You have too many fallow fields. Those acres are the difference between a profit and a loss for us this year. Cotton is up to forty-five cents a pound. We're going to miss out on a peak year. Prices will fall again by next year as supply increases."

"There weren't enough workers to plant them," said Grayson. "Too many Negroes left after the war. Most of the women don't want to work in the fields anymore. They want to stay home with their children like white women. And the spring rains delayed planting some of the fields."

"Why didn't you hire white men to help plant, then?" said Aaron.

"White men don't want to work side-by-side with Blacks," said Grayson. "It's beneath them. Why don't you see that?"

"Plenty of men, former soldiers and otherwise, are looking for work. If offered the wage and a place to stay, separate from the Black workers, you could have hired enough," said Aaron.

"Well, we didn't have quarters for them to stay in, so I don't think so. They don't mix. They aren't going to work in the fields with 'em."

"You've got to let go of the way things were," said Aaron. "Things aren't going back to the way they were. You can only move forward. We're going to build a bunkhouse for white workers this winter once the crops are in."

"You think because you read that book by that Doctor Barbee, from DeSoto county, that you know better how to make a farm profitable. That book was written to convince Northerners to invest in the South, but it doesn't have all the answers."

"Maybe so," said Aaron, "but to make this farm profitable again, we've got to change. What do you propose we do? We barely have enough labor to tend our planted acreage this year. How will we manage next year when we plant every available field?"

"The young ones don't work anymore, because of the school," said Grayson. "That's a loss. Some of those teenage boys were the most productive ones we had. I've apprenticed two I found whose parents left them; Freedmen's Bureau permitted a contract. They're working for me until they're eighteen. I'm trying to get some of the other strong ones to stop going to that new school, at least during the peak times, so that they can work in the fields."

"Well, those are creative ideas. That's what I need you to do," said Aaron.

"This is my farm. You're talking down at me like you own it."

"Elliot, this is *our* farm now. I've paid you over half of the value of the land. I won't allow your mismanagement to sink me."

"Mismanagement? You are accusing me of mismanagement?" said Grayson.

"You've underplanted, don't have enough labor, and can't

seem to keep our tools, mules, or horses from being stolen."

"Hell, you had one of our horses stolen right out from under your ass," said Grayson. "Why is this my fault? I can't help it if the scum are stealing and selling our supplies. I can't control the weather. You're full of shit, blaming all that on me."

"You're the residing owner. Your job is to oversee the operations. If you can't do it, then I will."

"Bloody hell," Grayson screamed. "I won't be told what to do by some Yankee lawyer who read a book on farming."

Evan, the house manager, knocked on the office door. "Excuse me, Mr. Grayson, Mr. Johnson."

"What is it?" shouted Grayson.

"I'm sorry, sir, but the pantry was cleaned out last night. They took most of the supplies. We don't have anything to make dinner with."

"Holy hell," shouted Grayson. "They pilfer my food. Let 'em eat what they stole. No dinner tonight."

"What about your family, sir?" said Evan.

"There's nothing?"

"A little cornmeal, some eggs. We can pick some greens," said the house manager.

"Fine, fix them something, anything. I don't care."

"Yes, sir," said the man as he left the room.

Aaron said, "You have to feed the hands."

"It will do them some good to go hungry," said Grayson. "I can't whip 'em to teach them a lesson anymore."

"We have to provide them food. It's part of our contract," said Aaron. "If we can't keep them satisfied, they'll go to work down the road. They have choices now."

Grayson screamed, "Damn Yankees! How are we supposed to do this?" He left the room.

Aaron called Evan back into the office. "Make a list of what you need. Send a man into town to buy the supplies and a lock for the pantry door. No one goes into the pantry unless you are there to supervise them, you understand? I'm going to create a ledger for the food, and you will log all of it in and out. I will hold you responsible for food supplies, you understand?"

"Yes, sir."

CHAPTER 9

Paris, Kentucky – Summer 1866

Dressed in shorts, Oskar called out the exercises to Thomas and Joseph. Catherine sat on the back steps watching them in the yard.

"Raise the bricks over your head like this," directed Oskar. "Five more. Come on, keep going," he encouraged. After that, they took turns with the jump rope and finished with a sprint around the yard.

"Enough," complained Joseph, bent over, and breathing heavily.

Catherine clapped. "Excellent, boys. Healthy bodies make for sharp minds."

Oskar ran across the yard and executed several front flips, turned, and did two more. He stood in front of Catherine and stretched his arms in front and to either side. Catherine couldn't help but admire his powerful physique.

"Show off," said Thomas.

"How do you move like that?" asked Joseph. "I'm out of breath from the calisthenics alone."

"It's disciplined conditioning. I trained with the Turners three times a week. I'm trying to maintain a regular schedule here. I'm bringing you two along. You'll be as fit as me before you know it."

"That sounds like an excessive amount of unnecessary movement," said Joseph.

Mrs. Stewart called from the back porch. "Supper is about ready. You boys want to wash up before dinner?"

"Thank you, Mrs. Stewart," said Oskar. "We'll be right in."

After they cleaned up, they all sat around the widow's dining room table, said grace, and feasted on her home cooking.

"Oskar tells me you're teaching the Negroes to read. How are they responding to you?" Mrs. Stewart said to Catherine.

"They're quite eager generally. Like any group of children, some are more focused than others," said Catherine.

"Do they have the ability to learn?"

"Oh, yes, only a few students are struggling. I'm looking for volunteers to help tutor if you're interested."

"Well, I'm not sure I'm suited to working with Negroes," said Mrs. Stewart. "I don't see the point of it. It's a lot of effort just to have field hands that can read."

"If we ever hope for the Negroes to support themselves, we have to give them the educational foundation to do more than farm," said Catherine. "We're starting with reading, but basic arithmetic is next. People need to be able to read, write, and figure to get along in the world—work, vote someday."

"Vote!?" said Mrs. Stewart. "Not here in Kentucky. Y'all can do that in your states up North. Freedom for the Negro is one thing, but what do they know about politics? They start rising up and acting like us, and there are men in this state that will put them in their place."

"Congress is about to pass another constitutional amendment that makes Negroes and anyone else born in the country citizens and guarantees them equal protection under the law. They're also considering reducing a state's congressional representation if anyone over twenty-one is denied the right to vote. Times are changing, Mrs. Stewart," said Oskar.

"Well, I don't think they mean Negroes when they say anyone over twenty-one."

"Oh, that's *exactly* who they mean," said Oskar.

"Hmm. It seems like Congress is unfairly picking on states like Kentucky. We never left the Union, and now they're trying to treat us like the Rebel states. Why can't they leave us alone? It's enough they let all the help go free."

Oskar rolled his eyes at his friends and let it drop.

"This chicken is delicious, Mrs. Stewart," said Catherine. "Where did you learn to cook?"

"My mother was a wonderful cook. She started teaching me her recipes when I was a young girl. Watching and then doing; it's the only way to learn anything."

"I agree. That's the same philosophy I use with reading," said Catherine.

"You were a teacher up there in Ohio?" the widow asked.

"Yes, I taught in the common schools in Cincinnati until I married. Then I started keeping house."

"How did you come to Paris, then?"

"My husband died in the war. I wanted to go back to work to keep my mind busy. I thought living in another part of the country would be an adventure, so here I am."

"Came here on your own. You spend an awful lot of time with these men. Not proper for a widow," said Mrs. Stewart.

"Most people have been fairly charitable toward me," said Catherine. "They recognize the work I'm doing under less-than-ideal circumstances."

"Well, you best watch it. People will start talking."

"I'll do that. Please let me know if you hear of anyone talking critically of me. I do appreciate you watching out for me."

After dinner, Oskar walked Catherine several blocks to her boarding house.

"Mrs. Stewart is like a mother watching over us," said Oskar.

"A Confederate mother who doesn't approve of the work we're doing or the company we're keeping," said Catherine.

"We need to stay clear of her. She's the first one in town who will start talking if she gets the wrong idea."

"Does she have the wrong idea?" said Catherine.

Oskar stopped and turned toward her. "She has a point. In some circles, it's considered improper for an unmarried woman to spend so much time in the company of men."

"I'm here in this town alone. I'm doing a job for the government, assigned to work for men alongside men. What else am I supposed to do? The people in this town have no interest in me, a Northerner, a widow. Do you think my behavior is inappropriate?"

"No, of course not," he said.

"Mrs. Stewart was commenting on more than my work situation. She was talking about us."

"What about us?" said Oskar.

"She can tell there's more between you and me than our working relationship."

"Is there more?" said Oskar.

Catherine looked at Oskar. "What do you think? Is there?"

Oskar stammered. "Well, maybe. It's unstated."

"Maybe we need to state it, then," she said.

"I don't know how to state it, exactly."

"Why don't you try?"

Oskar took a deep breath. "You want me to state what I think our relationship is?"

"That would be nice," she said.

"You work for me as a teacher, and we've become friendly. Friends. We enjoy each other's company."

"I agree with all that. Anything else?" she said.

"I like you," he said slowly.

"And I like you."

"And I find you attractive, beautiful," he said.

"I find you attractive. Handsome."

Oskar blushed. He attended the all-male St. Xavier College for ten years and had little experience talking with women beyond his sisters and neighbors.

"I'm drawn to you, but it's not right," he said.

"What's not right about it?"

"You were married."

"I'm not married now. I don't want to be alone for the

rest of my life. I'm allowed to have feelings for men and court again."

"And you are under my supervision. It doesn't seem right," said Oskar.

"Anything else?" she said.

Oskar took a deep breath. "To be honest, I've never felt this way about anyone. I only know that when we are working, having dinner together, or walking, I feel you're the most important person in the world, and I don't want to leave you. I don't know what to do with that feeling."

They stood looking at each other. Catherine broke their silence by leaning in and kissing him. He returned the kiss, then more eagerly, then put his arms around her. He broke the kiss. "My goodness."

"What?" she said.

"That was a surprise. And wonderful."

"I have feelings for you, too, Oskar. I love being with you. You reassure me and comfort me and make me feel alive again. I'm sorry for being so forward. It's just that I know what love feels like, and I wasn't sure if I'd ever feel it again, and now I do. I don't want to let it go. I hope you don't think me improper."

"No, I don't think that. I don't know what to think," he said.

"Maybe you shouldn't think too much."

He took her hand in his and kissed her again.

She withdrew. "We should go. Someone may see us and start talking," she laughed.

"Yes, there's likely more than one Mrs. Stewart in town who would love to scandalize the Bureau staff." They continued walking. "So what do we do now?"

She laughed again, "We wake up tomorrow and go on like before."

"I can't do that," he said. "I can't pretend this didn't happen; just ignore it."

"We don't need to do that, but we need to be discreet. Keep our affections out of school and the office."

"You expect me to turn off my affections at work?"

"You must. I can't have you fawning over me at school. What would the children say? Or Joseph or Thomas?" said Catherine.

"I live with them. I can't keep this bottled up. They're going to find out."

"They already know you're sweet on me," she said.

"They do?"

"Goodness, yes. It's been obvious since the day I arrived."

"But they don't know *this*," he said, waving his hand between them. "They don't know that you're sweet on me."

"I think they know," she nodded. "My, in the weeks I've known you, I've never seen you so flustered. You truly are sweet on me, aren't you?"

"I am," he said. "But we need to keep this secret."

"My affection for you is unbound, but I agree we must maintain proper appearances."

Oskar said, "I'll talk to the boys. I think they will keep our confidence."

"I should be getting home."

"Wait. One more kiss."

#

"I need your help," said the man sitting across the desk from Oskar.

"What's your name?" asked Oskar.

"Michael."

"It's good to meet you, Michael. Do you have a surname?"

"No, sir."

"You can choose one, then."

"Any name I want?"

"Yes," said Oskar.

"How about Lincoln?"

"That's a good name. Michael Lincoln." Oskar noted it in his notebook. "What can I help you with, Michael?"

"I heard you help men with disagreements with the

plantation owners."

"That's right. Are you working for one now?" said Oskar.

"I was up until yesterday. It was payday, and I was due my month's wages, but Mister Lang said I would have to wait until next month. He paid everyone else except me."

"Did you work a full month?" said Oskar.

"I started some time back. He said I only worked half a month, so I wasn't owed anything. Said the food and cabin was enough for half a month's work."

"Did you sign a contract with Mr. Lang?"

"No, sir."

"Do you know if other workers have contracts?"

"I dunno. Contracts is new to me. Mr. Lang said he doesn't need contracts for his workers."

Oskar pulled a sample contract from a folder and set it before the man. "I'll talk to Mr. Lang about that. Can you read?"

Michael shook his head.

"That's all right. This is a basic Freedmen's Bureau contract. It's a promise that you and the planter make to each other, and once you make your mark on it and the planter signs it, you both have to do what it says and work together. Usually, the contract says that you'll work on his farm six days a week for this year. In exchange for working for him, he must pay you a monthly wage. We write the amount on the contract. He also has to supply you with food, a place to live, and fuel for heating."

Oskar waited until Michael registered understanding with his face before continuing. "We put all that in writing, and one of my agents or I can review it and watch you make your mark. Then, you both must abide by it. If he doesn't pay or give you food, you come to the Bureau. And you have to work every day. If you're not working, you're deemed a vagrant, and the sheriff can arrest you for that. So you have to take responsibility for yourself now. Understand?"

"Yes, sir, but what about my pay for last month?"

"I'll visit Mr. Lang's plantation. I haven't met him yet. I'll talk to him about getting you a partial month's pay—that would be fair to both of you. I'll also talk to him about a contract for you and the other workers."

Oskar let it sink in, then asked him, "Do you have any children or a wife?"

"I have two young'uns."

"Are they old enough to work?"

"They did before we were free," said Michael.

"We have a school here in Paris. Do you want them to go to school?"

"That would be good for them, but it's a long way. It took me over an hour to walk here. They're too little for that."

"Mr. Lang's farm. It's near Centerville?" said Oskar.

"Yes, sir."

"Do you know where the Baptist Church is?"

"Yes, sir. We attend the African Baptist Church services there."

"Can your children walk there for school?" said Oskar.

"Yes, sir. They could manage that."

"Our teacher is starting classes a few days a week there soon. We're also going to do night classes for adults. I hope you can attend those. Are you married?"

"Amy is my wife, but we ain't married legally."

"Do you want to be?" asked Oskar.

"Yes, sir."

"Talk to your preacher about that. If he sanctions your marriage, I can record it in the books here. The Bureau records are just as good as the courthouse."

"Thank you, sir."

"Can Amy read?" asked Oskar.

"A little. She worked in the master's house back when."

"She can go to night classes too. The teacher is looking for anyone that can read to help her with classes. Maybe Amy would want to do that? Help teach the children?"

"I'll ask her," said Michael.

"Have you been to the army depot to get some clothes?"

"Yes, sir, we all got something. That was really nice to get them. I got some boots too. They're a little big, but they're new and don't have any holes."

"Good," said Oskar. "Anything else today?"

"No, sir."

Oskar stood and extended his hand. "It was nice to meet you, Michael. You head back to work now, and remember you must hold up your end of the agreement. You're only going to get paid if you work. I'll stop out and see Mr. Lang about your pay and contract tomorrow."

"Thank you, Mr. Mueller. Thank you."

Oskar made notes in his notebook, then walked out to the lobby. "Who's next?"

#

At the end of the long day, while Oskar's two agents recorded the day's work, Oskar walked over to the Episcopal church and knocked on the rectory door.

Reverend Thompson invited him in, and they sat.

The reverend said, "Your Mrs. Albert is quite a teacher. Her resourcefulness and ability to get the students to learn so quickly is impressive. She's divided the day into fourths. Two classes in the morning and two in the afternoon."

"She could use some help," said Oskar. "Have you had any success in recruiting any tutors?"

"I've appealed from the pulpit, and I even approached several ladies that I thought might be sympathetic to the mission, but so far, no. I can't get anyone to step up. The people in this town are not supportive of helping raise the Negro above their current standing. I thought I had one woman ready to volunteer, but suddenly, she changed her mind. I think others influenced her."

"That's disappointing," said Oskar. "Don't people realize we're trying to help the freedmen become self-sufficient? Do they want them to be wards of the government forever?"

"I'm afraid most of the community want nothing to do with helping Negroes. Some are poor themselves and resent the help that the government is providing to the freedmen."

"What can we do to change that?" said Oskar.

"I keep preaching the Christian word, but they don't want to hear the last shall be first. I think it's going to take time."

"I could use your help with something else," said Oskar. "I need to appoint a special agent to hear cases in a new Bureau court. It will take on civil and criminal cases where the freedmen's rights have been violated, or they are not given fair hearings. Do you know anyone who might be a good fit for the position? Someone that could be fair in hearing the freedmen's complaints?"

"Hmm. No one comes to mind. That sounds like a precarious position," said the reverend.

"I suppose it could be. We'll be careful in selecting cases to hear—only the most egregious ones where it's blatant that justice is not being served."

"I see the need. Some of the county judges' definitions of justice seem to change based on the individual's skin color. Judge Hawes is notorious."

"Who is he?" asked Oskar.

"Richard Hawes was a judge and state legislator before the war. He was named Confederate governor of Kentucky when the Rebels took Frankfort. The Union army ran him off, but he returned home and was re-seated on the Bourbon County bench. He has open hostility toward the Blacks and no patience for Union interference in his jurisdiction. Your new court appointee will want to stay clear of him."

"Thank you for the warning. Let me know if anyone comes to mind. We need this, especially with people like Judge Hawes in positions of power. Anything else I should know?"

The reverend said, "I've received some complaints from townspeople about using the church for the Negro school."

"What's the nature of the complaints?"

"Nothing in particular. General crankiness about educating the freedmen."

"Anything to worry about?" said Oskar.

"Not these folks. They're talking to me about it. It's the silent ones I worry about. Those with hate in their hearts. I worry about what they might do."

"What do you think they're capable of?"

"Some of those boys might try to disrupt the school."

"Stop classes?" said Oskar.

"Maybe," the reverend said.

"How would they do that?"

"Block the doors, attack the students or the teacher."

"You think they might go that far? Violence?"

"It's a peaceful town, so I don't think it would be open violence, but we should be vigilant."

"Can I count on the sheriff to help if there's violence?" said Oskar.

"Mm. I wouldn't count on it. Better to use your Bureau militia."

"I'll make them aware. I don't want to prompt violence by introducing them if I don't have to."

"I think that's wise. Most folks resent the soldiers' presence here."

"I worry for Catherine… Mrs. Albert," said Oskar. "She spends a lot of time alone in the classroom."

"You have a soft spot for her," said the reverend.

"Is it obvious? I'm trying to be discreet."

"Son, you wear it on your face whenever you're in the same room with her."

Oskar reddened.

"It's all right. You're both young, doing God's work. I understand why you're attracted to each other. Just remember the Lord's commandments."

"Thank you, Reverend. I'm trying."

"You must do, not just try," said the reverend.

#

Oskar found Catherine finishing up with a group of night students. He watched her working from the back of the classroom.

Once they all departed, he closed the door, and they embraced and kissed. "How was your day?" he asked.

"The days fly by. They're learning. The adults are eager to read. They don't learn as quickly and get frustrated more easily, but they want to learn. How was your day?" Catherine asked.

"Full of new challenges but invigorating," said Oskar. "I had twenty cases today; the line is never-ending. Our mission is waged one person at a time. I need more people. Joseph and Thomas aren't enough."

"Do you anticipate getting any more agents to help you here?"

"I don't think so. I've sent a letter to John Ely, who heads up the Bureau for Kentucky, but I think his hands are tied. It would be up to General Fisk, who oversees Kentucky and Tennessee. I think Tennessee is the priority—they have greater needs, with more freedmen and the task of rehabilitating the state."

"Any chance for another teacher?" Catherine asked with a hopeful expression.

"Not from the Bureau. But I'm working on it through the Western Freedmen's Association in Cincinnati. I've written a letter to my brother. He and his wife have connections there. I'm hopeful."

"I could do so much more for the students if I had another teacher," she said.

"Anything I can do for you in the meantime?"

She leaned in and kissed him. "Seeing you at the end of each day is motivation to get through the long days."

"Anything else?" Oskar said.

"Would you consider helping me tutor in the evening?"

"Me?"

"Yes, you. You went to college. You're certainly capable of teaching reading fundamentals, aren't you?"

"Well, yes," he said.

"And it would give us more time together."

"That is a benefit I hadn't considered. Yes, I'll be your assistant."

"Wonderful!" She kissed him again.

"I met with Reverend Thompson today," said Oskar. "He has noticed my affection for you and reminded me of God's commandments."

"Now we have a mother *and* a father watching over us," said Catherine. "We might as well be living at home."

"He also cautioned me that people in town might try to disrupt the school. You'll tell me if you notice anything that concerns you?"

"Why would anyone want to interfere with the education of children? I think he's being a bit paranoid, don't you?" she said.

"He has a good handle on the pulse of the community here. We're outsiders. We don't yet. We should heed his warning. Promise me you'll tell me if you see or hear anything," said Oskar.

"I promise," she said.

CHAPTER 10

Catherine walked around the classroom at the day's end, collecting the books. She stacked them on the bookshelf next to her desk and turned to find four figures clad in white pointed hoods, their penetrating eyes glaring through holes.

The men moved quickly toward her.

"What do you want?" said Catherine.

"You need to stop teaching these Negroes to read," said one of the men.

"I…I…I'm doing my job."

"You're making the problem worse. A learned Negro starts asking questions and wants more and more."

"They deserve an education," said Catherine, trying to keep her eyes on all four men moving to surround her.

"They don't deserve shit," spat one of the men.

"They need to go back to work. All this time in learning keeps them from doing what they do best, and that's farming," said another.

"They're children. They don't need to work."

The tallest man stood inches from Catherine, looking down at her from behind his hood. She stepped back, hitting her desk.

"You're a pretty lady. We're here today with a friendly warning. You take heed of it, and there will be no trouble. You keep teaching, and it will be a problem. You hear me?"

"What do you propose to do?" she said.

"We're not saying we'll do anything, but someone in the county might. You and your blond boyfriend and his agents are not welcome here. We don't need the Bureau interfering in the peaceful goings on in Bourbon County."

"Our intention is not to interfere," said Catherine. "We're trying to help. We want to help you peacefully integrate the freedmen into the community."

"No. No. No," said the tall one. "There'll be no integrating Negroes into anything. Not here. You need to pack up and leave. All of you."

"I…I…We can't."

"You can. Just pack your things and get on the train back north, where you belong. Do it, for everyone's sake. Let's go, boys."

The men shoved desks aside as they filed out of the room.

Catherine sat down in a chair, shaking.

#

Oskar, Thomas, and Joseph sat at a table at the Duncan Tavern. It had become their favorite place to gather after work. They could have a drink with their dinner, something Mrs. Stewart didn't condone.

Catherine approached their table with a concerned look on her face.

"Catherine, what are you doing here?" said Oskar.

The local patrons looked disapprovingly at the female presence in the pub and watched the scene. Oskar guided her into a seat next to his. "What's the matter?"

"Oh, it was awful. I'm frightened," she said.

"What, tell me?" said Oskar.

The three leaned in to hear her soft, quivering recounting of the incident. "Four men dressed in hoods came into my classroom."

"What?" said Joseph.

"Who?" said Oskar.

"I don't know. Locals," she said.

"What did they want?" said Oskar.

"They told me to stop teaching. Oh, it was terrible." She broke down crying.

Oskar put his arms around her, trying to calm her. Quiet sobs escaped his protective dome. He scanned the room at the prying eyes, then met Joseph and George's concerned faces.

"It's all right. We're here. Shh," comforted Oskar.

Her composure regained, she continued, "They said the Bureau should leave the county. That we were disrupting the way things are here, and if we don't, there will be trouble."

"What kind of trouble?" Oskar asked.

She shook her head. "They didn't say."

"Did they hurt you?"

She shook her head again. "What are we going to do?"

Joseph said, "Should we go to the sheriff?"

Oskar said, "Any idea who the men were?"

"No, they had hoods on. I have no idea."

Oskar said, "The sheriff can't pursue men we can't identify."

Joseph said, "We at least need to make him aware. Report it."

Oskar said, "We can do that, but I'm not sure how enthusiastically he'll work to protect us. I'll talk to Captain Hope. I think the army assigned to the Bureau is our best option. I'm beginning to question any of the locals' support of our mission."

"What do you think they'll do if I keep teaching?" said Catherine.

"I don't know," said Oskar.

"I don't know if I can do it. I'm frightened that they'll come back."

"You can. Your work is so important. We can't let these thugs scare us into retreat. That's what they're trying to do. Push us out so they can let things settle back into how things were before. The fighting is over, but the war against injustice has to continue."

Catherine bit her lip. Thomas offered Catherine his whiskey, "Sip this. It will help your nerves." She took a drink and winced.

"We're here with you," said Oskar. "I'll get a soldier posted at the school."

"That's terrible. Teaching with an armed guard in the classroom. What's happening to our country?" said Catherine. "How long will we have to do that?"

"As long as it takes," said Oskar.

#

One night after midnight the next week, Thomas burst into Oskar's bedroom, "Oskar!"

Oskar lifted his head and pushed himself up with his arms. "What?"

"Get up; there's a fire at the church," said Thomas.

Oskar dressed quickly and ran with Thomas and Joseph to the church. A crowd stood on the lawn, watching the wooden building ablaze in the night. A group of men had formed a bucket brigade and were dousing the lawn and school building next door with water from a cart to prevent the fire from spreading. Joseph and Thomas joined in.

Oskar found Reverend Thompson. "Reverend, what can I do?"

"It's too late. We saved some items from the sacristy, but the church is lost."

"I'm so sorry," said Oskar. They stood watching. They heard a loud crash and exclamations as the bell tower collapsed and fell to the ground with one muffled clank, wood splintering, and flames scattering on the lawn. The reverend exhaled.

The flames illuminated the concerned faces of the growing crowd. Several women wept. A line of Black adults and children stood at the far edge of the lawn. The massive flames mesmerized the spectators, stunned by the violence against their community.

Four men approached Oskar. "This is your fault." One pointed to the line of Black spectators. "You're bringing them into our church, school, and lives. This is not their town."

"No. This is not my fault," said Oskar. "I didn't set this fire. Someone with hate in their heart set fire to your church."

"Oskar," Reverend Thompson tried to quiet him.

Oskar said, "Someone who would rather destroy the church for everyone, rather than allow compassion for children who have been denied education."

"Oskar, now's not the time. Passions are high," said the reverend.

"And you all," Oskar motioned to the bystanders. "You stand by and let it happen. How can you attend this church on Sunday and then walk out and treat others as you do? You call yourselves Christians?"

The crowd erupted in jeers and shouts.

"No, you're the demon. Working against God's will," one said.

Others shouted. "Yankee pigs, go home," and "Negro-lover."

Oskar winced as a rock hit him on the shoulder. Another one pelted him, then two more. One hit him on the head, causing him to duck. He screamed, "Stop! For God's sake, stop."

Joseph and Thomas stepped in front of Oskar, scanning the crowd for the rock throwers. They were pelted. Joseph screamed, "Stop this."

Reverend Thompson held up his hands, "Please stop. Stop the violence. Stop." A rock hit the preacher.

A woman screamed and ran in front of him. "Don't hurt him. Listen to him."

The crowd softened, and the rocks ceased.

Reverend Thompson said, "You should leave. Your presence here will only agitate the troubled in the crowd. There's nothing else for you to do tonight. Come see me tomorrow."

Oskar took one last look at the church, then led his two men through the crowd. The spectators, including some children, taunted them with more shouts as they left. They stood across the street from the crowd and watched the pyre of the church burn to the ground.

Some of the freedmen approached them. "Thank you for what you've done, Mr. Mueller. For standing up for us."

"We're sorry about the church," another said.

"God bless you," several repeated.

CHAPTER 11

Cincinnati – Fall 1866

Annie nestled close to Max in the carriage as they made their way up the steep hillside just east of the city. On Sundays, Max loved riding in the suburbs or to the vast, park-like Spring Grove Cemetery to clear his head. He convinced Annie to join him this afternoon to explore the property the city would acquire for a new reservoir and park.

The land had previously been Nicholas Longworth's vineyard, where he grew Catawba grapes and produced world-renowned sparkling wines. Since Longworth's passing in 1863, the vines had slowly died back, overtaken by weeds and grasses. Longworth's son, Joseph, had agreed to lease the land to the city to construct the hilltop reservoir, which would supply Ohio River water to the city below it. Plans were being drawn for an extensive park surrounding it, tentatively called the Garden of Eden.

Annie placed her arm through Max's, "It's sad to see the vineyard dying out. I remember the day you brought me up here for a picnic, and we sat amongst the vines and looked down on the city. It's changed so much in ten years."

Max smiled, "Those were simpler times, weren't they? Our world seemed to be bound by the city. We didn't feel the weight of the world upon us."

"I felt that I was the only woman in Cincinnati who believed in women's rights at the time, but I know what you mean. Since the war, it seems national politics are more prominent. Tell me about the state convention in Columbus this week."

"It was an interesting several days," said Max. "Much debate about the Ohio Republican platform. Ultimately, we agreed to focus on what most voters can get behind—civil rights for the Negroes, and stronger demands of the Southern states before readmitting them into the Union. The state platform is pretty much in line with Congress's plan for Reconstruction."

"What about suffrage?" Annie said.

Max shook his head. "No, we're not going to support Negro suffrage. It's too radical for most Ohioans to support. The fear is if we back it, the Democrats will use it to sway voters to their side."

"So, even if it's the right thing to do, the party will do what's politically expedient?" said Annie.

"I'm afraid that's how politics work," said Max.

"What about universal suffrage—enfranchise all citizens—regardless of race or sex?"

"Not this year. That is as distasteful to many. We have to move slowly."

"It's too slow," said Annie. "It's too important. If we don't give the Negro the vote, their voice will be lost. They'll have to count on white men to speak on their behalf. It's treating them like wards of the electorate. It's the same for women—it puts us in a position where we depend on men's charity to act on our behalf. We'll never be equal if we wait for them to do it for us. And giving Blacks the vote now gives Republicans a boost. Most of the new voters will vote Republican."

"That's true, but their numbers aren't large enough to make a difference here in Ohio," said Max.

"It's frustrating to see the national debate focused only on the freedmen and their rights. I understand the need to advocate for them, especially in the South, but in the meantime, women's rights continue to be ignored. I can't sit by any longer."

"You aren't sitting by. You're doing plenty. How many letters did you and Mary send?" he said.

"Over a thousand," said Annie.

"That's not sitting by."

"Well, based on your report from the convention, it did us little good for this year's state election. Ohio Republican leaders are avoiding the suffrage issue. I have to do more."

"Annie, the time just isn't right," he said.

"It will never be the right time unless women force the issue. The Fourteenth Amendment that Congress is voting on has focused on the number of men in the population for determining state representation. If it passes, it further codifies the exclusion of women from our democracy. I've got to go."

"Go on tour with Elizabeth?" he said.

"Yes. It's time."

Max sighed. He knew this conversation was coming but hoped it could be delayed. "What about Lizzie? Marie and Wolf are leaving for South Dakota in a few weeks. Who will take care of her?"

"It's time to enroll her in a boarding school. I've written to several in New York."

"I don't think she will thrive so far away from us," Max said.

"Is it her or you that couldn't stand to be separated?" said Annie.

"I don't think it's right for either of us. We're not like you."

"Well, at least you're honest. I know your heart. You would struggle with it. What do you propose we do, then?" she said.

"Archbishop Purcell introduced me to a group of Ursuline nuns who have started a convent out in Brown County."

"You want Lizzie to become a nun?"

"No," said Max.

Annie continued, "Over my dead body. Talk about a

passive position for women."

"I don't mean as a novitiate. She would attend as a student there. They have a boarding school and a day school. She could stay during the week and come home on the weekends. It's only forty miles. There's a train."

"No. No." Annie shook her head. "You know how I feel about the Church. The papacy firmly places women below men. I agreed to let her attend church with you and be schooled in the Catholic faith, but I don't want her surrounded by that influence day and night. Besides, I can't imagine the curriculum is as rigorous as she needs."

"I met with Mother Julia, who runs the convent," said Max.

"You've gone and pursued this without me?"

"I had to explore it, just in case."

"In case what?" she said.

"In case you decided to run off."

"I'm not running off."

"You're leaving, and I'm left here to care for Lizzie," said Max.

"How does it feel to have your parental obligations stand in the way of your ambition?"

"Not very good," he shouted.

"Welcome to a woman's world," she shouted back at him.

Max closed his eyes, exasperated, and calmed himself. "Mother Julia is a lovely woman. The Ursulines aren't cloistered nuns. They go out in the world and do God's work. Their curriculum has the arts, the sciences, and mathematics. They would be a wonderful example for her."

"I'm sure she's a dear woman, but we're not sending Lizzie to a convent. Families who have nowhere else to turn to do that. She doesn't belong there."

"You're not willing to entertain this, are you?" he said.

"I'll take Lizzie with me before I allow that."

"That's not practical. We have to come up with something else."

"Hire a governess," Annie said.

"She needs to be with other students. That's not right for her," said Max.

"Mary Berry introduced me to a woman she worked with as a nurse in the war. Her name is Sarah Worthington King Peter. She has started a Ladies' Academy of Fine Arts. There's a young artist who is looking for work as a governess. She could come live at our house, look after Lizzie, and give her art lessons. Lizzie can continue going to her school."

"So you've been investigating options without me, too?" said Max.

"We both want what's best for her."

"Have you met this woman?"

"No, but she comes highly recommended. We can interview her. See what you think."

Max combed his blond locks with his fingers several times, thinking. "It may be our best option. Let's meet her."

"I'll arrange an interview," said Annie.

"You're going to do this?" he said.

"I must."

Max exhaled. "I understand."

They stopped at a ridge overlooking the river and across to the hills of Kentucky and took in the beauty of the fall colors.

"I'm going to have to hire a replacement for you at the shop," said Max. "You possess many skills. It will be difficult to find someone with the same blend you possess."

"Plenty of women could grow into the position as I did," said Annie.

"I wasn't thinking of a woman."

"Why not?" she said.

"Well, they typically don't have the background, and the men at the shop had difficulty accepting you. If you weren't my wife, I don't think they would have."

"Are you saying I was only successful in my duties because I was your wife?"

"No, that's not what I meant. You improved how we ran the business and handled your job efficiently and effectively."

"Thank you," she said. "Then why not hire another woman? I don't hold a monopoly on efficiency or effectiveness."

"There are more men with the relevant qualifications. And you must admit, it was difficult for you at first with the men until you showed them your capabilities and earned their trust," he said.

"The fact that more men have the qualifications is irrelevant. You only need one person—spend a little more time and find her."

Max pressed his lips together, suppressing further arguments, and changed the subject. "When do you think you'll leave?"

"As soon as we can arrange the governess."

"We're going to miss you terribly," he said.

"I'll miss you too, but I've put this off too long. You've seen it in me—my restlessness. I thought working, raising Lizzie, and my activities here supporting the women's movement would be enough. It's not enough anymore. You're so fulfilled with the shop and your work for the city. I want that too."

"Lizzie, though," he said.

"She'll adapt. She favors you over me. It's more important that she's with you than with me."

"No, she doesn't."

"She does. I see it." Tears formed in Annie's eyes. "I see the way she looks at you. The way she talks to you and listens to you and hangs on every word you say."

"It's just the nature of a father's role versus a mother's."

"You're so warm and comforting. She needs that," said Annie.

"She needs you, her mother. You're her model for womanhood."

"She's not like me," said Annie. "I know that. Her path will be very different from mine. I accept that. But I want to ensure she lives in a world where she can choose her path and not be told what she can't do. That's why I have to do this."

Max nodded as they rode on.

CHAPTER 12

Cincinnati – Fall 1866

Max and Patrick stood on the crowded public landing and watched the steamboat pass under the nearly-completed suspension bridge and maneuver into place on the bank of the Ohio River. The crowd rose in cheers and applause as the paddlewheels stopped and the shoremen put the gangway in place.

"Where's he coming from?" asked Patrick.

"The papers said Louisville was his last speech. I think he made a few stops along the way but didn't get off the steamer," said Max.

"That's one of the new ones, isn't it? *United States.*"

"Yes, I had the opportunity to take a trip on it to Louisville on its maiden run. The packet company wanted to entertain city council and other dignitaries."

"Another one of your extravagances paid for by shameless men hoping to suck from the tit of the city. What did you have to promise in return for that ride?" said Patrick.

"Nothing. Don't be so cynical. The packet company is an important partner with the city. Companies like theirs contribute to the city's success."

"Right, and all those men that take appointments from the president in the ever-growing federal government don't owe him any patronage, either," said Patrick.

"It's how our government works," said Max.

"This country's going to hell. First, Lincoln, and now Johnson is running us right into an aristocratic-run government that is counter to the Founding Fathers' vision of a country where every man has individual rights, unmolested by a central rule. Shit, we might as well go back to being ruled by the king."

"I thought you supported Johnson and the Democrats," said Max.

"Given the choices, I do, but the idea of forcing the Southern states back into a country they don't want to be a part of is un-American. I say if they want to leave the greatest country in the world, let them leave. Good riddance."

"They had no right to secede. There was no allowance for it in the Constitution. It's in everyone's best interest to reunite the country and get back to prosperity," said Max.

"Do you believe the path we're on will get us there?" said Patrick. "Forcing the Confederates to pledge allegiance to the government that trampled down their way of life? Dividing the Southern states into five military districts and placing federal troops there? Disenfranchising their former leaders and letting Black men vote in their states?"

"Johnson's plan for Reconstruction failed," said Max. "It put too much trust in the men who were traitors to our country. Congress had to act, or we'd end up right back where we were before the war—a divided country."

The crowd applauded and cheered as the president and his entourage descended the gangplank.

"There he is," said Patrick. "He looks like he's constipated. That scowl on his face. Why doesn't he smile? The crowd loves him."

"He doesn't look like he's having fun, does he?" said Max. "This tour must be wearing on him. He's calling it the 'swing around the circle.'"

"More like swinging from a rope in some of the towns. I heard the crowd in Cleveland was pretty unruly. They heckled him. They kept chanting for General Grant to speak instead of him, but Grant supposedly was too drunk to speak. Word is he's not happy about being forced to accompany the president on this tour. I'd like to be a fly on the wall when those two have private conversations about Reconstruction. Grant doesn't respect him at all."

"I have to agree with Grant and the crowd in Cleveland," said Max. "I find it shameful that Johnson vetoed the Civil Rights Bill, the Freedmen's Bureau Bill, and the Fourteenth Amendment. Thank God we have enough sensible men in Congress to override his vetoes. It must be very unpleasant to be the president right now."

"He's hoping this tour will sway public opinion to his side and force Congress to listen to the people's voice," said Patrick.

"I think he's done for," said Max. "They're working on articles of impeachment for him."

They watched the procession, followed by a marching band, walk up Broadway, adoring fans lining both sides. The group entered the Spencer House Hotel, which faced Front Street and overlooked the public landing. A few minutes later, Andrew Johnson and several other men in suits walked onto the hotel balcony and waved to the roaring crowd. A large banner with "WE WELCOME THE PRESIDENT" hung across the wrought iron balcony.

"Who's the young lady?" asked Patrick. "Andy have a traveling companion?"

"Get your mind out of the gutter. It's his daughter, Martha. Her husband, David Patterson, was elected to the president's vacated congressional seat in Tennessee."

"A regular royal family. Why bring them along?" said Patrick.

"She fills the role of the First Lady in many respects. The president's wife is not well—tuberculosis."

"I'm sorry to hear about Mrs. Johnson, but disappointed to learn the young lady is a daughter. A mistress would be more interesting," said Patrick, winking.

Max shook his head in amusement. The band stopped playing, and the audience quieted as a man stepped to the podium on the balcony.

"Who's that?" asked Patrick.

"Senator Groesbeck. He's one of Johnson's local toadies."

Groesbeck welcomed the crowd and introduced the president, praising him for rejecting the Freedmen's Bureau Bill. "A strong national government is a danger to the people." Groesbeck continued his remarks, interrupted numerous times by generous applause. "Slavery is gone, and we want peace and a government as our fathers made it. We dread experiments and movement toward centralization and despotism that war brings to government. It was a fratricidal war. We and the South are brothers. Common ancestry related by blood and other ties. We exchange almost daily greetings." He closed with, "Your fallen predecessor spoke of charity for all, malice toward none. Your Christian sentiment to Reconstruction will not injure people or country."

President Johnson shook hands with Groesbeck and stepped to the podium amidst wild applause.

The president thanked the crowd for the warm welcome and began his speech. "I have the same goals of preserving the Union and Constitution as when I visited Cincinnati several years ago as a senator. Can any man say I have departed from my principles since Lincoln and I were elected? If fidelity to my country and the Constitution is treason, then I stand before you a traitor. I have risen from little to the highest position in the world. I have nothing to gain and am not a traitor.

"I vetoed the Freedmen's Bureau, but this is not traitorous. It was never part of the platform Lincoln and I were elected on. The cost of implementing the bill is twelve million dollars and would cost the treasury fifty to sixty million a year to sustain. This is three times the cost of John Quincy Adams' administration. They propose to saddle another expense on the government.

"Where is the man who has contributed to more than I to the cause of abolition and emancipation? The slaves have been set free and placed on a footing where they have a fair chance in life. Some say they're not competent to take care of themselves. These same men say the freedmen are competent enough to take charge of the affairs of the state. If this is to be done, let the states do it. They each have the right to do so. Let each state take charge of its affairs without interference from Congress."

Max said, "He's abdicating all responsibility to mend the nation."

Patrick said, "He's right, though. The states have the right to govern themselves within their borders."

"The South can't be trusted to do the right thing," said Max.

"So you want Congress to regulate morality now? I thought you appreciated your freedom to worship as a Catholic. That will be the next thing to go."

They both quieted to hear Johnson. "The Freedmen's Bureau Bill authorizes me to appoint thousands of agents across the South in every county, parish, and civil district and put the Army and Navy in place in the South. It places me over millions of dollars of expense. The Civil Rights Bill I vetoed could have proclaimed myself dictator, but I said no."

The crowd erupted.

"Oh please," muttered Max. "How big of him."

The president continued, "I have been denounced as a traitor because I dare execute the power of the veto of bills that encroach upon the Constitution. I will continue to stand on my position. Others call me traitor for using my pardoning power for some Southern men. Who among us has not erred at some point in our lives? Who believes a man cannot repent and become better? I use the pardon with discretion. There are those in Congress who want to punish…. If they want more blood, let them erect an altar, and I offer my life as the last libation for the Union and the preservation of the Constitution."

As the audience cheered, Max said, "He sees himself as the savior, doesn't he?"

Johnson continued, "Now, if I know myself, I live for my country; I devote the best energies of my life to it. I have always trusted the people. They have never deserted me and never will desert me. Never. Never. The powers of the earth or below cannot drive me from the Constitution.... In conclusion, please accept my thanks for the cordial welcome you have given me here today. I invoke the best blessing of heaven upon this people."

Johnson smiled and waved to the applauding audience. A group started chanting, "Grant, Grant, Grant." Johnson frowned, then extended his hand toward the general, sparking an even louder round of applause. Much to the crowd's disappointment, Grant only stepped forward, bowed, and then retreated to his place.

"It's disheartening. He's the man we're counting on to restore our country to greatness," said Max.

"He's greeting citizens inside," said Patrick, pointing to a long line forming at the hotel entrance. "Want to go in and meet him?"

"No, I couldn't shake hands and hold my tongue. Do you want to meet him?"

"Me?" Patrick said, holding up his hook. "No. Shaking hands with politicians is your thing."

CHAPTER 13

Cincinnati – December 1866

Annie awoke in the dark bedroom and felt the weight of Max on her bosom. He was still except for his slow, steady breathing. She could feel his heart beating against her chest. She wanted to remember this feeling, unsure when they would be together again.

"You're awake, aren't you?" she whispered.

"Yes," said Max.

"How long have you been awake?" she said.

"I don't know. I didn't sleep much." He moved his hand slowly across her soft skin.

"It's going to be fine. Everything's going to be fine," she said, placing her hand on his.

She felt him taking deep, controlled breaths. They lay quietly for several minutes.

"I need to get up. I have to finish packing," she said.

He hugged her tightly. "We've never been apart this long. The longest was the week I spent during the city's siege in the war."

"We're both independent. We're strong. We'll write."

"Won't your heart ache without us?" he said.

"Of course, it will. It's difficult for me too, but I don't bleed on the outside as you do. You know me. I learned as a child to put on my shell and keep my feelings inside. It doesn't mean I don't love you or won't miss you."

"This is so difficult," he said.

"I know. It is. For you. My rock. You have to be a rock for Lizzie. If you falter, she'll follow your lead."

"I know."

"Be happy for me," she said. "I'm starting a new adventure. I'm doing work that means so much to me. We've always embraced the unconventional and supported each other in our marriage. Please don't give up on me now. I need your support more than ever. I love you for your ability to see me as your equal."

She sensed his chest heave with another deep breath and felt him nodding into her. He kissed her skin, then moved up to a lingering kiss. They held each other tightly until he loosened his embrace.

"Time to get up," he said.

They rose. Annie finished packing and woke Lizzie.

The three sat in the hired carriage on their way to the Little Miami train station.

"How long will the train ride take?" asked Lizzie.

"I'll be in New York City by dinner tomorrow," said Annie.

"That's a long time. Won't you get hungry?"

"There's a dining car where I'll take my meals, and I reserved a bed on the sleeper car for overnight tonight."

"Where will you stay in New York?" said Lizzie.

"I'm staying with friends for a few nights. A dear family I knew when I lived in New York as a child. After that, I'll stay with cousin Elizabeth."

"And then you're going to travel to other places?" said Lizzie.

"That's right. I'll be assisting Elizabeth and Miss Anthony in writing speeches and delivering them to audiences across the country."

"I'm going to miss you, Mother."

"I'm going to miss you too, and Papa, but this new job is my responsibility, and I must do it. It's important work—advocating for equal rights for the freedmen and women. We all have to make sacrifices to fulfill our responsibilities. I'm sacrificing time with you and Papa for my job, but I do it gladly. It's the right thing. Do you understand?"

"Yes, Mother."

"I'm starting a new adventure, just like you're starting yours at Mrs. Coons' Day School for Missus and Young Ladies. Papa will be here for you, and I'll write you letters. You'll never be far from my thoughts. I'll be home in a couple weeks for Christmas, and we'll have a grand holiday in our new house. That's something special to look forward to."

"Will you bring me a Christmas present from New York? Something beautiful?" Lizzie asked.

"If that's what you'd like, then I will," said Annie.

"I have something special for both of you," said Max.

"A present? Now?" said Lizzie.

Max nodded as he reached into his waistcoat pocket. He pulled out two small boxes with bows on top and handed them to Lizzie and Annie. "Go on, open them."

They each opened a jewelry box to find a heart-shaped gold locket.

"How beautiful," said Annie.

"Oh yes, they're identical," said Lizzie. "I've never had anything so beautiful."

Annie said, "I think it opens. See, right here." She showed Lizzie as she opened hers, revealing a photograph of Lizzie.

"That's my portrait," said Lizzie. Lizzie opened hers. "I have your portrait inside mine."

"They're wonderful. Thank you," said Annie. "I'll always have you with me, Lizzie. And you'll have me with you. Any time you want to think of me, you'll have it."

"Thank you, Papa," said Lizzie as she jumped across the seat into a hug.

Max helped them put the lockets on.

They arrived at the train station, and a porter took Annie's trunks. They walked holding hands, Lizzie in the middle.

When it was time to board, Annie squatted down, "I love you, my dear. Be my strong girl." She kissed and hugged her, then stood, taking Max's hands. "Thank you for being my partner."

Max bit his lip and nodded, forcing a smile as his eyes glazed with tears. They kissed and embraced. Annie picked up her bag and climbed aboard. They watched her move inside the car and take a seat.

The whistle blew, and the train started down the track. Annie looked out her window, smiling and waving, watching the tall Max and pint-sized Lizzie, hand-in-hand, waving back.

#

Later that week, Abby Baker, the new governess, entered the dining room. "Would you like anything else, Mr. Mueller?"

"No, thank you, Abigail," said Max.

"Please, call me Abby. All my friends and family do."

Max smiled at her, "Abby, then. You need not go to all this trouble for me for breakfast. I'm happy with an egg and a piece of toast. No one's ever catered to me so."

"It's no trouble. Lizzie needs to have a good breakfast, and I can just as easily prepare it for the both of you."

"Are you finding everything in the kitchen all right?" said Max.

"I'm still exploring. I'll have it mastered in no time."

"Lizzie helped Marie quite a bit in the kitchen. If you can't find something, ask her."

Abby nodded. "I'll need some money to go to the market."

Max took several bills from his wallet and handed them to her. "Once you get a handle on our weekly needs, I can give it to you each week and let you manage it. Annie worked all the finances out with Marie, so I'm not sure how much you'll need. This should get you started."

"Thank you."

Max said, "Lizzie, can you put on one of your nice dresses today?"

"I couldn't find my blue one," said Lizzie.

"Did you look in your wardrobe?"

"Yes, Papa, but it's not there."

Max looked at Abby hopefully.

Abby shrugged, "I'm sure I'll run across it at some point. Lizzie is also missing a pair of shoes."

"I'm sorry, I don't know where anything is when it comes to Lizzie's things," said Max.

"I understand," said Abby. "We'll figure it out, won't we, Lizzie?"

"Yes, Miss Abby."

Max said, "Next week, I will need you to pack our things for the move to the new house. They'll deliver the crates and barrels on Monday. I know it's an extraordinary request, but Annie handled this sort of thing too."

"It will allow me to go through everything in the house."

"Thank you, Abby. I'm so thankful you're here. I'd be lost without you," said Max.

He turned to his daughter, "Lizzie, here's the plan for today. We'll all walk down to the riverfront, watch the ceremony, and then walk across the bridge together. After that, Abby will take you up on one of the Covington hilltops so you can sketch the bridge. How does that sound?"

"I'm looking forward to walking across it," said Lizzie. "We've been watching them build it for so long. I wish Mother could be here for the opening."

"Me too," he said.

"She hasn't written yet."

"Well, she's only been gone a few days. I know she misses you and will write when she has a free moment. Maybe you can put one of your sketches of the bridge in your next letter to her?"

"That's a grand idea. That will make her feel like she was here for the big day," said Lizzie.

"Finish your breakfast then. We'll leave at 8:30."

#

The three stood among the thousands awaiting the formal opening of the Covington and Cincinnati bridge. The project started in 1856 after Kentucky and Cincinnati passed legislation to support the construction. Many had objected to the bridge, fearing northern Kentucky businesses would rob Cincinnati of commerce or multitudes would use the bridge to escape slavery in Kentucky. Construction stalled during the war but resumed near its end, and it would now be the first bridge across the Ohio River at Cincinnati.

A small group of well-dressed men stepped into the street behind a band at the base of the bridge. The crowd cheered and applauded as the men waved.

"Who are those men getting into the carriages?" asked Lizzie.

"That's the man who designed the bridge, Mr. Roebling, and his son, who assisted him in the project. The others are members of the board of directors for the bridge company. That's Mr. Shinkle from Covington, Mr. Stevens, and Mr. Pendleton."

"Why do they get to ride across it first?" asked Lizzie.

"They have worked over the last few years to raise the money and lead the effort to build the bridge," answered Max.

"What about the other men?" asked Lizzie.

"What other men?"

"The ones we saw climbing up on the bridge and building it. Why don't they get to go across first, too?" she said.

"Well, everyone can't be part of the procession. I guess they didn't want to make a huge fuss," said Max.

"It doesn't seem fair that the men who did the building aren't part of it. Just the men in their suits. It's an injustice."

Max suppressed a smile. "I'm sure they were thanked for all their hard work. There are times when it's not practical to make everything exactly equal. Some things are not worth quibbling over. Save your battles for the things that are most important."

"Like women's rights," said Lizzie.

"Yes, like that," said Max.

The band began playing a march and led the carriages across the bridge. A steam-powered fire engine fell in behind them with a long toot of its whistle.

Max held Lizzie's hand with Abby at the girl's other side. He said, "It's beautiful—a hopeful sign of a peaceful, prosperous relationship between North and South. It will lead to progress we can't yet fathom." He took a deep breath, stopping his lower lip from quivering and squeezed his daughter's hand. "Ready to walk on water?"

"We're not walking on water. We're walking *over* the water," said Lizzie.

"That is more precise," he admitted. As they started toward the bridge, a series of cracks echoed across the river from Covington as a one-hundred-gun salute greeted the procession. The crowd cheered and applauded. They inched slowly toward the bridge behind the mass of people.

"Why is it moving so slowly?" asked Lizzie.

"Everyone has to buy a ticket to cross," said Max.

"Why do you need a ticket?"

"The bridge company charges a three-cent fare. A horse and buggy are fifteen cents. Larger carriages are twenty-five or thirty cents, depending on how many horses. They'll use the money to pay off the bonds. The bridge cost over two million dollars to build."

"That's an enormous sum of money," said Lizzie.

Abby laughed. "How do you know so much about money?"

"Papa taught me about money. He lets me count it."

Max bought a sheet of one hundred walking fares for $1.25, and they joined the line to walk up the base of the bridge. "Do you want to walk in the street, or do you want to walk on the pedestrian walkway outside?"

"Outside! I want to look down into the water," said Lizzie.

"Are you sure? They haven't finished the metal railings, so they only have those temporary wooden ones."

"Yes, outside."

"Over here then." Max directed them to an approach paved with large oak wooden blocks that led to the seven-foot-wide walkway outside the iron bridge structure. The bridge rose almost imperceptibly to the middle and then fell to the shore on the other side.

Lizzie walked along the edge, unfazed by the nearly one-hundred-foot drop to the water. She stopped midway across, looked down at the river and across the shorelines, then gazed upward at the massive wire cables holding up the structure. "Will the ropes hold all these people?"

"Yes, no need to worry about that," said Max. "The cables are made from wire. Five thousand wires stretch across, and they're wrapped with another wire to hold them together. It's very strong."

"How do you know so much about the bridge?" asked Abby.

"It's my business to know about things like this. At Miller Industries, we make all kinds of things from iron: fences, building trusses, plates, and specialty machines. I met with Mr. Roebling ten years ago when he first designed the bridge to discuss supplying some materials. He's from Prussia, and we hit it off, but I didn't pursue the contract."

"Why not?" asked Abby.

"For one, I knew that building the bridge would take years due to the politics involved. And Mr. Miles Greenwood of the Eagle Ironworks was president of the bridge company at the time. I believed his firm would have the advantage in winning the bid."

"I'm in awe of people like you who have the mind to imagine and build things like this," said Abby.

"Oh, I couldn't design this," said Max. "I understand the mechanics involved, but my engineering skills aren't a fraction of what Mr. Roebling or his son possess."

"You're very humble," said Abby. "I read the newspaper article about the new machines your company builds to cut metal and make locomotive tires. It said you have two patents.”

"You're interested in machines?" said Max.

"I'm fascinated by how things are put together."

"Would you like to see them sometime?"

"Oh, yes," said Abby.

"You and Lizzie should come to the shop for a tour then. We'll arrange it."

"That would be interesting. I would like that."

"Rest assured, though. I didn't design any of our machines. I have a skilled engineer, Mr. Gray, who does that."

"Papa, look. The steamship is going to pass under us. What are they doing?"

"They're lowering the smokestack to clear the bridge. The smaller steamboats can run right under, but big ones like that are too tall." They stood watching until the boat passed directly underneath. Lizzie exchanged waves with the crew and passengers on the decks.

"Let's continue and let some others have a look," said Max. They moved slowly with the crowd to the Covington side of the bridge.

"I must go to work now," said Max.

"Papa, can't you stay with us a little longer?" pleaded Lizzie.

"Abby will help you find a nice vantage point to sketch the bridge from. I'll see your drawings tonight." He kissed the top of her head.

"Yes, Papa."

Max placed his hand on Abby's forearm, "Thank you. I'll see you at home tonight."

Abby nodded and smiled. "Ready, Miss Lizzie?"

"Ready! Bye, Papa!"

Max stood and watched them start their way up the hillside, then returned to the queue to cross back over the bridge.

#

A couple of weeks later, Max and Patrick met for a drink at the end of the day.

"How is it going without Annie?" asked Patrick

"I miss her terribly. So does Lizzie. I worry she doesn't have a woman's touch, just my rough edges."

"Don't take offense, but I think Annie has rougher edges than you. You're one of the most caring people there is. Lizzie's got you, and she's got the maid; what's her name?"

"Abby. She's a governess," said Max.

"Right, well, a governess sounds even better than a maid. What's Lizzie missing?"

"Her mother. Annie took care of Lizzie. She ensured she ate well, dressed appropriately, and did her lessons. She talked to her about things I don't."

"Like what?" said Patrick.

"I don't know. Womanly things. Topics I don't know much about. Who will she turn to when she matures or starts showing interest in boys?"

"You're getting on all right. Children adapt well to change. Mine got along fine when I was in the army. I think you worry too much," said Patrick.

"Thanks, but I don't know. She needs a woman to look up to."

"This governess. Isn't she there for Lizzie?" said Patrick.

"She is, but she's no Annie."

"There are few women like Annie. That may not be all bad for Lizzie."

Max said, "I know most people find Annie unconventional, but she stands up for herself and women. Lizzie and your daughters' lives will be better off because of women like her. Abby is sufficient in the day-to-day care of Lizzie but lacks Annie's drive and ambition. I want Lizzie to emulate those aspects of her mother."

"She'll be who she's destined to be. You're overthinking this," said Patrick.

"She's my only child. I want her to have all she wants from life."

"How are you getting along with this Abby?"

"Fine. She's very accommodating."

Patrick raised his eyebrows and grinned mischievously. "How accommodating? Filling in for the hole left by Annie's absence."

"No, nothing like that. We have a very proper relationship. She cares deeply for Lizzie's well-being," said Max.

"I'm sure she does. What about your well-being? Aren't you lonely without your wife?"

"Of course, but that doesn't mean I'm… that's not why she's here."

Patrick shrugged. "A man gets lonely. A pretty young woman under his roof. A relationship of convenience often results."

"I'm not like that. I would never," said Max.

"I know. I'm sorry. You've always been above temptation."

CHAPTER 14

New York City – December 1866

Annie sat, reading the morning newspaper at Elizabeth Cady Stanton's large dining room table. After a week in the city, she quickly readjusted to its constant activity and living as an independent woman with no family responsibilities. It brought her back to her teen years when her family lived in the city, and she had access to its culture, shops, and salons full of interesting people.

Her father's cousin had welcomed Annie into the fold of women's rights leaders who often assembled at her home and strategized the movement's activities. Since arriving, Annie had studied many of Elizabeth's speeches and attended several lectures on the topics of Negro suffrage and women's equality. She had also begun editing and proofing documents drafted by Elizabeth and her longtime partner, Susan B. Anthony. Annie was skilled at persuasive speech writing but was in awe of the two women's ability to craft their arguments. She aspired to be like them.

When Annie returned from the kitchen with her second cup of coffee, a short woman greeted her in a soft voice, "Good morning. I'm Lucy Stone."

Annie introduced herself. "I'm honored to meet you, Mrs. Stone. I heard you speak at the Women's Rights Convention in Cincinnati in 1855. You gave a moving speech on your disappointments as a woman. It inspired me. I'm here today because of you and the other women who spoke at that convention."

"It's nice to meet you, Annie. It's always encouraging to hear that our work inspires others. Please, call me Lucy. Is there coffee?"

Annie accompanied her to the kitchen and shared her background and how she came to stay with Elizabeth. Lucy explained that she was part of the executive committee of the recently formed American Equal Rights Association. She had arrived on the morning train from Boston and missed the leaders meeting. While waiting for Elizabeth to return from the meeting, they sat at the dining table and continued their conversation.

"I'm a Lucy Stoner, too," said Annie. "When I married, I kept my last name."

Lucy chuckled. "It's embarrassing for me to hear people say that. It's not like I am the only woman to insist on maintaining a sense of identity after marriage."

"You should be proud. Keeping our maiden names is a visible badge of what we stand for. It is a statement of my independence when I have to correct someone to use my name versus my husband's. However, it can confuse people. Sometimes, I let it slide and accept being called Mrs. Mueller, especially when we're with my daughter."

"I've found that as well. How old is your daughter?" asked Lucy.

"Lizzie is ten. We named her after Elizabeth. She was another inspiration to me. She showed me that a woman could be married and still have a vocation."

"My daughter, Alice, is ten also. I've been introducing her to my work. She attends some of my meetings and speeches in Boston."

"Do you find it difficult? Being away from her." asked Annie.

"I try not to be gone too long. I miss her when I'm on the road. Since she was born, most of my work has been in Massachusetts."

"Do you have a governess?"

"Yes, she's indispensable with our schedules, but I try to be home as much as possible," said Lucy.

"Does Mr. Blackwell contribute to Alice's care?" said Annie.

"Heavens, no. He doesn't see that as his place and isn't suited. Does your husband?"

"Not the hands-on of maintaining the house or Lizzie's day, but he engages with her intimately."

"That's uncommon, a man with the demeanor and patience. You're fortunate."

"Hmm. How do you and Mr. Blackwell manage to balance both of your ambitions? I'm aware of his abolitionist activities from the press," said Annie.

"Before we married, we redefined what marriage would be for us. We denounced the laws giving the husband the dominant position. We signed a contract that protects my financial position. We each retain what we brought to the marriage and share what we jointly reap. We agreed each of us could pursue our interests unencumbered by the other. We're true equals in the marriage."

"That's what Max and I strove for when we married, but it hasn't worked out that way. How do you do it?"

"It hasn't been without its challenges," said Lucy. "We have our difficulties, but we work through them. Communication and mutual respect, I think."

They heard women's voices in the foyer. Annie and Lucy joined Elizabeth and Susan B. Anthony in the parlor.

"I apologize for missing the meeting this morning," said Lucy. "I intended to be on the last train yesterday, but it was canceled. I was on the first one this morning and arrived just a few minutes ago. What happened at the meeting?"

"Our first topic was the Fourteenth Amendment and how to respond to its final wording," said Elizabeth. "We all agreed that the inclusion of the word *male* in the congressional representation clause further entrenches men's hold over the political structure of the country."

Susan said, "It does grant all persons born within our borders citizenship and guarantees all equal protection under the law. We presume all persons includes women, but it would have been better if it had been clearer. Like so much in the Constitution, it leaves room for interpretation, and until it is tested, we can't assume men won't use the vagaries to their advantage."

Elizabeth said, "It's frustrating. We lobbied congressmen to remove the male references, but they left them in—all the more reason to fight for suffrage, which was our next topic. We agreed to shift our focus to universal suffrage. Women won't have a voice in government until we are part of the electorate choosing our elected officials."

Lucy asked, "Were any immediate priorities agreed to?"

"We are going to lobby the Anti-Slavery Society to accept the goal of universal suffrage—add women to the Negro's cause. Join us in the battle," said Elizabeth.

"That seems like a tall ask?" said Lucy. "I remember the speech that Frances Ellen Watkins Harper gave at the convention in May. Her words were, 'White women speak of rights, Black women speak of wrongs.' She felt that women's plight paled compared to the wrongs against Negroes, which are life and death. Can we make a case to expand their cause to universal suffrage?"

"This is the Negro's hour," said Elizabeth. "We must push in beside him. We're both wronged by the aristocracy of men above women and Negroes."

"I wonder if we shouldn't tread more carefully going forward," said Lucy. "You and Susan came across as obstinate in opposing the Fourteenth Amendment. It made our cause look obstructionist."

Elizabeth shot back sharply. "We were against the amendment as worded, not in spirit. As we advance, we must be strategic. Align our causes."

"Henry and I are not convinced that is the wisest path," said Lucy. "We believe momentum is with the Negro's position and gaining his rights first will pave the way for women. Many men won't support women's suffrage because they believe it subverts their position."

"Giving women the vote won't degrade men, but will push them to do better, rather than accept their elevated position. We have to challenge them," said Elizabeth.

"I am not saying it will degrade men; I'm saying that most men believe it will degrade them," said Lucy.

"Do we accept that the lowliest men deserve the right to vote over educated and proper women?" said Elizabeth. "No. I am tired of the aristocracy of the male sex. It is odorous and an insult to women."

"I agree," said Lucy. "You need not convince me, but I'm not sure how we get men to see it that way."

"Women's qualities will save the nation," said Elizabeth. "Men created the chaos that led to the war and threaten to propagate its undemocratic inequities. Lucy, I'm sorry you weren't at the meeting to provide your perspective, but our position was decided."

Susan said, "Our efforts will move to two fronts. Influence the federal legislation to ensure it includes women and lobby the states most receptive to universal or women's suffrage. If we can get some state-level wins, that will help move the nation's sentiment and make ratification of any future amendments a reality. States such as New York and Kansas, where women's rights or suffrage are part of upcoming legislation or ballot initiatives."

Elizabeth said, "It's a tremendous amount of ground to cover, but we mustn't falter. Annie, are you ready to take an active role in the cause?"

"I am," said Annie. "I'm going home for the holidays but will return in the new year. Tell me how I can best assist."

#

The next day, Elizabeth held an afternoon parlor meeting. She invited a dozen New York women to discuss the topics of marriage and maternity. Annie conversed with the women over tea as they settled in.

Elizabeth began the discussion with some introductory comments. "As I work to support the American Equal Rights Association, I find it helpful to host these informal discussions periodically to gain the opinions of women like yourselves on topics of importance to you. The Association is focused on the vote for women, but there are other areas where there is an opportunity to improve the lives of our sisters across the nation.

"Today, I'd like to discuss marriage within our society. I spoke before the judiciary committee of the New York Senate as they debated changes to New York's divorce laws. In that address, I encouraged the men in the legislature to reconsider the divorce *and* marriage laws. New York has since made some progress, but men's rights are still assumed supreme, and the laws use the sanctity of God's blessing on a marriage to keep the couple in it long after love and civility have gone out of it. Marriage law must allow a woman to terminate a marriage that was entered with hope in her youth but becomes a cage of misfortune over time."

Elizabeth shared stories of unjust marriages and the detriments they forced on women. She railed against men in these marriages, the men who created the laws, and the men who enforced them.

Annie felt that Elizabeth over-dramatized, and her positions bordered on recklessness and cheapened marriage. She kept her thoughts to herself.

Elizabeth continued, "Couples enter into marriages under many circumstances. Most are well-intended, but we are human, and many fall far short of loving or even civil unions. The laws vary from state to state regarding divorce. Many women still are at the mercy of their husbands because of laws created by men years ago. It's time to make changes to protect the rights of all men, women, and children. Set aside notions of marriage laws as divinely inspired and recognize that individuals' rights to life and happiness are universal.

"I advocate for more liberal divorce laws which allow a

woman to escape an unhealthy or abusive relationship with her dignity and property intact. Too many women are forced to stay in loveless or abusive relationships. Ladies, these laws keep women at the feet of their husbands and gaining the vote will equip us with power at the ballot box to chip away at another corner of the patriarchal foundation of our society."

The ladies applauded as Elizabeth nodded firmly.

#

That evening, while Elizabeth and Susan worked behind closed doors, Annie sat with Lucy in the parlor.

"You're headed home to Cincinnati tomorrow?" asked Lucy.

"Yes, the first train in the morning."

"Tell me a little more about your family."

"My husband Max is a city councilman and owns an ironworks and machine fabrication enterprise. Lizzie is our only child. She's very bright and artistic. She draws and paints, plays the piano."

"She sounds advanced for her age. Does she get her creativity from you?" said Lucy.

"Oh, I suppose. I play piano. When I was younger, I liked to draw. I drew political cartoons and submitted them to local publications for a while. I had several make the paper. They caused quite a stir in conservative Cincinnati. The majority there still hold women in a traditional light. When my mother remarried and moved our family from New York to Cincinnati, I thought I would suffocate. Moving west was like taking a step back in time. I was young and unprepared for so much hostility toward my beliefs that women should own their destiny, unfettered by the traditions of society.

"Then I met Max, and he understood my frustrations because he, as a child of German parents, felt repression due to anti-immigrant sentiments. We connected and fell in love. He taught me to channel my energies in more productive ways. He's naturally gifted at reading people, considering their points of view, and approaching things rationally. I think it's his secret to success in business and politics."

"It sounds like you complement each other well," said Lucy.

"I think we do."

"Do you miss them, being away?"

"I do, but I've been unhappy with my life in Cincinnati," said Annie. "When Max and I courted, I agonized over the decision to marry, fearing I would give up my independence, many of my rights, and the freedom to make my own decisions. I almost didn't marry. I sought Elizabeth's council, and she described her marriage to Henry and their egalitarian relationship. It sounded manageable at the time. It turned out to be harder than I thought."

"How so?"

"Even though Max and I agreed we would treat each other as equals, I, as the woman, ended up being responsible for the domestic duties and rearing Lizzie. Thus, in addition to working and my activities with the Sanitary Commission during the war, I also bore the burdens of motherhood. I had domestic help and couldn't have done without it, but the attention to the myriad of little things weighed on my mind constantly. Men don't have those burdens. How can they move through life almost unaware of so much? Be unfettered, oblivious? I find it maddening."

"Society will take a while to change," said Lucy.

"Yes. Boys and girls are taught the expectations of the sexes from the time they're little ones. Max tries to make our marriage fair, but even he falls into the unspoken places of men over women."

"I understand. Henry and I wrestle with similar challenges in our marriage."

"You do?" said Annie.

"All the time," said Lucy.

"I suppose I thought you were above that."

"Hardly. Marriage is a set of compromises. We can't

always get what we want, can we?"

"No, that's a schoolgirl's fantasy that still invades my dreams," said Annie. She sipped her tea. It was reassuring to her that Lucy Stone, the national figure for women's rights, struggled with some of the same inner conflicts as she did.

"What prompted you to leave home and join Elizabeth and the cause?" asked Lucy.

"During the war, the advancement of women's causes was pushed to the background, overshadowed by the conflict within the country and the abolitionist movement. I don't have to tell you that. Just when I started to see hope, the war became another reason to put off women's rights for a later time. It wore on me. With all the men off to war, women worked in jobs that men had always done, in factories, stores, and government offices. When the war ended, men wanted their places back and begrudgingly acknowledged women's accomplishments, but as a temporary accommodation.

"I look at Lizzie and can't accept that she is destined to be a second-class citizen. America can be better. I could no longer sit on the sidelines and wait for others to make change happen. So much progress has been made for the Negroes. I see the opportunity before us and feel the time is now."

"Your story is similar to so many other women's," said Lucy. "We need young women like you to get involved with the cause. Elizabeth, Susan, and I are twenty years older than you. This fight will take generations. Sometimes I think Elizabeth deludes herself into thinking victory is upon us."

"I feel her frustration and impatience," said Annie.

"As do I," said Lucy. "It fuels our souls to action. But some of her ideas are so radical that they may hinder progress. The populace may not be ready for them."

"Like her ideas on divorce?" said Annie.

"For one, yes. I worry that her zeal for her positions may set us back. I'm more patient than she."

"Elizabeth has been a beacon to me since I was a girl. I try not to find fault," said Annie.

"No doubt she has become a powerful voice, but we each

have to decide how hard and fast to push things."

Annie reflected on this. "I have to catch the early train. I think I'll turn in."

"Annie, there's something I want to ask of you," said Lucy.

"What is it?"

"Out in Kansas, the state legislature is looking at changes to their state constitution to allow women and Negroes to vote. If the legislature passes the measures, they'll put it on the ballot as a referendum to the voters in November. This is the first time votes for women will be put before the people on a state ballot. Kansas has a history of progressiveness. They fought against slavery from the beginning. I think there's a good chance we could win there."

"That's encouraging," said Annie.

"It's far from guaranteed that it will pass. The Republicans are organizing against the measure for women; they say this is the Negro's time. That's why we need to organize and campaign in Kansas. We'd love to have you join us there."

"Oh, I don't know. I've been working in Ohio to get the state legislature to consider women's suffrage. We have the momentum to get a referendum to Ohio voters this fall for Negro suffrage. I don't want to disappoint the women I have been working with in Ohio."

"Kansas has the support to put both women and Black suffrage on the ballot. It's not a sure thing in Ohio, is it?" said Lucy.

"No, far from it, unfortunately," said Annie.

"Then, I ask you to consider the national picture. If we can win in Kansas, we can build momentum from there. A win there could be the start of changing minds across the country. You can do more good in Kansas right now."

"What do you need me to do?"

"I know it would be a hardship on you and your family, but will you come to Kansas and make speeches with us?" asked Lucy.

Annie reacted swiftly. "I think I could be of more use in a

supporting role. I couldn't give convincing speeches like you or Susan or Elizabeth. Who am I?"

"Annie. You are an accomplished woman who has worked in a business while being a mother and wife. You're articulate and would make an excellent impression on audiences."

"I don't know if I'm ready," said Annie.

"We need you. Kansas is a big state with many small towns. Spreading the word across it will take a cast of speakers. I'm recruiting others. I'd like you to be part of the corp."

"That's flattering, but I told Elizabeth I'd return to New York after the holidays to assist her."

"Your talents are under-utilized in editing speeches and articles. This may be your calling," said Lucy.

"May I think about it?"

"Of course. Go home and talk about it with Max. It won't be glamorous. Kansas is the West; it's not New York, but it may be just the place to prove yourself."

"I'll consider it. Thank you, Lucy."

Lucy took Annie's hand and held it firmly. "Follow your heart."

Annie returned her smile. "Good night."

"Good night, dear. I look forward to working with you."

CHAPTER 15

Cincinnati – December 1866

Working together in the kitchen of their new home, Annie handed Lizzie the last plate from the metal tub of water and dried it with the towel.

"Where do these belong?" said Annie.

"In that cupboard there," said Lizzie, pointing to the china cabinet.

Annie placed the stacks of plates and cups on the shelf.

"No, not like that," said Lizzie.

"Where then?" said Annie.

"They can't be messy like that. Put all the large plates in one stack and the small plates in another. Cups on the shelf above."

Annie looked at her daughter and said, "Papa insists the kitchen be organized?"

Lizzie nodded.

"Like everything else," Annie said as she took the dishes down, restacked them, and returned them to the shelves. "Is that acceptable?"

Lizzie nodded again.

"Time for piano practice," said Annie. "Do your scales first, then show me what you've learned while I was gone. Then we can play together."

They moved into a large room with sunshine streaming in from the tall windows, still lacking window treatments. A grand piano stood in one corner, and an artist's easel sat atop a canvas tarp in another. Several upholstered chairs were arranged in front of a large fireplace with a tiled hearth and ornately carved mantel. A large, framed daguerreotype of Annie, Max, and Lizzie was propped on the mantel.

Lizzie began playing.

Annie stood behind her and watched for a few minutes. She quietly moved to the painter's corner and leafed through the paintings on the artist's bench. There were several of the new bridge. Annie admired them, amazed at her daughter's ability to capture its essence and the varying skies of daytime and dusk. She thought of the political cartoons she had drawn as a young woman, thinking of how differently her daughter applied her artistic talents.

"Can we play a duet now?" said Lizzie.

"Which one?" said Annie as she sat on the bench beside her.

"You choose."

Annie rifled through the sheet music on top of the piano and placed the pages in front of them. "'Schubert's Fantasy.'"

They played the piece. Annie was rusty and made more mistakes than Lizzie. When they played the final note of the eight-minute arrangement, Annie rested her hands on the keyboard, letting the music fade to silence. "You play beautifully. I'm so proud of you." She hugged Lizzie.

"I wish you could be here for my piano recital."

"I wish I could be there too," said Annie. "Papa will be there, I'm sure."

"You'll be in New York?"

"Yes, dear. I'm leaving tomorrow to go back."

"He was at the last recital. It's just that, at the reception afterward, we had tea and cakes. Some of the students' mothers *and* fathers were both there. He was the only father alone," said Lizzie.

"You know how proud of you I am. I hope you don't need me there to believe that."

"No, it's not that. It's …"

"What, dear? Did he do something?" said Annie.

"No, the mothers had a gay time with him, but I think they wondered why you weren't there."

"Oh. I don't think that's anything to worry about, do you? It's not their concern. You know I love and support you, and my work requires me to be away."

Lizzie nodded. "Some of the girls say unkind things about you."

"That's not very charitable of them. What do they say?"

Lizzie hesitated, distressed by the conversation. "They say you're unwomanly. They call you odd."

Annie thought for a moment. "I've been called names ever since I was a little girl. It hurts to hear it, but I've learned to ignore it. Yes, I'm different from most women. But different isn't bad; people shouldn't judge someone harshly because they're different. I advocate for my right, women's right, to be treated the same as men. I don't accept that I must do everything society says a woman must do. Some people want to keep things the way they are, where women have to be a certain way, the way it's been in the past. They are against women doing things differently. Just like some people are against the Negroes gaining rights and freedom. They don't like change, and they resist it. I know it's hard to hear people criticize your family, but you must be strong. Try to ignore the criticism. Do you understand?"

Lizzie nodded. "When will you come home, for good?"

"I don't know when. There's so much that needs to be done."

They heard the front door open, and Abby called, "Hello? Anyone home?"

"Miss Abby!" Lizzie jumped up and ran to the front foyer.

Annie followed and found Lizzie in Abby's arms, her travel bags on the floor beside her.

"What a warm greeting," said Abby. "Did you have a nice Christmas with your family?"

"Yes, it was wonderful. We had a big tree, and we opened presents and made strudel. I made you an ornament; come see," said Lizzie, pulling her arm toward the music room.

"I will, just a minute." Abby closed the front door. "Hello, Mrs. Bennett."

"Hello, Abby. Welcome back. Did you enjoy your holiday?" said Annie.

"Yes, thank you. It was so nice to be with my family and spend some time in Boston."

"Wonderful. I'll let you unpack and get settled. There are a few things I'd like to discuss with you regarding Lizzie, but that can wait. Max and I are going to a New Year's party tonight. You're prepared to stay with Lizzie this evening?"

"Yes, that's fine," said Abby. "I'll take my things up to my room."

"Can I come help you unpack?" said Lizzie.

"Yes, I want to hear about your Christmas," said Abby.

"Lizzie, you need to do your reading now," said Annie.

"Oh, may I do it after? I missed Abby so much," said Lizzie.

"No, thirty minutes of reading. There will be plenty of time to visit with Abby."

"Yes, ma'am."

#

Max held Annie's hand as she stepped down from the carriage. He instructed the driver to pick them up at half past ten, then took Annie's hands in his. "You look beautiful tonight. I'm happy to be at your side."

She smiled at him and took his arm as they approached the Metropolitan Building at Ninth and Walnut Streets. They filed into the lobby and stood in line to check their coats. Annie wore an evening dress of green silk fabric, fringe at the sleeve openings and across the front, and a narrow waist and fit that accentuated her still trim figure at thirty years. They moved into the main hall of the building and greeted the hosts, Charles and Olivia Grainger.

"Good evening, Charles. This is my wife, Annie Bennett,"

said Max.

"My wife, Olivia," said Charles.

"Thank you for having us. It's so good to be able to attend celebrations again," said Max.

"Indeed," said Charles. "The world is finally returning to normal, and the future looks bright, doesn't it?"

"It does. Has your business picked up?" said Max.

"It's up. Not yet at pre-war levels, but I'm encouraged, though, as every month gets better and better. I'd love a shot at some of the city's projects—maybe the new hospital that council is discussing?"

"You should have a fair opportunity to bid. I'll make sure you're on the vendor list," said Max.

"Thank you. Anything you can do is appreciated. I hope you and Mrs. Mueller enjoy the evening."

"Thank you. Annie and I have to bow out before midnight. We have another engagement. My apologies, and thank you again for your hospitality."

The Graingers nodded and greeted the next guests in line.

"He thinks you're off to some official city function after this. No inkling that we're headed to a beer garden and a much livelier time than this stodgy crowd," Annie said.

"Come now, my dear. This will be fun. Look, they have an orchestra."

"You know I detest wearing this dress and putting on appearances," said Annie.

"But you're so lovely in it. I do enjoy seeing you like this now and then. Most of the crowd here is unpretentious. I know them from the Mechanics Institute. They're men who have worked hard to get where they are."

"Do they all want something from you, like Charles?"

"Well, they're all trying to advance their enterprises, just like I am. That's how it works."

"Networking and favors amongst the boys' clubs. It's how our democracy works. I'm learning firsthand," said Annie. "As we've tried to get woman's suffrage on the state legislative agenda, the men won't even talk to us. I wish I could join some of their organizations. That's where they discuss things, and we aren't even allowed in the door."

"I'm sorry it's been so difficult for you," said Max. "Can we forget about that tonight? Our last night together. Enjoy ourselves. We have so much to be thankful for and so many blessings."

"In the spirit of the season, I will suspend talk of women's rights for the evening."

"Thank you," said Max.

They took champagne flutes from a waiter's tray and sipped.

"Max! Annie!" Patrick and Molly Sweeney approached. Patrick shook his hook, ringing a bell tied to it with a red ribbon. "Happy New Year!"

"Well, aren't you festively attired," said Max.

"I had a mistletoe tied on it for Christmas. It was a lively opening line at the pubs," said Patrick.

"You're happily married. Aren't you past gimmicks to get young ladies to kiss you," said Max.

"Hah," said Molly. "He uses that thing to his advantage to score sympathy points with anyone. Women in saloons, businessmen, his children. He's shameless."

"I am a crippled Union soldier, and I deserve every ounce of sympathy I get," said Patrick.

"It doesn't seem to be slowing you down," said Annie.

"Annie, you look lovely. Can I say that?" said Patrick.

"Patrick," Molly said sternly. "He's already had a few."

"How nice of you to say, Patrick. Thank you," said Annie.

"Will you dance with me?" asked Patrick.

"Why yes, I will," said Annie. "I'm feeling exceptionally charitable tonight. Of course, I also dance with Negroes. I'm not averse to any man, except those who can't accept women as their equals."

Annie took Patrick's arm and gave Max a smile and a nod as they passed to the dance floor.

"Molly, would you care to dance?" asked Max.

"Yes, thank you," said Molly.

"Let me know if I'm poking you with it," said Patrick as they began to dance. "You put me in the same class as Negroes?"

"You're a man," Annie said. "You're all the same to me."

"You've become quite the radical since you've been out on your own."

"My views haven't changed much over the past year. I've always advocated for equal treatment of all men and women. My priorities have shifted slightly. Securing the vote for men and women, Black and white, will empower the disempowered to change the system over time."

"You truly believe this country is ready for Negroes and women to vote?" said Patrick.

"Whether they're ready for it is irrelevant. Many weren't ready for the emancipation of slaves, and look now."

"I don't want to argue with you, Annie; it will darken the festive mood and nice effects of the whiskey. Can we agree to a truce for tonight?"

"For tonight, yes. I already promised Max I'd leave the issues at home. Tomorrow's another day, though. We won't keep it locked up forever," said Annie.

"There is one thing I have to say, though," said Patrick.

"What is it?" she said.

"I don't care what causes you want to fight for or how you do it. That's your business. But Max, I don't like seeing you abuse him like you do."

Annie stopped dancing, and Patrick dropped his arms from her. She stepped back, somewhat alarmed.

"What on earth are you talking about? I couldn't abuse Max. That's what men do to women," said Annie.

"You don't physically abuse him, but you torment him just as cruelly," said Patrick.

Annie took another step back and scoffed. "Who do you think you are, talking to me like that?"

She turned to walk away, but he grabbed her arm with his good hand. Annie let out a cry. "Unhand me."

"You know what you're doing. You emasculate him with

your antics. He's one of the kindest, most Christian men on this earth, and you take advantage of him." He scoffed. "I guess you are just like a man." He released her as she stomped off the dance floor.

Max saw Annie fleeing from Patrick. "Molly, excuse me. Something's wrong," he said, nodding toward their spouses.

Max caught up with Patrick, Molly right behind him. "What happened?" said Max.

"I'm sorry, Max. I couldn't stand by any longer without saying something. You've always been there for me. Someone had to say something to her."

Max held up his palms in a gesture of confusion.

"She needed to be brought down a few pegs. I knew you wouldn't do it," said Patrick.

"What in God's name did you say to her?" said Max.

"She'll tell you. I hope she takes it to heart. I'm sorry, Max."

Max left them to find Annie.

Molly said to Patrick, "You had no business."

"I love him too much. I couldn't take it anymore," said Patrick.

"Paddy."

Max found Annie in a corridor off the main room, the music echoing in the empty hall. Her face was red, and she dabbed at her eyes with her handkerchief.

"Are you all right?" said Max.

"Yes, I'm fine," she sniffed, patting at her nose.

Max embraced her. "I'm so sorry. What did he say to you?"

She shook her head. "He doesn't understand what we have. What we agreed to."

"What did he say?" asked Max.

"Can we go? I don't feel much in a party mood anymore."

"Don't let Patrick ruin your evening. Come on. It's Patrick. He's been drinking."

"It wasn't the drink talking. He meant every word," said Annie.

"Please tell me what he said."

"In the carriage," she said. "I don't want to discuss it here."

"All right, I'll send the valet for our driver. This way."

Annie insisted they stand outside to wait for their carriage. Max was accosted by citizens who wanted to shake his hand or put a bug in his ear about this street needing sewers or that corner needing better police oversight. Annie stood by, as usual, and forced smiles.

The city solicitor, Edward Noyes, stepped out of a carriage with his wife. "Max, good evening." He looked at Annie, face flushed and tried to reconcile what he'd heard about Councilman Mueller's radical, women's movement wife with the attractive woman in an evening dress.

They introduced their wives. Annie made painful small talk with Mrs. Noyes while the men spoke.

Edward said, "I've drafted the letter to the Kentucky governor regarding our proposed railroad. Will you have time to look at it next week?"

"Thank you, yes. Can you send it to my office?" said Max.

"I'll send a courier. Is everything all right?"

"Fine, why?"

"Your wife. She appears upset?" said Noyes.

"She's not feeling herself tonight," said Max.

Once inside the carriage, Max said, "I'm sorry that took so long. Are you cold?"

"No, I'm so bound up by the layers of this dress."

"Are you sure? Want me to rub your hands."

"I said I am not cold. Give me some space, please," Annie said, her tone sharper than intended. "I'm sorry."

He inched away from her. "Are you sure you're feeling up to going to my family's?"

"Yes, I'm not feeling ill. I'm angry at Patrick. I don't need to be coddled."

"Will you tell me what he said to upset you?"

"He said I was abusing you," she said.

"I don't understand," said Max.

"He thinks I emasculate you by being a women's rights advocate and that I take advantage of your kind heart and have selfishly abandoned you to pursue my own endeavors."

They rode along in the dark.

"Is that how you feel?" she said, breaking the silence.

She tried reading his face but couldn't see. "Tell me."

He took a deep breath, and when he spoke, his voice quivered. "It's very challenging having to look out for Lizzie's well-being and think about the shop and work to keep our city thriving. Some days, I feel overwhelmed. It's hard to bear all that alone."

"I know how you feel. That's how I felt," said Annie. "That's how all women feel when they want to be anything in addition to being a mother. Imagine what it was like when Lizzie couldn't walk or talk, and I had to be at her side twenty-four hours a day."

Max said, "I think it's more difficult now. When Lizzie was a baby, Marie could feed, bathe, and clothe her, but I don't want to leave Lizzie's maturing years in the care of some hired girl. She needs her parents now."

"You mean, she needs her mother now, don't you?" said Annie.

"I think she does. How can I replace her mother? I don't know how to be that."

"You worry too much. She loves you. She's thriving. I've watched her since I've been home. You're doing a wonderful job. I'm almost in the way now."

"No. That's not the case," he insisted.

"It is. You and she have your routine," said Annie. "You've found your rhythm together. She seems enamored with Abby. It's like she has a sister and a mother. My coming home is disruptive."

"No, you're reading it wrong. I'm trying to make everything appear right, but it's not. This is the hardest thing I've ever done in my life. I want you back home," said Max.

"That's not the answer. I'm not the answer. You are a caring and resourceful person. You're enough for Lizzie.

You'll see."

"That's it. You don't have any lingering doubts that this is the best thing for her?" said Max.

"I have scores of doubts, but this is what I must do now. I'm sorry. I wish I could bring myself to a different answer. If I don't go, I'll fall back into the melancholy I wrestled with for so long. It's my time now."

"I'm not sure which is more emasculating," said Max. "Making me a mother, or you choosing yourself over me."

"That's not what I'm doing," she said.

"That is what you're doing. That's not love." Max banged on the roof of the carriage. "Driver, stop."

"Max," pleaded Annie.

Max got out of the carriage. "Please take Mrs. Bennett home. I'll walk from here."

"Yes, sir. Good night, sir."

Max watched the carriage pull away. He stood next to the canal, replaying their conversation. It happened so fast. He said words he had been thinking for weeks but had been too considerate to vocalize. She had to know how he felt. Now she knew, and it didn't matter. He feared losing what they had built together. He put his hand over his mouth to suppress crying. He took deep breaths to regain his composure. He combed his fingers through his hair, then a few vigorous strokes to prepare his façade for the rest of the evening. Max Mueller would remain calm and composed on the outside, as expected.

CHAPTER 16

During the three-block walk from where the carriage dropped him to the Eichen Garten, Max reconciled himself to his immediate future without Annie by his side. He was sad for himself and Lizzie, but he had never let adversity defeat him. As he walked into the saloon, he felt the embrace of the neighbors who had stood by his family in good times and bad. Throughout his life, he felt most at ease among his people in the German neighborhood. He needed their solace tonight.

He stopped at the bar, greeted his sister, and downed a beer.

"Mother upstairs?" Max inquired.

Helene nodded. "She's happy to leave the late nights to me and the hired help."

"Nice crowd tonight."

"People are happy to say goodbye to 1866. Where's Annie?"

"She wasn't feeling herself. Another?" Max said, handing her his mug.

Helene poured the lager, foam running down the side. "She's leaving again?"

"Tomorrow," he nodded.

"It weighs on you, the separation," said Helene.

"It's what she wants. She's doing important work."

"And leaving you to fend for yourself."

"I knew what I was getting into when I married," he said.

"Did you? I'm worried about you. You've lost your usual cheerful demeanor."

He downed the second beer and handed her his mug.

She took it. "You're not going to find your happiness in the beer. Papa searched it for years."

"Tonight, I'm looking to get lost, not find anything."

"Max," said Helene.

"I'm all right."

She filled his mug from the keg at the end of the bar. "Oskar and Peter are out back. Oskar's lady friend is with him. He's smitten."

"Well, let me go meet this woman who has captured the heart of our baby brother."

Helene squeezed Max's forearm and gave him a supportive smile. He nodded and then pushed through the crowd onto the patio. A large group stood warming themselves around a fire in the back corner. He found his brothers and Catherine at a table.

"Catherine, this is my big brother, Max," said Oskar.

Max took her hand, "So nice to finally meet you," said Max. "Oskar tells me of your wonderful work with the freedmen. It's admirable. I'm sorry Annie couldn't be here to meet you. She taught in the school here in Over-the-Rhine. She would empathize with some of your challenges."

"Where is Annie tonight?" said Oskar.

"She wasn't feeling herself. She's spending a last night at home with Lizzie."

"I'm sorry to hear that," said Oskar. "Anything serious?"

"I'm sure she'll feel well enough to travel in the morning," said Max.

"Max was like a second father to me," Oskar explained to Catherine. "He took an interest in my education and success after our father died. He paid my tuition for college."

Max squeezed Oskar's shoulder. "My little brother has grown into quite a remarkable man."

Oskar flicked Max's hand away. "Coddled me incessantly.

I resented him like a father for a while, but I came to appreciate what he taught me."

"What did you do today?" asked Max.

"Oskar took me to a gymnastics exhibition," said Catherine.

"At the Turner Hall?" said Max.

"It wasn't the Turners," said Oskar. "The Young Men's Gymnastics Club put it on at Mozart Hall. Two brothers in the club have become somewhat famous in gymnastics circles. I met them at competitions back when I was practicing. Their act was fabulous. Some amazing moves on the parallel bars. Some of their somersaults off the board were the most complex I've ever seen. They brought in some magicians for entertainment. Magic dice, other tricks."

"They had a fortune teller," said Catherine.

"Catherine went up on stage," added Oskar, smiling.

"And what did he say?" asked Max.

Catherine blushed.

Oskar said, "She has a second chance at a long and happy life."

"Well, now, that's encouraging," said Max. "On this New Year's Eve, I'm hopeful we all will have a second chance at happiness."

"*Prost!*" they toasted.

Oskar said, "Who needs another one? Catherine and I will get them." He collected the mugs and left Peter and Max.

"She's pretty. And charming," said Max.

"They seem very happy together," said Peter.

"How are you doing?" said Max. "How's the new job?"

"It's been nonstop. Along with two other reporters, I cover Congress for the *Washington Post*. The paper is much bigger than the *Daily Commercial*. There is so much to report. I cover the western states' activities."

"I'm glad to hear you're doing well. What's your read on Congress's Reconstruction efforts? Are they going to overcome Johnson's foot-dragging?"

"I think so," said Peter. "Johnson has fired disloyal

appointees in Washington and across the country, trying to build up support around him, but I think the momentum toward breaking the Southern political stronghold is too great."

"I saw Johnson when he spoke here during his 'swing around the circle' tour," said Max. "He speaks as if what he says is gospel. He says things with enough conviction and repetition that it becomes the truth, at least in his mind. Plenty of the audience here in town was aligned with him. He spoke to his supporters."

"The tour was a valiant effort," said Peter, "but I think the tide is turning against him. The riots in New Orleans and Memphis created enough outrage against his soft stance toward the Southerners."

"Good," said Max. "We need the states to ratify the Fourteenth Amendment and put Reconstruction to bed. Then we can get on with expanding and strengthening the country."

"I'm optimistic looking into next year, but it's no sure thing the amendment will get enough states' support to pass. Kentucky won't support it, and it's unclear whether Ohio will vote for it either," said Peter.

"We'll pass it," said Max confidently.

Oskar and Catherine returned with the beers.

"Oskar, tell us how things are progressing at the Bureau?" said Max.

"I feel like we are making a significant impact on the lives of many," said Oskar. "For so long, these people were deprived of so much. I can't imagine living in the conditions they endured. I'm constantly amazed by their resilience and desire to become fully part of society. They are appreciative of the work we're doing. Beyond food and shelter, the education Catherine and her volunteers provide is the greatest impact we're making."

Catherine nodded in agreement.

"Are the schools like ours here in Cincinnati?" asked Peter.

Oskar motioned to Catherine to respond.

"No, nothing at all like them. First of all, we don't have a school building. We've moved around. Currently, we're in an old army depot building. We have limited books and supplies. Due to the large number of students, we created a rotation to use the classrooms. Each student attends for about ten hours a week and has assignments between classes. I teach night classes for the adults who want to learn reading or arithmetic."

"Do they have the same capacity to learn as the white children you've taught?" asked Peter.

"On the whole, yes. Like any class, some are more advanced than others. Much of it is about motivation. I see most Negro parents stressing the importance of education to their children. They recognize education is a prerequisite to participate in society and be accepted by the broader community."

"I'm sorry for all the questions," said Peter. "I talk frequently with congressmen about the effectiveness of the Freedmen's Bureau. I appreciate your first-hand information."

"I appreciate the interest," said Catherine.

"It sounds like you've had to create a school from nothing," said Max. "I assumed the Bureau provided more."

"The Bureau is drastically underfunded and understaffed," said Oskar. "There are close to four million freedmen across the country. We're helping them create lives one family at a time, and we have to make it up as we go along."

"Isn't there a prescribed program to follow?" asked Max.

"There are briefs distributed across the agents and plenty of bureaucratic procedures and reports to complete, but most of that focuses on tracking how the money is spent. Each Bureau office is pretty much on its own," said Oskar.

"It was horrible how the Klan burned down your church. Have you had any problems since you moved the school to the armory? Are the locals supporting you?" asked Peter.

"We haven't seen anything from the Klan since then. We have the posted soldiers to thank for that, I suppose. Some of the locals are supportive and want the freedmen to succeed. They see the value in getting them to a place where they can care for themselves. Most, however, want us to go away."

"I know you won't let them deter you, Oskar," said Max. "You're one resourceful and determined man. This is the man who snuck into a Confederate army camp, posing as a Kentucky local to gain enemy intelligence."

"You did?" said Catherine. "You never told me that."

Oskar downplayed it, and Max told how Oskar had done just that.

Max said, "The work you're doing, both of you, it's inspiring. I'm thankful we have people like you on the ground. You'll fix it."

"That's kind of you, Max, but I think the beer has made you a bit happy," said Oskar. "Let's not overstate the abilities of the Bureau to fix a century of injustice. It will take years."

Max, now tipsy, said, "Peter, do you have a girl in Washington?"

"There's a girl, yes," said Peter.

"What's her name?"

"Maria."

"She doesn't sound German," said Max.

"No, she's Italian."

"You couldn't find any German girls?"

"You didn't marry a German girl," said Peter.

"No, I didn't. Maybe I should have," said Max.

"She's beautiful. Dark hair, big brown eyes."

"Where did you meet her?"

"I was doing a story at the U.S. Treasury about the women they hired during the war and what they are doing now. She was hired as a clerk to trim paper money. She's been working there ever since."

"A working girl. Annie would be proud," said Max.

"I see her almost every weekend. She loves the theater,"

said Peter.

"Think twice before marrying her," interrupted Max.

Peter and Oskar looked at each other, unsure what to think of Max's uncharacteristic comments.

Helene arrived with fresh beers and passed them around. "It's almost midnight," she said, raising her mug and toasting, "*Prost Neujahr!*"

"*Prost Neujahr!*" they cheered, clinking glasses. They took sips while Max downed his, set his glass on the table, and belched. "Happy New Year, family. May 1867 be a better year for all."

"Thirsty Max?" said Helene.

"I'm just trying to forget the bad parts of the last six years. Better days."

"All right, then. Another?" she said, taking his mug.

"Yes, please," Max said, a broad smile across his face.

Oskar shook his head.

"I'm back to the bar. Happy New Year!" Pointing at Max, Helene said to Peter. "You'll look after this one?"

The bar erupted in cheers of Happy New Year and *Prost Neujahr*. A young man came running out of the saloon screaming "Happy New Year!" as he completed a lap around the beer garden and went inside shrieking. Oskar kissed Catherine as others around the bar did the same in celebration.

Max hugged his brothers and Catherine, then went through the crowd greeting and hugging old friends. His ebullience faded as he reached the state of intoxication where he felt as if he were looking at himself from the outside. He found himself in front of the saloon and looked up and down the street. The neighborhood was deserted, except for the occasional partiers on their way home, their voices echoing against the buildings. He started walking east on Twelfth Street. He moved slowly as if in a fog, his mind knowing the way without thinking. He turned left onto Sycamore and started walking up one of the steepest hills in the city.

His pace became slower and slower until he stopped.

"Christ, this bloody hill. Why did I build a house up here?" he breathed heavily. He turned around and looked down at the city, the lights shining back up at him. "Ah, that's why." He stood for a few minutes, gazing at the view below. A wave of nausea replaced the wave of nostalgia. He leaned over, his hands on his knees to steady himself, and vomited in the street. He stood, wiped his mouth on his jacket, and resumed walking.

He let himself in the house and went to the kitchen. He opened a metal box and pulled out a half-eaten apple pie. He cut a piece, ate it with his fingers, and drank a glass of water. He used the water closet and considered going upstairs. Instead, he went into the parlor and fumbled around in a chest until he found a quilt. He pulled off his jacket and shoes and sat down on the sofa.

He was surprised to look up and see Abby standing in the doorway in her dressing gown. "Max, is everything all right? I heard noises down here," she whispered.

"Abby. Come in," said Max.

"Shh. You'll wake everyone," said Abby entering the room.

"Oh, sorry," whispered Max, laughing a little. "How was Lizzie tonight?"

"We had a nice evening. We played chess and made a pie."

"I had a piece. You're an excellent baker."

"Do you need anything?" she asked.

"No. Come sit and talk with me, will you?"

She sat in the chair across from the sofa.

"How was your night?" he mumbled.

"As I said, Lizzie and I had a nice evening."

"Yes, the pie."

"Yes," said Abby.

"Did Mrs. Bennett come home?" said Max.

"Yes, about half past nine. She said she wasn't feeling well."

"No, she wasn't. She came home, so I celebrated the new year without her."

Abby sat quietly.

"Happy New Year," he said a little too loudly.

"Happy New Year," she said.

"In German, we say *Prost Neujahr* and give hugs and kisses," said Max.

Abby sat perfectly still.

"That's what we did tonight at the Eichen Garten. It was nice to see my old friends."

"What's going on here?" Annie said from the doorway.

"Annie," said Max. "Abby and I were talking about New Year's."

"You're drunk, aren't you?" said Annie.

"I am. I'm sorry. No, I'm not sorry. I'm allowed to celebrate once in a while. That's my right as a man."

Abby got up and hurried up the stairs.

"You're a father," Annie said with a hint of disgust. "What kind of example is this? Drunk, alone in a room with an unmarried young woman in her nightclothes. Is this how it goes when I'm away?"

"No, it's not," he said.

"How can I trust you? With her?"

"Don't do this, please. We were just talking," he said.

"Who knows what might have happened if I hadn't come in?"

"Stop. You know I wouldn't."

"The apple doesn't fall far from the tree, Max," said Annie.

"What does that mean?"

"Your father, William. Alone in his house with a young girl. We know how that turned out."

"Why are you being so cruel?" pleaded Max.

"You're drunk. There's no reasoning with you tonight. We'll talk in the morning." She went upstairs.

Max sunk into the couch, pulled the quilt over himself, and fell asleep.

#

Dressed in his rumpled clothes from the previous night, Max entered their bedroom and quietly closed the door. "Good morning," he said softly.

"Good morning," Annie replied without turning from her packing.

"I had too much to drink last night. I'm sorry," he said.

"You did."

"Maybe I shouldn't have said everything I did last night, but it's how I feel."

"Now we both know where each other stands. It doesn't make it any easier, but it's out in the open," said Annie.

She continued packing without looking at him, so he went to the bathroom to freshen up.

When he returned, Annie said, "We need to find a new governess."

"Why? Abby is wonderful with Lizzie."

"I can't trust you in the house with her," she said.

"Annie, you're imagining something that isn't there."

"She's young and pretty. You're a man. It's a volatile mix."

Max sighed heavily. "Don't be unreasonable. I've never strayed. It is a sin I cannot commit." He looked her in the eyes, holding his breath, heart quickening as he prayed she would feel his sincerity.

She stared at him intently. "God, it's true."

He relaxed. "My vow is sacred. I'll never betray you that way."

"I don't see any reason for you and Lizzie to come to the station with me. The driver can manage my trunk," said Annie.

"She might feel better if she's able to see you off. Can you ask her?" he said.

"All right. We'll leave it up to her. Will you carry my trunk downstairs, please?"

"Of course," he said.

She looked around the room for the final time in how long, she didn't know, then went downstairs.

Abby was serving Lizzie breakfast in the dining room. "Good morning Mrs. Bennett."

"Good morning, Mother," said Lizzie cheerfully.

"Good morning, my darling," said Annie.

"Can I make you an omelet? Something substantial for your day of travel?" asked Abby.

"Yes, thank you—an omelet. I appreciate it," said Annie.

Max came in and kissed the top of Lizzie's head. "Good morning, daughter."

"Good morning, Father."

"Good morning Max. Would you like an omelet?" said Abby.

"No, thank you. I'll just have coffee."

Abby brought Max a cup from the kitchen. Max sat at the table across from Annie and took a sip. They sat in silence.

"Why isn't anyone talking?" said Lizzie.

"I have a headache this morning," said Max.

"I have a lot on my mind getting ready for my trip," said Annie. "Lizzie, do you want to go to the train station to see me off this morning? It's up to you. We can say our farewells here if you prefer."

"I'd like to go," said Lizzie. "That way, I can see you longer and won't forget what you look like."

Annie said, "You have your locket. You can always look at my likeness inside it. You didn't forget what I looked like last time I was gone, did you?"

"I looked at the picture often," said Lizzie. "I saw you, but I forgot the details. And how you smelled and felt and the colors in your hair. I don't want to forget those things."

"That's one of the loveliest things anyone has ever said to me," said Annie. "Thank you." Annie took Lizzie's face in her hands and looked into her eyes. "I want to remember all your details too." She smiled and kissed her.

CHAPTER 17

Max entered the small school building near the corner of Court and John Streets and scanned the room. Among the small, primarily Black audience of parents, he recognized another councilman, a few city leaders, and Peter Clark, the school principal who was a long-time champion for Colored schools in Cincinnati. He spotted his half-brother John and took a seat next to him. "John, good to see you."

"Good morning, Max. How is Miss Annie?" said John.

"She's traveling the country, championing the causes of women and suffrage for all."

"She's a forceful woman and a generous spirit. My mother enjoyed our dinner at your home. Annie made her feel welcome."

"How is Jenny adjusting to her new city?" said Max.

"She's getting along pretty well," said John. "She's working at the Brighton House Hotel. They took her on, happy to have her experience from the hotel in Jackson. She's trying to find a community at church, but she doesn't feel comfortable yet. I don't know if it will ever feel like home for her."

The school principal, Mr. Clark, began, "Thank you all for coming today to help us celebrate the first graduates of the Gaines High School. We opened this school just a year ago to provide the Colored boys and girls of Cincinnati an education beyond the primary grades. It has long been a vision of the Colored school board to provide our children the same opportunity for high school as that given to the children in the white schools. I want to thank those who donated funds and worked to help us get the school off the ground."

As the principal continued his opening remarks, John tapped his hand on Max's knee, recognizing his substantial donation to the school. Max nodded at John.

The two half-brothers didn't acknowledge their blood relationship in public. In getting to know John, Max came to accept him, cast off most of his racist beliefs, and became an abolitionist. However, he still feared the public's reaction and his family's learning of his illegitimate birth and his relationship to John.

They watched the students sing songs and read poems and essays. Reverend Towler thanked Mr. Clark for his tireless efforts on behalf of Colored education in Cincinnati.

After the ceremony, Max greeted Mr. Clark and the reverend. "Thank you for coming today, Mr. Mueller. We are pleased to have a city representative take an interest in the success of our school. And more so, we appreciate your voice in council as a constant reminder that we are here. Your donation to the education of students in our school was generous. Thank you."

"I feel blessed to be able to assist," said Max.

The two men moved on to a family, the young student sporting a white achievement ribbon on his chest.

"John, I'm headed downtown. Which direction are you going?" said Max.

"I'm going to the barbershop," said John.

"Will you walk with me?" They started the mile walk southeast toward the central business district. "How are your brother and sister doing? Have you heard from them?"

"Yes," said John. "They're going to come to live with my mother and me here in Cincinnati."

"That's wonderful news," said Max.

"Now that slavery is dead, they're not afraid to return. The slave catchers are all out of business, thank the Lord. Even though there's no slavery in Canada, the white people there weren't very welcoming."

"Tell me, honestly, John. Do you think they'll feel more welcome here in Cincinnati?" said Max.

"I don't know what it was like in Canada, just the little bit in Martha's letters," said John. "I find that most white folk leave us Black folk alone as long as we don't bring too much attention to ourselves. And so we find it most pleasant to live amongst our people. We have our churches and schools. We have our clubs. We stick to our neighborhoods unless we have a reason to shop or such. It's not too bad. It's better than the other life we had before."

"I think it will take time," said Max. "Congress is working on trying to do more to help the Negroes than President Johnson thought necessary. I have hope."

"We are a patient people," said John. "We put up with so much for so long. However, I am worried about all the freedmen arriving from the South. They need a way to earn money and places to live. I don't know where they are all going to go."

"It's not just Blacks who need work," said Max. "Many white men are looking for work too. Business isn't booming right now. We have to bring more commerce and jobs here. I'm working with city council on it. That's going to take time too. Where are your brother and sister going to live?"

"I found a house to rent over on Gest Street in the West End. It is big enough for all of us. We hope to buy the house someday."

"That sounds nice. Your family will all be living together again. I'm happy for you."

"Thank you. I know I'm lucky to inherit that money from Master William and to have a job. Many are not so lucky," said John. "How's your brother, Oskar, doing? He's working for the Bureau now, isn't he?"

Max nodded. "He's doing pretty well. He's working hard."

"Where's he at?"

"He's in Paris, Kentucky. Not too far from your old home at Given House."

"I'm sorry for Oskar. I'm happy if I never step foot on that soil again as long as I live," said John.

Max nodded again.

"Have you heard anything from Aaron?" asked John.

"No. His wife packed up their belongings and moved to Mississippi with the children. You heard anything?"

"No," John scoffed. "Last I saw him, he was fixin' to buy a plantation. He was confident he could turn it around and make himself rich."

"Aaron has a history of finding enterprises to make him money," said Max. "I hope this one is more successful than the smuggling that led to his imprisonment during the war."

"I'll never understand him," said John. "We were friendly as boys, then he turned his back on me, and most recently, I don't know how he feels. He seemed uncomfortable just being around me."

"I can't say that he and I ever felt comfortable around each other either," said Max. "I think he was raised to believe that he was above you, me, and nearly everyone else. When he encountered anything that challenged that, he didn't know how to deal with it."

"Well, the one thing he did that I'm grateful for is send Jenny to me."

"I guess we can pray that he finds redemption in this stage of his life," said Max.

"Amen to that."

CHAPTER 18

Lawrence, Kansas – Spring 1867

Annie sat at a table in the dining room of the Hotel Eldridge with Lucy Stone and Olympia Brown.

"How was your trip in?" Lucy asked Annie.

"Long. The train was delayed for several hours. I didn't arrive until after midnight last night," said Annie.

"I'm sorry. Was your room comfortable?" said Lucy.

"Very. It's a beautiful hotel," said Annie.

"It's only about ten years old. The original hotel was burned to the ground by pro-slavery rioters. A group of anti-slavery settlers founded Lawrence, and it was a hotbed of conflict throughout the war."

"The landscape in this part of the country is so different from Ohio or New York," said Annie. "I'm looking forward to seeing more of it."

Lucy said, "With the limited rail lines in the state, you'll have plenty of opportunity. Most of your travel will be by coach or other means."

"I'm excited to get started," said Annie. "A little nervous."

"Don't worry. Olympia will be with you. She's quite experienced at the speaking circuit. Olympia, why don't you share your background with Annie."

"Happy to," said Olympia. "I was raised in Michigan and then attended Antioch College in Ohio. At the time, it was one of the few colleges to accept women and Negroes. Co-education was called 'the great experiment.' College was where I learned to confront society's barriers against women.

"Each year, the college brought accomplished men on campus to lecture. We inquired why no women were ever invited to speak, and the professors gave us a bunch of excuses: there were no women comparable to the men speakers, or no woman's voice could fill the chapel— senseless arguments. I organized a fund drive and raised the money to invite Antoinette Brown Blackwell, the first ordained woman minister in the country, to speak. The lecture was well attended, and Miss Blackwell inspired me to become a minister."

"Is Miss Blackwell related to your husband, Lucy?" asked Annie.

"Yes, by marriage. Her husband Samuel is Henry's brother," said Lucy. "It's a small world, isn't it? The Blackwell family lived in Cincinnati for a while. Did you know of them?"

"I'm afraid not," said Annie. "I'm sorry, Olympia; please proceed with your story."

"It was difficult for Antoinette. She faced criticism and was discounted as a preacher. After several years, she married and retired. I decided to pick up where she left off and become a preacher. It was difficult to find a college to accept me. I attended the theology school of St. Lawrence University in New York and was the first woman in the country to be awarded a theology degree. After I graduated, the faculty refused to ordain me, so I appealed to the Universalist Church council and finally was ordained the first female in the Universalist Church in 1863. I have been preaching in communities in Massachusetts and Connecticut since.

"At first, I faced ridicule and skepticism, but as my congregants got to know me, they became warmer and more open. I have preached and lectured on equality for all men and women. I find that some people only see the need for equality for Black men but deny it for women. When Henry and Lucy contacted me to help with this campaign, I felt this effort aligned with my ministry."

"You've overcome so much in the face of tremendous obstacles," said Annie. "I feel inadequate to share a podium with you. I haven't accomplished a fraction of what you have."

"Lucy has told me of you. Of your passion and your fight against inequality. Many people will relate more to you than to me," said Olympia.

"That's very kind of you to say, but I'm not sure I believe it," said Annie.

"Don't underestimate the power of the connection you have. Many women find themselves in marriages with children, wanting to use their skills beyond the home. Men will see that equal rights don't have to mean giving up their place. You are a living example."

"But I've never spoken on a campaign circuit to audiences," said Annie. "I was a schoolteacher, but those audiences were eager young minds. I know our meetings will be filled with hostile thinkers. I'm not sure I'm ready."

Lucy said, "That's what the next few days are about. We're going to help you prepare your speeches so you're ready. We're in this with you."

#

Annie had read many of Lucy's, Elizabeth's, and Susan's speeches on women's rights. She read Lucy's articles and lectures for the Kansas campaign. Lucy's position centered around three arguments. The first was that the case for Negro suffrage applied equally to women. The power in a democracy comes from the people it governs—thus, all of the people should have the right to participate through the vote. It is unjust and degrading to give the vote to Black men only.

The second was that introducing women's voice into the vote would raise the standards of politics, curb intemperance, and improve the laws. Her final argument countered the claim that giving women the vote would harm womanhood and families. Annie digested Lucy's positions, compared them to the other women's rights leaders, and developed a take of her own, which had evolved to promote equality for all oppressed and disenfranchised people so they could contribute to the nation's prosperity.

The three spent hours in a hotel room helping Annie refine her messages, practice delivery, and prepare for audience reactions and questions. The women took turns conducting dry runs of their speeches, and they became comfortable critiquing and supporting each other.

After four days, they sat at their usual dining table, sharing one last dinner.

Lucy said, "Henry and I are traveling tomorrow to meet Susan and Elizabeth at the New York state constitutional convention." Lucy reviewed the tentative schedule for the next week. "You two will start in Anderson County and travel south. We have two other teams arriving next week that will cover the state's northern and western parts. In addition to organized lectures and meetings, you'll meet with as many newspapers as possible to drum up coverage.

"Dr. Joseph Root, from the local American Equal Rights Association, has spread the word and posted notices about your appearances. He's arranged for you to speak across the county over the next week. Some will be in churches, some in homes; one will be on the porch of a saloon. Beggars can't be choosy. After that, Sam Wood, the chairman of the Kansas Republican central committee, has made arrangements for one or two meetings every day for the next few months across the southern part of the state. The meetings are planned, but you'll need to arrange your travel and lodging with the locals as you go."

Annie said with a hint of concern, "The Association hasn't secured accommodations for us?"

"I'm afraid not," said Lucy. "We don't have the resources."

"But we don't know the territory or the people? How are we supposed to manage?" said Annie.

Olympia said, "The Lord will watch over us. He'll guide us. Have faith in him."

"There's faith, and there's practicality," said Annie. "I didn't know we'd be left on our own."

"Kansas is full of good-hearted people," said Lucy. "Open yourself to them."

Annie looked skeptically at Lucy, then at Olympia.

Olympia said, "Don't be dismayed. Our work is tremendously important. Remember, every voter in the state will get to cast his ballot on the three constitutional changes regarding voting—the one to remove the word *male*, the second to remove the word *white*, and the third to exclude men disloyal to the Union. Every vote counts."

Lucy added, "That's right. Kansas is the first state where women's suffrage is being considered. If we can win here, we can build on the momentum. The Kansas Republican party is supportive, but there are plenty of skeptics. We must convince the men of this state to open up the vote. I've made several speeches and will be back later in the summer. Elizabeth and Susan are also planning to campaign when their schedules allow it. You're part of a greater force."

A bellman approached their table. "Mrs. Bennett. This letter arrived for you today."

"Thank you," said Annie, taking the envelope from him.

"Another letter," said Olympia. "Max is quite a prolific writer."

"He's actually quite concise in his writing. Never one to waste words. I think it comes from his German mother."

"Still, it must be nice to hear a word from home so often," said Olympia.

"Oh, Lizzie addressed this one," said Annie excitedly, ripping open the envelope. She pulled out a single page. As she examined an elaborate pencil drawing, she regained her positivity. Lizzie had drawn Athena, the Greek goddess of War and Wisdom, atop a podium donning flowing robes and a helmet. In the background was the new suspension bridge. The Goddess's face was a likeness of Annie. A banner strung across the top of the page declared, "Fighting for Equality for All."

Annie held it up, tears forming in her eyes, a broad smile across her face. "Lizzie drew it."

"Annie, champion of liberty," said Lucy. "Lizzie knows her mother."

"Amen, Amen," said Olympia.

#

Olympia and Annie sat in the hired carriage as it jostled over twenty-five miles of winding roads with little more than two wheel ruts in the mud. The driver stopped at farmhouses several times to ask for directions. Winds rocked the vehicle from side to side as the two women conversed, watching the monotonous prairies roll by. They ate from their basket of food.

As sunset neared, the driver stopped at a remote farmhouse. They knocked on the door and arranged to spend the night and board the two horses in the barn. The farmer's wife was excited to have adult guests to converse with for the evening. They joined the six children on benches at a large oak table for supper. The family had homesteaded their farm ten years prior, moving from Ohio, and were eager to hear Annie's news of Cincinnati and learn of their crusade for enfranchisement. The family had little since their corn and wheat crops had been decimated by grasshopper infestations the prior year, but they were generous with what they had to offer.

When it came time to retire, Olympia and Annie were given a bed to share in the children's room while the displaced girls slept on blankets on the floor. The driver slept on the floor of the main room. Annie spent a fitful night pressed against the wall, listening to the children's turning, coughs, and other noises. After an early, hearty breakfast of eggs, bacon, and biscuits, they bid a heartfelt farewell and were back on the road shortly after dawn.

Annie's body ached from the previous day's ride, and she had a headache from lack of sleep. They watched the long horizons of newly-planted corn fields broken up by occasional stands of trees with few traces of civilization. Annie tried to write a letter home but gave up after just a few sentences of illegible text. She rehearsed her speech, then fell into a light sleep repeatedly interrupted by the carriage's jolts.

After dark, they heard the driver shouting down at them. "I see a light."

Annie leaned out to spy a dim lantern in the belvedere of a house ahead. "Tonight, we'll sleep in a hotel," said Annie.

"Thank the Lord," said Olympia.

They checked in to the Garnett House Hotel in the center of the small town of Garnett. The wooden structure with its large porch looked more like a farmhouse than a hotel but offered a dining room for patrons of its four guest rooms. They spent a restful night and explored the town in the morning, learning what they could about the counties where they would speak. Nearly two dozen wood-frame buildings comprised the growing town center, including several dry goods stores, saloons, a butcher, blacksmiths, a boarding house, a tin shop, and two drug stores.

Annie took the opportunity to write a letter to Max and Lizzie and mailed it at the post office window in the back of the City Drug Store. In her conversations, she learned of the area's history. Natives inhabited the land before the opening of the Kansas territory. The Potawatomi people, who were removed from Indiana, settled in 1833. European settlers began migrating and establishing homesteads in 1854. Bloody violence between Free Soiler settlers from the East and slave advocates from nearby Missouri gained national attention between the period of the Kansas-Nebraska Act and the Civil War, as the national debate between free versus slave states played out.

In talking with the locals, Annie gleaned a range of

attitudes about the upcoming ballot initiatives. She gauged most were anti-slavery but not necessarily pro-Black, and few would voice an opinion about giving women the right to vote. There was strong sentiment against anyone who had been disloyal to the Union and for preventing them from re-establishing power, making the loyalty amendment the most popular of the three referendums. Although cordial and curious, the residents were preoccupied with a successful farming season. As the afternoon wore on, Annie became more anxious about her debut speech.

It was finally time for the meeting. Annie and Olympia walked the three blocks to Bruns' Hall, a two-story building. They entered the large main room, which also served as the county courtroom. About twenty men and women conversed in groups.

Annie approached a circle of men and women and introduced herself. A balding man with a long beard and mustache bowed. "I'm Charles Robinson."

Another man explained, "Mr. Robinson was one of the original settlers in the Kansas territory and served as our first governor at the beginning of the war."

"It's an honor to meet you," said Annie.

"The honor is mine," said Mr. Robinson. "Thank you for coming to our state and continuing our fight for freedom for all. I've heard of the reverend, Miss Brown, but I am unfamiliar with your background."

"I'm a wife, mother and manager in one of the largest machine building foundries in the West," said Annie. "I speak on behalf of those who seek equal opportunity to pursue their vocation of choice."

"A businesswoman?" said Mr. Robinson.

"One of the hats I wear, yes. I shall expound upon my others in my remarks. Will you be in the audience this afternoon?"

"Yes. Mr. Wood from the Republican central committee asked me to come today and introduce you and Miss Brown."

"We're grateful for your support," said Annie.

"It's a noble cause and continues on the principles of freedom that Kansas was founded on. I've recommended that we champion our causes under the banner of 'impartial suffrage.' I'd be obliged if you could use that term in your meetings."

"Why not universal suffrage?" asked Annie.

"Impartial is a term we've used here in the state and is generally understood to mean suffrage for Black and white men loyal to the Union," said Mr. Robinson.

"And women?" said Annie.

"The term *impartial* is vague enough to allow the inclusion of women as well. Trust me; it is more likely to garner the support of the Republicans in this state."

"Well, thank you for your advice," said Annie.

"I hope all of the referendums will pass, and this will signal to the Copperheads and former Confederate states that their influence over the nation has passed," said Mr. Robinson.

"Do you believe most Kansas men support the vote as retribution and political gain over the South, more than an advancement of democracy for women and Black men?" asked Annie.

"Well, it can be both, can't it? There is a range of motivations," said Mr. Robinson.

"Of course. It's never that simple, is it?"

"I'm looking forward to your and Miss Brown's remarks today to understand your arguments in your appeal to our voters. We're attempting to set up a suffrage association in each county, distribute pamphlets and so on, but your appearances are vital to our success. Thank you for being here."

Olympia joined the group and introduced Dr. Root, the local leader who had arranged the meeting. He asked everyone to be seated so they could begin. Annie looked around at the crowd, which had grown to over thirty. She took a deep breath and sat behind the podium with Olympia.

Dr. Root welcomed the audience and introduced former Governor Robinson. After his remarks, in support of the referendums, Dr. Root introduced Olympia.

Olympia spoke eloquently, impressing the audience with her accomplishments, inspiring them with an appeal to their sense of morality and Christian faith and entertaining them with stories of the people she had worked beside in the name of anti-slavery and women's rights over the years. She name-dropped national figures the audience had read about in the papers: Frederick Douglass, William Lloyd Garrison, Wendell Phillips, Lucy Stone, Susan B. Anthony, Lucretia Mott, and Elizabeth Cady Stanton. She articulated the logical arguments for why suffrage was needed and deserved by Black men and women.

As Annie listened, she pushed away her recurring doubt that she didn't merit a place at the same podium as Olympia and the names she mentioned. A lifetime of frustration and burning to be treated as an individual, not just a woman, had led Annie to this point. She was ready to give her first speech, telling her story and hoping to inspire and persuade others to change. She took several deep breaths as she stood and took her place before the crowd, all eyes on her.

Most of the audience's lives centered around their families and their farms. They lived in rural areas with few of the conveniences that the eastern cities had. Kansans saw the meetings as a social outing and a rare opportunity for entertainment. To many, hearing a woman speak in public was a novelty in itself. Annie didn't look like the other feminist speakers that Olympia had rattled off. Most of them were ten to twenty-five years older than she. Annie had smooth skin and shiny hair that had become more auburn than red as she matured, pulled back in a loose bun. Annie smiled at the sun-weathered faces and received smiles in return.

She started in a loud, clear voice, "I am a mother, a wife, a manager, a teacher, an aide, an advocate, an American. I will contribute to society using the talents that God has given me.

"I stand before you today, the men and women of Anderson County, with much empathy for your position. I come from Cincinnati, the Queen City of the West. It was once like Kansas—a place that is growing and building—a place of opportunity. Your history is an honorable one as a Free Soil state and champion for freedom. Each and every one of us wants a fair chance to build our life and prosper from the bounty of our great nation. Voting for the state referendums to grant suffrage to women and all men will allow each to pursue that and multiply the human talents that can contribute to Kansas's success."

Annie told her story for forty minutes as an "everywoman" who demonstrated that she could have a family and a career as a teacher and then as the office manager of their family business. She had worked on the Underground Railroad, organized a volunteer corp of women and worked as a nurse's aide during the Civil War. She let the other women's rights speakers articulate all the arguments about why women and Blacks deserved equal rights and the vote. Her speech augmented the other speakers' by saying what women could contribute to enterprise and society if given the opportunity. As she spoke, her fear diminished, and she began to enjoy herself. She was energized and spoke more fluently and expressively. She found herself making eye contact with the audience, nodding and smiling.

Annie closed with, "My daughter is ten years old. Many of you have children. America has changed so much in the last five years and will continue to change. We have the power to shape the country into a place where the Founding Fathers' vision of a nation where all its children are equal citizens becomes a reality. Please vote for the referendums. For our children."

The audience, led by Mr. Robinson, applauded. He shook Annie's hand and made a few closing remarks as she sat down.

Olympia leaned in and whispered, "That was wonderful. You connected with them."

"Thank you," Annie said. She felt an adrenaline rush and was excited to do it again.

The editor of the local weekly paper, the *Garnett Plain Dealer*, interviewed Annie afterward. He was interested in her ability to work and be a mother. She played down the fact that she had a paid caregiver, something that most women in the audience couldn't afford. As she talked about her family back in Cincinnati, she felt brief pangs of guilt but pushed them aside. She and Olympia entertained questions from a polite audience for over an hour, then left the hall with Mr. Robinson.

Mr. Robinson walked them to the lumber yard, where they met their driver, an Indian employed by the yard. He secured their things on the back of a large wagon loaded with boards. They climbed into the driver's seat with him and began the fifteen-mile ride to their evening meeting.

#

Annie adjusted to the punishing schedule of touring. She and Olympia held one or two meetings every day, including Sundays. Their accommodations were rough, but their hosts were gracious.

One evening they held a meeting for six people in a farmer's barn. After the meeting, the farmer and his wife invited the speakers to spend the night with them. They walked across a field to their one-room cabin. Olympia and Annie helped Evelyn prepare dinner while her husband, Elliot, tended to his animals. Annie prepared the utensils and plates while Olympia followed Evelyn's instructions to mix the batter for the skillet biscuits.

"What do you think about the ballot referendum to give women the vote?" Annie asked Evelyn.

"Well, Elliott usually makes the decisions for our family, so I don't know why I need to vote," said Evelyn earnestly.

"Aren't there things you care about that you'd like to have a say in?" said Annie.

"I don't know. Politics doesn't impact my life much. Property rights maybe or the prices of feed and livestock, but

Elliott handles those."

"Anything else that is on your mind?" said Annie.

"We haven't had any Indian raids around here the last few years. That used to worry me. Now it's all I can do to feed us, keep Elliott's clothes mended, and help him with the planting and harvesting."

"Do you hope to have children someday?" Annie asked.

"Oh yes. We had a baby, but she came early and didn't make it."

"I'm sorry. That must have been difficult," said Annie. "What about schools? Don't you believe a mother should have a say in the schools her children attend?"

"Well, yes, but here in Kansas, women get to vote in school elections. We've already got that, and we have a say in the liquor trade too. I think the things women care about are already considered here. I thought your speeches tonight were most interesting, and you both have done some extraordinary things, but those aren't things that I would ever see myself doing. I wouldn't want to create more hardship for Elliott by neglecting my duties at home or carrying on in an unwomanly way."

"Is that what you think of me?" asked Annie.

"Well, I don't know what's acceptable in Ohio for a woman, but some of what you do would be cause for shame here."

"What things?"

"Well, traveling without your husband or a manly escort for one. It opens yourself to all kinds of things, real dangers or improprieties, or the suspicion of them," said Evelyn.

"I appreciate your concern, but it's unwarranted," said Annie. "Olympia and I have been traveling for weeks with no harm to either of us, and I assure you neither of us has engaged in anything improper. We try not to worry about others' imagined improprieties."

"I'm sure you are both good women. Christian women, too, I think," said Evelyn.

"We are."

"Miss Brown is a reverend, and I assumed you were a believer from your speech. I'm not one to cast a stone," said Evelyn.

"Well, we all come from different backgrounds and live in different circumstances," said Annie. "All my life, I have felt that our country's laws and customs have been skewed toward the men in power. Women and Colored people aren't given equal opportunities. Our country can do better in living up to our principles. That's why I campaign for suffrage. Participating in the elections gives a voice to those who are impacted by the laws that are passed. I want my daughter to grow up with more rights than I had."

"Can I ask you something?" said Evelyn.

"Of course," said Annie.

"Your daughter. I was wondering. Who cares for your husband and daughter while you're here?"

Annie blushed. "Well, we have a governess that looks after Lizzie and cooks and cleans the house."

"Is she kin of yours?"

"No."

"Does she live in your house with your daughter and husband?"

"Yes. That way, she's there whenever Lizzie needs something."

Evelyn considered Annie's response without saying anything. "Looks like those biscuits are about ready. I'll see if I can get Elliott to join us." She stepped outside, and they heard a loud bell clanging.

Annie said to Olympia, "Their life is so removed from ours. These people are worried about making it through this season and surviving day to day in the meantime. They don't care about suffrage for their wives or Black men. Why are we trying to pass this in Kansas first?"

Evelyn came back inside. "He's going to be a little while longer. He said to start without him."

"No, of course not," said Olympia. "The soup will stay nice and hot in the pot."

It was after ten o'clock when they finally ate. They helped Evelyn clean up afterward and then washed up in a basin of cold water at the dry sink. Elliott and Evelyn insisted that the ladies take their bed, and they retired to the barn for the night. Annie and Olympia used the outhouse, changed into their nightclothes, and climbed into bed. The summer night was warm enough to dispense with any covers. Annie blew out the lamp, and darkness enveloped them. Annie let out a long sigh.

"How are you faring?" Olympia asked Annie.

"I'm all right. You?"

"I'm exhausted."

"It's not what I expected," said Annie.

"Nor I. It's quite an adventure Lucy sent us on, isn't it?"

"Is it a wild goose chase? Is there any chance the men of Kansas will vote for suffrage?"

"It seems dim right now," said Olympia. "It's hard for us to see the forest for the trees. We're in the thick of it. I have hope. They're good people. They're good Christians with good hearts. Don't lose faith."

"You're right. We must somehow communicate why the vote is the Christian thing to do. Appeal to that. I need to work on my speech," said Annie.

They lay quietly, sleep coming quickly.

#

Annie's scream pierced the dead silence in the remote cabin. She clawed at her face, then down her chest.

"What? What is it?" said Olympia.

"A mouse! I think. It ran across my face," said Annie sitting up.

"Oh, dear. Is it gone?"

"I think so." Annie started to cry. She was tired and discouraged. She was disappointed. The reality was nothing like her dream of joining the women's movement and making speeches across the country. She missed Max terribly and wished he were there to hold her in his arms. He was so reassuring when she needed it.

Annie lit the lamp, and they let it burn the rest of the night.

CHAPTER 19

Cincinnati – Summer 1867

After work, Max walked into the Niemes Café and scanned
the bar for Patrick. He instead found Mayor Charles Wilstach
standing at the bar with Councilman Nate Bartlett. He
stopped to greet them. The mayor nodded, and Nate's face
lit up. They exchanged pleasantries.

The mayor said, "Max, are you acquainted with Mr. Henry
Probasco?"

"Yes, I did business with him for years. He and the late
Mr. Tyler Davidson had the hardware business. Probasco
recently sold the store and retired."

"That's him. Is he a good man?"

"I think so. Honest, fair. Why?" said Max.

"I received a letter from him. He's abroad in Italy but has
offered to build a grand statue at the Fifth Street Market in
memory of Mr. Davidson, his business partner, and he's
offered to do it fully at his own expense," said the mayor.

"Probasco inherited the entire company when his partner
died, so he's quite wealthy," said Max. "He has no children,
so this may be his legacy. What a great idea."

"You think so?"

"A fountain in the middle of town. I think it's a unique
enhancement worth considering," said Max.

"He's included some stipulations."

"Ah. It seems unsolicited gifts always have strings

attached. What has he requested?"

"Nothing too onerous," said the mayor. "The city commits to providing fresh drinking water for the public forever, that we maintain it, and staff someone to take care of it and keep it secure around the clock."

"Well, *forever* sounds like a clause our lawyers need to shorten, but it sounds nice, especially at the cost of zero dollars to the city," said Max.

"He estimates the cost to build at $30,000, but he'll bear it fully. We'll have to include the maintenance of the fountain in the budget. Do you think he'll follow through on a commitment of this magnitude? I'd hate to get halfway into it and find out we're on the hook for a chunk of it."

"As I said, all my dealings with him have been positive."

"Good, I'll put it on next week's council agenda."

"It would be a nice win," said Max. "We need more of those. Last year's commerce figures are out, and we're still not growing like before the war."

"Any word on the state legislature's roadblock on funding railroads?" asked the mayor.

"Our proposed legislation is being considered, but nothing to report yet."

The mayor grunted. "Columbus bureaucrats."

"Please excuse me; my friend is waiting," said Max. "Good to see you both."

Max greeted Patrick, who sat at a table, sipping a whiskey. "Sorry, I'm late."

"Don't worry about me. My liquid friend here kept me company," Patrick said, raising his glass. "I understand. I saw you had important business to discuss with the mayor. How's Charlie?"

"Mayor Wilstach is fine, thank you," said Max.

"Did you solve all the city's problems?"

"Hardly, but he shared some good news. Henry Probasco plans to donate a fountain to the city to be built at the Fifth Street Market."

"Nice to see rich men share their wealth," said Patrick.

"It would be a nice addition to the city. The more we can do to make it an attractive and inviting place to live and visit, the more successful we'll be at growing our businesses and keeping people employed."

"I think things are looking pretty good," said Patrick.

Max shook his head. "Maybe from your vantage point, but it's spotty. I've seen the commerce numbers for last year. Manufacturing is slowing. Meatpacking is down. Less trade came through our ports again last year. The population is up, but we aren't keeping pace with enough jobs for workers, especially immigrants and Blacks."

"Don't get me started on the Blacks coming into town and taking jobs from hard-working Americans," said Patrick.

"Black men are hard-working Americans, too," said Max.

"I don't know. A lot of them are leeching off the Freedmen's Bureau. They don't have the smarts or the work ethic that we do."

"We're working on better public schools for them," said Max.

"It's a waste of resources. They don't have the capacity to learn."

"They do, Patrick. I've visited the Gaines High School and met Black students. My brother oversees a school for the freedmen in central Kentucky. The teacher there says they're just as quick to learn as white children on the whole. What are you basing your comments on?"

"It's common knowledge," stated Patrick.

"It's common bigotry that the Democrats use for political purposes. What's wrong with you today? You're in a sour mood." said Max.

"We had a Friendly Sons of St. Patrick's meeting last night. It was a late one. I need a refill, and you need a drink." Patrick waved a waiter over to their table.

They caught up on their families until the food arrived.

"How are you getting along without Annie?" asked Patrick.

"Lizzie and I have settled into our new routine. Abby is

terrific for her. With no siblings, I'm comforted that Lizzie has someone that is part caregiver, part companion. Abby is helping her develop her artistic skills."

"And you?"

"I'm fine," said Max.

"Are you?"

"I miss her. I wish she were back home, but I know she's happy doing what she's doing, and she would regret it if she came home now. So I get along."

Patrick shook his head.

"What?" said Max.

"It's not right. She's a selfish suffrage shrew."

"Please don't speak about my wife that way," said Max calmly.

"What part of that isn't true?"

"She's not selfish, and she's not a shrew," Max said.

"She does what she wants to do without regard for others. That's the definition of selfish."

"How is what she's doing different than what you, I, or any other man does? Pursue our jobs and leave our spouses to stay home and care for the home and family?"

"It's different. Women are suited to those domains. Besides, she isn't making any money, is she?" said Patrick.

"I'd say women have historically done those roles, but it doesn't mean that's their destiny."

"Do you believe that?"

"Yes. Just like the Negro wasn't destined to be enslaved. And you and I weren't destined to accept our place at the bottom of society as sons of immigrants. We're all due the opportunity to raise ourselves up."

"Lord, you have become a full-fledged radical," said Patrick. "Back in school, you never stepped out of line."

Max smiled. "You can call me a radical, but I haven't changed that much. I'm still trying to follow Christ's teachings."

"It always comes back to that for you, doesn't it?"

"I try," said Max.

"All right. If you say you're fine, then I'm happy. We need another drink."

"One more. I want to get home to Lizzie before she goes to bed."

The waiter took their plates and brought another round of drinks.

"You need an afternoon out," said Patrick. "Come be my guest at one of the Cincinnati Baseball Club's games. They're a load of fun."

"I don't think so. Watching a bunch of men run around a field doesn't sound like a productive way to spend an afternoon," said Max.

"We can make a bet to make it more interesting. When you have a dollar invested in the game, it makes your heart beat a little faster. It'll be just the thing to liven your spirits."

"That I won't do. Bet with the cranks who spend their days at the grounds. I'm a councilman," said Max.

"I beg your pardon, sir. I didn't mean to offend you. No one is getting hurt by some friendly wagers on the games."

"You're really into this game, aren't you?" said Max.

"I am. Aaron Champion has turned the club into a real enterprise. We've over three hundred men in the club now."

"Aaron Champion. He's the attorney with Tilden, Sherman, & Moulton, isn't he?" said Max.

"Yes, he's put some money into the old Union Cricket Club grounds," said Patrick. "They've sodded the field and built a grandstand. You won't have to stand all afternoon. We've seats. He's put together a real team. The nine are undefeated so far this season."

"I'm busy. I don't see the point, but I am interested in what Mr. Champion sees in this investment in the club."

"There you go. Champion's a civic booster. Right up your alley. You're going. I won't take no for an answer. Come out and get a little fresh air. Live a little."

"Enough. I'll join you for a game," agreed Max.

"Good. The Washington Nationals are coming into town. They're supposed to be the best in the country. We'll cheer our boys on."

#

Max and Patrick took the twenty-minute horse-drawn streetcar ride west across town and then walked to the end of Hopkins Street to the Union grounds. Buggies lined up, dropping off the more privileged of the city in front of the stadium gates. Men huddled in groups outside, some placing bets, others staking positions along the fence to secure a view of the ballfield.

Patrick pushed their way to the club members' entrance. They walked underneath the gates into a crowd of more than three thousand men and women. The grandstand, called the Grand Duchess, sported a Red Stockings pennant from its steeple and had stands along both baselines. The buzz of the crowd filled the stadium. Patrick led them to the section reserved for club members.

They greeted other club members, men who paid dues to support the budding team. The ladies in attendance wore colorful dresses and hats.

"All of these people are here to watch a baseball game? Is it always like this?" asked Max.

"Like what?" said Patrick.

"So alive. Full of energy. Everyone's happy."

"It has been this year. We haven't lost a game yet."

"It's wonderful. To see people enjoying themselves," said Max.

"Mr. Champion is hell-bent on making the Red Stockings a team that will bring national attention to Cincinnati."

"I applaud Mr. Champion," said Max as he studied the stadium.

"The Nationals. They're a force. This will be a tough game for our starting nine," said Patrick. They watched the coin toss to decide which team would bat first. The Nationals, dressed in blue caps, white shirts, blue pants, and red belts, took their seats on the benches along the third baseline, while the Red Stockings, dressed in red and white, took theirs along the first baseline.

"Who's the man in the coat and top hat?" asked Max.

"He's the umpire. That's Mr. Brockway of the Live Oaks Baseball Club here in town. He's a tough one; he won't let any cranks or players intimidate him, although they'll try. The fans can get downright nasty with their shouts. I've even seen them throw things at the umpire if they don't like his calls."

The Red Stockings batted first and scored no runs in the first inning. The Nationals scored two. At the end of the third, it was six to five Nationals. Then the floodgates broke loose, and the Nationals scored eleven runs in the fourth and kept pounding from there.

In the seventh inning, the Nationals had seven runs and two outs. The Red Stockings' shortstop, Mr. Neff, grabbed a solid hit with both hands to end the carnage. The crowd cheered as Neff dropped to his knees, holding his right hand with his left.

"Oh Christ," said Patrick. "Shit. Looks like he's done for the day."

"What happened?" said Max.

"I'd venture he broke something by how he's holding his hand. It happens. Those balls are hard. The boys have callouses plenty from catching so many balls, but lots of broken fingers and torn fingernails. It's part of the game."

"Can someone else play for him?" asked Max.

"They have two substitutes on the roster. They'll likely move Crooks from center field to shortstop and then put a substitute out in the field where there's less action. But it's not looking good for us. We're already down thirty-seven to nine."

"Most of the fans don't seem to care that their team is losing the game," observed Max.

"Today is an anomaly. They haven't lost a game yet this year. Don't worry. The Red Stockings are on a streak. Mr. Champion is confident that with a little more investment, we can be the best team in the nation."

"What would you think of holding an industrial exposition in Cincinnati?" said Max.

"What? Are you even watching this game?" said Patrick.

"Yes, I am," said Max. "It's nice to be outside in the fresh air. It clears the mind. I was just thinking. Something similar to the exhibitions that the Mechanics Institute held before the war, but on a grander scale. Invite commercial enterprises to put their products on display and demonstrate them. Publicize it across the West in as many newspapers as we can. Showcase all that Cincinnati offers and position us as the best place to establish or grow your business?"

"I enjoyed attending the Mechanics Institute events," said Patrick. "I always learned something. It sounds like a lot of effort and expense. Who would fund it?"

"I don't know. I haven't thought it through. It's just an idea at this point. You think there'd be interest?"

"I do. It's an opportunity for men to showcase their companies and for us all to learn from each other."

"That's what I'm thinking," said Max. "It could lead to new ideas and maybe some partnerships. But most of all, it could put Cincinnati back at the center of industry in the West."

They watched the game for several innings.

"I wanted to ask you about my engineer, George Gray," said Max. "When you and he traveled to the East Coast to visit the factories, did he give you any indication that he might be looking to leave my employ?"

"Hmm. Not outright, but he talked about a couple of other men in town who have started a machine shop."

"Do you recall their names?" asked Max.

"One was James Gaff, the other, surname Gordon, I think. You worried he'll leave you?"

"George is brilliant. He started as an apprentice for Miles Greenwood at Eagle Ironworks. I met him during the war. Greenwood had him build the models of the experimental Gatling gun. He helped me catch Aaron smuggling arms to the Confederates. Anyway, I built a friendship with him that led to my bringing him on. He's done great work for me. I moved him from being a machinist to designing some of our newest machine tools. He's been the key designer for our new drills and the author of several of our patents. I'd hate to lose him."

"One evening, after a few drinks, he did go on about wanting to be his own man, stop working for someone else," said Patrick. "At the time, I didn't think twice about it. If he's that critical to Miller Industries, you best hold on to him."

"Sounds like I need to pay him more, but if he gets the capital to go out on his own, I won't be able to hold him back. I understand the attraction of building your own company over working for someone," said Max.

"There are times I envy you, owning your own factory, but I see the worries it brings you," said Patrick. "Competitors will swoop in and take your business if you stand still. Look at Greenwood. He used to dominate the ironworks business in town. You've blown past him with your machine tools."

"Greenwood made some missteps," said Max. "He took on a project for the government during the war to build a specialized ship. The government screwed it up, and he got left holding the bag for all he had invested. He didn't want to file a claim due to his patriotism for the Union, but his loyalty nearly ruined him. His sons are taking over the business, and they don't have the mind that Miles had. They've asked the Mechanics Institute for a loan to keep them afloat."

"Why would the Mechanics Institute loan Greenwood money?"

"He provided significant financial backing to help start the Institute. It would never have gotten off the ground if it weren't for him. I hate to see him in such a state. Although he's been a competitor, I respect him and all the good he's done for the city over the years. Seeing him go down reminds me that nothing is for sure. That's why I'm worried about losing George. No one is immune to competitive progress."

At the end of the ballgame, the Nationals crushed

Cincinnati fifty-three to ten.

"Thanks for getting me out today," said Max.

"I'm glad you enjoyed yourself," said Patrick. "You should do it more often. I'm just sorry you had to see their one loss this year."

CHAPTER 20

Kansas – Fall 1867

Annie and Olympia held over one hundred meetings across Kansas over four months. They returned to Lawrence for a break and meetings with the campaign organizers at the beginning of September. They sat at a table in the dining room of the Hotel Eldridge with Lucy Stone, her husband, Henry Blackwell, and Susan and Elizabeth, who had arrived to help with the final push before the state elections.

They caught up, with Olympia and Annie relaying their rustic adventures, now able to laugh about them. Then they got down to business, updating each other on the current state of the campaigns. Women's suffrage had been defeated at the New York constitutional convention. Congress was considering a Fifteenth Amendment granting suffrage to Black men, but there were still no politicians willing to include women in the amendment.

Annie summarized the statistics on the Kansas meetings, the number of attendees, and the cities and towns they covered. "We were not able to cover some of the northwestern counties. There have been reports of Indian raids opposing the plans to run the railroads through their reservations. We also had to cancel a couple of meetings due to cholera outbreaks. We were willing to submit ourselves to many prairie hardships but felt it prudent to avoid those."

"Of course. These poor people. I can't imagine. Still

concerned with Indian attacks," said Lucy. "How would you characterize the reception of your audiences?"

Annie said, "Most attendees seemed fairly neutral on the issues of women and Negro suffrage. They're not concerned with the issues and don't see the relevance or advantage to their lives. We've been called de-sexed, bloomerized women, and worse."

Elizabeth said, "You're not letting those ignorant attacks upset you, are you, dear?"

"No, I'm used to them now. More maddening is the disregard or positioning our whole cause as inconsequential."

"How do you mean?"

Annie said, "Some newspaper men paint us as dainty women, only commenting on our appearance, voice, or manners. They don't report any of our arguments."

"Yes, that's an intentional tactic. Belittle us to discredit our message," said Elizabeth.

Annie added, "And some men who speak against us won't share a podium with us. They say it would be ungentlemanly to debate on the same stage. More like cowardly."

Olympia summarized the prevailing newspaper reports. "A group of influential men across the state has been campaigning to advocate for patriotic and Black suffrage over women's. Some are quite detrimental to our cause. Charles Eskridge, one of Kansas's former governors, wrote some nasty letters to the papers. He likened the damage that female suffrage would do to the grasshopper damage done to the state's agriculture. He made some personal attacks on Mr. Wood for supporting it and went after you, Lucy, and Henry."

"Us? What's his beef with us?" asked Henry.

"Same story that the opponents have been citing for years. The two of you were never married, that you're living in sin, and women's suffrage is bringing free love to Kansas," said Olympia.

"That story will never die," said Lucy. "We've produced our marriage certificate multiple times. Journalists love a racy story, don't they?"

"Indeed they do. True or not, it fires up their base. Have they attacked either of you two?" Elizabeth asked.

Olympia answered. "No, we've seen little of that. Lucy is a known name and sells more papers."

"Lucky me," said Lucy.

Olympia continued, "Mr. Wood wrote a rebuttal to the attacks, and there has been some back and forth in the papers. Mr. Wood's opponents are calling his motives into question, implying that his support of our cause is only for political reasons. Some have intimated that he only supports women's suffrage to dilute support for Negro suffrage."

Annie added, "I wish they'd confront us directly in our meetings so we could address their arguments head-on. Having it all play out in the media is so frustrating. We can't control it."

Olympia said, "The overall sentiment is shifting toward separating the two causes. The state Republican leadership is now supporting Black male suffrage and distancing themselves from our cause. They're neutral at best."

"What are the main arguments? Anything new here that we haven't heard in other states?" asked Lucy.

"Nothing new," said Olympia. "But here, I think the arguments center on the damage that suffrage will do to womanhood, the detriment to families. Some position women's suffrage as frivolous and unnecessary—a political maneuver. The newspapers are starting to take positions as the election nears." She pulled a clipping from the *Ottowa Western Home Journal*. "The editor of this one asserts that a woman's natural state is married, and her equality with man is best exemplified in the control men and women exert over their respective spheres. He goes on to describe the loss of purity and the decline of the family resulting from women leaving their natural sphere and descending into the world of men."

Annie laughed, "Descending. At least he described the relative position of men accurately."

Susan said, "It's the same thing we've seen in New York and Michigan. The Republicans fighting for Negro suffrage fear that attaching women's suffrage to the issue will cause both to fail. Some Democrats are supporting us for the same reason—hoping that it will aid in defeating Black suffrage."

Lucy said, "Well, ladies, thank you for the months of campaigning. You've communicated our message to thousands of Kansans. The women of our country appreciate your work and the hardships you've endured. I fear, however, that the Republican party here in Kansas is showing the same signs we've seen elsewhere. Support for the women's amendment in Kansas is waning. It's no fault of yours."

Henry Blackwell said, "That's right. Horace Greeley had been a long supporter, and politics caused him to desert the women's cause in New York. Republicans here are most concerned with the third amendment—limiting voting rights to those loyal to the Union.

"I met with the local AERA leader yesterday. He tells me that the radical Republicans met in Lawrence last week and are organizing a campaign in favor of Negro and opposed to female suffrage. We only have seven weeks until the election, so we need a focused effort to counter their efforts. Lucy and I are leaving on the train home tomorrow, so it will be up to you all for the final push."

"That's why we're here," said Elizabeth. "Susan and I will start making appearances."

"You two have name recognition, and the papers hold you in high regard, Elizabeth, even if they're opposed to the cause," said Henry. "You'll make an impact."

"Thank you, Henry," said Elizabeth.

Henry said, "I've sent a pamphlet that I used in the Southern states that argues the case for women enfranchisement to the legislators here in Kansas. In addition, Lucy worked with the Kansas Impartial Suffrage Association on this flyer that addresses the major arguments against the referendum. It will be distributed to voters across the state."

Elizabeth scanned the flyer without comment, then handed it to Susan for inspection. "On the train ride here, Susan and I discussed enlisting the help of the Democrats."

Annie said, "What? Those who were against the war and fought the anti-slavery movement?"

"Yes," stated Elizabeth.

"I'm not sure my conscience will allow me to align with Copperheads," said Annie.

"Dear, this is a political battle. We need every vote, not just Republican ones," said Elizabeth.

"But many of those men will vote against the Negro suffrage referendum," said Annie.

"That may be, but they're separate referendums, and we women must look out for ourselves," said Elizabeth.

Annie sat back, silent and uncomfortable with Elizabeth's position. She looked to Lucy for solidarity, but Lucy maintained a neutral facial expression and avoided eye contact with any of them.

Henry said, "How do you propose enlisting the Democrats?"

"We've arranged to have George Francis Train come to Kansas to speak on behalf of the referendum," said Elizabeth.

"You've already made these arrangements?" said Lucy. "Without discussing them with us?"

"You and Henry are leaving this campaign in Susan's and my hands. We will take the necessary steps to win it," said Elizabeth.

Olympia said, "Mr. Train is known to be against Black suffrage."

Annie asked, "Who is Mr. Train?"

Elizabeth answered, "He's a wealthy businessman. He's financing the Union Pacific Railroad across the Rocky Mountains. He's a supporter of women and women's suffrage, quite famous, an entertaining speaker, and he's offered to do this gratis."

"He'll alienate many Republican voters due to his

positions against the war," said Henry.

"And he'll bring much-needed publicity that hasn't materialized in the months you've been managing this campaign," said Elizabeth with a somewhat accusatory tone.

"That's not fair," said Lucy. "There has been plenty of press here in Kansas. The meetings these two and the others held made an impression."

"The papers back East have little mention of the Kansas campaign. It's as if it's not going on," said Elizabeth.

"The referendum voters are in Kansas. We're not trying to influence New Yorkers a thousand miles across the country," said Lucy.

"Of course we are," retorted Elizabeth. "This campaign is of national importance. The political leaders in the East and the South are keenly interested in the outcome of this election. For heaven's sake," said Elizabeth condescendingly, shaking her head.

"I don't think this is a good idea," said Henry.

"It's done. Arranged. There may be some who are offended, but on the whole, this is good for the campaign," said Elizabeth.

"I guess we'll see in seven weeks," said Lucy. "Anything else we need to discuss?"

"No, I think we'll take it from here," said Elizabeth.

Elizabeth and Susan said a curt goodbye to Lucy and Henry and went to their room. Henry retired to write some letters.

Lucy, Annie, and Olympia remained at the table.

Annie said, "Lucy, I'm sorry Elizabeth has treated you this way. I was quite taken aback."

Olympia said, "Her remarks about the campaign's effectiveness were unjustified."

"It's quite all right. Thank you both," said Lucy. "I've grown used to her blunt assertion of her ways. It's part of what makes her such a force."

"She was quite brash," said Olympia.

"Had a man behaved as she, you wouldn't say that," said

Lucy.

"I'm surprised at her stance for the women's movement at the expense of the Negro and employing a known Copperhead," said Annie. "He sounds like a dynamic individual, but is he the right spokesman for our cause?"

"I know Elizabeth's heart is in the right place. She will fight to win," said Lucy.

"You're very charitable," said Olympia.

"It's in her hands: hers and Susan's. The two of them can be insular at times. I wish they would have discussed this with Henry and me, but I won't dwell on it. I'm looking forward to getting home to Alice. Annie, you must miss Lizzie?"

"I do, yes. I'll be heading home as soon as the election is over," said Annie.

"You must be getting anxious to go home."

"I can't wait to share my stories with Lizzie and Max, but I'm here to the end."

As they left the dining room and moved toward the stairway to their rooms, Lucy and Annie hugged.

"Don't let tonight dampen your enthusiasm," said Lucy. "You have done so much for the cause."

Annie said, "I try to look at it as another wrinkle in the long fight for equality. I know the journey is full of highs and lows. Since I was a girl, I've encountered the entrenched ways and the forces of politics, war, and humanity that keep us from getting there. I still have hope."

"Good," said Lucy as they climbed the stairs to their rooms.

#

Annie and Olympia went back on the road for the final push, holding meetings over the last few weeks. The press mostly ignored them, centering their coverage on Elizabeth, Lucy, and Francis Train's appearances.

Olympia and Annie had laid out the arguments for Negro and women's suffrage. Elizabeth's speeches directly addressed the main arguments against women's suffrage that the press had repeatedly printed.

Elizabeth impressed the people of Kansas as a reasonable advocate of her cause, a woman of knowledge who appealed directly to the citizens of Kansas with relatable arguments. Of all the campaign speakers, she was the most favorably reviewed by both pro- and anti-newspapers.

Francis Train's appearances amused the Kansas audiences. He alienated many Republicans because of his publicized activities against the war, but his speeches never failed to entertain. He rambled across many other topics besides the women's movement and took questions from the audience, often answering with witty, sarcastic responses that brought the audience to laughter. He inserted plugs for himself as a future candidate for president.

On election day, November 5, the speakers fanned out and made a last appeal to voters at the polls. Although seven thousand men voted for the women's suffrage amendment, almost twenty thousand voted against it, and the referendum failed. The Negro amendment was defeated by a similar margin. Kansas approved the amendment restricting the franchise to those loyal to the Union. The voters in Kansas reflected much of the North's perspective. They weren't comfortable granting suffrage to women or Blacks, as they were still concerned with a post-war Southern backlash and a need to reunite the country in a way that returned prosperity to its citizens.

#

Annie walked across the stage of Mozart Hall in Cincinnati, followed by Francis Train, Susan, and Elizabeth. The half-filled auditorium of four hundred people stood, applauded, and cheered, none louder than the corner where Max, Lizzie, Mary Berry, and a cadre of Annie's friends sat. It was Thanksgiving Day, and the event had been hastily arranged with little publicity.

Annie stood at the podium, smiling, and waited for the crowd to quiet before she began, "Good evening, Cincinnatians. Thank you for joining us tonight to hear from three of the nation's most ardent advocates of equal rights. On this national day of Thanksgiving that President Lincoln introduced, it is fitting that we come together and recognize that although we as a nation have much to be thankful for, the work Mr. Lincoln championed during his truncated presidency remains unfinished. Too many men and women in this country still suffer the injustices of discriminatory laws and practices holding back over half of our population from contributing to our prosperity." Annie's fans led another round of applause.

"Those of you who know me know that my husband, Max Mueller, and I have worked on numerous fronts to advance the disadvantaged, gain equal rights for women and Negroes, and build a stronger, more prosperous Queen City. I'm working on the campaign to gain suffrage for the Negro in Ohio. I also recently returned from an extended campaign speaking across Kansas with these three distinguished freedom fighters. The state's voters cast seven thousand votes for women's suffrage and nearly the same amount for non-white suffrage. They are here tonight to speak for those who don't currently have the vote—a voice in the laws that govern their lives. Please welcome Mr. George Francis Train." Annie held out her hand toward him as Train stood, raised his arms, and turned to one side of the room then the other like the showman he was, encouraging the audience to continue applauding him.

The audience quieted, and Mr. Train took the podium. "Isn't she beautiful," Train said as he held his hand toward Annie. "Cincinnati's own women's movement champion, Mrs. Annie Bennett."

Train was a stylishly-dressed, handsome man. He spoke theatrically and moved about the stage as he addressed the audience.

He relayed the highlights of the Kansas campaign

presentations that Elizabeth, Susan, Annie, and he made that contributed to the large number of votes for women's suffrage. He said, "Five votes were a victory, five hundred a triumph, and five thousand a revolution. We got seven thousand votes, and woman, thank God, is emancipated in this country forever!"

He finally stopped talking and introduced Susan B. Anthony.

Susan spoke for twenty minutes, explaining why women were capable, yet denied the vote. At the end of her speech, she recognized and thanked women's new champion, Francis Train.

Mr. Train then introduced Elizabeth, who received a standing ovation. Her speech argued that they asked for the vote not as women but as citizens of the republic. Women in America asked the same thing as the Working Party in England and the Republican Party for Blacks in America. The principles of government, natural rights, and the Bible demanded suffrage. The question to decide is if it is in the nation's best interest.

Elizabeth looked out at the audience. "Miss Anthony spoke of the Negro. I am very glad that the Northern states have voted against suffrage for them. I protest in the name of women against the enfranchisement of another man, white or Black, until women are crowned with all their political rights. We need the refinement and virtue of the women of the country to stay the incoming of poverty and vice that is now threatening the nation." Half of the audience applauded in agreement.

Elizabeth continued in a forceful voice, with the crowd intently listening to her words. She concluded, "You worry about women corrupting politics, but our politics are corrupt today.... Our danger at this hour is not in the centralization of power, not in Andy Johnson's assumption of authority, but in the corruption of people. We propose to introduce a new and moral power into politics that will have a purifying, elevating, and civilizing influence upon it." Elizabeth waited for the applause to quiet. "I do not claim that woman is better than man; for some of the noblest spirits I have known on earth were men. I simply claim that men and women have a most elevating power over each other.

"In this nineteenth century, so marked for inventions and discoveries, with our telegraph bringing nations together, and with all the great internal improvements of the age, linking together the Atlantic and Pacific Oceans, and binding the nations in one, let us, in these great moral questions, be as great and as grand as we are already in our material improvements.... Our life work is not to build up civil and ecclesiastical institutions, creeds, and codes, but by the instrumentalities of civilization, of Christianity, to roll off the mountains of superstition that they shall never oppress the human soul and will set the imprisoned angel free." The audience applauded as Elizabeth stood back, smiled, and waved to the crowd.

Mr. Train retook the podium and sped through a series of entertaining topics, bringing the audience to repeated applause and laughter. He then returned to a serious tone and recalled the great women leaders of the world, Catherine the Great, Queens Anne, Mary, and Elizabeth of England, as evidence that women had the capacity to participate in government affairs. He insisted it was unjust to place women below uneducated immigrants and Negroes, should they obtain the vote before women. His final words were an enthusiastic advertisement for himself as president of the United States.

As the crowd departed the auditorium, a group gathered around the speakers at the foot of the stage. Lizzie and Max waited for the mass to exit, then moved to the front of the auditorium. They stood back until Lizzie lost patience. "May I go see her, Papa?"

"Go on," said Max.

Lizzie ran around the crowd and slid in behind Annie. She tapped her mother's arm. Annie looked down, smiled, and pulled Lizzie in front of her, placing her hands on the girl's shoulders.

"Who is this?" said one of the women.

"This is my daughter, Lizzie," said Annie.

The women introduced themselves. One said, "Your mother is an inspiration and true leader."

"What did you think of your mother being on stage?" asked another.

"I was happy to see her doing her women's movement. I've only read her letters and newspaper accounts," said Lizzie.

"What's it like having her for a mother?"

"She loves me."

"Is it difficult having her away so much with her travel?"

"Papa and I miss her dearly when she's gone, but we have our routines."

Another asked, "Are you a little suffragette yourself?"

Lizzie said, "What is a suffragette?"

"I mean, are you, like your mother, an advocate for women and the vote?"

"I don't do what she does, but I have my own favorite things."

Max joined them, and Lizzie took his hand for reassurance.

Annie introduced him. The ladies sized him up, curious about the man behind the woman.

"What do you think of your wife's work?" one of them asked Max.

"I'm very proud of the work that Annie is doing for the disenfranchised and the disadvantaged in our city and the nation."

A man in the group said, "Mr. Mueller, how can you let your wife go off galivanting across the country, stinting the moral development of your daughter?"

Max responded, "I assure you that her moral development is well tended to."

"But without a model of true womanhood at home, what will become of her as she comes of age?"

"I am confident that she will use her God-given talents to lead a moral and productive life, just as any parent wishes for their child," said Max.

"You must admit that your family is unconventional."

"I admit it is different than most, by today's standards, but we are in the midst of a changing world," said Max. "I've never been one to accept commonly held standards if they are unjust. Jesus didn't shy away from change that was the right thing to do."

The man responded, "Are you comparing yourself to Jesus and invoking Christianity to support your radical positions?"

"I don't liken myself to Jesus but rather hold myself to his teaching that I should stand up for those who have been pushed aside."

"Jesus didn't intend for his teachings to warp God's order of things," pressed the man.

Max said, "Man has done an adequate job himself of warping the world into an order that is far from just. I can only follow my conscience and assure you I don't harbor reservations about my support of my wife or daughter."

"Hmmph," said the man, deciding to step away from the dagger-like gazes of the women in the group.

After the supporters dissipated, Annie pulled Elizabeth aside.

"Lizzie, this is Mrs. Stanton. You were named after her."

"Lizzie, it is so nice to meet you, finally. I have heard so much about you," said Elizabeth.

"I've read some of your speeches in the newspapers, Mrs. Stanton," said Lizzie.

"Have you? You're a bit younger than my intended audience, but I hope my words encourage you."

"Mother told me about staying with you on your farm when she was a girl after her father died. And that you helped her decide to marry Papa."

"She gives me too much credit. Your parents decided to marry each other on their own. I was happy to be there for them." Elizabeth looked up from Lizzie. "Max, it's lovely to see you. I'm delighted to see what the three of you have become. You're a model of what we're fighting for. Truly."

Max smiled, "Thank you, Elizabeth. We hold a special place in our hearts for you. We are eternally grateful for your kindness and support."

"That's very kind of you to say."

"How are Henry and the children?" asked Max.

"Henry is writing for several papers now, less visible, but still advocating for Republican causes. We have three children left at home. The other four are off into the world. Thank you for asking."

Max said, "Mr. Train is quite the entertainer and an unapologetic self-promoter."

"Yes, he's that," said Elizabeth. "I have found the larger the personality, the larger the audience. We need that. Susan, Annie, Lucy, me—our energy doesn't fill a room like his. I know some people don't agree with some of his positions, but he has stepped forward to support women. He gives his time and has offered to fund a newspaper focused on the movement. The paper will give us a voice that we can control. Today, we're at the mercy of the editors. Lucy and I are hoping to start publication soon."

"That's very generous of him. It's a smart move," said Max.

"We feel like we need to seize the hearts and minds of the electorate now. Support for Black suffrage isn't gaining traction. We saw it in New York."

"It's similar here in Ohio," said Max. "The state constitutional amendment only received forty percent support from the voters. The Democrats played to people's fears and prejudices. Across the state, Democrat candidates won in a backlash against the Republican positions on Black suffrage."

"That's why I'm trying to distance women's cause from the Negro's. We must take control of our destiny," said Elizabeth.

Annie said, "I won't give up on universal suffrage. They're talking about impeaching President Johnson. The Republicans will continue to advocate for Black suffrage to overcome the Southern push to regain power. I think our best opportunity is to align with them."

Elizabeth said, "I'm afraid you and I are of different minds on this. I've been betrayed once too often by Republican leadership. I don't trust them."

"In the end, we all want the same thing," said Annie. "Our only discord is in tactics."

"Agreed, then," said Elizabeth. "I apologize, but I must depart. I am traveling to Oxford tonight. Henry's brother, Robert, is president at Miami University, and I will spend the night with his family. Annie, thank you for arranging this meeting. And for all your efforts in Kansas."

They embraced. "Keep in touch," said Elizabeth.

CHAPTER 21

Cincinnati – Summer 1868

Jenny, Martha, Harry, and John had not lived together since their time at Given House. Harry and Martha moved from Canada and joined John and Jenny in the West End neighborhood in one of the clusters of more well-to-do Black families. John used some of his savings to buy furniture and housewares. After a few months, they settled into a routine.

John continued working as a barber while Jenny worked at the Brighton House Hotel. Martha worked as a washerwoman, doing laundry for several white families. Harry went to work on the U.S. Mail line packet steamer *America* as a steward and maintenance man.

In the dining room, Martha set bowls of stew before John, Jenny, and their guest, Stephen Evans, a carpenter. After John said a prayer, they began to eat the soup and bread.

"This is delicious, Martha," said Stephen.

"With the fresh vegetables this time of year, it's so much easier to make something good," said Martha.

"John has told me you're a fine cook, and I have to agree with him," said Stephen.

"I've been cooking since I was a little girl. Started in the master's house after Jenny was sold."

"What was the name of that girl that worked in the house with us?" said Jenny.

"That was Miss Clara," said Martha.

"That's right," Jenny nodded. "Clara always knew what was going on with everybody. You wanted to know who was kissing who or who was mad at who, you asked Clara."

"She took good care of John and me after you were gone," said Martha.

"Whatever happened to her?"

"She died about the time I was sixteen," said Martha. "I don't recall what she died of."

"How about you, Stephen," said Jenny. "You lived here all your life?"

"Yes, ma'am," said Stephen. "My parents were free in Pennsylvania, so I was born free. They moved here before I was born. My daddy taught me the carpenter business. We've built over a hundred houses around the city between him and me."

"A hundred, Lordy," said Jenny. "That is like magic, what you do. Create something so beautiful from the ground up. I've seen some of the fine houses here. There are some pretty ones."

"Stephen built the house he lives in up in Walnut Hills," said John. "It's as grand as any house on the street."

"Oh, I'd like to see it sometime," said Jenny.

"My wife and I will have you to dinner," said Stephen. "You two, Martha, and your brother, Harry."

"We don't see much of Harry. He'll visit when the *America* is in for repairs, but other than that, he goes up and down the river to Louisville," said Martha.

"His home is on that boat," said Jenny. "But he's lucky to have that job. He couldn't find work in town. Even though he's smart and knows how to do a lot of things, white men don't want to work with Black men."

"It's been that way ever since I started working," said Stephen. "Most of my customers are Black. The whites, they prefer to work with white carpenters. The war and emancipation haven't changed much in this town."

Martha passed the bread plate to Stephen, who took a slice and handed it to John.

"Jenny has a tooth that's been hurting her for a while now," said John. "Do you know a dentist that she could see?"

"Dr. Turner is the Colored dentist," said Stephen. "His office is on Seventh Street. You go see him; he'll take care of it for you."

"I'm all right," said Jenny.

"There's no reason for you to be in pain," said John.

"I don't want to spend money on something I can just live with," said Jenny.

"If you're afraid, I'll go with you," said John. "And it won't cost much."

"You do what John says," said Martha. "We have money for a dentist."

"I want us to be able to buy this house," said Jenny. "I want it to be ours."

"We're all working and saving," said John. "We're doing fine. Let me worry about that."

"Everything costs money living in the city," said Jenny. "I don't want to end up like those ones I see down by the river begging and stealing just to get along."

"That's not going to happen," said John. "We're all earning, and we'll take care of each other. I won't let that happen to us."

"I just worry," said Jenny.

"Don't. Please," said John, patting his mother's arm.

"You're a good son," said Jenny. "Where are you two going this evening?"

"We have a Colored School Board meeting," said John.

"What do you do at those meetings?" said Jenny.

"We work on improving the Colored schools. Tonight we'll be talking about how to fend off the proposal to merge the Colored and white school boards," said John.

"Why do people want to do that?" said Jenny.

"In Columbus and Cleveland, they're integrating the schools," said Stephen. "Proponents say that it provides a better education for the Black students. They argue our Colored schools provide an inferior education. Those of us on the Colored School Board don't agree. We have excellent schools with Black teachers who better understand our students."

"If we merged the schools and the school boards," said John, "our voice would get lost in the larger picture. And I don't think anyone in Cincinnati, Black or white, really wants mixed schools."

"If we integrated the schools, we'd lose one of the few places besides the churches to gather as a community. What would happen to our libraries and meeting rooms? Places where we feel comfortable?" said Stephen. "John and I are going to fight it."

"What are you two doing after supper?" said John.

"We're going to hear a speech at the Female Seminary," said Martha. "A man is lecturing on temperance. After that, Mrs. Tinsley is going to play music."

"That sounds like a nice evening. You enjoy yourselves," said John. "Stephen and I need to be off."

"Thank you for dinner," said Stephen. "It was nice to meet you both."

As the two men walked to the meeting, Stephen asked, "How are your mother and Martha adapting?"

John said, "I think they're still getting used to everything. I went through a similar adjustment after I was freed. All those years of someone else controlling so much of my life. It was overwhelming to think about what to do with my time. Martha has been free in Canada since before the war, so for her, it's adjusting to a new community. Jenny is still feeling lost I'm afraid. She works at the hotel and is taking it all in. So much is foreign to her. The city, the way the Northern whites put up with you, but don't want to see you. She comes home and doesn't want to go out much. Other than my sister and brother and me, she's got no one. I'm trying to get her involved with the ladies at church, but she doesn't fit in with their class."

"Have you considered another church, maybe?" said Stephen. "I know the congregation at the Union Baptist

Church can be a little rigid and proper. Jenny might be more comfortable at another church, maybe the Allen Chapel. I think they have more newly emancipated members. There are more like her from the South."

"We'll look into it; thank you," said John.

CHAPTER 22

Paris, Kentucky – Summer 1868

Oskar and Thomas rode in the carriage beside Captain John Hope on horseback. Two of Hope's mounted soldiers followed.

"I'm hoping we don't need your assistance this afternoon," said Oskar, "I hate to trouble you, but your presence reassures me. Three freedmen came into the office complaining of their treatment by Mr. Sinclair. He's in violation of the contracts that he signed with his workers. I tried to see him yesterday, but his foreman threatened me with a shotgun."

"That's why we're here, Oskar. It's no trouble at all," said Captain Hope.

"Have your men seen any signs of concern at the school?"

"It's been quiet, but they'll remain on guard. They understand the importance of remaining vigilant."

"Thank you. I don't want to see the students' lessons interrupted by the regulators' activities," said Oskar.

They turned off the dirt road and up the driveway toward the house. Workers dotted the field, some stopping to watch them ride past. The foreman, shotgun in hand, started walking from the field toward the house.

As Oskar and the others dismounted, the foreman moved in between them and the porch.

"I'm here to speak with Mr. Sinclair," said Oskar.

"He's not receiving visitors today. What's your business?" asked the foreman.

"Official business of the Freedmen's Bureau concerning his contracts with his workers."

"I oversee the workers. What are they crying about now?"

"This is between Mr. Sinclair and the Bureau. Where is he?" said Oskar.

"I already said he's not receiving visitors today."

Oskar started toward the house.

The foreman raised his gun. "Hold on there."

The three federal soldiers pointed their guns at the foreman in return.

"I'm not looking for a confrontation. I'm here to have a discussion with Mr. Sinclair," said Oskar.

Captain Hope said, "Put the gun down. There's no need for violence."

The foreman eyed him distastefully, sized up the soldiers, then lowered his gun.

Oskar moved past him and climbed the steps. As he approached the door, it opened, and a thin man stepped outside.

"Mr. Sinclair?" said Oskar.

The man nodded.

"I'm Oskar Mueller, from the Freedmen's Bureau, Paris office." He extended his hand, and Sinclair shook it. "How are you today, sir?"

"I'm a busy man. What can I do for you?" Sinclair scanned the armed party on the lawn.

"I don't intend to take up too much of your time. I'm hoping we can quickly address some complaints from some of your workers."

"What's the complaint?" said Sinclair.

"Several reported that you haven't provided meals and supplies in accordance with the sharecropping contracts you signed with them. They said you threatened not to pay them if they filed complaints with the Bureau."

Sinclair sighed. "I'm doing the best I can. Things are tight.

Our labor cost has risen significantly, so we're a little short on cash. You look like a smart man. You may not understand the numbers involved in farming, but you understand that when your costs triple, it's a problem, don't you?"

"I admit I don't know the economics. I know it's a challenging endeavor, farming," said Oskar.

"We don't have the money to buy the supplies we need. They need to accept things like they used to. No one's going to starve if they skip a few meals," said Sinclair.

"You need to feed your people," said Oskar. "They work in the fields for you, day after day, in the hot sun. It's not right to drop your end of the bargain."

"What do you want me to do? Did you hear me? I don't have the money. Look, my family's doing without too. We're barely hanging on."

"I'm sorry," said Oskar. "I'm sure it's difficult."

"That's an understatement. Damn United States government and your Bureau. How are we supposed to make this work? The price of crops isn't going up enough to cover the increased costs. Can your government fix that?" said Sinclair.

"I can't control that. I just know you need to treat these people fairly," said Oskar.

Sinclair shook his head back and forth. "Tell me. Tell me what I'm supposed to do."

"You could start by sitting down with your workers and explaining the situation. You're all in this together. They have a stake in the success of the season too. Don't treat them like children."

Sinclair scoffed.

"Look at what you might harvest and use from your farm. Or, let them grow some gardens to help feed themselves. You have to come up with something. You can't not feed them," said Oskar.

"What's going to happen if I don't?"

"You'll be in violation of your contracts, and they'll be free to look for other work. You don't want that."

"Let them try. Where are they going to go?" said Sinclair. "Besides, these contracts aren't enforceable, anyway."

"What makes you say that?" said Oskar.

"Judge Hawes told us we don't have to follow these contracts. He said the Bureau doesn't have the right to be in Kentucky. We weren't part of the Confederate States."

"Judge Hawes is not correct," said Oskar.

"I'm not saying I want them to leave, or I want to break contracts, but it ain't right leaving us to figure this out for ourselves. Damn national government sticking its nose in good people's lives," said Sinclair.

"We can't go back on that," said Oskar. "The country's moved forward, and we all want to get to a new place where we can prosper peacefully. Everyone involved loses if you can't make your farm work. That's not what we're trying to do. We want to help. I can get you some rations from the Bureau allotment to help you get by for a few days. But you need to meet with them. Talk to your workers and treat them like they're part of the solution. You might be surprised at the cooperation you get if you treat them with decency."

Sinclair scowled.

"Can you try that?" said Oskar.

"Yeah, I'll talk to them," he said.

"Good. Send a wagon to the Bureau's depot. We'll load up some rations for you." Oskar extended his hand, and Sinclair shook it.

The foreman stepped back as Oskar moved past him and climbed into the carriage. He tapped his finger on his shotgun and smirked. "You boys, have yourself a nice day."

#

Oskar approached the Bourbon County courthouse, a stone building with a tall spire rising above the other buildings in Paris. Since it was a court day, more people were on the grounds than typical. A man stood on the stone ledge that lined the courthouse lawn, reading from a list of prices for livestock. Men tended to horses and cows, awaiting the beginning of an auction. Oskar walked past several carts where merchants sold their wares. One offered household metal items: pans, cups, spoons, and knives; another sold spices, ground wheat flour, and cornmeal. Several farmers displayed fresh vegetables.

Oskar found the office with Judge Hawes's name on a plaque next to the doorway. He entered and introduced himself to a man at a desk.

"The judge is still in court," said the man.

"I'll wait," said Oskar. He sat in a hardwood chair, pulled his notebook from his satchel, and reviewed the most recent Bureau reports.

Almost an hour later, a slightly stooped man of about seventy with white hair entered the office.

"Judge, this man is here to see you," said the man at the desk.

The judge turned to Oskar as he stood, "Who are you?"

"I'm Oskar Mueller from the Freedmen's Bureau."

The judge grunted. "What do you want?"

"I'd like to discuss some of your recent rulings. You've negated some of the labor contracts between freedmen and farmers."

"That's correct."

"Can we sit and talk?" said Oskar, motioning toward the inner office.

Oskar followed the man into his office. A large Confederate flag covered most of the wall behind the desk. The judge shuffled around the desk and sat, motioning for Oskar to take one of the two chairs across from him.

"So you run the Freedmen's Bureau in Paris?" said the judge.

"Yes, sir."

"Jesus, no wonder it's such a shambles. Boys running the show," the judge mumbled.

"Sir?" said Oskar.

"Look at you. How old are you?"

"I don't think that's relevant."

"Eh, where you from?"

"Cincinnati."

"You say your name is Mueller?" said the judge.

"That's right."

"Any relation to Max Mueller?"

"Yes, he's my brother. How do you know him?"

"I oversaw the settlement of his father's estate over in Scott County. If I recall, he and his half-brother each netted a nice sum from the sale of the plantation and the slaves."

"You must be mistaken," said Oskar. "My brother was born in Cincinnati. He's not related to anyone in Scott County and wouldn't profit from the sale of the enslaved."

"I'm not mistaken. Max Mueller from Cincinnati was the bastard son of William Johnson. Johnson left him half of his estate," said the judge.

"You must be confusing him with someone else," said Oskar.

"I'm old, but I'm not senile. I settled the case. I'm not arguing with you. What do you want?"

Oskar pushed aside his confusion. "You need to stop nullifying the contracts the freedmen have with the farmers."

"I will not. Those contracts are invalid, and in my jurisdiction, I will protect the rights of the hard-working landowners who bring their grievances before me."

"Sir, those contracts are valid and necessary to protect the rights of the freedmen," said Oskar.

"They don't have any rights," stated the judge.

"Sir, the Thirteenth and Fourteenth Amendments to the Constitution...," said Oskar.

"Those amendments weren't passed here in Kentucky."

"Regardless, Kentucky is bound by the Constitution and its amendments," said Oskar.

The judge scoffed. "You want to argue law with me, son? The act establishing the Freedmen's Bureau authorized it in those states which rebelled against the Union. Kentucky did not secede and, thus, is not subject to its rules or its so-called courts. I am the law here in Bourbon County, not your Bureau military courts. It's a trampling of the state's rights that this nation was founded on."

"Sir, the Bureau does have jurisdiction here, and since the passing of the Civil Rights Act in 1866, the freedmen now have the option of taking their cases to federal courts, if necessary, to seek justice," said Oskar.

"Well, then let them. This is Kentucky. We will not be told what to do by a bunch of pencil pushers forcing us to stoop to the level of the Black man. We've more pride than that. Now, I'm a busy man."

"Victor," shouted the judge. "See this boy out."

#

Thomas came into Oskar's office. "You need to come see this."

Oskar followed him into the lobby, where a man, a woman, and two children sat on the bench, clinging to each other. The man's shirt was shredded into blood-stained tatters of cloth. He looked up as Oskar approached, then lowered his eyes again. The children cowered in their mother's lap.

"What happened to you?" asked Oskar.

None of them responded. Oskar approached the man gently. "Can I see your back?"

The man stood slowly and turned. Deep cuts crisscrossed his back, scraps of material embedded in places. His back was dark red, and his trousers were soaked with blood.

Oskar took a deep breath. "Who did this to you?"

The family remained mute.

"Thomas, go down to the store and buy some salve. Joseph, get some water and a cloth."

Oskar squatted down in front of the man. "I'm Oskar. I'm sorry this happened to you. Can you tell me what happened?"

"We didn't know where else to come. Folks said you might be able to help us," said the man.

"You did the right thing. We're here to help you."

Joseph poured water from a pitcher into a glass and handed it to the man, who gratefully took and drank it down. "The children," he said, pointing.

Joseph gave them each a drink.

"What's your name?" asked Oskar.

"Ely. This is Mary and Sarah and Tom."

Joseph handed each of them an apple.

"Where are you from?" said Oskar.

"Woodford County," said Ely. "We were working on Mr. Thompson's farm."

Oskar pulled up a chair and sat. "Can you tell me what happened?"

"Two nights ago, we were sleeping, and the regulators, about six of them, busted in and pulled me outside. They tied me to a tree, then made the others in the house come out to watch. They whipped me until I blacked out."

"Did you know the men?"

Ely shook his head. "Never seen them before. They said they were doing their duty to restore order, and I was an example for everyone to learn from."

Mary spoke, "This isn't the first time. The regulators hung another man for talking back to a white man in town. They came and pulled him out of bed too. Ely lucky to be alive."

"Why did they attack you?" said Oskar.

"We had a party," said Mary.

"What?" said Oskar, not understanding.

"We had a party a few nights ago for Sarah's birthday. We sat outside with our friends and made some music. Some white folk came over and told us to shut it down. They told us we had no reason to be acting like we's king of ourselves. Said we were getting too big for our own good."

"Then what happened?" said Oskar.

"We shut it down and went to bed. We didn't want any trouble. I guess these men wanted to make sure we didn't have no more parties," she said.

Oskar sighed. "Lord, help us."

"Morning after the regulators left and Ely could see straight, we left," said Mary.

"You walked here? What, it's about twenty miles?" said Oskar.

Mary nodded.

Thomas returned with supplies and began to wash and dress Ely's wounds.

"We'll get you a place to sleep for a few nights," said Oskar. "Then I want you to come with me to the sheriff's office to file charges."

Ely shook his head. "I'm not going back to Woodford County. Ever. Sheriff there is not interested in helping the Black man."

"We'll take a couple of soldiers with us. Nothing's going to happen to you."

"For all I know, these men are friends of the sheriff. They are doing his business to keep the white man on top in Woodford County. They told us that's how it's been, and that's how it's going to be. We've got to go someplace else. Can you help us move somewhere?"

"Yes, I can help you do that, but I need your testimony. I can file the report and take it to the sheriff. We might need you to testify in a courtroom, though," said Oskar.

"No sir, not me. I'm not going to cross them. I want to go somewhere my freedom means more. Please. Help me find that place."

"All right, Ely. We'll find a place for you."

#

Oskar and Catherine sat in their favorite spot near the bank of the creek, a short walk from town. They liked to relax amongst the trees, away from the prying eyes of the townspeople and talk about their days. Oskar rested against a large oak tree with Catherine leaning back into him.

"Do you feel like we're making a difference?" asked Oskar.

"Yes, we are. I'm certain of it. Don't you?" asked Catherine.

"Usually I do, but then I have weeks like this one. Hearing about the regulators' attack on Ely makes me wonder if the war and the amendments and laws can break through the hatred and fear that so many harbor toward the Negroes. Here in the South, men don't even attempt to hide their distaste. At least at home, most are civil or ignore Black people. The Democrats have retaken the congressional seats in Kentucky and reinstated most of the politicians who were against emancipation before the war. They're trying to reconstruct the state's social order as it was—the only difference is they're freedmen now and not slaves. The freedmen are still relegated to the bottom of society's ladder by the laws, customs, and treatment by their neighbors."

"But we have made an impact," said Catherine. "Think about where Bourbon County was when we arrived. There were a lot of freedmen not working or working without any contracts to corral the landowners. Some were starving. Few could read. They had no recourse if they had a legal problem. That is significant progress. They have a path to prosperity now."

"It still seems so daunting," said Oskar.

"It's a long path they're on. We're trying to change mores that were a hundred years in the making. You are a man who doesn't like sitting still. It will take time. We need to keep working."

"I think the brightest spot is the school you've established. You are giving so many the foundation they need to continue down the path." He hugged her. "You are an amazing woman."

Catherine put her hand aside his face and pulled him into a kiss.

"It's been so rewarding to see the students' progress. It does give me hope," she said. "I was ready to quit when the church was burned, and we had to start over."

"But you didn't," said Oskar. "We can't let them win.

These regulators and Ku Kluxers are using intimidation anywhere they can. They're cowards, though. They pick on the defenseless, hide their identities."

"It's reassuring to have the federal soldiers at our sides. I don't know what we'd do without them," said Catherine. "I would have been too afraid to return to the classroom without them."

"Thank God Grant was elected president," said Oskar. "If the white man's candidate, Seymour, had won, the Democrats would have tried to undo everything that Congress has done. I am worried that sentiment will eventually turn against having Federal troops stationed in the South. All of the states but three have been reinstated in the Union. I'm not sure we should have let them back in so easily. Like in Kentucky, many people in the South are not aligned with the goals of Congress's Reconstruction plan."

"Yes, thank the Lord for President Grant. And good riddance to that awful man, Andrew Johnson," she said.

"Grant won by a landslide in the electoral college, thanks in part to the newly enfranchised Blacks in the South, but he barely had a majority of the popular vote. That worries me," Oskar said.

"Why does that bother you so?"

"It could signal that there were many voters in all the states that supported Seymour, meaning a lot more people than we think are against equality for the freedmen; in the South *and* the North."

"Even more reason to persevere, then," said Catherine.

"It's so peaceful here," said Oskar.

"Do you ever miss home?" she said.

"Sometimes. I miss my family."

"I miss the city sometimes," said Catherine.

"I think about what they're all up to. Lizzie is almost twelve. She's growing up so fast. I lived with Max and Annie when Lizzie was young. She's like a little sister to me. And Annie's off somewhere. Who knows where. I wonder how Max is faring without her.

"The other day, Judge Hawes made the queerest comment about Max when I met with him."

"What did he say?" she asked.

"He said that Max was the bastard of a Scott County plantation owner, and he received a significant inheritance from the man from the sale of his property and slaves."

"That doesn't make any sense. What do you think he was talking about?"

"I don't know," said Oskar.

"The man is ancient, isn't he? He must have confused Max with someone else."

"That's what I thought, but he was adamant. I'm going to make some inquiries, but I want to stay clear of the judge."

#

"Well, this is a pleasant surprise," said Catherine.

Oskar entered her classroom and closed the door. They embraced and lingered in a kiss.

"I thought we were meeting after dinner and taking a stroll down by the creek?" she said.

"I had to see Captain Hope. I was here and thought I could walk you home. Maybe we could have dinner together in town at the inn?" said Oskar.

"I would love nothing more. Will you collect those books?"

Oskar helped her straighten the room, and they walked to the inn. The staff knew Oskar and Catherine and gave them their preferred table in the corner. They ordered their meal, and Oskar ordered a second beer.

"I had a visit today from General Fisk, the Bureau Assistant Commissioner," said Oskar.

"He's the boss, right?" said Catherine.

Oskar nodded, "He oversees all the Bureau operations in Tennessee and Kentucky."

"He traveled all this way to your little field office. How did you find him?"

"He's a military man and also has a commerce background. Very competent. He's started a university in Nashville for the freedmen. I wish I could have met him sooner."

"You sound disheartened. What's the matter?" she asked.

"They're shutting us down. The Freedmen's Bureau," said Oskar.

"What?"

"They're closing the Bureau offices."

"How can they? There's so much more to do," she said. Oskar nodded slowly.

"No, they can't. These poor people. They're not ready. They'll be devoured. Oh, Oskar." Catherine began to cry softly.

"General Fisk said that our office must be closed by year-end, but the school can remain, at least for now."

"Did he say why? Is he unhappy with the performance of the office?" she said.

"No, nothing like that. They'll be closing all the Bureau offices. Congress won't extend funding for the Bureau. The electorate wants to be done with Reconstruction. They're ready to move on."

"But the job's not finished," said Catherine. "It's too fragile. The Southern Democrats have already started to put things back the way they were. Left unchecked, it's only a matter of time before all we've gained will be lost."

"I know," said Oskar. "It's disappointing."

"Oh, Oskar."

He reached across the table and took her hand in his. "I know."

They sat in silence. The waiter brought their dinner, and they ate.

"The school should remain open," said Oskar. "General Fisk said that you'll be paid, but he anticipates that school funding will dry up sometime next year."

"That's terrible," she said.

"I don't want you to stay," he said.

"I have to, I must, or the school will fold," said Catherine.

"You should prepare the school to operate without you. Put local teachers in place."

"That will take time. Right now, no one could step up. I have volunteers, but no one with the capacity to run the school."

"They'll have to figure it out without you," he said.

"I don't see how they…"

Oskar blurted, "I want you to come home with me. Be with me. I don't want to live without you. I want you to marry me so we can always be together."

"I want that too." She squeezed his hands. "But I don't want to leave now. Not with still so much to do. I don't want to abandon my students."

"They're going to pull the soldiers too. You won't have any protection," said Oskar.

"Oh. Maybe we can both stay. Here. Build our life in Kentucky. You can protect me," she said.

"No. Not me," said Oskar. "I don't want to live among these people who smile and nod at us, then spew hate the moment we turn our backs. I don't want to have to constantly look over our shoulders, wondering who might attack us next. I want to go home, live amongst our people, and continue the fight from there."

"I would feel guilty leaving. Like I'm abandoning the children," said Catherine.

"You have to let that go," he said.

"How am I supposed to do that? It doesn't seem right."

"I had similar feelings in the war. Men who lost their lives or were wounded while I walked away unscathed. It will eat you alive if you linger on those thoughts."

"I don't know if I can do that," she said.

"It will become easier over time. Look, this is happening, and we can't change it. We can only control what we do in response to it," said Oskar.

"Maybe we should stay and make the school more permanent. Be a force against the regulators and people who want to return things to how they used to be," she said.

"We'll have a family," said Oskar. "I don't want to put you or them in harm's way. If we stay, that's what we face. We have to think about ourselves too."

"How can I leave and be happy knowing the pain of the people we're leaving behind?" said Catherine.

"I know. It's tragic. I wish the world were fair, but it's not. That's heaven. There's no heaven on earth," said Oskar.

"Can you just walk away from these people?"

"I can. And so can you. You need to allow yourself to be happy. Please. Will you come home with me?"

"Oskar, I love you and want to be with you. I can't stay here alone. Yes, I will."

CHAPTER 23

Hinds County, Mississippi – Fall 1868

Aaron and Mary Johnson sat on the freshly painted porch of the plantation house, looking across a cotton field bursting with white bolls.

"I think the worst is over," said Aaron. "Picking has started, and we're going to have a larger crop than I ever dreamed. The hands are anxious to get it all picked. I feel like we're all working for the same thing. Switching to sharecropping was the wisest thing I've done since taking over the farm."

"It couldn't get much worse than the last two years. Thank God for the weather this year," said Mary.

"I think things are going our way now. Don't you, dear?"

Mary didn't respond.

"Mary, aren't you feeling settled now?" said Aaron. "The house is repaired. You're furnishing it. It's almost as grand as Given House was. You and I will be lord and lady of the county. The politics are settling down. Mississippi will be restored to Congress soon. President Grant wants peace. By this time next year, we can host a big party. It will be fun. You can plan it."

"Aaron, I'm worried," she said.

"Why? We're sitting high. My investment is finally paying off."

"It's like you've created an island here, and shark-infested waters surround us."

"Honey, why these troubled thoughts?" he said.

"I was in town today. I heard some men talking about you."

"What did they say?" he said.

"They were saying that you bought your election to the statehouse. Bribed the Negroes to vote for you with favors. That you're a carpetbagger who's only here to suck out what the Union armies didn't already take," said Mary.

"Oh, you know these Southern boys. They're angry that they're not allowed to vote. Their pride has been hurt in losing the war, and the enfranchisement of Black men over them is salt in the wound."

"Did you, though? Did you buy your workers' votes?" Mary asked.

"I didn't buy them. I encouraged them to vote for me. I'm a better representative for this county than others they might have voted for. They trust me. I've been fair to them. I took them all into town to register to vote and told them why I was the best candidate. It was me or Clem Dixon from Gleason's farm. Hell, he can't even read; how could he serve in the legislature? I will serve them well."

"Those men make me nervous. They were cussing up a storm about you."

"Aw, they're just sore about how things are turning out. Try not to worry yourself. Let me do the worrying," said Aaron.

"It's not just them," said Mary. "The women at church are acting even colder to me than they used to. Sylvia told me it's because we ran the Graysons off their plantation. Many of them hate us for that. The rest hate us just because we're Northerners. Like we personally took up arms and killed their sons and husbands. I don't even try to explain how you were neutral during the war."

"I'm sorry you have to put up with all that. They don't understand business. I made a fair deal with Grayson and paid him one and a half times over what his property was worth. Grayson caused his own demise. He couldn't get past his anger. He refused to work with the freedmen. He stuck his head in the sand and hoped things would return to how they were. It's his own damn fault. I tried to tell him."

"I know you did, but the ladies in town can't see past their pride either."

"Things will get better. You'll see."

"You've been telling me that for two years," she said.

"And haven't they improved?"

"Yes, they have."

"See," he said.

"It's just so lonely at times."

Their two sons, James and Evan, rode up the road and waved as they passed on their way to the barn.

"They're both becoming fine horsemen," said Aaron. "It reminds me of my youth."

"They love to ride," said Mary. "James will be fifteen. We can't wait any longer. He has to go to school this fall."

"I know. He'll hate it, going off to Boston. Leaving this."

"I don't think he will. He's lonely too," said Mary. "The Southern boys don't accept him any more than their parents accept us. It's going to be harder for Evan to be left here without him."

"We should probably look at boarding school for Evan then," said Aaron. "Schools here are shit."

"I agree, we should. I was thinking I might visit my father in Boston when James goes off to school. I can take Evan and Nan with me. We'll find a school for Evan near my sister. She can look in on him."

"That would be good for you. Go home and see your family."

#

Mary took the children by steamboat and train to Boston. Aaron rattled around the large house by himself.

Late one night, Aaron awoke to the strong smell of smoke.

He jumped from his bed. In the dark, he sensed that the room was filled with smoke and heard a rushing sound. Flickering light drew his attention to the window.

A row of figures stood across the front lawn, dressed in pointed white hoods that evoked the ghosts of Confederate soldiers. They stood, watching the large house, now fully aflame, light the yard. The front corner of the wooden house collapsed and crashed to the ground, sending sparks and flames across the grass.

Aaron heard the boom as the pieces hit the ground. He ran to the door of his bedroom. He grabbed the doorknob and then yanked his hand back from the heat. "Christ," he screamed. He picked up a shirt from the floor and used it to turn the knob. When he opened the door, a rush of hot air smacked him. The floor and doors in the hallway were ablaze. He slammed the door shut and ran for the window.

The men and women from the cabins stood in a line to the side of the hooded men, watching the scene.

"Help, someone!" cried Aaron from the second-story window.

The hooded men stood silently.

Several workers moved toward the fire but stepped back from the heat. "Mr. Johnson," one of them called. More pieces of the house tumbled down in flames.

"Ricky!" Aaron started coughing, now finding it difficult to talk. "Fetch a ladder from the barn."

Ricky and another man ran to the barn. Some of the women began praying. One of the men yelled, "Hold on, Mr. Johnson. They're going for the ladder."

They returned with the ladder and assessed the flames blazing high into the sky, lighting the night, and warming everything in its aura. They pulled up their shirts to cover their mouths and noses and approached the house.

A shot rang out above the roar of the fire. "Stay back. Let the devil burn," one of the hooded men shouted. The row of vigilantes moved several steps toward them.

The workers retreated with the ladder and laid it down.

They looked to the now empty window, searching for signs of Aaron. They heard a faint cry coming from the house, then silence.

One woman dropped to her knees in prayer, while another turned away and shielded her daughter from the scene. They were powerless to combat the forces against them.

After a few minutes, the entire roof collapsed, disappearing into the flames. Several workers cried out. They comforted each other as they watched the house continue to burn. With the destruction of the house and Aaron's murder, their future was again uncertain and at the mercy of men who were immune to their struggles.

The hooded men retreated down the driveway, disappearing into the dark.

CHAPTER 24

Cincinnati – Fall 1868

After Sunday mass, Lizzie and Max took a carriage several miles north of downtown to the Spring Grove Cemetery. Max loved the expanses of grass, lush trees and shrubs, and the quiet of the grounds. It reminded him of the days in his youth when the boys of St. Xavier would spend the afternoon playing at Archbishop Purcell's mansion in the once-rural suburb of Walnut Hills.

Lizzie loved their afternoon rides and walks for the uninterrupted time with her father; no employees, no businessmen, no citizens with complaints or requests for favors from the councilman. He was all hers.

"Mother said in her letter that they are changing the newspaper's motto to be 'Men, their rights, and nothing more; Women, their rights, and nothing less.' It doesn't sound equal to me," said Lizzie.

"Well, maybe that's the point," said Max. "Men have had more opportunities historically, so the paper's position is it's time to give more to women, starting with their rights."

"She said she'll be home for Christmas and stay until the new year."

"It will be nice to have her home, won't it? We'll have to make the most of our time together. Soon, you'll be away too," said Max.

"I know I need to get a proper education, but why do I

have to go away to school?" said Lizzie.

"Your mother and I want you to have the best education possible."

"You went to school here, and Mother didn't go to college."

"The world is different now than when we were your age. An education from a highly regarded college will prepare you for the rest of your life. To attend a reputable college, you must attend a rigorous prep school. Mother is looking into options for you in New York. You could both end up living there."

"So we'd be in New York, and you'd be here by yourself?" said Lizzie.

"That's one option we're looking at. I think you'd like New York. You could continue painting there."

"Abby says that I should start looking at other art forms. Women aren't respected as painters. She said maybe pottery," said Lizzie.

"Is that so? What do you think of that?" said Max.

"I love to paint and draw, but I might like pottery."

"Do you think men have something special that makes them better at painting?" asked Max.

Lizzie thought for a minute. "I can't think of anything, but there must be something because all the famous artists are men."

"I would argue that if you dedicate yourself to painting, learn from great teachers, and practice, you could become an excellent painter. As good as a man. I don't think your sex has anything to do with it. As Abby suggests, most famous artists are men because women have been discouraged from painting. If you love painting and want to pursue it, then keep painting. That's one of the reasons we want you to go to college. There, you can learn about other things. Some of those things might use your God-given talents, but you won't know unless you explore them."

"How am I supposed to know what to study?" said Lizzie.

"That's why you need to attend a prep school. You have

time to think about it."

A flock of birds flew off as they drove past a small spring-fed lake. Max took a road to the right and steered the horses onto the grass. He tied them to a tree and took Lizzie's hand. The cemetery grounds were landscaped with a mix of planted species amidst the established oak, maple, and ash trees that had been there for decades.

They walked toward one of the tallest monuments in the cemetery—a granite obelisk atop a square base. Max stopped in front of it.

Lizzie looked up the column toward the sky, then read the name on the base, "Longworth. Who is it, Papa?"

"This is the Longworth family plot. Nicholas Longworth was a very generous man in Cincinnati. He gave money to many causes and helped those that others ignored. He also supported artists by buying their art and paying for their trips abroad to study."

"Why did you stop here?" she asked.

"Old Nick, that's what we called him, was very special to me. As a little boy, I lived in Over-the-Rhine with Oma and my Papa and brothers and sisters in the house over the Eichen Garten. I sold newspapers at the Fifth Street Market. I watched the businessmen go to and from work and wished to be like them someday. Old Nick would buy a paper from me every morning, and we began to know each other. He asked my parents if he could pay for my schooling at St. Xavier. So I went and lived in the dormitory there for six years and received my degree. That led to me getting my job and eventually being able to buy Miller Industries."

Max put his hand against the tall shaft and looked to the top. "If it weren't for Mr. Longworth, I might still be working at the Eichen Garten, and I would never have met your mother."

"Why did he pick you to pay for your schooling?" said Lizzie.

"Hmm. That's a good question. One I've asked myself many times since I was a boy. The only answer I can come up with is that God sent him. There were other boys selling newspapers at the market. There were other boys from Over-the-Rhine who needed a little help. Hundreds of boys and girls across the city from families who couldn't afford to pay for an education. I was lucky.

"We're all born into our circumstances. Some more fortunate than others. We start from that. What we do with our blessings and gifts is up to us. But it sure makes it easier if we're one of the lucky ones. You understand that you're very fortunate."

"I know, Papa. We have our nice house. I have nice dresses and my paints."

"Yes, and you have two parents who love and care for you and want the best for you. The children we visit at the orphanage, the people we see begging in the streets, and the Blacks born into slavery, weren't so lucky. We have to remember that we're no better than them; we were just born luckier than them. And if God gives us much, it's our duty to help others."

"I know, Papa."

"We're so very blessed," he said as he kissed her head.

"So thank you, old Nick," Max said as he patted the granite. "Shall we ride on?"

They got back in their carriage and rode further into the cemetery to the Soldier's Monument. A bronze Union soldier standing guard with his rifle rested atop a granite pedestal. Hundreds of soldiers' graves encircled it. They dismounted the carriage and walked along the white gravestones.

Max stopped and slowly rotated 360 degrees, Lizzie watching him silently.

"So many men killed in the war, Lizzie," said Max.

"How many?"

"Hundreds are buried here, but over 500,000 men died from the North and South."

"Aunt Marie's Hugo died," she said.

"Yes, she lost Hugo to the war. He was a brave soldier in *Die Neuner*, the German regiment."

"Jo's papa, Mr. March, didn't fight in the war, just like you didn't, Papa," said Lizzie.

"Who's Jo? A friend of yours?"

"No, in my book, *Little Women*."

"Oh."

"He was a chaplain," she said.

"Sounds like maybe he was like me," said Max.

"Jo and her sisters had to live without their papa being home, just like I live without mother. They get along. They're lucky, though, because they have each other. I wish I had sisters. They're not lucky, though, because their father lost his wealth when he loaned a friend money. I hope that doesn't happen to us."

"I don't think you need worry about that," said Max. "I'm careful with my money, as one should be."

"Jo is temperamental like her mother, Marmee. Marmee gets frustrated, but Mr. March helps her control her temper. Like you and Mother."

"Well, you're relating to all kinds of things in this book," said Max.

"The girls in *Little Women* are fortunate to have Marmee. She is easy to talk to and has good advice."

"Do you wish Mother were here more?" said Max.

"Yes, I do. Marmee talks to her daughters about boys and courting. I wish Mother and I could talk about things like that."

"I'm sorry you miss her so. I do my best, but there are some things I'm afraid I'm not very good at being a substitute for your mother."

"I'm sorry, Papa. I didn't intend to make you feel bad," said Lizzie. "You're the best father a girl could ever want. You're even better than Mr. March."

"Thank you. It's nice to know I compare favorably to the fictional Mr. March. You're a sweet girl to worry about my feelings. I think we get along rather well when we need to, just the two of us."

"I do too. I know *Little Women* is a made-up story, but the characters seem real. I do love the book. I like Amy best because she's an artist, even though she's a bit too fussy. I think I'm most like Beth. She plays the piano and tries to help everyone to get along."

"Well, it sounds like this author has written quite a gripping novel," he said.

"Oh, yes, Mrs. Coons said that it is one of the most popular books in the country right now. All the girls at school are reading it," said Lizzie.

"Maybe I should read it then too. So I am up to date on young ladies' literature."

CHAPTER 25

Ohio River, North of Warsaw, Kentucky – December 1868

The *America* was part of the Cincinnati & Louisville Packet Company's fleet that regularly ran between the two cities on the Ohio River, carrying mail, manufactured and farm goods, and passengers. Working on the riverboats was among the few occupations available to Black men in Cincinnati. Most positions were unskilled: deckhands and firemen who tended the boilers. A few were employed as porters or stewards. With the advent of the railroad, riverboat traffic declined, and steamboat-related jobs diminished in number and status.

Harry, dressed in his black steward uniform, entered the crew's dim bunkroom of the *America*. The white crewman observed him as he walked through their section of the bunkroom and stood next to Colin's bunk.

"Colin," whispered Harry.

Colin opened his eyes. "What is it, Harry?"

"Sorry to wake you," said Harry, handing Colin a folded piece of paper. "Mrs. Garrison handed me this."

"What is it?" said Colin.

Harry shrugged and shook his head.

Colin stood, walked over to one of the oil lanterns in the room, and read the message. "After the band stops playing, they want a bottle of wine in their cabin tonight at eleven o'clock." He handed the note back. "Anything else?"

"No. Thank you," said Harry tucking it into his breast

pocket.

"What are you two going on about over there?" said Greg, one of the other white stewards.

"Nothing. Colin is just helping me out," said Harry.

"Why do you help that darkie out?" Greg said to Colin. "If he can't read, he isn't qualified for the job. You keep helping him, and you keep one of ours from a job they deserve."

"Harry's all right. Leave him be," said Colin.

"It's one's like him driving the wages down for all of us," said Greg. "You a Negro lover?"

"I've no problem with Africans," said Colin.

"I guess you are," Greg said to Colin, then turned to Harry. "How'd you end up with this job? It don't make no sense. You know somebody special? Maybe you sucking up to the captain? That must be it."

"I fix things," said Harry.

"What things?" said Greg.

"I repair things on the ship when they break. That's why they hired me," said Harry.

"Well, aren't you a special Negro. A regular fix-it man," said Greg.

"I don't want any trouble," said Harry.

"Just let him be," said Colin. "We all have to get along. You do your job and let us do ours, and we'll all get to keep our jobs. You pick a fight, and you'll get us all thrown off the crew."

"Negro lover and his special Negro. I got my eyes on you two," said Greg. "On this boat, we have to get along, but when we dock, if I see you—we'll see."

Harry started down the narrow aisle toward the door. He turned sideways to pass Greg to avoid brushing against him.

When Harry was gone, Greg said to Colin, "You call yourself an Irishman. Where's your sense of dignity?"

"Piss off," said Colin as he climbed back into his bunk.

#

A little after eleven o'clock, Harry delivered the bottle of wine and two glasses to the Garrisons' stateroom, his last task for the day. He met Colin on the hurricane deck for a smoke. Harry had become friends with many of the Black workers on board but had found it helpful to befriend Colin and learn as much as he could from him to do his job. They often met at the end of the day, in the darkness, so as not to draw too much attention.

They sat in the dark of the cloudy night, whispering.

"Thank you for standing up for me today with Greg," said Harry.

"It's all right. Being stuck on this boat day after day is hard enough without guys like him making things more miserable than they already are," said Colin. "But you best stay clear of him."

"I've encountered plenty of men like him since freedom. There's no reasoning with the likes of him. Unfortunately, there are only so many places a man can go on this boat, so staying clear isn't easy."

"Who's that up in the pilot house with the captain?" said Colin.

"That's Mr. Jenkins. He's sitting in for the Frenchman," said Harry.

"Where's Dufour?" said Colin.

"He's off for the next two days. They borrowed Jenkins from the boat that goes to New Orleans."

Harry and Colin spied the lanterns of an approaching steamboat headed downriver.

"There's the *United States*," said Colin.

The substitute pilot, Jenkins, gave two blares of the whistle, indicating he would pass to the left of the *United States*, contrary to the regular nightly passing protocol.

"What the hell," said Colin, "Why's he passing left?"

The *United States* sounded a single blare in return as the *America* moved into its path.

"Holy Jesus," said Colin as the two steamboats collided

with a jolt, knocking both men to the deck, and then rocking the boat back and forth. The crack of the *America's* splintering hull was followed by shouts of passengers and crew from both vessels.

Harry could feel the boat slowly listing as its bow spun slowly toward downriver and drifted toward the Indiana shore. Passengers emerged from their staterooms and stood on the deck in confusion.

A loud boom rang across the water as flames shot high into the sky and out the sides of the main deck of the *United States*. The fire quickly consumed the wood railings, decks, and walls. Passengers stood outside, screaming. Flames landed on the decks of the *America,* catching it on fire, too.

Harry and Colin ran down to the boiler deck and shouted to the men and women standing on the side of the *United States*, which was now banging against the *America* and burning quickly. Harry called to the panicked passengers, waving his hands, "Jump, jump!"

Passengers began to jump from the *United States* to the *America.* The crewmembers rushed to their aid and helped them up and out of the way. Within five minutes, the *United States* was a large bonfire lighting the sky. Harry yelled to the remaining passengers, "Jump!" but they refused. He heard screams as a woman's dress caught fire. Then, more cries as the water overtook the boat's hull. Seconds later, the steamboat sunk into the Ohio. Men and women jumped into the river amongst flaming debris.

Harry watched in horror. The pilot had maneuvered the *America* toward the shore. Harry saw passengers jumping from the shore-side of the boat and wading to safety. He led passengers around the deck, pushing some, and shouting directions. Most jumped, but some hesitated, afraid. The *America* was sinking. Harry knew they would be lost if the remaining people didn't abandon ship. He screamed for them to jump as he grabbed a man's arm and pushed him over the rail. Then he grabbed another, who fought him off. He shoved a screaming woman over the side.

He felt a drop and a sharp listing of the boat as it began to submerge. As passengers slid toward the water, he pushed two passengers and followed them in. He paddled with his hands until he found he could stand on the mucky bottom. He pulled a woman out of the water to the shore and returned repeatedly until all the survivors were safe on the riverbank.

Exhausted, he sat down and watched the floating debris and pools of burning fuel, the only remains of the two steamboats.

CHAPTER 26

Cincinnati – December 1868

John stood behind the man, one of his regulars. The banker came into the barbershop on Monday mornings for a shave and hair trim. He read his newspaper and had little interest in conversing with John or any of the men in the barbershop, but John didn't mind. He was a faithful customer who tipped well. John preferred his kind to the men who made condescending remarks or insults.

The man stood, brushed himself off, handed John his tip, and nodded before departing. As John tidied his station and a boy swept up the hair from under his chair, Thomas, one of the other barbers, approached. "John, doesn't your brother work on the steamboat *America*?"

"That's right," said John.

"You hear about the accident?"

John shook his head, "Nuh uh, what accident?"

"The last man I cut said there's talk down on the levee that the *America* didn't come in this morning. Word is it collided with the *United States* steamer about halfway from Louisville. The *United States* caught fire. Both boats sank," said Thomas.

"Oh my God. Anyone hurt?" said John.

"He said it was bad. A lot of people drowned."

John cleared it with William Watson, the shop owner, and ran down to the packet line office on Front Street. He stood outside the crowd of people blocking the small office door. Several reporters lingered amidst family members of passengers. Several were crying and consoling each other.

John asked what happened but was ignored. He tried to piece together events from the numerous conversations around him.

"Excuse me, sir," he said to a man. "What's happened? I heard there was an accident on the America."

"That's right," said the man. "It struck the *United States* near Warsaw, Kentucky."

"What's happened to the crew?" said John.

"I have no idea," said the man, turning back toward the building.

John considered pushing his way inside but realized it was futile.

After several minutes, a man emerged from the office. "If you'll all quiet down, I'll make an announcement. At about half past eleven last night, the America, upbound, collided mid-river with the downbound *United States* on their regular runs. The *United States* caught fire and sunk, and the *America* sank soon after. There were casualties, but I don't know how many. We have sent another steamer to retrieve the survivors. That's all I know right now."

The crowd shouted questions at the man, some pushing forward.

"I'm sorry. I don't have any more information right now," said the man.

John watched the fracas for a while, then returned to work.

#

Max and Annie sat with Max's siblings at a table in the corner of the Eichen Garten. Oskar and Catherine had announced their engagement, and both had moved back to Cincinnati.

"What are you going to do now?" asked Max.

"I'm exploring a couple of opportunities," said Oskar. "St.

Ann's School for Colored Children is looking for someone, and Father Henni has a position at St. Aloysius's orphanage."

"Doing what?" asked Max.

"Running it. I'd be the administrator. He's going to retire in a few years. I'd support him until he does, and then I'd take over everything."

"Will they pay you a sufficient salary to live on? You're planning to have a family," said Max.

"The money will be adequate to support our lifestyle. Some of us don't require china in the dining room," said Oskar.

"You have an education. You may be settling for less than you're worth. One day, you may wish you'd gone a different direction."

"I'm not settling. We're not all like you," said Oskar.

"Max, I think it's wonderful that Oskar wants to continue to serve others," said Annie. "He'd be a wonderful administrator for St. Aloysius or St. Ann's."

"He was blessed with an education," said Max. "I don't want to see him waste it."

"Waste it," said Oskar. "Just because I wish to contribute more to my community than making money, you deem that a waste? You don't speak like the son of a German immigrant. Where do your values come from?" said Oskar.

"The same place as yours. Our youth and our Catholic educations," said Max.

"Do we come from the same place, Max?" Oskar stood and stared intently at Max.

Max stood in response. Oskar moved toward his brother, so their faces were now inches apart.

Max reddened in the face and stared into Oskar's eyes, trying to read his meaning.

"Do we?" Oskar repeated, pressing his finger into his brother's chest.

Max pushed Oskar from him, "Outside," he muttered.

"Max, Oskar," said Annie.

"Leave us be," snapped Max as he motioned Oskar

toward the door and followed him. They stormed through the bar and out the front door. Oskar stopped in the street.

"Not here," Max demanded as he walked down the street toward the canal. He stepped into an alley, out of earshot of anyone.

"What do you have to say to me?" Max said.

"What do you have to say for yourself?" said Oskar.

"Yes, I'm fortunate. I'm blessed with wealth beyond anything I dreamed of, but I've shared it. With charities, with the Church, with the family, with you. I practically raised you and paid for your education. Will you judge me for my good fortune?"

"No, not for that, but for what you've kept from us—that which separates us," said Oskar.

"What?" said Max.

"Who is William Johnson?" said Oskar.

Max froze. "How do you know that name?"

"Who is he?" said Oskar. "Tell me."

After a long silence, Max said, "He was my father."

"What the bloody hell? You've lied to us all these years. Acted as if you were our brother when you weren't."

"I am your brother," said Max.

"Ha. I understand you have two other brothers, too."

"Yes. You're all my half-brothers. Let me explain. Withhold judgment of me, please. I never told the family because I wanted to protect Mother. There was nothing to be gained by dredging it all up."

"Dredging what up?" said Oskar.

"Just listen. When Mother first arrived in America, she worked as a domestic for a man in town, William Johnson. He had his way with her, and she became with child. He was married and had another house in Scott County, Kentucky. William paid her to go away quietly. Mother could barely speak English, was young, and didn't know what to do. Papa agreed to marry her to save her reputation."

"Is this true?"

"I'm afraid it is," said Max.

"Oh, Christ. Poor Mother," said Oskar.

"They never told anyone. Papa raised me as his own but resented me. After Papa died, Mother told me he wasn't my father, but she didn't reveal who was. Just before the war, William Johnson died, and in his will, he left half of his estate to me and the other half to Aaron Johnson."

"Your friend," said Oskar.

"My half-brother. His lawyer contacted me, and I learned my father's identity."

"And John Johnson," said Oskar. "I did some checking at the Scott County courthouse. He's also your half-brother." Oskar explained how he came to learn of Max's secret.

"Mother doesn't know any of this?" said Oskar.

"She knew nothing of William's death or will or that I knew who he was. She's been through enough, and I didn't want to open old wounds—things she couldn't do anything about but would be painful for her to relive and explain to others. Annie and my friend Patrick know, but I've told no one else," said Max.

"But you've been living a lie all this time. You're not truly German. It's not a big surprise if you look closely at how you live. You're only German when it suits you. You were happy to take that man's inheritance and use it to prop yourself up. And you ignore your relation to John even more than to us. Your true colors aren't as pretty as the ones you project to the world."

"Oskar, please. None of this is easy for me. From the time I was a boy, I felt different and was treated differently by Papa. It made it easier for me to chase the American life. Then when I found out he wasn't my father and that I was a bastard child of a man who raped my mother and paid her off to make me, the problem, go away. How do you think that made me feel? William didn't acknowledge me my whole life and tried to make up for it in his will."

"The nice sum you inherited must have made it somewhat more tolerable," said Oskar.

"I didn't care about the money. I only received a fraction

of it. William's brother-in-law owed me the rest, but he went bankrupt when the war came. Most of what I did get, Annie and I gave to charity. We never felt right about taking it."

"The courthouse records said there were slaves in the estate?" said Oskar.

"There were."

"Besides John?"

"Yes, there were others," Max said with a painful recollection.

"What happened to them?"

"I tried to emancipate them as part of the estate settlement. I tried everything, but William's brother-in-law insisted they stay on his plantation."

"How could you?" said Oskar. "Benefit from the sale of another human life?"

"I tried. There was nothing I could do."

"You freed John. Why not the rest?" said Oskar.

"No. William manumitted John in his will. Annie and I brought him to Cincinnati to help him get his start."

"But you wouldn't acknowledge him as your blood relative?" said Oskar.

"How could I? That would have meant I had to tell everything. William, the rape, to explain how I was related to John," said Max.

"And it might have hurt your reputation in town. The councilman has a Black brother. Might have hurt your business's bottom line too, isn't that right?"

"Yes, people would judge. Most in this city aren't open-minded enough to accept it. Think about it. Even I had trouble accepting John. I grew up with the same beliefs."

"I used to respect you," said Oskar.

"I had to get to know John," said Max. "I had never known a Black man before. I held the common belief that Black men were a race below ours, but by knowing him, I learned differently. I changed my politics and my stance on the war."

"How does John feel about his brother not

acknowledging his heritage? Not fully acknowledging him?" said Oskar.

"I don't know."

"I know a little bit about how it feels, Max. At least you call me your brother, even though you've suppressed your German heritage when it was convenient. I can't imagine how he feels to have you pretend he's someone else. I spent the last year living among the freedmen and trying to help them. In addition to education and employment, they're trying to gain dignity and be accepted. You say you've helped your brother John, but by hiding your relation to him, you're refusing to see him as the person he is. You're keeping him in his place as much as the men in Kentucky who won't look him in the eye on the street."

"Oskar, it's complicated."

"No, it's not," said Oskar. "I thought you aspired to follow the teachings of Christ. Whatever you did for one of these least brothers of mine, you did for me."

"I have a family. I have to consider my reputation. Some day, when you have a family, you'll understand. Oskar, please," said Max.

"It's not *my* forgiveness you should be asking for."

With a pained look, Max said, "Will you keep this to yourself? Please? Not tell the family. For Mother's sake?"

"Sure, Max. It's your cross to bear." Oskar turned and walked back to the saloon.

Max collected himself and rejoined his family at their table. He attempted to remain nonchalant. Oskar ignored Max, signaling that an unresolved rift between the brothers remained, and the family tread carefully. After several beers, Max and Annie said goodnight and walked to the stables to retrieve their carriage.

They began the ride home. Annie took Max's arm. "What happened between you and Oskar?"

"Oskar learned of my father and my relationship to Aaron and John," Max said.

"How did he come to know about it?"

"He met a judge in central Kentucky who heard William's probate case. He recognized the Mueller name and asked Oskar if he was related to me. From there, Oskar made inquiries at the courthouse."

"I take it the conversation didn't go well. What was Oskar's reaction?" said Annie.

"Sadness for Mother. Contempt for me for keeping it a secret from the family and denying full acceptance of John. He also shamed me for not securing the release of the slaves at Given House."

"You tried," said Annie.

Max nodded.

"I'm sorry. I'm sure it was a difficult conversation. Is he going to tell the rest of the family?"

"I don't think so," said Max.

They rode on in silence.

"What was I supposed to do?" said Max. "I agonized over whether to tell them. I did what I thought was the right thing at the time. It would have only brought sadness for Mother."

Annie squeezed his arm. "I know you did. I remember how distraught you were."

"He accused me of putting my interests and success ahead of my morals. He believes I subjugate John by not openly recognizing my kinship."

"You do what you believe is right. That's all any of us can do," said Annie.

"Do you think it's right?" asked Max.

"Do you honestly want to know what I think?"

"Of course."

"I think that in your position, you must protect your reputation. Just like when you married me, you were cautious about how much you shared about my women's movement positions in order to be elected. Over time, you have let that guard down, and you're now comfortable defending your position on women's rights while balancing it with limiting any offense to the electorate. I think you're still testing the waters on your public positions on the Negroes' place. I think inside, you're there, but you're still cautious."

"So you're joining Oskar in 'beat down Max day'?"

"No. You asked me what I thought. I'm telling you what I see. You accept and respect John, but I don't think you're comfortable giving all Negroes the same position," said Annie.

"Why do you say that?"

"You haven't embraced his family. You haven't hired any Black men at the shop."

"I have trouble finding white men with the skills to do the work, let alone a Black man. My workmen would struggle to accept a Black man," said Max.

"If you were ready, you would have found an opportunity to hire a Black man and make it work. I'm not judging you. You are a good man. One of the most righteous I have ever known. Sometimes, your ambition blinds you to what your morals tell you to do. You're not the first man to suffer from it. I've met many politicians in the last year that are guilty of the same."

"I'm part of that lot now? The politicians?" said Max.

"I'm afraid, councilman, you are. But every day is a new opportunity to change."

#

They arrived home, and Max delivered the horse and carriage to the groom in the carriage house. He undressed and joined Annie in bed.

"It's so nice to have you home," he said, putting his arms around her. They easily reclaimed the familiar comfort of each other that they both missed when they were apart.

Afterward, Max dozed off while Annie lay with her thoughts.

He awoke and sensed her restlessness. "You can't sleep?" he said.

"No. I learned to sleep anywhere in Kansas, but I have a lot on my mind," said Annie.

"Will you tell me?"

"When I come home, I love being with you and Lizzie. The simple things. Sharing a meal, reading the newspaper together. Watching her paint or play the piano. But worries about work find me. I feel I should be back in New York doing something about them."

"Learning to push those thoughts of work away when I'm home with Lizzie is something I've trained myself to do, but I know it's not easy," said Max.

"*The Revolution* is struggling," said Annie. "Mr. Train disappeared as quickly as he arrived. He only delivered a fraction of the money he promised to fund the newspaper. He went off to England soon after we started it up. Word is he's been jailed for supporting Irish independence. He's a bit of a lunatic."

"He was an unlikely partner for the Association. I thought Elizabeth and Susan had more sense than to partner with someone like him," said Max.

"Lucy and I were against it, but there's no stopping those two. I understand why they did it. At the time, they had little support from the establishment. He was a man who drew an audience, and he was willing to write checks—for a while, anyway. *The Revolution* has given us a platform to cover women's issues from our perspective. Most newspaper editors have stopped covering women's suffrage and focused solely on the vote for the Negro. Elizabeth, as editor, has full control of the content. Lately, though, she seems more radical in some of her articles, alienating some of our subscribers. We've grown circulation to three thousand across the country. With some of her positions on marital relations and divorce, I think she's damaging our ability to expand our audience."

"Some of her articles stretch the bounds of what readers are comfortable with," said Max.

"I tend to agree with the ones she's written on women's rights, but lately, she has become more combative against the abolitionist movement that promotes suffrage for the freedmen. That is what's most troubling to me.

"She no longer supports universal suffrage for all. She will not support giving the vote to one more man before women get the vote. It's creating a divide within the movement and hurting us."

"How so?" said Max.

"Some of her comments have been hurtful to Black men and women, saying things like Sambo doesn't have the intelligence that enlightened women do. She's angered men like Frederick Douglass, who has made statements against her positions. Lucy and Henry are this close to creating a separate organization from the AERA. Lucy's confided in me that she's considering starting a competing, more conservative newspaper."

"It must be stressful to be in the middle of all that," said Max.

"It is. I agree with Lucy and Henry's positions, but I feel allegiance to Elizabeth. Like turning away from her would be turning from my father."

"No, let go of that," he said.

"We're coming to a critical point in the lobbying for the Fifteenth Amendment. Elizabeth has withdrawn support because the current wording only prohibits denying the vote based on race, color, or previous enslavement. It doesn't explicitly grant the right to vote to anyone—man or woman—putting the real power back in the hands of the states. She has put a stake in the ground that it is all or nothing. I don't agree; I'll take any progress over nothing."

"You're wise in your strategy," said Max. "You've come a long way."

"How do you mean?"

"I remember a young woman who made a scene at the Burnet House Hotel because they wouldn't allow you in the gentlemen's dining room. It was all or nothing for you back then."

Annie laughed. "You taught me the value of regulating my passion. We've been a good team, you and I."

"We are," he agreed.

#

John and his family spent the next three days worrying and praying for Harry. The newspaper reported seventy-five casualties from the *United States*. All but four aboard the *America* survived. John learned from the packet company office that the survivors were taken by steamboat to Louisville. He prayed that Harry was not one of the four lost.

Arriving home after work the following day, John found Harry sitting with Martha and Jenny at the table. They celebrated his safe return, and Harry gave them a complete account of the accident and rescue.

"I don't have a job no more," said Harry.

"Can't they put you on another boat?" said John.

Harry shook his head. "The company only had three steamboats running the route. Two of them sunk. Only the *General Lytle* is left. Most of the *United States* crew died, but I'm going up against all the other men on the *America* for the remaining jobs. Most of them are white men."

"What about other steamship companies?" said John.

"I don't know any. I can try and get work on the levee, but even those jobs are hard to come by," said Harry.

"Don't you worry about a job," said Jenny. "You let yourself rest for a few days. There's time for that."

"He has to find a job," said John. "What's he going to do all day, sitting around here? I'll ask around. We'll find you something."

CHAPTER 27

Cincinnati – Spring 1869

Max sat with the mayor in his office.

"The Red Stockings are getting quite a bit of national coverage. They're having another winning season," said Max. "They're a valuable asset for the city."

"*The Enquirer* described Harry Wright as a baseball Edison," said Mayor Wilstach.

"He seems to be adept at both finding players that can win and coaching them on the field, but I hear he's struggling to make the numbers work."

"Is it bad?" said the mayor.

"Rumor has it that the club is in financial peril. They haven't figured out how to make the economics work. Becoming the first all-professional team has made them winners, but proven to be very expensive."

"Maybe we should help," said the mayor. "The Red Stockings are nationwide promotion for the city."

"Use public funds to prop up a private sports enterprise?" said Max. "I think most taxpayers would find that unacceptable, given the city's other needs."

"What if we invested in the Union grounds? Made it free for all walks of life to attend the games?"

"The fans would like that, but I don't see how that helps the economics of the club. They count on gate revenue to pay the players."

"Let's think more about it," said the mayor. "I'm meeting with the club president, Mr. Champion, again next week. I want to help. The Red Stockings have become the pride of the city. Champion has proposed flooding the Union grounds' field in winter to create a skating rink to generate more revenue. Maybe we can help with that."

"It's a creative idea but doesn't sound like enough. I have a friend who is a club member. He says that the club keeps asking for more money from the members. At some point, they're going to say *enough*."

"On another topic," said the mayor. "I've been thinking about the growth the city is experiencing. The building of new houses in the suburbs is unprecedented. It's good for all of us, but we must invest in the city services to keep up. Those suburban streets need sewers, street car lines, and parks. Our new water reservoir can't come soon enough, but that project is estimated to cost over a million dollars. All these things will take money we don't have."

"Are you thinking of an increase in the tax?" said Max.

"Not politically viable," said the mayor. "Not if I want to be reelected. What do you think about increasing the city's debt to finance some of these projects?"

"If we do it responsibly, limit the bonds to reasonable debt payments, then yes. But we have to include something for everyone, not just those building homes in the suburbs. The relief union's needs are increasing, and merchants' donations are down. Can we increase the city's contributions to relief? The city also has to look out for working men and hard-up people."

"I realize they vote too, and I suspect more will soon," said the mayor.

"And it's the right thing to do. What about a free library?"

The mayor looked at Max quizzically. "Books?"

"Yes, provide access to books to further the education of everyone. Books shouldn't be a luxury for the privileged class who can afford a subscription."

"We've got the reading room. What more do we need?"

said the mayor.

"We need to adequately fund and expand it so it's accessible to everyone."

"Are you suggesting a public library for both Coloreds and whites?"

"Yes," said Max. "Why should there be a distinction? We all need to educate ourselves."

"Many people in this town don't want to rub elbows with that kind."

"We've got to stop thinking like that," said Max. "I'm talking about a new library for people who can't afford a membership at the Mercantile or other private libraries. I recognize the privileged of the city won't mix with the lower classes, but the lower classes should have access to this benefit, regardless of their color. Supplement the good work we're doing with schools. It's an investment in our citizens."

"Maybe we can find some benefactors to help establish it. But it will take annual funding to operate it. I question its priority," said the mayor. "We need a new building to house the city offices."

"I don't think the timing for that is right," said Max. "That doesn't help the working people of this city who have real needs right now."

"Look at this place," said the mayor, motioning around his office. "It's a small step up from a log cabin. It doesn't project the aura of one of America's great cities."

"I don't see it making a difference in our prosperity."

"Max, you don't think big enough. People who invest want to invest in success. We have to project success in all aspects. Mark my words. We'll get the new city building the Queen City warrants."

"I'll support you, but it's not foremost on my list of priorities," said Max. "Remember our discussion about a grand industrial exposition?"

"Yes, what's the latest on that?" said the mayor.

"The Ohio Mechanics Institute put together a committee to evaluate the idea. We sent out a survey to four hundred potential exhibitors. The response was tepid. We only received twenty-six responses. The committee recommended we table the project."

"I don't understand. Last year, the Woolen Manufacturers' Association had a successful convention in David Sinton's building. It brought hundreds of visitors to town."

"I'm not giving up on the idea, but deferring it. The economic climate may be better next year.

"With Grant in office, I'm hoping the whole country returns to prosperity. We can put all this fighting over reuniting the country behind us," said the mayor.

"Amen to that," agreed Max.

#

Max stood with George Gray, his chief designer and foreman, looking at plans for an addition to the Miller Industries factory.

"It's a lot of space," said George. "Almost three hundred square feet. What are we going to do with it all?"

"George, in two years, we could use double this space if our orders continue to grow at the current rate," said Max.

"It just seems like a lot of money. Aren't you worried? What if the growth doesn't materialize? Won't it bankrupt you?"

"That's not my concern. This has been our best year for sales and profits ever. The machines we make are building the future for industries all across the West."

"What are you worried about then?" asked George.

"I am concerned we won't find enough men with the skills to work on the new machines. I'm working with the Mechanics Institute to develop new training classes, but I'm worried the demand will come before the workers."

Two men dressed in dirty work clothes knocked on the door to the office.

"Come in," said Max. "You're the men from the

Cincinnati Lumber Company in Sedamsville?"

"Yes, sir. I'm John Yost, the foreman. This is Cyrus. He runs our millwork operation. Mr. Gazley sent us to talk about the bat."

"Right. Mr. Gazley said you need a special lathe to make a prize of some sort?" said Max.

"It's for the Red Stockings," said Yost. "Mr. Gazley wants to present the team with an award for their season on behalf of the company. He said you'd be willing to donate the use of one of your lathes to make it. The ones in our shop aren't big enough to make what he has in mind."

"We're happy to help promote the Red Stockings," said Max. "Have you been to a game?"

"No, but we hear plenty about them," said Yost. "Papers say they're tearing it up in the East."

"Some are saying it's not fair, with them being all paid players," said Cyrus, the laborer. "No other teams are doing that. Like a lot of things—if you have the cash…"

Yost retorted, "Professional teams are the way it should be. It gives the common man a shot at playing the game—don't have to be from one of those snooty universities. It's turning the game into every man's game."

Max interrupted their banter. "The rule change allowing professional players has certainly captured the public's attention. Now, tell me about the project Mr. Gazley has in mind."

"He wants us to make a baseball bat to present to the team at the exhibition game against the picked nine when the club returns from their road trip next week. There's going to be a tribute celebration for the team. We've got an ash tree trunk in the lumber yard. The boss wants it turned into a twenty-eight-foot baseball bat that he'll present to the team at the game."

Max whistled. "That's huge. Do you have a drawing with the specifications?"

Yost handed over a rough sketch of the bat. George and Max studied it. The bat was twenty-seven and a half feet long and eighteen inches in diameter at its bat end. The words *Champion Bat* and all the players' initials were to be carved into it.

"What's the estimated weight?" asked Max.

"We figure it will be over a thousand pounds. The tree will be a third more than that before we start turning it. You got a lathe that can handle that heft?"

"Sure. We can make some adjustments to one of ours to handle the length. George, can you take them downstairs and introduce them to our lathe man? You two can discuss the specifics of making this with him."

#

At the adjournment of the city council meeting, Mayor Wilstach led the council members outside to a line of carriages on the street. The men rode from downtown to Henry Probasco's residence, Oakwood, which stood on twenty-nine acres, just south of the Miami and Erie Canal in the Clifton suburb. The driveway curved from the iron gates on Lafayette Avenue through the grounds, past benches, fountains, lakes, and landscaped gardens. The massive limestone and sandstone Norman revival home looked more like a castle than a residence, with its arched entryway, tall windows, ornate stone carvings, and cross-adorned turret.

Waitstaff took their coats in the foyer. A chunky, hand-carved, wooden staircase matched thick wooden carved doors and window frames and inlaid wooden ceilings. Henry and his wife Julia greeted their guests and gave them a tour of their home, which displayed an impressive collection of art and an extensive book collection in its library.

Councilman Nate Bartlett whispered to Max, "Who knew hardware was such a lucrative business."

"All those fittings and screws I purchased over the years paid for this. It's incredible," Max whispered back.

The party moved to the main hall, where Probasco unveiled a bronze model of the fountain that the artist had shipped from Germany. The statue was entitled *Genius of Water*, a homage to the many forms of the blessings of water. The replica detailed the statue's three tiers and the numerous individual bronze figures—each a work of art telling its own story. At the top, a robed lady stood with outstretched arms to allow water to flow from them down to the middle basin. She rested on a platform adorned with the inscription "To the People of Cincinnati."

Perched one level below the lady, four groups of figures adorned water basins, each depicting uses of water: a farmer seeking rain, a Venus-like mother and child at the bath, a daughter and her aged father, a man with a bucket to extinguish a fire. On the lower level, figures of children enjoying water—fishing, skating, and seeking shells on the beach, adorned the outside corners and housed the drinking fountains. It evoked the finest statues from European masters.

Probasco provided an update on construction in Germany and then shared a drawing of the suggested site between Main and Walnut Streets. The rendering made it clear that there was insufficient room for the large fountain in the planned location. He proposed changing the site to the square between Vine and Walnut Streets, currently occupied by the Fifth Street Market House.

"Holy shit," Nate whispered to Max. "He's suggesting we tear down the market house that's been a staple of the community for years. What hubris."

Max whispered, "He brought it to the mayor several weeks ago. The mayor is supportive. The market house is an eyesore. There will be some squawking from the merchants who rent stalls there, but council will approve the move."

Probasco shared several drawings of a proposed "Fountain Square" esplanade to be built in place of the market house with his fountain at its center. A raised oval promenade with trees and lampposts would surround it, creating a new park at the city's center. The men nodded in approval.

The hosts served a light buffet in the dining room before Mayor Wilstach began his remarks. He thanked the Probascos for their hospitality, generosity to the city, and foresight in adding a public fountain to the landmarks that would define Cincinnati as it continued its preeminent place among American cities.

The mayor concluded with, "Let us, in the erection of this magnificent fountain, signify to the country and to the world that Cincinnati is destined to be not only the seat of learning and literature but of high art, the beautiful relics of which are found in the classic lands of Greece and old Rome. Surely, no more honorable or appropriate tribute can be paid to the memory of the late Tyler Davidson than this noble work."

Probasco then spoke of the honor of bringing a work of art to the city that would place the Queen City among the greatest cities in Europe. He was pleased to contribute to making the city more attractive for its residents and visitors by placing the first public fountain to supply clean, fresh drinking water for all.

Probasco closed with, "May we not, then, dedicate the Fifth Street market space, between Vine and Walnut streets, forevermore to the people and their fountain? Let us have running water in the heart of this great city. It will refresh the laborer in the morning as he wends his way to the day of toil. It will slake his thirst in the blazing, sultry heat of noonday. Tear away these dark, damp, disease-creating market buildings, as they are doing in Paris and elsewhere, and give us sunshine, light, air, and water. Shall not the work of German artists, appealing to our German citizens from the fatherland, stimulate them with the desire and hope that we shall continue to beautify and adorn every part of our city?"

CHAPTER 28

Cincinnati – Spring 1869

Harry looked for work for months. Through John's connections, he made repairs and painted walls in the Colored school buildings, but when those jobs were completed, he was again unemployed. He read the want ads in the papers and applied but found most wouldn't hire a Black man. John encouraged him to attend night classes to improve his reading, but Harry found the lessons difficult and lost interest. One evening, instead of going to class, he made his way down to Front Street on the riverfront. He remembered his co-workers on the *America* talking about the saloons where they spent their evenings while in port in Cincinnati.

A host of businesses, hotels, saloons, and brothels situated along the riverfront catered to those who made their living from river-related jobs. Much of this activity remained hidden from the broader community, confined to the blocks along the levee between Broadway and Sycamore.

Harry walked along the portion of Front Street known as "Rat Row" and found a saloon, where he heard piano music and laughter. He stood outside and observed. A group of Irishmen, likely roustabouts from the riverfront, laughing and speaking loudly, went inside. Another white man, then two more, went in. A group of men came out and stumbled down the street. Harry moved on.

He repeated the vetting at the next saloon with the same outcome. The dock men and boat workers either ignored him or looked at him suspiciously, but he drew the same conclusion. This was for white men.

At 7 Front Street, two white women with painted faces stood outside a sign-less building. He kept his eyes on the ground as he walked by.

One of the ladies touched his arm as he passed. "Good evening, friend," one of them said.

Harry looked up and found she was looking directly at him. "Evening ma'am." He nodded and resumed walking.

She grabbed his coat sleeve, "Hey, what's the rush? It's all right. You from one of the riverboats?"

"No, uh, I used to work on the *America* until she sank," said Harry.

"What are you doing in town?" she said.

"I'm just looking for a place to have a drink," said Harry.

"You can have a drink in here. We can also offer you a little company if that's what you want."

"You serve Blacks?" he said tentatively.

"Sure, Miss Pearl welcomes everybody. You want a white girl?"

"No," said Harry. "That would get me arrested."

"We won't tell. A Black girl then?"

"No, I don't. No. I'm just looking for a drink," said Harry. "Just a saloon. Do you know which ones allow Black men?"

"Sure, right next door, here, this one's for Blacks. Just down there, Pickett's Tavern—Mr. Pickett lets anybody in as long as you don't make any trouble."

"Thank you," said Harry, tipping his hat.

He walked to the end of the block and found Pickett's Tavern. He opened the door cautiously to the sound of music and a crowd. He stepped inside and was relieved to see a mixed group of men and women dancing in a large ballroom. Three men played on a stage—one banjo, one fiddle, and one guitar. No one paid any attention to him as he walked around the dance floor's perimeter. Harry smiled, hearing music for the first time since he'd left Canada. The couples on the dance floor finished a quadrille and applauded. Harry watched the dancers for several minutes; they seemed to forget the outside world and their struggles. He noticed a man slide up behind another man and pull several bills from his pocket. Harry checked his own pocket to ensure his money was still there.

Men and women moved up and down the staircases on either side of the room. Harry took the wooden stairs up into a dark hall. Couples stood along the wall, talking, some kissing. He peered into the first room with dining tables. The next room was a packed, noisy tavern with two bars and tables.

He was happy to find half a dozen of his former crewmates from the *America* drinking around a table in the center of the room, accompanied by several white women. He greeted his friends, who responded with shouts and hugs. Harry bought himself a drink and joined them.

"So Harry, what are you doing now?" said Daniel.

"Me, I've done some jobs for the Colored schools. I'm still looking for steady work. What about you two?"

"I'm a drayman for the Hauck & Windisch brewery," said Daniel.

"I'm driving a hack," said Abel.

"Did the packet company hire any of us back?" asked Harry.

"I don't think so," said Daniel. "A few of the boys are working on the docks." He pointed to a crowd of white men around a nearby table, including Greg from the *America*. "Where are you living?"

"I'm staying with my family," said Harry. "My brother, sister, mother, and I are in a house on Gest Street. You?"

"I have a room at a boarding house in Bucktown," said Daniel.

"I move around. Right now, I'm staying with a friend," said Abel.

"It's a lady friend," said Daniel. "Abel may grow roots

now that he ain't always on a boat."

"You ought to come down and meet her sometime. We play pool over at Luke Midas Hall," said Abel.

"I'd like that," said Harry. "I'll do that. I miss you all."

George, a fireman from the *America*, pushed into their circle, each arm around a white woman. "Harry, nice to see you."

"George, you're looking fine. And who are these two ladies?" asked Harry.

"This is Katie and Vickie," said George.

"Harry worked on the steamship with us," said George. "Although he wore a uniform. Sucked up to the ladies and gentlemen."

They all laughed.

"We called him 'the fixer,'" said Abel.

"Why's that?" asked Katie.

"Because he can fix things. Harry was called in to save the day if a railing was loose or a doorknob wouldn't turn."

"Sounds like you're quite handy," said Vickie.

"Harry rubbed elbows with the passengers and with those kinds," said Daniel, pointing at the table of Irishmen.

"Those kinds are brutes," said Katie. "We prefer your type. Not so full of yourselves."

"What do they think of you, hanging around Black men?" asked Harry. "That cause trouble?"

"Those ones don't have any interest in us. They like theirs with ribbons in their hair and mouths that stay shut. They leave us alone, and we leave them alone, and no one talks about what goes on down here," said Katie.

"Where are you from, Harry?" asked Vickie.

"I moved here from Canada last year," said Harry.

"What was Canada like?"

"There was no slavery there, but things were difficult. Just like here, jobs were hard to come by, making it hard to get ahead," said Harry.

Vickie touched Harry's arm as she asked, "Why did you move here?"

Harry began to relax, sensing these girls were comfortable around Black men, maybe even intrigued by them. "After the war, I didn't have to run from the slave catchers anymore. My brother found my mammy and brought her here to Cincinnati. My sister and I came to stay with them."

"That's a really nice story," said Vickie. "I take it your story before Canada wasn't so nice?"

"No, I don't want to talk about that," said Harry.

"Of course, whatever you say," said Vickie. "You want to buy me a drink? Then maybe we can go downstairs and dance?"

"Go on, Harry," said George. "We'll see you later."

#

Harry spent several nights a week on the levee. He stopped going to night classes and church events during the week. He worked occasional odd jobs but stopped seriously looking for employment. John asked him to sit on the front steps with him one evening.

"Harry, I'm concerned about you," John said.

"What are you worried about?" said Harry.

"You've been spending a lot of time down on the riverfront. You're drinking and getting in late, and I don't know what else you're getting into down there. It's not a place for Christian men."

"I'm a grown man. I don't need you fussing over me, telling me how to live my life. I'm not bothering nobody," said Harry.

"You need to find work, Harry," said John.

"I work. I work. I don't put on a smile for whitey, hawking for tips, like you, but I work."

"You need a real job. One that pays you enough money to live on."

"I don't need much," said Harry. "Leave me be."

"It's not right. You are living off of the rest of us. Mammy is working, Martha and me. We're saving money to buy this house, and you're off spending it," said John.

"I work too."

"You're taking money from our savings and blowing it on tobacco and alcohol, and who knows what."

"Is that what this about?" said Harry.

"It's not just the money. It's the kind of folk you're associating with," said John. "The good Lord gave us our freedom, brought us back together, and gave us the chance to build our lives here. We've got to hold ourselves to a high standard and better ourselves. We've got to make the white man respect us by showing him that we are as good or better than he is. You go running around with the wrong crowd, and you bring us all down. You put us right back where he had us before we were free."

"I don't want the white man's respect if it means I have to become like him," said Harry. "You may want that, but I want to be respected as I am. Why do you want to be like them? You think if you get a job, go to church, build your schools and clubs, and do all the things that white men do, you'll be just like them. That's a fool's game. You're a fool. Even with your light skin, they never going to let you be one of them."

"Harry, please," said John. "We can't make progress if we don't try. Sure, we were dealt a sorry hand in life, but we have a chance to improve it. We deserve a better life, but no one is going to hand it to us. We have to stick together and fight for it. God is by our side, be open to his guidance."

"God has abandoned us," said Harry. "We're on our own."

"No, we're not," said John.

"How can you believe that? Our years of bondage at Given House. Now told we're free but left to fight for a living at the bottom of a world of people who still don't see us as worthy. I don't want to live in their world. There ain't nothing there for me. I want to live with my people, on my own terms, or I don't want to live at all."

"I don't believe that," said John. "You're a fighter. You

escaped with Martha to freedom. You saved yourself and all those people on that steamboat. You can stand up. Let God continue to walk by your side. Things are going to get better."

"What do you think's going to make things better? They shot President Lincoln. President Johnson didn't change things. Are you waiting for President Grant now? Nobody gives a lick about us. Look around."

"We have to fight to change things. That's what I'm trying to do. We have people on our side," said John.

"What people? White people don't want us here. You can't change what's in people's hearts," said Harry. "I don't see the point of trying."

John hugged his brother. "I know it's difficult. Please don't give up. We can change people's hearts by showing them ours."

Harry pulled from their embrace. "I'm not like you," he said. "Just let me be." He turned and started down the street.

CHAPTER 29

New York City – Spring 1869

Annie was excited to attend the annual meeting of the American Equal Rights Association, held in Steinway Hall in New York City. Ever since her first Women's Rights Convention in Cincinnati in 1856, she tried to attend regional and national gatherings of like-minded women and men. She always came away energized about the cause.

She sat next to Margaret Longley, a Cincinnati teacher whom she had worked with on some local initiatives. The delegates to the meeting included representatives from organizations across the country. Many were famous suffrage advocates, including Elizabeth Cady Stanton, Susan B. Anthony, Lucy Stone, Antoinette Brown Blackwell, Amelia Bloomer, and Frederick Douglass.

Elizabeth chaired the meeting and opened the session. Lucy Stone gave an executive committee report detailing the petitions and conventions held across the country over the prior year. She noted the successes of the previous year's debates and votes on women's suffrage—an improvement over being discounted or ignored. In addition, state constitutional changes to incorporate women's suffrage had been voted on in several states.

Reverend Octavius Frothingham, a Unitarian abolitionist, opened with a prayer and initial remarks supporting women's suffrage, optimistically noting that suffrage was the remaining question to be decided for women. "She is a teacher, artist, and preacher and has places in the literary and scientific worlds. The one position she does not hold is voter."

The first order of business was the announcement of the officers for the following year.

Mr. Stephen Foster, an abolitionist, stood and objected to Elizabeth Cady Stanton as president because she had publicly repudiated the principles of the Association. He objected to her support for "educated suffrage," declaring he was an enemy of any kind of suffrage other than universal suffrage. "Massachusetts abolitionists cannot cooperate with the society if it elects officers who ridicule the Negro, call the Fifteenth Amendment infamous, and endorse Francis Train."

Henry Blackwell tried to calm the hubbub from Mr. Foster's comment. "*The Revolution* has published unwise things in its pages, but they have severed ties with Mr. Train. I do not think Miss Anthony and Mrs. Stanton mean to antagonize relations between the women and the Negro suffrage questions."

Frederick Douglass stood, and the room quieted as attention focused on the most famous Black abolitionist in the country. "There is no greater name in women's rights and equal rights than Mrs. Stanton, but I have to object to her use of names in *The Revolution*. In her commentary, she has used names such as 'Sambo,' 'the gardener,' and 'the bootblack' that I cannot ignore."

Margaret whispered to Annie, "Did Mrs. Stanton actually write those things? In those words?"

"I'm afraid so," said Annie.

Frederick Douglass continued, "I do not see how anyone can pretend that there is the same urgency in the giving of the ballot to women as to the Negro. With us, the matter is a question of life and death. When women, because they are women, are hunted down through the cities of New York and New Orleans; when they are dragged from their houses and hung upon lampposts; when their children are torn from their arms, and their brains dashed out upon the pavement; when they are objects of insult and outrage at every turn; when they are in danger of having their homes burnt down over their heads; when their children are not allowed to enter schools; then they will have an urgency to obtain the ballot equal to our own."

The audience applauded.

A man shouted, "Is that not all true about Black women?"

Mr. Douglass answered, "Yes, yes, yes; it is true of the Black woman, but not because she is a woman, but because she is Black."

More applause.

Susan B. Anthony stood. "The old anti-slavery school says women must stand back and wait until the Negroes shall be recognized. But we say, if you will not give the whole loaf of suffrage to the entire people, give it to the most intelligent first. If intelligence, justice, and morality are to have precedence in the government, let the question of woman be brought up first and that of the Negro last."

Some in the audience booed while others applauded.

Annie whispered, "They've become somewhat elitist with their positions. This is not good for the cause."

Other speakers stood and enthusiastically stated their positions for either women's or universal suffrage. One gentleman tried to dredge up the tired story that Lucy Stone and Henry Blackwell's marriage was free love. Lucy rebuked the argument as smear politics with no basis.

The meeting was getting nowhere, so Elizabeth redirected the conversation to the Fifteenth Amendment. The room argued over the wording of a resolution that the Association should pass regarding support for it. People began speaking over the top of one another, and the meeting devolved into chaos with hisses and shouting.

Annie leaned over to Margaret Longley. "Is this meeting always so contentious?"

"No, in prior years, there was much more spirit of cooperation. I wonder if this factionalism is due to the heightened importance of the issues. Are we victims of our own success?" said Margaret.

"There are numerous causes, but I'm not proud to be part of it," said Annie. "People show little respect for each other's right to voice their position. I'm saddened to see such lack of decorum and democratic principles."

Elizabeth banged her gavel multiple times, finally restoring order.

Ernestine L. Rose, a popular national figure for women's suffrage and abolition, proposed changing the society's name from the American Equal Rights Association to the Woman's Suffrage Association.

Lucy Stone argued against the name change as it would cause a loss of support from the public and hinder their progress.

A gentleman stood and countered with the name Universal Franchise Association to emphasize that they advocated for universal suffrage as opposed to impartial suffrage—which was taken to apply to men only.

Once again, Elizabeth shut down the discussion by stating that the constitution of the Association required a month's notice before a vote could be taken on a name change.

She then began her remarks to conclude the meeting, hoping to rally the women in the audience. She chastised the men present for disrespectful behavior, which brought some applause. "I propose a monster petition of a million names to the legislature for suffrage. How about it, ladies?" She raised her arms to the audience. They responded with enthusiastic applause. Elizabeth cued the Hutchinson Family, a music group from Chicago, and they began their closing song.

Elizabeth gathered her papers from the podium and moved off stage to the exit without acknowledging any of the women who vied for her attention.

Annie said, "Well, that was a waste of a morning. We accomplished nothing."

"She bolted off that stage like she was late for a train,"

said Margaret.

At the end of the week, a group of leaders from the Association met in the Women's Bureau offices. The annual meeting and after-discussions had made it clear that there were two distinct schools of thought on the suffrage issue, pitting the Republicans and abolitionists against a subset of the leaders of the women's suffrage movement. The assembled ladies created a charter for a new organization called the National Woman Suffrage Association. They debated excluding men entirely but could not get enough to agree, so they compromised by restricting elected officers to women only. Elizabeth was elected president.

The new organization began to meet weekly and worked on plans for a sixteenth amendment giving women the vote. Annie stayed in New York through the summer. She supported the organization's activities, drafting editorials, responding to correspondence, assisting with meeting planning, and participating in discussions with Elizabeth, Susan, and others. Dissension among the ranks continued, and Annie felt less and less comfortable with the organization's direction and the tone set by Elizabeth's callous remarks.

In August, Lucy Stone came to New York and invited Annie to lunch at her hotel.

"How is progress at the NWSA?" asked Lucy.

"We held two conventions over the summer," said Annie. "One in Newport and another in Saratoga. We had large audiences from across the country. We distributed reprints of issues of *The Revolution*. That was good exposure for the paper. I hope some of the women will subscribe. We could use the money."

"You seem discouraged," said Lucy.

"I don't know. I'm not comfortable with many of the positions of the organization. It makes it harder to do the work when my heart isn't fully behind it," said Annie.

"Do you see any softening in Elizabeth and Susan's positions?"

"No, if anything, they're even more determined that they won't support giving the vote to one more person unless women are given the vote first. I don't think that's realistic, given where sentiment is across the nation right now."

"You know I agree with you," said Lucy. "The Fifteenth Amendment will be passed, and Black men will gain the right to vote. Then we'll be right back to where we were before, with women trying to gain suffrage. All she's doing is creating disagreement and disruption, and I don't know if that's her objective or if there's something more to be gained by this splintering off of part of the movement. Do you see it—is there something I'm missing?"

"I'm afraid I don't," said Annie. "I've had several conversations with Elizabeth and tried to get her to justify her rationale, but I haven't been successful. She becomes frustrated with me and even insults me for not seeing it her way. She's started to shut me out of things."

"I'm sorry, dear. It must be difficult," said Lucy.

"Thank you. It is. Elizabeth has been an inspiration for me since I was a teenager. She had a major influence on me and has been a source of motivation for my work, but I can't align with her stance of women first while degrading the Black man. I just can't do that. I can't." Annie started crying.

Lucy reached across the table and took Annie's hand.

"I feel like all of the work I've done to promote equality for all people is for naught. If Elizabeth abandons universal equality, is it right for me to continue fighting?" said Annie, putting her hands over her face and sobbing into them. "I don't know if I can go on."

"It is worth fighting for, and you can," assured Lucy.

"I'm so disillusioned. The days are long, and I struggle to find joy anywhere in them."

"I have a proposition for you," said Lucy. "Henry and I are forming a new organization. The old AERA is dead. We're going to call it the American Woman Suffrage Association. We'll continue the push for universal suffrage by focusing on the states with momentum. The same strategy we've followed. We'll support the Fifteenth Amendment and use it as a stepping stone. Our sole focus will be suffrage. We won't be distracted by some of the other issues Elizabeth continues to push for."

"That's more in line with my position," said Annie. "But I don't know. I feel like I'm betraying Elizabeth."

"I know you have a personal, family connection with her. But I think it's she that has betrayed the principles that you believe in."

Annie pondered Lucy's statement. "I hate to see this division. We're arguing with each other instead of focusing on making progress. It's senseless."

"I know. I wish it were different," said Lucy.

"But I can't go on working with them. I'm so distraught. I'm not productive. I know something needs to change," said Annie.

"We're going to run the organization from Boston. We have been recruiting women and men to be part of it. Henry is going to lead it initially. We could use you. Will you join us?"

"I'd be honored to be a part of it," said Annie.

"Good."

#

One evening, after a meeting of the core group in Elizabeth's parlor, Annie remained with Elizabeth.

"Annie, have you mailed the letter I drafted to the Cincinnati papers yet?" said Elizabeth.

"I'm sorry, but I can't do it," said Annie.

"Why not?"

"You ask me to submit a letter under my good name, known in Cincinnati, that encourages the electorate not to support the Fifteenth Amendment. I can't, in good faith, pen my name to it," said Annie.

"But that's our position," said Elizabeth. "You must set aside your beliefs for the organization's goals."

"I am not a sheep," said Annie. "I'll do no such thing when it violates my moral code. We've discussed this. I've made my position clear."

"I think you're making too much of your moral code. We both know the amendment is going to pass. I'm asking you to register the injustice of the amendment toward the educated women across this nation that remain below the lowest of cretins," said Elizabeth.

"And if it's going to be passed by the men in a majority of the states and become the law of the land regardless, why is this so important?" said Annie.

Elizabeth huffed in frustration, "You can't see the bigger picture. We must position ourselves for the next move—like a chess game. Your father used to talk about what a bright girl you were. I wonder what he would say if he were here today."

Annie was incensed by Elizabeth's trying to guilt her into her position by invoking the memory of her father. Elizabeth knew Annie's strong motivation to please him. Annie said, "He would respect my standing my ground in defense of the humanity and dignity of all people."

Elizabeth considered her comment, then said, "You were just a girl when he passed. He would be disappointed in your rash judgment to recede from our cause."

Annie took several deep breaths to remain composed. "Elizabeth, I have the utmost respect for your accomplishments and leadership. You are a visionary thinker, but some of your ideas tend toward the theoretical. Your work has been limited to philosophizing, authoring, and orating, some of which are so extreme they alienate all but the most radical feminists. They're so far removed from the experience of most women that people have stopped listening. I share your passion for equality and justice for women, but I will not achieve it by pushing down others so we may rise up."

"That's not what I'm doing," stated Elizabeth.

"It is what you're doing and it tarnishes the golden

reputation you've spent your entire life building."

"I will not be lectured to by a young pup who is a feminist in name only."

"You label me and anyone else who disagrees with your flavor of the cause or tactics as uncommitted. That makes you feel elevated but sows dissension amongst those you need to make progress. You're old enough to be my mother. I don't have your years of life to draw from, but I have learned from experience that we can't recklessly push to have it be our way or no way. If we want to effect change, we must push but also know when to relent and take smaller steps toward our goals. In this case, that means continuing to partner with man suffrage advocates to gain suffrage for all."

"I am tired of waiting. Putting men before us," said Elizabeth.

"I am, too," said Annie. "But there is our desire, and there is the reality of the situation. We must accept reality."

"You're taking the wrong path," said Elizabeth.

"You don't know that."

"No one can know exactly what the right path is. We can only do what we feel to be right."

"Agreed," said Annie. She could hear her heart pounding inside her head. "That's why I've decided to join Lucy and Henry in the American Woman Suffrage Organization. I'm grateful for everything you've done for me and for women, but I must follow my heart."

Annie continued to hear only her heartbeats for what seemed like minutes as she and Elizabeth faced off.

Finally, Elizabeth said, "I'm very sorry to hear that. If that's your decision, I wish you well, dear. You've become a force, and you have made a difference. My hope is you will continue to do so."

CHAPTER 30

Fall 1869

After tying up loose ends in New York, Annie took the train to Boston and rented a room from a friend of Lucy Stone in her hometown of Dorchester, Massachusetts. She helped the new American Woman Suffrage Organization establish a mailing list and network of supporters across the country. Max and Lizzie's letters and the anticipation of her visit home sustained her as she worked into the fall.

She traveled home to Cincinnati in early September to conduct an inaugural meeting of a new Ohio women's suffrage organization. Her homecoming was sweet. Max and Lizzie met her at the train station, flowers in hand. They had a quiet dinner at home.

When they were finally alone in their bedroom, Annie and Max embraced tentatively and then released their pent-up passion. Annie guided Max's hands and kisses and pulled him to their bed.

Max fell asleep, and Annie lay thinking. She loved lying next to him, their bodies touching. She took in his scent, something she had tried to conjure in her months alone. Her body was now at peace, but her mind continued to race. She couldn't put the Association's activities out of her mind. Even when she sat with Lizzie and Max that day and should have been enjoying their reunion, she was plagued. The unfinished tasks, the expectations of the Ohio meeting, the constant insistence of universal and woman suffragettes that their position was right, and the elusive goal of equality. She received bursts of satisfaction from victories along the way but was obsessed with the work. It was all-consuming.

She knew her work was crucial and core to her being, but she wanted to be able to enjoy the moments with her family. Lizzie was almost thirteen and looked more like a young woman, no longer a girl. Annie longed to be more involved in her life.

#

Max stepped into Simon Arnold's tavern on Eighth Street and walked along the occupied stools at the bar that spanned the depth of the building. The bartender nodded at Max in recognition.

"Have you seen Patrick Sweeney?" Max asked.

The barkeep nodded to a booth at the back.

"Whose lager are you pouring?" asked Max.

"Moerlein's"

"I'll have one." Max looked around the dimly lit room while he waited. "Thanks," he said, sipping the head off the beer as he walked to the back booth. He found Patrick reading his newspaper.

"Governor," said Patrick standing and embracing Max.

"What is that?" said Max, pointing to a red cloth threaded through several holes onto Patrick's prosthetic hook.

"It's my team spirit." He held out his arm and unfurled the mini flag, revealing a large white *C* in the center. "The Red Stockings are still undefeated. I won't take it off. It might be bad luck and break their streak. They're on course for a perfect season."

"I'm well aware of the success of the nine," said Max. "Technically, though, their season's not perfect. Their game against the Haymakers of Troy, New York, was a tie."

"Such a stickler for details. Enjoy their success."

"I am. They're bringing good press to the city and lifting

spirits across town."

"There now. Will you join me for another game soon? They've only a dozen or so left in the season," said Patrick.

"We'll see. That thing looks ridiculous," said Max.

"It's my good luck charm."

"It's a filthy rag. Have Molly give it a washing."

"I told you I'm not taking it off. What's new with you?"

"Annie's home," said Max.

"For good?"

"No, for a convention here in town. She's worked with women across the state to form an Ohio Woman Suffrage Association. They're meeting today to vote on their constitution and kick things off."

"Good for her."

"Patrick," said Max.

"I'm happy for you. Your wife will sleep in your bed tonight. As it should be."

Max took a drink of his beer. "I want you to consider doing something for me."

Patrick eyed him suspiciously. "You've never asked me for anything. Ever that I can think of."

"Then you're due. Will you consider something?"

"Yes, for my emasculated friend. What do you need?"

Max ignored the jab. "Are you familiar with the Peter Claver Society?"

"I read about it in the *Catholic Telegraph*. Our pastor has made appeals from the pulpit repeatedly. It's evidently a priority for Archbishop Purcell and his brother, the Vicar General."

"It is. Will you join?"

Patrick made groaning noises and shook his head in hesitancy.

"Come on," said Max.

"Do we need another Black school in town?"

"Yes, we do. And this one is a Catholic school. Right now, there are freedmen coming from the South that were attending mass on their plantations, and they don't have a

Catholic parish to turn to. The white Catholic churches haven't been very welcoming, so they're joining protestant churches. How would you feel if new Irishmen came to town and didn't have a Catholic church to join, so they became Protestants? We must give them a place to feel at home in the faith."

Patrick groaned some more.

"We started the parish and school to fill the void. My brother, Oskar, is running the school now. The church is $3,000 in debt. We're asking men to join the Peter Claver Society to support St. Ann's. This is not just another charity; it's a moral obligation that we Catholics have to spread the ministry right here in our community. We send missionaries around the world to convert people, yet there are seeking souls right here in our city."

"How much?" asked Patrick.

"To join the society, we're asking for one dollar per week. For one hundred dollars, you're a lifetime member. Come on. If you don't join, I will ask Father Hill or Father Weninger from St. Xavier to reach out to you personally. You don't want to have to take a meeting with one of them, do you?"

"Sic the old Jesuits from school on me. You're relentless. If I agree, will you come to a baseball game with me?"

"Yes."

"Fine, then. I'll join," said Patrick.

"Great, you're a good Catholic man."

"You've always been there to make sure I was." Patrick took a drink from his glass. "I saw Brian McManus yesterday. He had some disturbing news. About Aaron."

"What about him?" said Max.

"Some vigilantes, the Ku Klux Klan. Last fall, they burned his plantation house to the ground."

"Oh, Lord, that's terrible. Why'd they go after his house?" said Max.

"It wasn't just his house, I'm afraid," said Patrick, hesitating. "He was in it. He died in the fire."

Max closed his eyes, recalling the fire at the Eichen Garten that killed his stepfather and youngest sister. He had to identify their charred remains for the coroner. The smell of their burned bodies came back to him. He let out a long slow breath as he thought of his half-brother subjected to a similar fate.

"I'm sorry," said Patrick. "He was our classmate, but I know he was your kin."

"What about Mary and his children?"

"No, they were up East, visiting her family."

"Thank God," said Max. "How? Why?"

"Brian didn't have all the specifics, but the word was Aaron had taken over a plantation and was running it, employing freedmen, and doing it well, better than many of the neighboring farms. He was elected state representative with the support of the freedmen who worked for him. The locals didn't appreciate his successes. They torched him."

"Jesus," said Max. "How can they let men take things into their own hands like that? Where's the law?"

"It's a different world down there. You read the papers. If it weren't for President Grant's sending troops to the South, those boys would restart the war to put things back like they were."

"I hoped we were past all that."

"Not down there," said Patrick.

"Poor Mary. I wonder what she'll do," said Max.

"Brian said she's here in town to settle things and sell their house, but she's moved up East with her parents. There's a memorial mass on Friday at St. Xavier. I thought you should know since he's family."

"Aaron and I are related by blood, but we never really became family," said Max. "Aaron was a shit. From the time we were in school, he treated me like dirt because of my heritage. His treatment of John and his selling arms to the Confederates during the war; the man had a troubled soul."

"Yeah, he was a slippery one," said Patrick.

"I don't wish his fate on anyone, though," said Max. "What those men did to him. But I won't miss his presence here on earth. I'll pray for his soul."

"It could probably use your prayers," said Patrick. "To Aaron's soul." He lifted his glass in a toast.

#

After meeting with Patrick, Max walked to the Pike Opera House and sat at the back of the evening session of the inaugural convention of the Ohio Woman Suffrage Association. Nearly one thousand people, mostly women, crowded the room. After a full day of meetings, the air was heavy, and the open windows supplied only humid September air.

Max surveyed the people on the stage. He recognized Lucy Stone and Henry Blackwell, Susan B. Anthony, Mrs. Leander Crall, wife of an advertising agent Max had done business with, and Mrs. Elias Longley, wife of *The Weekly Chronicle* newspaper editor, and Annie. The rest were faces he did not recognize, presumably women from other Ohio cities who had worked with Annie to form the new organization.

Max could barely hear Susan B. Anthony over the chatter and shifting of chairs in the audience. When she turned toward him, he caught her words. She scolded those politicians who opposed women's suffrage and declared a warning that men from both political parties would regret their stance once women had the vote. The crowd cheered as she pounded the podium with her fist. She concluded with an appeal to form committees in every district in the state to create petitions to bring to the national meeting in Washington in December for the introduction of a Sixteenth Amendment for women's suffrage. The audience cheered again.

Another woman took the stage and denounced several common objections to women's suffrage. "To give every woman the vote will not debase womanhood as these men claim. That is not a rational fear. Instead, it will elevate politics as women's moral influence counters men's natural instincts."

The convention chair rose and took the woman's hand, and they raised arms together, inciting the audience to further applause. The chair thanked the committees for their work, the audience for attending, and guests Susan B. Anthony, Henry Blackwell, and Lucy Stone for joining the meeting. "We have had a productive meeting, ratified our organization's constitution, and elected our officers. We have accomplished much, and we have so much yet to achieve. It will take all women, from all states and all local and national organizations, to achieve woman suffrage and make our government what it is in theory—a government of the people!"

As the crowd applauded, the chair signaled a small band that began playing, and the entire room broke into a chorus of the Doxology hymn. The women hugged, some cried, and they exited the hall in enthusiastic conversation and laughter. Max watched the attendees file out, and once the aisle to the stage was clear, he made his way forward and found Annie in the dwindling crowd.

They walked to Max's shop and retrieved their carriage. Annie relayed the meeting's events as they drove home.

"You're so quiet," Annie said. "What's on your mind?"

"I learned some bad news today," he said. "Aaron. He was killed in a fire at his plantation house last year."

"Oh, my, that's awful," she said. "How did it happen?"

"A group of Ku Klux Klan set fire to his house. He was inside."

"Oh, Max. That's terrible."

Max turned his face away from her to hide his tears, his guard down in her presence.

Annie put an arm around him. "Max, I'm sorry."

"I can't help but think about what it must have been like for Aaron. To be burned to death. He was a flawed man, but he didn't deserve this. No one does. There's still so much animosity. How do we end it?"

"I don't know," said Annie.

Max wiped his misted eyes with his sleeve. "There's a mass on Friday. Will you come with me to support Mary and his children?"

"Of course. We should ask them back to our house afterward. I'll make the arrangements. Will you invite John and his family?"

"I don't know. That could be awkward," said Max.

"This situation may warrant you putting your discomfort aside. For John's sake, even for Mary's. John stood by Aaron's family even when Aaron didn't deserve it. They should be allowed to grieve together."

Max ran his fingers through his hair several times.

"What are you afraid of?" said Annie.

"People's reaction to having John and his family there. It may raise questions."

"This is an opportunity to chip away at the wall. Stop waiting."

Max closed his eyes. "I know you're right."

"Let go of your fears," she said.

CHAPTER 31

Cincinnati – Fall 1869

Max entered William Watson's barber shop on Third Street. William looked up from shaving his client. "Good day, Mr. Mueller. You back already? You were just in last week."

"Good afternoon, William. I was hoping to talk to John," said Max.

"He's in the back." William sent the young boy sweeping to get John.

"Max," said John, walking toward the front of the shop. "You need a shave today?"

"No, thanks. There's something I wanted to discuss. Do you have a few minutes?"

"Sure."

"Can you take a walk with me?" asked Max.

John retrieved his coat, and they walked to the riverfront and sat on a bench in front of one of the stores overlooking the public landing.

"I have some disturbing news. About Aaron."

"Oh?" said John.

"Aaron was killed in a fire at his plantation house. A group of Klansmen set fire to it, while he was sleeping."

"You sure?"

"Yes. Mary's in town to settle his affairs here. I saw her yesterday." Max relayed the story.

"Hmm. That's awful. A shame," said John. "The Lord

sure works in mysterious ways. Klan burning up white men. I don't try to make sense of it anymore."

"I can't make sense of it either," said Max. "Pointless killing of men. Mary said Aaron was hated by most of their neighbors for his success and for taking over the plantation when the owner ran out of money. He was doing pretty well at farming. He had built a good rapport with the freedmen working for him. They helped elect him to the legislature. The locals couldn't stand to see Aaron's success."

John nodded.

Max said, "A couple of rogue men allowed to take Aaron's life, devastate his family."

"It's not just a couple of men," said John.

"Well, we don't know how many it was. We need to root them out and hold them accountable."

"It's everywhere. Across the South, in the North. Even here, in Cincinnati," said John.

"No, we don't allow them here," said Max.

"You don't see it. They're here, amongst us," said John.

Max looked at John with a puzzled expression.

"It takes the killing of a white man you knew for you to realize it," said John. "Hundreds of Black men and women are being harassed and killed across the South. Those that can are leaving. Many are coming here. They're escaping the vigilantes with torches and nooses, but what they find here is not the freedom they hoped for. It's worlds better than before, but our freedom doesn't look like your freedom, Max. We face potential hatred in every white person we meet."

Max took in John's perspective. It was the first time John ever called Max out for his position. "I'm sorry, John. I get caught up in my own world. I'm sorry."

John softened. "You don't have to be sorry. You do what you can. We're a long way from true freedom. We need you to keep doing whatever you can for us."

Max nodded. "There is a mass for him on Friday at St. Xavier. Mary would be happy to have you and your family there. Afterward, we're inviting his friends and family to our house for lunch. I hope you'll come."

#

After the memorial mass, friends and family gathered at Max and Annie's house. Annie had caterers serve food from the dining room table. The guests milled about in the parlor and music room and spilled out onto the back lawn overlooking the city. Lizzie entertained the children with games in the carriage house. As the afternoon faded, the guests dwindled to Mary, John, and Max's families.

Max and Mary stood together outside.

"It was a nice mass," said Max. "Father said some nice things about Aaron."

"He was very charitable," said Mary. "Everyone was so kind today. It reminded me of how much we missed living here. We never felt welcome in Mississippi."

"It must have been difficult for you and the children."

"It was. It's almost over. David Janitz at Aaron's old firm is going to take care of selling our house here. The children and I are settled in Massachusetts. It's a comfort to be near my family."

"I'm so sorry Mary. That you've had to go through all this and now go on without him," said Max.

"You're so kind," she said. "Thank you for all you've done—today and before."

"Well, I caused some heartache for you over the years, too," said Max. "Turning Aaron into the Union army. I know that was hard on you."

"I can't blame you for that. Aaron brought that on himself. My husband tried to be a good man, but he let his ambition get in the way sometimes."

"Annie has told me I suffer from the same. I think all men struggle with that," said Max.

Mary looked down into the city. "He thought you were above that. He admired your ability to live according to your principles."

"Oh, I don't think he admired me," said Max.

"He did, but he also resented you sometimes because he couldn't live up to your standards. He was a complicated man. It must have been confusing for him to grow up the son of a Southern belle and a Northern businessman. I know he was uncomfortable with the idea of slavery, but his mother's family believed that the slaves on their plantation were born to serve them. His father had different ideas. By the time we moved to Mississippi, I think Aaron accepted that slavery was wrong. That's what I want to believe about him anyway."

"Many in this country have taken a long time to come to that conclusion. Unfortunately, there are still many who haven't," said Max.

Max's mother, Katharina, and John's mother, Jenny, sat in the corner of the music room, watching their families and making occasional small talk. Katharina, who immigrated to and lived in the insular Over-the-Rhine German neighborhood for thirty-five years, still struggled to follow English conversations.

Jenny said, "Your son Max, he has a kind heart and a soul of an angel. He and Annie have been good to my family. When William died, and Max met John at Given House, Max treated John better than Aaron did. They're an unlikely lot. Three boys, three mommas, one daddy, and William dying brought them all together."

Katharina picked up on the name William. She had never discussed William's rape of her or the identity of Max's father with anyone other than her deceased husband and Max. "William?" she asked.

"I understand he took to you like he did me." said Jenny.

Katharina said, "William is John's father?"

"Yes," said Jenny, "And Max's."

Katharina put her hand over her mouth, and her eyes widened with realization. "No, No, No. Shh. Shh." She put her finger to her mouth, indicating silence and shook her head.

Jenny said, "It's all right, dear. We had no say in the

matter. He took what he wanted. Left us to raise our sons."

"No," Katharina repeated. "Say nothing." Katharina rose and went in search of her daughter, Helene.

Jenny rose and followed her. "Katharina, it's all right."

Katharina called into the parlor, "Helene, Helene."

Annie heard Katharina's distress and saw her movements with Jenny following. "Katharina, what is it?"

"Helene, Helene," cried Katharina.

"Max," Annie called. "Come in here, your mother."

Max entered the parlor, followed by Oskar, Helene, John, and Martha.

"What is it, Mother?" said Max.

Katharina began speaking to Max in German; only the Muellers could understand what she was saying. Katharina pointed at Jenny.

Jenny tried to speak above Katharina. "What is she saying? I didn't mean to upset her."

Katharina said in German, "She said she knows William, the man who was your father. She says William was John's father too. Is this so? Do you know this?"

Max replied in German, "Mother, yes. She speaks the truth. I have learned William Johnson was my father. He was also John's father—and Aaron's."

"And Aaron's?" Katharina put her hands to her cheeks, then covered her eyes.

"Mother, there's no shame. It was not your fault. It was William."

"How do you know this?" said Katharina.

"What are they saying?" said Jenny. "What's the matter?"

Knowing the family secret, Oskar said, "My mother didn't know of William Johnson's other children or that Max knew who he was. This is a surprise to her. Please, let's let them have privacy." Oskar guided them all out of the room, leaving only Max and Katharina.

"I don't understand," said Katharina. "What is she saying? Why does she know this?"

"Mother, Mother, please. Calm down. I will explain," said

Max.

He sat her in a chair. He explained how he learned of William after his death, the will, the inheritance, John, and Aaron. "I didn't tell you because I didn't want to cause you any pain. It is in the past."

"When did you learn this?" she asked.

"About ten years ago," said Max.

"Did you know him?"

"William? No."

"You knew all this time? Who did you tell?" Katharina said.

"Only Annie and Oskar knew," said Max.

"And these people know?"

"Yes. They knew William. They were all slaves on William's plantation. John was his son."

Katharina put her hand in front of her mouth and whispered, "He made his son a slave?"

"Yes," Max nodded.

Tears streamed down Katharina's face. She closed her eyes.

When she opened them, she saw Max's face, tears forming in his eyes too.

"I'm sorry," he said.

She hugged him. "My son. My son." She kissed him on the cheek.

Katharina collected herself and told Max she wanted Helene to take her home.

She put on her overcoat with Oskar and Helene by her side, doting on her. They started for the front door.

"Wait," Katharina said. She went into the music room, where Jenny, John, and Martha sat. The others followed.

Katharina approached Jenny. She took Jenny's hands in hers. "I'm sorry. I didn't know."

Jenny said, "It's all right. I didn't know either."

Katharina took Martha's hands and smiled at her. She moved to John, who stood. Katharina took his hands, stood on her toes, and kissed his cheek. She gripped his hands with both of hers and forced a smile.

#

Max and Annie sat at their dining room table over breakfast the following day.

Annie looked up from her newspaper to find Max gazing at her.

"What?" she said.

"I'm just happy to have you here," he said, smiling. He took her hand.

"It's nice to be home. To be where I feel I belong, not just visiting. And surrounded by people who truly care about me," said Annie.

"Your co-campaigners don't show you love as I do?" said Max.

"No one loves me as you do," she said. "Lucy is a dear, and so are the other women, but I'm growing weary of living out of a bag. Boston is a bustling city, but I don't know the number of people that I did in New York. Bostonians tend to stick more to themselves. They all have families and circles of friends. I'm lonely there."

Max cracked a smile.

"What?" she said.

"Nothing."

"What?" she insisted.

"You're allowed to come home. No one will judge you if you decide it's time," said Max.

"I know I'm allowed."

"The only person who might judge you is yourself. It's not a sign of weakness."

"I don't think that," she said.

"All right, but you've nothing to prove to anyone. Lizzie and I would love to have you back."

"I have been thinking," Annie said. "With the momentum here, it might be time for me to focus on Ohio and progress in Columbus. I can leave the national organization to the ladies of the East."

After a few moments of silence, she continued, "Much needs to be done right here. Ohio is a long way off from recognizing women in our legislature. There's plenty to do."

Annie waited for a response. "Well, aren't you going to say anything, one way or the other?"

"I think that sounds wonderful," said Max.

"Don't patronize me."

"I'm not. It's just I know my opinion is irrelevant. You will do what you will do. Just as I do what I do," said Max.

"I want to know what you think. I value your opinion. And take the emotion out of it. I know you want me home, but what's the right thing to do?"

"Me? Emotion in a decision? I never," said Max.

"Tell me what you think."

"I think you were devastated by the direction Elizabeth took the NWSA, and you're worn out from the infighting between the organizations. You would benefit from a break from the travel before you can truly give your full self to the AWSA. If you go back to Boston, they won't be getting the full benefit of Annie Bennett's talents. Right now, you can be most helpful, putting your heart, soul, and time into the Ohio organization, and if you do, there's a young woman who will be ecstatic to have her mother around more, and that's a huge plus. And later, next year, or when Lizzie goes off to college, you will find the next place where you can make a significant difference in the lives of others, just like you always have."

Annie burst into tears and sobbed with relief. Max hugged her.

"It's been so difficult," she said. "Progress seems to elude us. Just when I think we're making headway, we are dealt a blow. The world we're trying to create, where everyone is given an equal chance, is so distant from the reality of today. We have so little support."

"You're taking on centuries of customs and a way of life. It's difficult, I know," said Max.

"I missed your reassuring, supportive embrace. I need it."

"I'm here. I'll always be here."

Their hug was interrupted by Lizzie. "Papa, Mother, what's the matter?"

Max stood. "We're all right. We've missed each other."

"Me too!" She joined them in another hug.

Lizzie sat down and spread butter on a biscuit.

"Lizzie, what would you think if I began working with the Ohio Woman Suffrage organization instead of the national one in Boston," said Annie.

"Would that mean you would be home?"

"Yes. It means I'd be living at home and traveling much less frequently," said Annie.

"Then I think it's a wonderful promotion."

"Well, it's not a promotion but a change in my focus."

"It sounds like a promotion to me," said Lizzie, causing them all to laugh. "If you're home with us, it will be like Marmee and her girls. We can talk and you can counsel me about boys and other things."

"Who is Marmee, and what boys?" said Annie.

"Mrs. March," said Lizzie. "Laurie and Professor Bhaer."

"What are you talking about?"

"*Little Women*," said Max.

"What little women?" said Annie.

"Mother, you are behind the times. Everyone's reading it. I'm already reading the second book, and you don't even know about the first one," said Lizzie.

"Even I've read it. Miss Louisa May Alcott has penned a bona fide hit," said Max.

They finished their breakfast and sent Lizzie off to school.

Annie said, "The Burnet House Hotel has consented to letting us hold today's social reception for all the convention attendees in their parlor. Can you steal away from work and join us?"

Max laughed. "Did you arrange that?"

"I did."

"Why did you choose there? When they threw us out years ago, I thought you vowed never to step foot in that hotel again."

"I thought it would be poetic justice," said Annie. "When we courted, the hotel wouldn't admit me to the main dining room because I was a woman. Now, they are catering an event in support of equality for women."

"See," said Max. "You *are* making progress."

#

After the city council meeting adjourned, Max stayed behind with the new council president, Alfred Goshorn, a heavyset mutton-chop-bearded man, and fellow councilman, Nate Bartlett. Nate pulled a bottle of Ward & Irwin Rye from his coat pocket and held it up.

"A drink to toast the new city leadership?" said Nate.

"I'll drink to it," said Alfred. Max nodded.

Nate poured three glasses and they toasted. "Welcome to city politics," said Nate. "It's great to have you at the helm, sir. You've been a beacon in promoting Cincinnati, starting with your support of the early Red Stockings teams."

"Well, thank you. I love this city and want it to shine. And drop the 'sir.' My friends call me 'General,'" said Alfred.

"Let's hope the new mayor can continue the progress that Mayor Wilstach has made over the last four years," said Max. "I don't know if Mayor Torrence understands the urgency of the city's situation. We are competing with Chicago, Louisville, St. Louis—all cities that could overtake us as the preeminent city in the West."

"I think you made it blatantly clear to him in the council meeting," said Nate. "You couldn't stop talking about the Cincinnati Southern Railway to Chattanooga."

"It's critical!" said Max. "If we don't build a direct rail line to the South, commerce will bypass us. Our natural advantage on the river has faded."

"You don't need to convince me," said Nate.

"We finally got the law change in Columbus to allow us to raise funds for railroad investment, and the city approved ten million dollars in bonds. Now we need to convince Kentucky to approve it," said Max.

Alfred said, "That will take some greasing of the skids. The men in Louisville will lobby against a new railroad, even though central Kentuckians want it."

"How much grease?" asked Max.

"I don't know how much it will take. Miles Greenwood has started lobbying some of the Kentucky legislators, but if the railroad is built, it will severely impact the trade through Louisville. All the more reason to push forward with the idea of an industrial exposition," said Alfred.

"Yes. Let's talk about that. We've been mulling the idea over for a couple of years now," said Max. "You turned down the role of president of the committee at the Board of Trade to lead the effort. Is your support waning?"

"No, not at all," said Alfred. "It's just I can't run the exposition committee and lead the city council at the same time. Wilstach will do a fine job chairing the committee for this year. He's got the Board of Trade president Greenwood's support. We also have the Chamber of Commerce and the Mechanic's Institute on board. Each organization has pledged $1,000 to the guarantee fund."

"That's a solid start," said Max. "How will we fund the rest?"

"We're proposing to sell subscriptions. Businesses pay in, get publicity for it, and at the end of the exposition, assuming it's profitable, we return everyone's investment from the proceeds. My paint company has committed," said Alfred. "Are you in, Max?"

"Count Miller Industries in. If we do this right, it puts the Queen City back in the center of commerce and industry."

"We're also looking at including the arts?"

"How so?" said Max.

"We're going to add a classification for artists to exhibit and compete for awards," said Alfred.

"I like it," said Max. "This has the potential to have a greater impact than the new fountain on the city's reputation."

"Much greater," said Alfred.

"Max, I heard you won the bid for the ironwork for the new park around the fountain. You get some help from the city's purchasing agent?" said Nate, implying Max had preferential treatment as a councilman.

"Our contract award was all on the up and up," said Max. "We had the low bid, beat out Eagle Iron Works and Clements. We're building the decorative boxes and grates that will surround the trees and installing the plumbing for the refrigeration chamber. It's a nice contract for us."

"What's the refrigeration chamber?" asked Nate.

"It's ingenious. Colonel von Miller designed an underground chamber that will be filled with blocks of ice in the summer. The drinking fountain water pipes will run through it to chill the water. Nothing like it has ever been built."

"So cold water on a hot day," said Nate. "It's novel, but that esplanade is costing the city an unplanned $46,000. Mr. Probasco snuck that one in on us."

"It's going to be worth it," said Max. "The market is an eyesore. The fountain will be a magnificent symbol of the city's prosperity and hope for the future. Probasco has been generous."

Alfred added, "Henry is a neighbor and friend of mine. I don't believe he tried to slip anything by the city. The original site was just too small for the fountain. This is the right thing."

"The merchants who rent those stands in the market are going to push back when we inform them that we're not renewing their leases," said Nate.

"They will, and they'll get over it," said Alfred. "We can't let a few vegetable peddlers get in the way of progress. We must look at the bigger picture. What's good for the whole instead of the few."

CHAPTER 32

Cincinnati – Spring 1870

The Ohio Republican-controlled legislature narrowly approved the Fifteenth Amendment in January of 1870 after an initial defeat by the Democratic-controlled state body the prior year. The amendment prohibiting voting discrimination became part of the U.S. Constitution in February 1870. Most Northerners were still reluctant to grant the freedmen equal political rights. Still, enough feared a resurgence of Southern Democrat control of the nation that they supported its passing in hopes that the "Negro question" would finally be settled.

Black citizens in Cincinnati and across the country voted for the first time in 1870. The elections were primarily peaceful in the North, but intimidation, poll taxes, and other means were used throughout the South to prevent the freedmen from exercising their new civil right.

A committee of Black leaders in Cincinnati organized a "Day of Jubilee" celebration to recognize the significance of voting as citizens. Led by Peter Clark, the education champion, the committee planned a full day of festivities a week after the election. Many prominent Blacks and others gathered in the morning at the Fifth Street Market to form a parade.

Max secured his carriage with a stable groomsman, and he and Annie walked to the market. They strolled along the row of horses, carriages, wagons, and floats lined up on Elm Street. Hundreds of Black men, women and children were gathered, dressed in their finest clothes, many in red, white, and blue attire made for the occasion.

As citizens accosted Max in the street, Annie patiently waited until he dispensed with them. A man dressed in a dark suit, with a newspaper under his arms, stopped them. "Mr. Mueller, congratulations on your re-election to council."

"Thank you," said Max. "I'm honored to continue to serve the people."

"This spectacle this morning," said the man, motioning across the market and to the street. "I could hardly make my way through the market. Ever since election day, they've been running about town as if they owned the place. I do hope, after this pomp today, they go back to where they came from."

"They're citizens of our city, sir," said Max. "They're from here, like you and I."

"You know what I mean," said the man, surprised by Max's misalignment with his perspective. "Good day, sir," he said, tipping his hat.

"Well," said Annie, "It seems some are having difficulty accepting the freedmen's new rights."

They approached the front of the parade line to find several horses draped in patriotic colors, followed by a row of carriages. Men stood around them, some wearing sashes across their chests. They spotted John among the group.

"It's a glorious day," said Annie. "We're thrilled to celebrate with you."

"It is," said John, a broad smile on his face. "Let me introduce you to some of the men. Gentlemen, this is my good friend, Max Mueller, councilman and Board of Trade secretary. He and his wife, Annie, strongly support Colored causes in Cincinnati."

"This is Major Isaac Delaney, the first grand marshal for today. Major Delaney and I served in the Black Brigade together in the war," said John. "You know Peter Clark. Peter is the president of the jubilee committee. These fine men are the marshal's assistants for today."

"Congratulations to you all on your first of many elections," said Max. "My fellow Republicans and I appreciate the support you added to the ticket. As you know, many other parts of the country are succumbing to the Democrats' influence that moves us further from our country's ideals and values. Your vote mattered." They talked for a few more minutes, then left them to their preparations.

"Will you be at the ceremony?" asked John.

"We will. We'll talk to you then," said Max.

Annie and Max walked down Sixth Street, where there was plenty of room on the sidewalk. They exchanged pleasantries with two Black women and their children who had come out to watch the parade. Annie reached inside a basket and offered them slices of apple strudel that Lizzie had baked. The children looked to the women before accepting and then thanked Annie.

"Lizzie so wanted to miss school and see today," said Annie. "I wish I could capture the image of gratitude from them so she could see the reaction to her thoughtfulness."

"She has a generous heart and a skillful hand in the kitchen," said Max.

"Qualities she obtained from her father's side of the family," said Annie. "The kind heart from you and the baking from Marie."

"I'm glad someone in the family likes to work in the kitchen," he said.

"I agree. I'm just glad she sees it as only part of her identity. I think she is growing into a pragmatic feminist. It will serve her better than my variety of it," said Annie.

A band began to play, and the marshals on horseback led the parade toward them. Max nodded to the marshals as they passed, followed by the decorated carriages carrying the city's Black leaders. The marching band followed, then several expensive-looking carriages.

"Who are they?" asked Annie.

"Some of the city's wealthy Black families."

"The ladies are well dressed," observed Annie.

"There's a caste system within the caste system," said Max.

"Does John associate with that class?"

"No, he doesn't have their wealth. He knows some of them from church and his literary club."

"There's the St. Ann's wagon," pointed Max. Oskar stood on the wagon bed, towering above a mass of students dressed up for the occasion. A paperboard sign on the wagon's side read "St. Ann's Catholic School."

Max called to Oskar and waved. "We'll meet you after the parade."

Oskar's new bride, Catherine, walked beside the horse-drawn cart with students and several nuns dressed in black with white yoke collars. Catherine stepped out of the line to hug Max and Annie and then caught up with the float.

Next came another band, then a fire engine from the city fire department. A half dozen girls were crammed into an eight-horse carriage. The sign on the door read, "Goddess of Liberty presides over the states of the Union."

A company of Black soldiers marched, sporting a banner that read "In the War for the Union 200,000 Strong." The Colored Orphan Asylum's float carried children and a man holding a mammoth American flag. More groups processed, including the United Brethren and a large group of men from the Good Samaritans.

Two men held a banner for The Good Templars, followed by two hundred men and women marching in support of temperance.

"Not these noisemakers," muttered Max, maintaining his politician's smile.

"They have a right to march, along with everyone else," said Annie.

"They think drinking beer fills the workhouse. They can't imagine that the men who end up in the workhouse drink out of desperation to fill a hopeless life. It's a symptom, not a cause. I'd love for these agitators to put their energies into helping create more opportunities for men rather than locking them up and closing down the saloons."

Annie laughed. "I don't think you need to worry that they'll close down the saloons."

"Brewing and distilling provide hundreds of men work in this town. They need to be careful what they advocate for," said Max.

"Not to worry. There are too many saloons," said Annie.

"You, of all people, should know better than to underestimate the power of enraged women."

"I think your beer is safe," she said.

Another band brought up the rear. The Black spectators left their spots and joined the parade in front of the final marching band.

The streets quieted, and city life returned to normal. A few spectators watched from their upper-floor windows as the tail end of the parade turned onto Vine Street and disappeared, but most of the white citizens had hardly registered the event.

Annie and Max walked to the West End and joined the crowd assembling in the rink across from Lincoln Park. Children splashed in the pond. As the parade reached the park, its participants disbanded, and people filed into the building.

Annie and Max approached the St. Ann's wagon. Oskar was lifting the children down.

"Good morning, Sister Regis, Sister Marie Monica," said Max. "So nice to see you in the parade."

The two nuns gushed as Max approached. "Mr. Mueller. How are you? We are so blessed to have your brother and Mrs. Mueller guiding the boys and girls in our school," said Sister Regis.

"God is good," said Sister Marie Monica. "This day celebrates the spirit of the Lord that has found its way into our politics and bodes for a brighter future for our pupils."

"The children have the day off?" Annie asked Catherine, nodding to the dozens circling the wagon.

"This is a day of celebration for them too. Father declared a holiday so we could all attend," said Catherine.

"How is the new position?" asked Annie.

"I'm teaching the upper grades since the nuns aren't allowed to teach boys older than ten. It's nice to have the structure of the school. And it's refreshing not to have to worry about any violence."

"I'm so happy for you. Both you and Oskar," said Annie.

Tears clouded Catherine's eyes.

"What is it?" said Annie. "What's the matter?"

They stepped away. "Oh, Annie, just when things were settling in, seemed perfect."

"What?" said Annie.

"I'm going to have a baby."

"Oh, Catherine." Annie took her forearm. "Are you happy?"

"Yes, I'm happy. Oskar wants a family, and so do I, but we didn't expect it yet. I've just established a rapport with the children. Now I'll have to leave them."

Annie appreciated the disappointment of foregoing a career when motherhood arrived. "I'm sorry," she said, embracing Catherine. "You can return to the classroom after the baby is born if that's what you want."

Catherine shook her head. "I don't think so."

"It's so archaic," said Annie. "This practice of insisting that women cannot be parents and teachers simultaneously. Men do it all the time. Nothing's changed in the fifteen years since I was a teacher."

"The Church won't support it," said Catherine.

"Oskar and Max will advocate for you."

"It's the Church. Maybe in the common schools, but not here."

"Don't dismay," said Annie. "There's time. For now, be happy about your baby. That's what you should focus on now. We can talk about all this later."

They embraced. "Celebrate today. You have much to celebrate," said Annie.

Meanwhile, Oskar and Max caught up.

"Nice to see you out supporting the freedmen," said Oskar. "Your generosity to St. Ann's and the other Negro charities in town is acknowledged and greatly appreciated. I'm sorry I doubted your motivations."

"Thank you for saying it," said Max.

"In managing the affairs of St. Ann's, I've learned first-hand the benefit of tempering my support for integration of the Negro when interacting with the power brokers of the city. I depend on them for the funds to keep the school open. I've learned to bite my tongue when necessary. The donors are happy to support the school, as long as the Black families accept their place and don't try to upset the unwritten rules that allow us to live side by side."

"I know it's difficult," said Max. "Keep reminding yourself you're doing good work. God's work. Imagine how hard it must be for the freedmen to do this dance. You're making the best of the situation."

"Thank you," said Oskar. "I've good news."

"Tell me."

"Catherine's going to have a baby."

"Congratulations," said Max. "You've wasted no time. Another reason to practice pragmatism. A family will do that."

They joined their wives.

"Shall we go in?" said Max.

They entered the newly constructed, vast hall, which was less than half full, with fifteen hundred people, mostly Black, seated and standing. Children ran around and ducked in and out of the side rooms. Oskar directed them to chairs for the ladies, and he and Max stood behind them. When the band in the corner concluded their song, Peter Clark called the meeting to order. The assembly all sang "America, My Country 'Tis of Thee." One of the Black preachers gave the opening prayer, followed by reading of several government official's proclamations.

Peter Clark re-took the podium and made his opening

remarks, "'The Star-Spangled Banner'—that flag now waves over only free men…. This great reform inflicts credit on both white and Black. For two hundred years, the Blacks had whips and thumb screws and had not been allowed to own their own wives; but all this time, thousands of philanthropic white men and women had naught in their friendship for the Black."

Clark ended with, "We are a great and strong people. Any other people would long since have been swept away like the red men."

Clark and others read a long series of remarks and letters from dignitaries absent from the event, including Chief Justice Salmon Chase, the former Cincinnatian who had defended slaves in court cases long before the war. The Ohio governor, judges, and other prominent citizens' words were read to the increasingly antsy audience.

After three hours, Clark read a resolution, adopted by the Colored citizens of Hamilton County, thanking the President, Congress, and men who fought for freedom. "…Colored people now must educate our children and gain property. We must never forget Lincoln and the other men who led the fight. Resolved, that John Brown's body lies moldering in the clay, but his spirit is marching on. Glory, glory, hallelujah."

The crowd applauded and began dispersing. They stood in groups, hugging and laughing.

The Muellers found John and his family.

John said, "Thank you for being here. We will forever be thankful for the kindness that your family has shown us. We've got to raise ourselves up, but we thank God for people like you, who fight with us for the chance to do it. Too many people are happy to leave us with no chance."

Max and John embraced.

Max said, "God has blessed us, and today if he grants it, is the beginning of a new day for all men and women to be given the opportunities to reap his blessings. I pray we have turned a corner."

"Amen."

John's mother, Jenny, took Max's hands in hers. "You've given much, but more than anything, you give me hope—hope that people can look beyond the hate of the past and to better times. Mister Aaron—he's no longer with us. He didn't know how to undo what was done. You can't undo it all. I think he was sorry, and I believe he finally found love in his heart. He led me back to my children."

John said, "Would you like to join us? We're suppering with some friends in the neighborhood."

"No, thank you," said Max. "This is your celebration. Go be with your friends."

CHAPTER 33

Cincinnati – Fall 1870

After a year of planning, the first Cincinnati Industrial Exposition opened in the Saengerfest Hall, situated in Over-the-Rhine between Elm Street and the Canal. The large building stretched between Twelfth and Fourteenth Streets, standing 250 feet tall with scores of windows and flag-topped turrets. The building had once been an insane asylum and then an orphan's asylum before planners turned it into the exposition center. Organizers quickly constructed several outbuildings adjacent to the original structure to provide more space for the hundreds of exhibitors from twenty-four states.

Max worked tirelessly to help the former mayor, Charles Wilstach, and the others on the committee to make the event happen. For him, the expo symbolized the Queen City's return to prosperity that he had sought since the war.

The newspapers chronicled the exhibition daily, from the rush to finish the preparations to its final days of crowds that totaled more than 300,000 over the month-long event. It was a success by all measures, generating news stories across the country and taking in more than enough twenty-five cent admissions to cover all its costs and return the investments to the businessmen who had funded the event. Max invited Annie and Lizzie to spend an afternoon at the exposition on one of the final days.

They entered the large exhibition hall and admired the floral display and fountain. Hundreds of visitors stood in two lines for tickets in the entry promenade. Beyond the fountain were rows of wooden booths with people moving along them. Above the splash of water, a constant hum of voices and distant industrial noises filled the space.

"Do we need tickets, Papa?" said Lizzie.

"No, put these on," Max said, handing them blue "Exhibitor" ribbons.

They wandered through the Grand Central Hall, which featured categories of smaller items. Lizzie was interested in the household goods, which included kitchenware, furniture, linens, and home decorating items, including wallpapers, carpets, and rugs. There were also booths exhibiting clothing, boots, shoes, hats, and an assortment of other things: ropes, leather goods, soaps, candles, and oils.

"It's as if all the stores on Fifth and Sixth Streets relocated here," said Lizzie.

"Let's go into Power Hall," said Max, directing them to the large hall dedicated to machinery. Gears and pulleys attached to leather belts ran across the room near the ceiling. Belts stretched down, powering the various machines. "Steam engines outside the hall supply the power to the exhibits through these belts." They had to raise their voices above the sounds from the moving gears, turning belts, and machines.

Annie said, "It's an engineering marvel in itself. They built all this just for the exposition?"

"Yes," said Max. "It was the most efficient way to demonstrate all the equipment without having scores of steam engines puffing away in the exhibit hall. We had several engineers design it and then worked with the exhibitors to hook all their machines up."

"Look at that," said Lizzie as they approached an exhibit of large machines. "What are they?"

"That's a clothes washing machine, and that one is a clothes wringer," said Max.

"I didn't know there was a machine to do such a thing," said Lizzie as they watched a man demonstrate how it worked.

They admired the stoves and ice boxes, then moved to the industrial machine section. Miller Industries had a prime spot near the entrance. George Gray, Max's chief engineer and several employees stood near the machines on display. Annie greeted them, some of whom she knew from working at the factory.

"What's this contraption?" Lizzie asked the man.

"This is a tire lathe. It's used to shape and smooth locomotive wheels. Let me show you." The man pulled a lever, and the metal railroad wheel started turning. Once it built up speed, he pulled another lever and a sharp blade connected with the tire causing screeches and sparks. "The lathe removes any bumps or rough spots and ensures that it is perfectly round. The railroad companies re-shape their tires after they are worn down and damaged by miles on the railroad tracks."

Max pulled George aside while Annie and Lizzie watched demonstrations of the other machines. "What's traffic been like today?" he asked George.

"Constant flow again today. A man from the Union Pacific Railroad stopped by. He was very interested. We had a long conversation about the merits of our machine versus others. I gave him a leaflet."

"Did you get his name and address?" said Max.

"I put it in the log."

"Good. This exposition has allowed us to meet so many railroad men that we'd otherwise have to travel miles to do so."

They moved on to see other machines, including street sweepers, printing presses, grinders, and drills. They approached the Steptoe, McFarlan & Co. booth, where Patrick stood with a man before a wood lathe.

"Hello, Muellers." Patrick extended his arm for Lizzie to shake an ornate wooden chair leg in place of his hooked hand. "Feel how smooth it is. Look at the craftsmanship! A product of our lathes and jigs."

Lizzie refrained from touching it, not sure what to think.

"That's quite an attention-getter you have there, Patrick," said Max.

Patrick removed the leg from his arm and replaced it with another from a bin. "You like this one better?"

Lizzie shook her head.

"Ignore him," said Max.

Patrick pulled a wooden Christmas ornament from a barrel. "How about one of these? I know you could do a wonderful job painting it. How's your painting going?"

"I haven't been painting as much. School consumes so much of my time now," said Lizzie.

"Take it. Maybe you'll find time before Christmas," said Patrick.

"Thank you," said Lizzie.

"How's it been for you the last few days?" asked Max.

"Good. We had a great day today. The judge awarded us a silver medal for our universal milling machine," said Patrick, pointing to the medal hanging on the front of the booth.

"Congratulations!" said Max.

They crossed back through the Grand Central Hall and into the Floral Hall, elaborately landscaped and supplemented with fresh-cut flowers. The room's focal point was a fountain with a large pine tree in the center of a metal basin.

They passed through the music room, where merchants displayed various musical instruments. They stopped to listen to a pianist play a piece, then moved to the art gallery. Lizzie led them along wall after wall, admiring more than one thousand paintings, most of which had been borrowed from private collections.

After an hour, Max suggested they dine at the Keppler's Restaurant in the Grand Central Hall. They ordered and watched the people go by. A bird had found its way indoors and flew around the high ceiling, attracted by the large skylights.

Max nodded to two men passing by, and they approached the Muellers' table.

"Max, I have to say, the exposition has exceeded our expectations," said one of the men. "The city owes all of you on the committee a huge thank you for your vision and perseverance to make it happen."

"Thank you," said Max. "We are thrilled with the results and feel we've accomplished what we set out to do."

"You have to be exhausted."

"It's been exhilarating. I've been here most days, and the energy in the halls is nonstop. I almost wish it didn't have to end," said Max.

"Well, my New Jersey and Philadelphia customers have read about it and want to come next year. Cincinnati is the talk of the nation's commercial circles this month."

"Glad to hear it. I appreciate you stopping by," said Max.

After they left, Lizzie said, "Papa, you're so happy."

"I am at that. What did you think of the exposition?" asked Max.

"There was so much to see," said Lizzie. "I wish we could have stayed longer."

"It was an epic display of the range of products that Cincinnati has to offer. Very impressive. You and the committee are to be commended for your efforts," said Annie.

"Thank you," said Max proudly. "We're already discussing how to make it even more impressive next year."

CHAPTER 34

Cincinnati – Fall 1870

Harry's usual routine became dining in one of the Rat Row joints with his friends and drinking until his money ran out. Some nights he would save enough for a room at one of the riverfront hotels that catered to river workers, or he might crash on a friend's floor.

Late one evening at Pickett's, Harry and Vickie went downstairs with George and Katie to dance. It was a predominantly Black crowd, except for the few white women regulars.

The musicians played a few waltzes but quickly moved to what the crowd wanted, increasing the tempo and volume. The men and women moved their bodies in free-form dance. Men surrounded the dancers and patted juba, slapping their hands on their thighs and chests to the rhythm of the music. Harry and Vickie danced in a small circle with friends, shouting and clapping to the music.

Harry moved closer to Vickie, bumping his body against hers as they both jumped around and reveled in the music. They ignored the smoky, sweaty air and tight conditions, smiling and laughing as they focused on each other. Harry placed his hands on Vickie's hips and leaned in, touching foreheads with her. She pushed him away, laughing. He grabbed her hands, pulled her in, swung her around, and pulled her in again. She pushed him away again, laughing. The next time their faces touched, Harry kissed Vickie. They stopped dancing and lingered in the kiss, in their own world, until Harry was roughly pulled around by his shoulder and stood face to face with Greg, the Irish steward from the *America,* who had vowed to keep his eyes on Harry. Two rough-looking men stood on either side of Greg.

"Keep your dirty lips off of her," said Greg, still holding Harry's shoulder. The small circle of dancers spread out, surrounding the confrontation. The rest of the floor continued to dance to the music, oblivious.

Harry tried to shrug him off, but Greg held firmly.

"You leave him be," said Vickie, "He ain't bothering you. Why you gotta come in here and spoil our fun?"

"You," Greg said, turning to Vickie. "You're the lowliest of trash, cavorting with his kind. Letting him paw and mouth you like that."

"You talk so high and mighty, but you're here with the rest of us. There must be a reason you're at this crib instead of a white one. Maybe you're not so snobby when it comes to the color of women you paw and mouth either," Vickie said.

Greg whacked Vickie across the face with the back of his fist. She screamed as she sailed to the floor, crashing into the circle of onlookers.

Harry jumped at Greg, grabbing him by the throat with both hands and squeezing. Greg pawed at Harry's arms, swatting, trying to break his grip. Harry continued strangling and pushed Greg to the ground, climbing on top of him. Greg's two companions tried to pull Harry off, to no avail. Greg was kicking his legs and bucking, trying to free himself from under Harry's weight. The bystanders were screaming, and the room began to notice. The musicians stopped playing, leaving only the sound of the men's shouts, screams, and grunts.

George and several of Harry's friends shouted at him. "Harry, stop." "Let him up." "No, Harry." They pleaded for him to relent before he committed an unreversible act.

Two large Black doormen pushed their way through the crowd to the fight. One grabbed Harry by both arms and pulled him off of Greg. The other bouncer picked up Greg, who was out of breath and subdued. They pushed the two through the crowd and out onto Front Street, a small group following.

The man holding Greg released him, allowing Greg to place his hands on his thighs and catch his breath. The other man pushed Harry against the front of the building.

Greg stood. "I want him arrested for attacking me."

Harry said, "I was defending a lady."

"You. Quiet," said the bouncer.

"He struck this woman," said Harry.

Two police officers arrived on the scene.

"Shit," said George. "Button it, Harry."

The women and the Black men, except for George, left the scene.

"What's the trouble, here?" said Officer Jefferies. "Man came running down the street and said a Black man was killing a white man. Is that so?"

Harry shook his head. "No."

Officer Kappen asked Greg, "That true? Attempted to kill you?"

"Yes, sir," said Greg.

"Bullshit," said Harry.

"No one asked you." Officer Kappen said to Harry.

"You saying you want to press charges?" asked Officer Kappen.

"Damn right. He's a menace to society," said Greg.

"I hardly touched him," said Harry. "Look at him. He's fine."

"I said keep your mouth shut," said Officer Kappen.

Harry started speaking but stopped when the policeman jabbed his billy club into his stomach. He simmered with rage.

Officer Kappen sized up Greg. "You seem unharmed. Is this really necessary?"

Henry Pickett, the club's owner, came out the front door. "Good evening officers."

"Henry," Officer Jefferies nodded at the man.

"We don't like to have to come down here," said Officer Kappen. "You allowing mixing of the races leads to trouble like this."

"I'm sorry you officers had to rush down the street. I think it was just some boys had too much to drink and got a little testy with each other," said Pickett.

"He says it was serious," said Officer Jefferies, pointing at Greg. "That Negro tried to kill him."

Harry pursed his lips to keep from speaking and glared at Greg.

"This one," said Pickett, indicating Harry. "He look dangerous to you?"

"I don't trust any of you," said Officer Jefferies.

"I'm sorry you had to trouble yourselves. It's all under control here," said Pickett. "Can I give you something for your trouble?"

Pickett pulled two ten-dollar bills from a wad of cash and handed them to the officers.

"We don't want to hear any more problems from this end of the street tonight. You hear?" said Jefferies.

"This animal was forcing himself on a white woman," blurted Greg.

Officer Kappen turned back to Greg. "What's that?"

"On the dance floor," said Greg. "Against the laws of nature and the state. It was disgusting. You can't just let him go. What's to stop him from doing it again?"

Harry cursed under his breath.

"Did you accost a white woman in there?" said Officer Jefferies.

"No, sir," said Harry.

Officer Kappen said, "Anybody else see what he's claiming?"

"I did," said one of Greg's pals.

"Me too," said the other.

"I didn't do no such thing," said Harry.

"Who you going to believe?" said Greg, "One of his kind or three white men?"

"Where's this woman?" said Officer Jefferies.

"She ran off," said Greg.

"So which is it," said Officer Kappen. "Did he attack you, or did he molest a white woman?"

"Both," said Greg. "He was kissing and rubbing himself on her on the dance floor, so I tried to get him off her, and he attacked me."

"Is that what happened?" Officer Kappen said to Greg's pals.

They nodded. "Yes, sir," said one.

"Just like he said," said the other.

"Henry, this…we have to take him in for this," said Officer Kappen.

The bar owner nodded, knowing there was no way out for Harry.

The officers took Greg's name and led Harry down the street.

"I told you," Greg shouted after Harry. "You take our jobs and our women. There's a price to pay."

#

Max stood in front of the large boring machine, watching the operator drill out the inside of a thick metal rod, sparks flying from the point of contact. Over the noise of the grinding and the steam engine, he heard one of the shopmen, "Max! Max!"

Max stepped back from the machine. "What is it?"

"There's a Black man in the office to see you," the shop man shouted in his ear over the din.

"What's he want?" shouted Max.

The shopman shook his head, "He didn't say, just that he needed to talk to you."

Max nodded. "I'll be out in a minute." He watched the operator finish boring the hole and shut down the machine.

Max found John sitting in a chair in the business office, trying to ignore the gazes of the men who passed through. "John," said Max.

John stood, and they shook hands.

"I'm sorry to bother you at your workplace," said John. "I didn't know what else to do."

"Is everything all right?" asked Max.

"No, it's Harry. He's in trouble," said John.

"Let's step outside," said Max, leading him down the stairs and into the factory yard filled with piles of steel and wood crates.

"I hate bringing my problems on you. They're my problems, and you have enough of your own," said John. "Harry's in big trouble, and I fear no Black man can help him. Please..."

"I'll help if I can. What happened to Harry?" said Max.

John told Max about Harry's altercation and arrest at Pickett's Tavern the previous night. "I went down to the Hammond Street police station, where Harry's locked up. They said he was going to be transferred to the county jail on Court Street today and then charged with having relations with a white woman."

"Did Harry do that? With a white woman?" asked Max.

"I don't know," said John. "It doesn't sound like him, but they wouldn't let me talk to him. He's been spending time on the riverfront, drinking and otherwise disgracing himself and the family. I tried to steer him away from those temptations, but he's in with the riverboat crowd. I know he's responsible for what he's done, but he's my brother, and I'm afraid for him. What are they going to do to him? Black man accused of doing something like that. In Kentucky, they'd hang him for that. He don't deserve that."

"He didn't rape this woman, did he?" asked Max.

"No, they aren't saying that," said John.

"They're not going to hang him, then. I don't think you need to worry about that. Not here. The law prohibits interracial relations. If he was with a white woman, he may get jail time or be fined."

"Harry's a good man. He's just lost. He feels the whole world is against him. He doesn't need to go to a trial and all that. That's just more on top of what he's already fighting."

"I'm sorry, John," said Max.

"Is there anything you can do? You know lawyers and judges. You're somebody. I'll only ask this once, I promise," pleaded John.

"Let me see what I can do," said Max.

#

Harry sat alone in the dark cell behind bars. He went through a range of emotions during the night. At first, he felt rage at Greg and angry at the policemen for ignoring his side of the story and not even allowing him to plead his case.

In the quiet of the night, fear overtook anger. Harry imagined what his fate might be. He would be taken to the county courthouse and then go before a judge. He had no inkling of what it would entail, but assumed a white court would pass judgement on him and wouldn't be any more open to his story than the police were. He contemplated the worst—ending up imprisoned somewhere or sent to work on a chain gang. Enslaved again. He felt powerless to defend himself or influence his fate. He chastised himself for getting involved with Vickie. Then anger returned. Anger toward the white men in the bar, toward all white men and their society, anger at God for abandoning him again.

Mid-morning, the new officer on duty approached his cell with his keys. He unlocked the door. "You must have friends in high places."

"What you mean?" said Harry.

"You're free to go," said the deputy.

"Just like that?" said Harry.

"Mr. Ratterman, the city councilman who oversees the Police Committee told the captain to let you go."

"That's it? I can go?" said Harry.

"That's what he said."

Harry picked up his coat from the bench and hurried out of the cell and up the stairs. As he stepped outside, he found John on the sidewalk.

"Harry, you're all right. Thank God," said John.

Harry nodded. "Let's get away from here."

They walked along Fourth Street toward home.

"How'd you get me out?" said Harry.

"Max Mueller got you freed," said John.

"Your white brother. He got me out?"

"That's right," said John.

"They said I was going to the county jail and going to be put in front of a judge. I was afraid I'd be locked up forever, or worse," said Harry.

"I didn't know what was going to happen to you. I feared it would be bad, so I went to Max," said John. "He knows some important people in the city. He went to considerable trouble for you. Had to explain why he was so interested in a Black man on the riverfront. I reckon he was pretty ashamed to say he was a kin of sorts to you."

"Why did he do that for me?" said Harry.

"Because I asked him to."

"Why does he care about a Negro like me?"

"Because he's a good Christian man," said John.

"Hmm," said Harry.

"Harry, we're now living in this city, with all its good and bad. We have two choices. We can hate and sin and cry about our situation, or we can follow God's word and help each other make our lives better. We're living on earth amongst men, sinners, one and all. If we follow God's path, it will lead to a better life in heaven."

John folded his hands and raised them to the sky. "I pray for us all that we'll all be together in heaven one day, and I pray that in the meantime, we lean on each other to find what's good in the world we've been given. I pray that you will too.

"God's given us another chance here, in Cincinnati. He

led us from bondage to freedom. He's given you another chance to live right—he sent Max to get you out of that jail and avoid going to court. Brother, at some point, you're going to run out of chances. You best be looking at your life and make the most of this one."

CHAPTER 35

Cincinnati – Winter 1870

Oskar, Max, and Patrick sat at a table in the corner of the Eichen Garten, catching up over drinks.

"Why don't we come here more often?" said Patrick.

"You like it?" said Max.

"Not especially," said Patrick, "but the drinks are free."

Max pulled the glass of whiskey from in front of Patrick. "You're an ungrateful one. The least you could do is pretend. This is home for Oskar and me. We spent many hours in our youth delivering beers, swabbing tables, and emptying spittoons."

"I see the attraction, even beyond the free drinks. People here seem comfortable. You know everyone who walks through that door," said Patrick.

"Our parents opened the saloon the year Max was born. Generations have been coming here," said Oskar.

"Of course, the governor knows everyone in town, north and south of the canal," said Patrick. "Your brother is quite the politician. City's lucky to have him."

Oskar nodded.

"The city may go to the dogs if we don't turn some things around," said Max.

"Always the pessimist. What crisis do you need to turn around now?" said Patrick.

Helene brought them another round of drinks—beer for

the brothers and whiskey for Patrick.

"I would give my right hand for a sister like you," said Patrick raising his hook and smiling at Helene. "Thank you, love."

"Damn Louisville legislators. They killed the bill to approve the right of way for the Cincinnati Southern Railway to Tennessee. The second time," said Max.

"I thought there was strong support for it?" said Oskar.

"In central Kentucky, yes, but not Louisville. It's dead for now, anyway," said Max, shaking his head.

"You're not giving up?" said Patrick.

Max sighed. "No, but I'm at a loss as to the next steps. We need that rail line."

"You'll think of something. You always do," said Patrick.

"This problem is as dogged as Reconstruction. We have to convince people to change their thinking," said Max.

"Christ, Reconstruction is done. The nation's been put back together. Congress's enforcement acts are beating a dead horse," said Patrick.

"We're not done with it," demanded Oskar, pounding the table, and making their glasses jump.

Patrick said, "The slaves are free, they're citizens, and they have the vote. They have schools and churches. They have every opportunity that you, Max, and I had as poor immigrants' children."

"In what world are you living?" said Oskar.

"Calm down," said Patrick.

"Do you really believe that if we just declare we're done repairing the nation, the Black man will figure out how to pull himself out of the poverty handed to him as his version of American opportunity?"

"Some of them will. Some of them won't. We can't all be prosperous. It takes hard work, determination, and a little luck. Same for Blacks and whites," said Patrick.

"I lived in the South," said Oskar. "I saw the hatred of the Ku Kluxers, the Confederate men who believe that the war was an injustice against them and their way of life and will do anything to restore it to what it was before the war. You saw what they did to Aaron."

"I get that some still harbor the resentment," said Patrick. "Men are still committing heinous acts to defend their cause, but do you believe we should continue to saddle the country with the expense of settling the differences between men across the entire South? Congress's latest bill makes these crimes federal offenses. That crosses a line of state sovereignty that will be hard to step back from. The federal government will keep expanding and someday bankrupt the nation."

Oskar said, "The Democrats have already won control in Tennessee and Virginia. If we leave the Southern states to rule themselves, we might as well not have fought the war. Look at the sacrifice you made. Do you want that to be for nothing?"

Patrick shook his head. "It's time to let men stand up for themselves. I think it's time to let the voters in the states decide how they want things to go in their states. We can't force people to change through federal government control."

"That would be fine if it were a level playing field," said Oskar. "But it's not. Not even close!"

"Yes, the world's not fair," said Patrick. "It's not. It never has been. It never will be. There's always someone more fortunate than you and me, and there are also those less fortunate. We can help, but we'll never make it equal in all ways. That's not the way the world works."

"So you want to give up?" said Oskar.

Patrick shrugged.

Max said, "Patrick, that's your right, but Oskar and I won't. I used to think like you, but I can't anymore. I'll work to create as many opportunities for as many people as possible. I know I won't solve all the problems, but I'll lift as many people up as I can."

"Well, you've always done that, and God will reward you for it. I'm just saying, enough is enough from the government," said Patrick.

"People like you," muttered Oskar. "Bigoted to the core." He pushed himself back from the table and left.

Patrick smirked at Max. "Little brother is a bit of a hothead."

"He's passionate," said Max. "I feel the same as he, but I control my emotions better. Seeing John and his family try to make their life here. It's not right."

"Another cross you choose to bear, my friend," said Patrick. "I'm empty. Would you like another?" Patrick went to the bar.

He returned with their drinks and sat. "I've resigned from the baseball club."

Max said, "You're deserting them? They're a banner for the city."

"Have you read the papers? Last year they were the shining star. This year, a money-sucking mongrel on the tit of the club members. The fans stopped coming to the games. There's not enough money coming in. They keep asking members to subsidize the fat payrolls for the players. We were good with it as long as they kept winning and the fans were buying tickets."

Max said, "They won what, sixty-eight of their seventy-five games this year? They're still a great team."

"Last year, when they were undefeated, they seemed like gods," said Patrick. "The city, the country, and the club had Red Stocking fever. It faded quickly. At the end of this season, the club president and secretary resigned. When the new president came in, he announced that next year the team would go back to amateur status. We can't afford to pay the big salaries anymore. Chicago and a few other teams have the funding, and they've already hired away most of our players."

"So it's done? That's it?" asked Max.

"I'm afraid so," said Patrick. "I wish it were different."

"So, in addition to Reconstruction, you're giving up on the Red Stockings too?"

Patrick shrugged.

"I suppose you're not alone. Americans' support seems to

be easily diverted when things get a little rough," said Max.

CHAPTER 36

One year Later, Cincinnati – Fall 1871

Lizzie entered the kitchen to the smell of coffee. "Good morning, Mother," she said cheerfully.

"Would you like me to fix you some eggs for breakfast?" said Annie.

"Yes, please." Lizzie investigated the open door that looked out onto their back lawn. She saw Max standing at the far edge of the yard in the first morning light.

"What's Papa doing? He's just standing there."

"He's admiring his city," said Annie.

Lizzie crossed the dewy lawn and snuggled up beside him.

Max kissed the top of her head and put his arm around her. "Good morning."

"Good morning, Papa. What are you looking at?"

"All those buildings past the West End; they weren't there a few years ago," Max pointed. "People keep moving outward. The city's footprint has doubled, and we have over 200,000 people now."

Morning sunlight lit the hills west of the city, and whisps of fog floated over the Ohio River.

Annie joined them on Max's other side, taking his hand. They stood in silence.

"You came in late last night. How was your evening with Colonel Von Miller?" said Annie.

"The German singing societies paid tribute to him. They

were all there; the Orpheus, Maennerchor, St. Cecelia, Liederkranz, the Turner Singing Section, and the Druids Singing Society. They all lined up outside Saengerfest Hall. I brought the Colonel and a few others after dinner, and they surprised him by singing half a dozen songs in German. He loved it. Then we all walked downtown behind the German battalion to the Burnet House, picking up people along the way. We must have had over four thousand people by the time we reached the hotel. The Colonel made a speech in German—much to the pleasure of the assembled crowd, and then we went inside for refreshments. I think it made him feel like a piece of his homeland was here."

"Von Miller is the son of the artist?" said Annie.

"Yes, he arrived a month and a half ago to oversee the fountain's installation. He's a delightful young man."

"So today is the big day. The fountain is finally going to be unveiled," said Annie.

"Over four years of work by craftsman in Germany, the long voyage across the ocean and by train, the prep work on the esplanade," said Max. "It's a beautiful work of art. I can hardly believe it's here, in our city, in the middle of America. I think it's the finest public fountain in the world."

"You've seen it already?" said Lizzie.

"My crews helped test the piping underneath. I've been behind the wooden fence on and off for weeks now. Words can't do justice to its beauty."

"I can't wait to sketch it," said Lizzie.

"I've arranged for you and Abby to sit atop the temporary stand that Mr. Green built over the sidewalk in front of his store. You'll have an excellent view of the entire esplanade and all the festivities. It should make for a nice drawing spot."

"Thank you, Papa. Where will you be sitting?"

"They've reserved seats for city officials next to the fountain."

"How about Mother?"

"She and Mary Berry have reserved seats on the esplanade," said Max.

"Are you going to cry today, like you did for the Garden of Eden Park opening?" said Lizzie.

"I might," said Max.

"You love Cincinnati, don't you?" said Lizzie.

"I do. Almost as much as I love you two." He gave both of them a peck. He looked at his pocket watch. "I've got to go. I've some things to get done before the festivities start."

"What time should we be there?" asked Annie.

"They'll open the esplanade at half past ten; the exercises begin at eleven. There will be crowds. Leave early, especially if you hope to catch a street car from the bottom of Prospect Hill."

"I think we'll walk," said Annie. "It feels like it's going to be a gorgeous fall day."

Max left the house, and Annie and Lizzie spent a couple of hours working at the dining room table; Annie on her suffrage correspondence and Lizzie on her homework.

When it was time to go, Lizzie placed a tablet and pencils in her cloth bag and stood by the door. "Come on, Mother. Papa said there will be crowds."

"I'm coming," Annie answered down the stairs. She came down the steps. A large "VOTES FOR WOMEN" button pinned to her dress. She offered one to Lizzie.

"No, thank you," said Lizzie.

"You won't support the cause?"

"I support the cause, but I won't wear that thing. It's gigantic."

"Oh, come on now. What's the difference?" said Annie.

"Mother, please. I would look ridiculous wearing it."

"Why are you worried about how you look?" said Annie.

"I'm not old enough to vote."

"All right then." Annie dropped the button in her bag.

As they stepped down from the porch, a teenager called to Lizzie from the yard across the street and waved, "Good morning, Elizabeth."

Lizzie smiled. "Hi, Robert."

"I'm leaving today," he said.

"Mother, I must go say goodbye."

"Aren't you going to introduce me?" said Annie.

"No, stay here, please. Let me go. I'll just be a minute." Lizzie crossed the street without waiting for a reply.

Annie watched her interact with the young man. Lizzie chatted with him, laughing coyly as she had never seen her daughter behave; she was no longer a little girl. The pair embraced in a brief, awkward hug, and Lizzie returned, her face slightly flushed.

"Who is that young man?" asked Annie.

"Robert Benton. He's off to the Naval Academy in Maryland," said Lizzie.

"He sounds like an impressive young man. How do you know him?"

"He's lived across the street from us since we moved in."

"Of course. I gather you and he have spent time together?" said Annie.

"Nothing more than sitting in the garden together or talking on the porch. He's an only child too."

"He's handsome," said Annie.

"Mother," said Lizzie.

"I'm only making an observation. He called you Elizabeth."

"Yes, I prefer it. Lizzie sounds juvenile."

"I see. Do you want me to call you Elizabeth?" said Annie.

"No, I'm fine with Lizzie at home."

They began their walk toward the city. Annie found their conversation flowed more openly when they walked.

"Have you given any more thought to college?" asked Annie.

"Attending college is daunting to think about."

"What are you concerned about?"

"I don't want to look foolish. I can't imagine sitting in a class with boys like Robert, who are so smart," said Lizzie.

"I understand. I found some of the boys intimidating when I was young too."

"You did?"

"Yes. It's an awkward dance we have to do as women. We are expected to act womanly even if it means suppressing our innate nature. Some boys feel they must be superior to girls in all manners. It's what society expects of them, and they're considered weak by other men if they're not. If a woman challenges that superiority, a man might consider her unwomanly or decide she's not an attractive partner."

"So how am I supposed to act so I don't disappoint boys?" said Lizzie.

"First of all," said Annie, "Boys' judgment of you is their opinion. You are the one who decides what's right for you. You are in charge of yourself, not any boy, ever. Do you understand?"

"Yes," said Lizzie. "I know that when it comes to what I want, I'm not bound by what people think girls should do. That's the women's movement. But when it comes to boys, I have to do what boys like, or they won't like me."

Annie took a deep breath, realizing that this conversation was one of the most important she had ever had with her daughter. Lizzie was now facing one of the significant quandaries of being a woman—how to be strong and independent amid societal expectations that women be docile and secondary to men.

"No, you don't have to do what boys want, and you shouldn't do something you don't want to just because a boy says you should. Some boys will expect you to fall in line with their expectations of you. And other boys will accept you for who you are. As you begin to meet boys and court, you must choose wisely. Even if the boy is handsome and polite, he is not worthy of you if he won't respect you as you are. Your papa loves me for who I am. Even though he may not agree with everything I do, he respects my choices. That is the kind of boy who deserves your affection. Don't settle for anything less."

"It's all so confusing."

"I'm afraid it is," said Annie, "but I want you to come to me if you have questions. It's important we talk about these things you're wondering about."

Annie thought about Lizzie leaving for college. She had felt an all-women's institution like Vassar, where the women could support each other, might be the right place for her daughter. But their conversation gave her pause. Lizzie, with no brothers and now schooled at a private girls' school, needed to start interacting with boys. She needed to be comfortable with them, see them as peers and recognize that her intelligence was equal to many of theirs. Oberlin College had been co-ed for years. The University of Michigan was now co-ed. The new Cornell University would be opened as co-ed. She would investigate these.

"I'm glad you're home now. So we can talk," said Lizzie.

The conversation heartened Annie. She knew that being home now for Lizzie was where she needed to be. The movement would have to do with a little less of her time for a while.

#

Max greeted the boy selling newspapers on the market square. "Good morning, Fritz."

"Good day, Mr. Mueller. Today promises to be a day unlike the others. I can already see it."

"It sure will be. Tell me what you gleaned from the paper this morning?" said Max, repeating his exercise with the boy, encouraging him to learn from the newspapers he sold. "If you provide me some useful insight, there's an extra nickel for you."

"It's a slow news day. I think the reporters are saving up their good words for the new fountain," said Fritz.

"Come on now, give me something."

"Well, General Durbin of the Union army gave a speech at Mozart Hall. He wants us to forget the animosities of the last ten years and repeal the Ku Klux and bayonet laws."

"Do you think that's wise? Letting the Southern aristocrats regain control of the South?" quizzed Max.

"Well, my father says it's dangerous to give the federal government too much power," said the boy.

"Your father has a point, but wise use of power can protect the rights of men against abusive state governments. You need to decide what you think for yourself, you hear me?"

"Yes, sir."

"Anything else interesting?" asked Max.

"A boat full of rich people sunk off the coast of Massachusetts. They were all rescued."

"You sound disappointed," said Max.

"No, but it would have made a better story if somebody drowned."

"All right then." Max handed him a dime—five cents for the paper plus a tip.

"Thank you, sir." The boy tipped his hat.

Max approached the esplanade, where police had strung ropes to keep people out until the appointed hour. A wooden grandstand had been erected north of the fountain. Bleachers four rows high were hastily constructed along the north and south edges of the esplanade. Wooden benches filled every available space on the plaza. Four thousand seats were numbered, corresponding to the tickets distributed to guests.

Max greeted one of the policemen guarding the roped-off square, stated his business, and was admitted. He approached the fountain to find Colonel Von Miller and several other men making final preparations for the unveiling. The tall wood fence that had shielded the construction had been dismantled overnight, and cloths were now draped over the fountain.

After checking in at the shop, Max joined the other government dignitaries at ten thirty in front of the Burnet House. A committee worker gave him a large tasseled blue ribbon to pin to his jacket. It was printed with "Dedication of the Tyler Davidson Fountain" and the date. "City Government" was printed across the bottom to distinguish him from the presenters.

A German battalion outfitted in spiked helmets and Prussian uniforms marched behind a military band. Colonel Gustav Tafel, one of the most prominent Germans from Over-the-Rhine, rode the lead horse. The day's speakers walked behind the soldiers, and last in line were the invited government officials. They paraded up the street, entered the esplanade, and walked between the rows of benches, now filled with guests. The speakers mounted the platform; Max sat with the other dignitaries beside it. He waved to Annie and her friend, Mary. He had convinced Annie to leave her suffrage banner at home, but both ladies sported the large "VOTES FOR WOMEN" buttons.

As they were settling, a loud commotion started at one end of the plaza, then spread to the other, as the crowds standing outside the ropes plowed over them and filled in the spaces between the benches. There was nothing the police could do to stop it, and after a few minutes, every inch of the plaza and surrounding streets was filled with twenty thousand spectators.

From the grandstand, the committee chairman, Mr. George F. Davis, a meatpacking company owner, kicked off the day. Only those within two hundred feet could hear the orators; the rest gleaned what they could and patiently awaited the unveiling.

Max looked around the plaza at the crowd. He was awed by the number of people who showed up on a Friday morning, wanting to be a part of the momentous day in Cincinnati. The crowd was diverse—all classes, ages, neighborhoods, and races. Members of the Black community clustered around the edges—only a few had secured reserved seat numbers. Max had seen that John and his employer, William Watson, received tickets. He spotted them halfway back in the crowd.

Max wanted to believe everyone here felt pride in their city despite its problems. Days like today made his work promoting the city worthwhile.

Archbishop Purcell took the podium and made his

remarks, giving thanks for the blessings in Cincinnati. He praised it for its enterprise, industry, successful expositions and now wonders of the noble fountain.

The archbishop went on, "Who is there at the present hour who sees not in the near future the first signs of a conflict which may end in the dissolution of society, in the rupturing of the moral world to its center? I fear irrepressible conflict of rich and poor, of capital and labor."

After his dire warning, he turned more encouraging, praising men like Henry Probasco, patriotic citizens that contribute to the good of mankind. He challenged capitalists to give generously to causes such as schools, hospitals, widows' homes, orphanages, and all others in need.

Max had respected Purcell for many years and looked to him for inspiration. As he listened to the archbishop's plea, Max felt the clergyman was speaking directly to him. He thought back to his mentor, Nicholas Longworth, himself a great Cincinnati philanthropist. Longworth had paid for his education and told Max, "Make sure you put it to use and do some good on this earth."

Governor Hayes spoke next and celebrated the fountain's enhancements to the city. "It makes a pleasanter city, her homes happier, her aims worthier, and her future brighter." He praised Cincinnati as a central city in the nation, becoming a convention city of progress, as demonstrated by the second Industrial Exposition currently underway. He stressed the duty of its citizens to their community. He hoped the donation of the fountain would inspire other gifts of parks, schools, art galleries, libraries, and other improvements to benefit people.

A loud boom rang out across the square, stopping the governor mid-sentence. A flurry of shouting followed; a cloud of dust rose above a section of the risers that had collapsed. Max stood but saw that policemen and others in the area were attending to the people who had fallen in the crash. After several minutes, it appeared that no one was seriously injured.

The governor continued, reminding the gathered to "share beyond your heirs; share your fortune with the general public, and you will gratefully be remembered as someone who bestowed blessings on mankind." He closed by thanking Henry Probasco and his deceased partner, Tyler Davidson, for the gift that nobly honors them.

After a second speaker, pupils from the public high schools ascended the stage and sang an ode to the fountain.

The Reverend Dr. Max Lilienthal, Rabbi of the Jewish Synagogue on Mound Street, made the next address. Born and schooled in Munich, he expressed his pride in his German heritage and what German influence had brought to the city. He recalled a lecture on America by one of his professors who had said, "Europe will bring to America the arts and sciences, and America will give us, in return for them, liberty, civil and religious liberty, in the fullest sense of the word." The reverend spoke of Hiram Powers, a Cincinnati sculptor who gained fame in Europe with his piece, *The Greek Slave*.

Max remembered meeting the artist, Hiram Powers, one day at Longworth's mansion before he became famous. Like himself, Powers had also been a recipient of the man's charity to young men. Max was pulled out of his reminiscing by another loud crash, as a second set of bleachers collapsed under the weight of spectators, this one near the grandstand. Policemen quickly tended to the casualties and carried an injured woman from the stands.

Max looked around the plaza and to the stores beyond the railing. Most businesses had built makeshift stands above the sidewalks in front of their buildings. Each was stuffed with spectators. He worried that one of the precarious porches would fall next. A police officer shouted up from the street at one overcrowded platform. The inhabitants were ignoring the officers' pleas to lighten the load. Max looked behind him and saw Lizzie and Abby atop the platform above Mr. Green's storefront. He debated whether to push through the crowd and retrieve Lizzie from it, but he counted only eight on the stand and thought she would be safe. He said a quick prayer and returned his attention to the grandstand.

With the disturbance settled, the reverend returned to the podium. "Nobody killed," he announced, then continued his accolades for the fountain and Probasco. "And, sir, you have presented this donation in due and proper time. Cincinnati was losing her crown as Queen City of the West. You, today, inaugurated the era in which it will proudly replace it. Therefore, Mr. Probasco, once more, accept the heartfelt thanks of all your fellow citizens. We appreciate not only the beauty and grandeur of your gift; we also understand its meaning and importance. The motto of our city, *Juncta Juvant*, strength in unity, shall arouse all our means and energies."

The band played another piece, then Henry Probasco took the podium, greeted by extended applause. When the cheering quieted, he spoke of the history of the fountain. Artist August von Kreling and collaborator Ferdinand von Miller at the Royal Bronze Foundry in Bavaria designed the fountain but could not find anyone to fund its construction until Probasco visited Germany years later. Probasco worked with the artists to see it built and donated to the city.

Probasco introduced the artist's son, Colonel Von Miller, who briefly thanked the people of Cincinnati in his broken English. Probasco spoke for over twenty minutes on the beauty and the water theme of the *Genius of Water*. He addressed Mayor Davis.

"And now, Mr. Mayor, representatives of the municipal government, and fellow citizens of Cincinnati: In the name of Tyler Davidson, for the cause of our common city, and as a humble effort to encourage by the aid of art one form at least of philanthropy, this fountain is hereby absolutely given and entrusted to your custody, a possession for you and your children forever, with the earnest hope that the offering may not be without benefit to man and the blessing and favor of Almighty God."

The mayor stood to accept the gift. "Permit me, Mr. Probasco, again to thank you for this useful, beautiful, and exquisite work of art, and to assure you that the citizens and authorities of Cincinnati will ever cherish and preserve it, and associating your name with the names of Woodward and McMicken as benefactors of the city and its people, they will hold you in grateful remembrance."

As the mayor completed his remarks, Colonel Von Miller descended the platform stairs and pulled the cord holding the canvas, revealing the fountain. The plaza was still momentarily, then exploded with a thunderous celebration. The people on Vine and Walnut Streets at each end of the esplanade applauded with a fluttering wave. Water began to flow from the shining bronze statue's hands, and arcs of spray sprouted from the jets on the lower basin. The water droplets sparkled in the sunlight around the womanly figure. The drinking fountains began dispensing from their orifices as the water flowed down and overflowed to the base pool.

The mass of people moved to the fountain to see it up close and drink from the chilled fountains. An attendant brought out a dozen tin cups. Each drinker used a cup and passed it on to the next person.

As the sun faded, a city worker lit four calcium lights, illuminating the fountain. He periodically changed a filter throughout the evening, switching the light's color. A band from Newport barracks played music from the grandstand. At the east end of the esplanade, another worker set off a series of rockets and Roman candles.

Max found Annie lingering near the fountain with several of her sisters in the movement. She bid them good night and took Max's arm. Oskar and Catherine, baby Walter in her arms, approached. Abby delivered Lizzie to her parents, and John joined the group.

"Do you want to have a drink?" Max asked Lizzie.

They waited in the long line.

"The fountain's as wonderful as you said, Papa," said Lizzie. "It's as if she's holding her arms open, inviting everyone to join her."

"She's saying welcome to the Queen City," said Max.

When it was their turn, Lizzie took the cup and drank. A smile spread across her face, "It's so cold." She handed it to Catherine. Then Oskar and Annie.

Annie handed the cup to John. He placed it under the stream of water pouring from the mouth of a sea turtle, filling the cup.

A man standing in line behind Max shouted, "You can't use that cup."

John froze.

Several men surrounded the family and jeered at John. Oskar and Max stepped in front of John to shield him from the taunts.

John handed the cup toward Max.

Max shook his head. He turned to the crowd, his "City Government" ribbon still pinned to his coat. He pointed up at the words carved in the statue. "The fountain says 'To the people of Cincinnati.' It is given to all our people—Men, women, Black, white, rich, and poor."

Max hesitated. Annie encouraged him with her eyes. He put his hand on John's shoulder, "This man is my brother by blood, but he is a brother to all of us in the family of mankind." He nodded at John. "He deserves the same as any of us."

John hesitated amidst murmurs in the crowd. Max nodded again.

John took a drink from the cup. Several people began clapping, then a few more. Max took the cup from John and drank, then embraced John. John moved to each of the family, hugging them. A few approached John and shook his hand, smiling and wishing him well. Several men shouted insults, but the crowd quickly calmed and returned to their indifference.

They lingered on the square and talked with the dwindling crowd. Eventually, only a police officer and a few others remained. With their family surrounding them, Annie and Max stood hand-in-hand in front of the fountain, admiring it. The esplanade was quiet except for the sound of the splashing water. The babble echoed against the surrounding buildings and reached for a century into the future.

"It's a beautiful addition to the city," said Annie.

Max gazed at the fountain in the spotlight, the robed lady towering over the square. He thought back to his childhood, selling newspapers not far from where he stood. Cincinnati was the Queen of the West. People came in droves to make new lives in the booming city of opportunity. He had lived with his family Over-the-Rhine but wanted to shed the taint of being German and become an American. His education at St. Xavier paved his way to enter the world of commerce and service to his fellow Cincinnatians. He surrounded himself with hardworking people who were curious and advanced with the times. God blessed him with good fortune, and he tried to share his gifts.

Annie came into his life like a storm, and they made each other better. She had taught him to see injustice, push past his reservations, and let his goodness reign.

The city had evolved with him. German heritage was now a badge of pride forged by thousands like him who gave of themselves to make their home a better place. It demonstrated people's ability to accept others.

They survived the war and were adapting to more change in its aftermath. The dawn of industrialization was reshaping livelihoods and neighborhoods, pushing the city outward.

Agony amidst so much opportunity. Max saw it all—the realities of humanity. There was still much to do, but today's fountain opening brought his fellow citizens together to celebrate where they had come from and hope for the future.

"Yes," said Max. "It's a magnificent fountain."

AUTHOR'S NOTE

When I envisioned the *Queen of the West* series, I planned on three books and the periods they would cover, Antebellum, Civil War, and Reconstruction. In researching book three, *Queen's Moment in the Sun*, I read numerous books on Reconstruction, some written in the decades afterward, others written by contemporary authors. They covered a range of perspectives; Black, white, Southern, Northern, and specific state histories. Reconstruction is commonly defined as the period between 1863–1877—a broad timeframe covering too much ground for one novel, so I chose to end the book in 1871, a turning point.

At that time, the Southern Democrats and their allies were beginning to regain power and roll back the progress of Reconstruction. Many people still saw hope that we would reunite our country, return the South to prosperity, and incorporate the formerly enslaved into the new order.

It would be almost fifty years before women achieved the vote, but the movement persevered. Cincinnati's reign as the Queen of the West had arguably crested, but its champions continued to reinvent the city, making it a cherished home for generations. I chose to end the series at this point because I wanted to conclude with a theme of hope. Hope for the characters who represented the people of that time. Hope for the women's movement, the freedmen, and the city of Cincinnati.

Sadly, the country fell short of the goals for

Reconstruction and the years since have been fraught with many of the same feelings, fears, biases, and battles my characters experienced. The book's title comes from W. E. B. Du Bois's words, "The slave went free; stood a brief moment in the sun; then moved back again toward slavery." (*Black Reconstruction in America*, 1935). Du Bois's words capture the essence of the tragic arc of Reconstruction. Others had moments in the sun in the late nineteenth century: immigrants, women, aspiring entrepreneurs, and Cincinnati—as it strove to remain the Queen of the West.

In wrapping up the series, I inserted Annie into some of the significant women's movement activities of the time, including the Kansas campaigns, Francis Train's speech in Cincinnati, and the fallout between Elizabeth Cady Stanton's and Lucy Stone's camps. The conversations are imagined, but the circumstances and sentiments were taken from history.

Similarly, Oskar and Catherine's experience working for the Freedmen's Bureau is a fictional account created from historical books and Bureau records. There was a Paris, Kentucky Bureau office, but all of the book's events in Bourbon County are fiction.

Cincinnati held a series of Industrial Expositions in the 1870s that brought attention and visitors to the city and led to the construction of Music Hall. Alfred T. Goshorn was the father of the expositions, but I imagined Max as a primary champion and organizer. I also inserted Max into the city's activities to bring Henry Probasco's fountain to Fountain Square and the Cincinnati Southern Railway to the South.

Depending on their circumstances, Cincinnatians, both Black and White, held a range of views on Reconstruction. John and his brother Harry represent Black Americans' diverse sentiments about their newfound freedom and hope for the future. Nikki M. Taylor's book, *Frontiers of Freedom, Cincinnati's Black Community 1802–1868*, was an informative resource, as little has been written about Cincinnati's Black community in the era.

I included speeches of people to portray the historical

sentiments and the vernacular of the period. Their words convey national and civic pride and their obligation to serve their fellow citizens.

President Johnson's "Swing Around the Circle" speech in Cincinnati was excerpted from *Dubious Victory: The Reconstruction Debate in Ohio* by Robert D. Sawrey.

Elizabeth Cady Stanton's speech in Cincinnati on Thanksgiving Day exemplifies her strong opinion that women should be given the vote before Black men. Her positions evolved over her life. As all strong leaders do, she did what she felt was in the movement's best interest, even if it caused conflict. Her speech was reported in the *Cincinnati Commercial*, November 29, 1867.

Frederick Douglass's words justifying Black over women suffrage at the AERA meeting in May 1869 were so powerful that I didn't want to dilute them. I took them from *History of Women's Suffrage, Elizabeth Cady Stanton, Susan B. Anthony, Matilda Joslyn Gage, Vol 2, 1861–1876.*

I excerpted words from Peter Clark's Day of Jubilee speech to speak directly from his voice. The address was reported in the Cincinnati Commercial, April 16, 1870.

The Tyler Davidson Fountain: Given by Mr. Henry Probasco to the City of Cincinnati, by William Frederick Poole, available in the Cincinnati Public Library's digital collection, was published the year after the fountain dedication and included photographs and detailed descriptions of the fountain and its history. To capture the words of past Cincinnatians and the event's aura, I incorporated portions of the dedication speeches given by Archbishop Purcell, Governor Hayes, Mayor Davis, William Groesbeck, Reverend Dr. Max Lilienthal, and Henry Probasco.

History is filled with moments in the sun. I intended to share how Cincinnatians experienced the period after the Civil War through my characters' moments.

Like Max and Annie, I seek an America that provides more equitable opportunities for all its citizens. It will require each of us to have the courage to be open to new ideas, push past our discomfort, know and empathize with others, care for humankind, and change our minds and actions. These were daunting asks in the nineteenth century and remain so today.

ACKNOWLEDGEMENTS

I am grateful to the following for their help with this book. My trusted early readers who provided feedback and encouragement: Calista Hargrove, Mary Ann Russo, Beth Tschop, and Tari Williams. My friends, the "Fogeys on Fifteenth" readers, for their support and suggestions: Bob Gilbreath, Stephanie Gilbreath, Kevin Hassey, Roseann Hassey, Sarah Kiley, Andrea Klein, Jerry Koch, Marci Koch, Marilyn Maag, Jeff Roller, and Kim Roller. Ericka McIntyre for her edits and guiding questions. Jill Beitz at the Cincinnati History Library for her assistance with my research. And my wife, Peggy, for her continued encouragement, support, and championing of me and my work.

ABOUT THE AUTHOR

JR Zink enjoyed a successful career as a consultant and corporate leader before stepping away from the business world to develop his right-brain talents as an author. In addition to writing, he coaches high school swimming and enjoys running, backpacking, bicycling and travel. JR and his wife raised a family and now live in the historic Over-the-Rhine neighborhood in Cincinnati.